ACKNOWLEDGEMENTS

Thanks to Jakob Levinsen, Niels Lillelund, Michael Enggaard, Helle Vincentz, Peter Stein Larsen, Finn Stein Larsen, Martin Berg, Anders Bach and Hans Petter Hougen.

Thanks to Lene Juul, Charlotte Weiss, Nya Guldberg and all the other good people at JP/Politiken Publishing, who have helped my book along the way.

A special thank you to my editor Anne Christine Andersen.

Thanks to my wife, Anja, for believing in me the whole way through, and my daughters, Emilie and Hannah, for being who they are.

NØRREBRO
Copyright: Jesper Roug

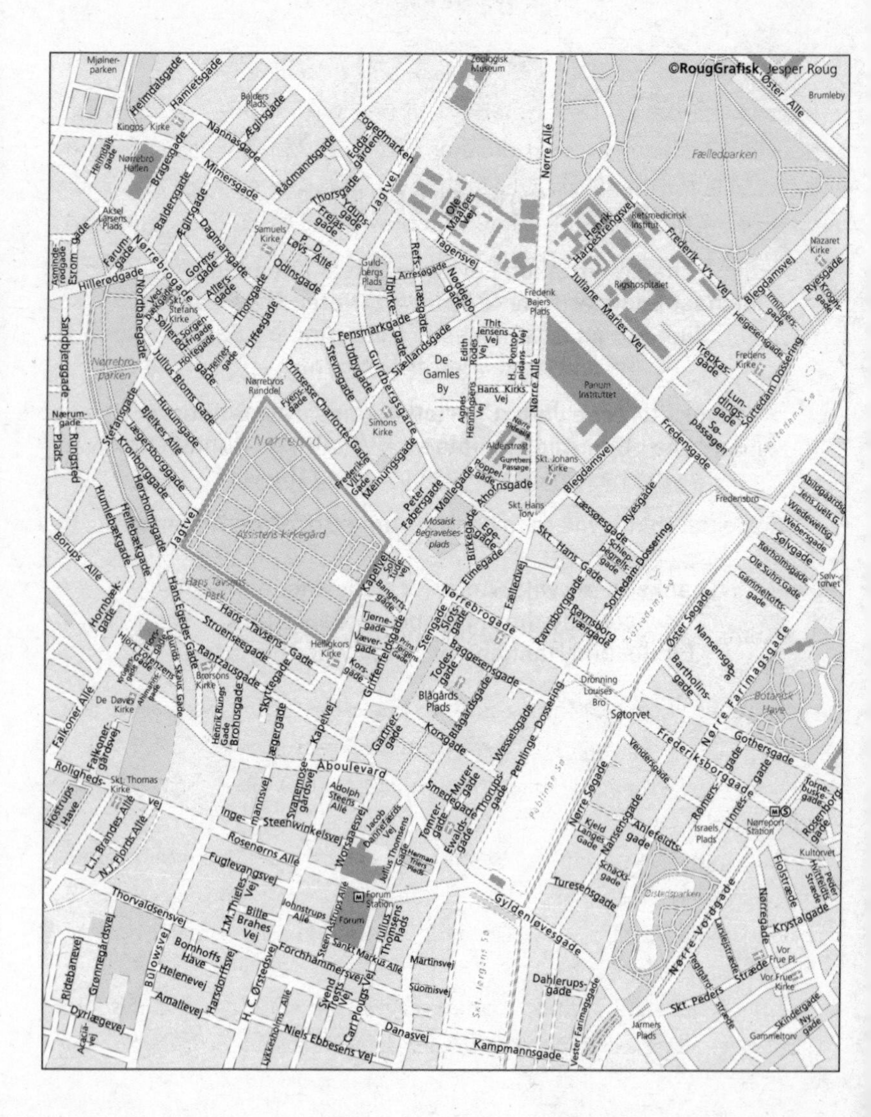
©RougGrafisk, Jesper Roug
Mjølner-parken
Heimdalsgade
Hamletsgade
Zoologisk Museum
Øster Allé
Brumleby
Fælledparken
Nørre Allé
Kingos Kirke
Nannasgade
Ægirsgade
Fogedmarken
Edda-gården
Mimersgade
Rådmandsgade
Bragesgade
Baldersgade
Thorsgade
Jagtvej
Ole Maaløes Vej
Retsmedicinsk Institut
Henrik Harpestrengsvej
Frederik V's Vej
Tagensvej
Nazaret Kirke
Dagmarsgade
Samuels Kirke
Nørrebrogade
Hillerødgade
Esrom Gade
Odinsgade
Arresøgade
Nøddebo-gade
Refsnæsgade
Fredenk Bajers Plads
Juliane Maries Vej
Rigshospitalet
Blegdamsvej
Ryesgade
Gorms-gade
Allersgade
Uffesgade
Fensmarkgade
Tibirkegade
Sjællandsgade
Thit Jensens Vej
Nordbanegade
Sandbjerggade
Nørrebroparken
Julius Bloms Gade
Udbygade
Stevnsgade
Guldbergsgade
De Gamles By
Hans Kirks Vej
Panum Instituttet
Trepkasgade
Fredens Kirke
Sortedam Dossering
Nørrebros Runddel
Prinsesse Charlottes Gade
Simons Kirke
Fredensgade
Husumgade
Bjelkes Allé
Jægersborggade
Stefansgade
Kronborggade
Hørsholmsgade
Rungsted Plads
Nørrebro
Meinungsgade
Peter Fabersgade
Møllegade
Ahornsgade
Skt. Johans Kirke
Skt. Hans Torv
Fredensbro
Humlebækgade
Hellebækgade
Borups Allé
Assistens Kirkegård
Mosaisk Begravelsesplads
Birkegade
Egegade
Elmegade
Skt. Hans Gade
Læssøesgade
Fælledvej
Hans Tavsens Park
Hans Egedes Gade
Kapelvej
Nørrebrogade
Ravnsborggade
Ravnsborg Tværgade
Sortedams Sø
Sølvgade
Hornbækgade
Hans Tavsens Gade
Struenseegade
Rantzausgade
Stengade
Slotsgade
Baggesensgade
Østersøgade
Nansensgade
Bartholinsgade
Nørre Farimagsgade
Botanisk Have
Falkoner Allé
Brorsons Kirke
Griffenfeldsgade
Skyttegade
Jægergade
Todesgade
Blågårds Plads
Blågårdsgade
Dronning Louises Bro
Søtorvet
Frederiksborggade
Gothersgade
Brohusgade
Gartnergade
Korsgade
Wesselsgade
Peblinge Dossering
Falkonergårdsvej
Rolighedsvej
Skt. Thomas Kirke
Åboulevard
Svanemøllevej
Adolph Steens Allé
Smedegade
Thorupsgade
Peblinge Sø
Nørre Søgade
Ahlefeldtsgade
Israels Plads
Nørreport Station
Rosenborggade
Hostrups Have
L.I. Brandes Allé
N.J. Fjords Allé
Ingemannsvej
Steenwinkelsvej
Rosenørns Allé
Worsaaesvej
Julius Thomsens Gade
Tømrergade
Ewaldsgade
Kultorvet
Fuglevangsvej
Thorvaldsensvej
Forum Station
Forum
Turesensgade
Gyldenløvesgade
Ørstedsparken
Nørre Voldgade
Nørregade
Fiolstræde
Krystalgade
J.M. Thieles Vej
Bille Brahes Vej
Julius Thomsens Plads
Bomhoffs Have
Grønnegårdsvej
Bülowsvej
Helenevej
Harsdorffsvej
Forchhammersvej
Sankt Markus Allé
Martinsvej
Skt. Jørgens Sø
Suomisvej
Dahlerupsgade
Vor Frue Kirke
Skt. Peders Stræde
Ridebanevej
Amalievej
H.C. Ørstedsvej
Carl Plougs Vej
Dyrlægevej
Niels Ebbesens Vej
Danasvej
Kampmannsgade
Vester Farimagsgade
Jarmers Plads
Gammeltorv
Skindergade
Nygade

1

Friday, March 2, 2007

It was fantastic sex. Better than it had ever been before. A bubble of pleasure and lust detached from time and place. He was making love to his ex-wife for the third night in a row. He looked into her eyes with their peculiar droplets of yellow in a brown-black net. They glistened with delight and desire. Desire for him. She sat on him and rode him with her round breasts dangling right in front of his lips.

There was a Heaven.

And a Hell.

As he realised when his ringtone smashed the dream to smithereens. The sound came like a slap in the face. And with it the recognition that he was lying alone in his bed on a cold sheet.

He rolled over onto his side, grabbed his mobile from the floor, looked at the display – unknown number – and pressed the button.

"Axel Steen."

"Antonsen from HQ. I've got one for you."

"What?"

"A man. Unidentified. Found him ourselves. Sitting up against the wall in Assistens – only 100 yards from the Youth House."

Assistens Cemetery. Green breathing space in a stone desert. Burial ground. Refuge. Crime scene.

Axel put the phone down and glanced at the four small black numbers divided by two dots on its luminous green background. 03:30. Friday morning. His shift. Tonight he was the duty officer for the Homicide Division.

After smoking a joint, he had managed to get an hour and a half's shut-eye, falling asleep to blue flashes and the glow of flames floating across the wall and the sound of sirens near and far – fire engine horns and electronic screams from ambulances and police cars.

He had spent the evening remote control in hand, zapping back and forth between the TV news channels, interrupted by trips to the bay windows, where he had an unobstructed view for about three-quarters of a mile down Nørrebrogade.

Everything was in flames.

Less than 24 hours ago, the police had cleared the Youth House, a cultural centre and meeting point for radical left-wing activists, and cordoned off the entire neighbourhood. At seven in the morning, the anti-terror squad from PET, the police intelligence service, had lowered officers carrying sub-machine guns from helicopters; the building had been wrapped in fire-extinguishing foam mixed with tear gas, the back doors smashed in with a battering ram, and the police had used maximum force, by Danish standards. Assistens Cemetery had been closed to the public and patrolled from within by a large police force.

Axel had despondently watched the disturbances spread throughout the morning. The young demonstrators and their many sympathisers had certainly been caught off guard, but in a few hours they had assembled an impressive crowd of desperate, furious people. They were fighting back in many places and the disturbances were spreading uncontrollably and destructively. Nørrebro had become a war zone, with burned-out cars, smashed windows, looted shops and bonfires several feet high made from rubbish bins and old furniture left out for collection. This was his part of the city. And that of 80,000 other people. Around midnight he had stood at the window and stared out over Copenhagen, appalled. The sky was hidden behind a thick blanket of smoke from the endless fires, a poisonous cloud over the glowing roofs. He had seen the hooligans roaming the streets below him. Only a few of them were Youth House users, autonomists or other radical left-wing activists; most of them were opportunists.

Now the weekend was approaching. Far too many people were off work and didn't have to get up the next day. It would get worse.

"Hello, you there?"

"Yes, where in Assistens is it?"

"Last entrance on Nørrebrogade coming from town. Know where that is?"

"I live 300 yards away."

"Right, thought so. Some people just can't get enough."

Axel ignored him. Nørrebro wasn't the most popular option for police officers wanting to settle in the capital. Over decades the district had built and stubbornly maintained its reputation as a battlefield between the police and squatters, second-generation immigrants, anarchists and autonomists. Axel didn't know any other officer, out of 3,000 stationed in the capital, who lived in Denmark's most densely populated neighbourhood.

"What happened? Are there any witnesses?"

"No, but..."

"What about forensics? They there?"

"There's only an ambulance doctor and our people who've been guarding the cemetery since YoHo was cleared. You're the first person I've called. They're cordoning off, but it's not that easy. There's half a dozen fires blazing up and down the street, and it's swarming with wankers, autonomists and drunken arseholes."

The vision of his ex-wife had vanished, but he could still feel the warmth of her skin. It was two years now. He still fucked her in his dreams while, in the real world, she was screwing a career lawyer in PET.

How do you describe a condition when being woken up is the worst feeling of all – because it's so much better being yourself in a dream. When despite knowing that something doesn't quite add up – it doesn't become completely unbearable until you wake up and face reality. Is that a dream, or a nightmare? Of all the women in the world, Cecilie Lind was the one he least wanted to get a hard-on over, because she had dumped him. Chosen someone else. But he still longed for her with every nerve in his body, and had to live with the agony of that longing.

Looking out of the bay window, he could now see a group of people dressed in black and wearing balaclavas and crash helmets rolling three big grey waste containers down by the next junction. They opened the lids. One of them pulled the cloth out of a clear bottle and sprayed liquid into the first container, as if it were a giant barbecue grill. Another one set fire to it.

"How the hell could someone be killed in there when there are so many of us around?"

"Don't ask me, but it's top priority. The boss is on his way down. And the public prosecutor's been informed."

Axel could feel his pulse rising. The public prosecutor only got involved if police officers were suspected of having done something illegal.

"Why?"

"The body's dressed in a balaclava, black clothes and military boots. He's probably an autonomist."

An autonomist killed somewhere closed off to everyone else except police officers. That explained everything.

"Why didn't you say that before?"

"I did try, but you never let me get a word in."

"Do we have anything to do with it?"

The line went quiet a moment.

"I don't know."

"Make sure nobody touches anything before I get there. And call the duty officers in technical and forensics. I'll be there in 10 minutes."

He looked up at the sky. An aircraft with flashing landing lights was floating straight towards him from the darkness in the west on its way to Kastrup airport.

He went out to the bathroom, switched on the light and looked at himself in the mirror: blue eyes, greying black hair, wrinkles.

The two smoothly shaven spots on his chest stared back at him. His latest ECG. His sixth in two years.

He put a hand on the hairless spot on the left side of his chest, even though he knew it would frighten him, but he had to check it out. It was beating – doggedly, rhythmically pulsing.

He moved his hand and closed his eyes, but the beating sensation didn't go away; he could feel it in his eyelids, in the tip of his tongue vibrating against his front tooth, in the bones of his neck. Even in his dreams, he sometimes saw that pulse, like a poisonous rhythm, a weak trail of light over the black screen of his consciousness.

"I'm 38, divorced, I have a five-year-old daughter. I have one of the world's most thoroughly tested hearts and I'm still terrified of dying," he said aloud. The sound of his own voice filled him with disgust.

He took his pulse and immediately knew that there was nothing to worry about. Beating in time with the second hand.

He went back to the window and looked down on the dark, devastated street. All the street lights had been put out of action last night, when bicycle chains had been thrown up to short-circuit the power lines. There was smoke and glowing embers from smouldering bonfires and piles of burned rubbish. Was there any way he could get down to Assistens Cemetery in his car? He thought about his bike, but if he had to go to HQ, or out to forensics afterwards, he had to have his car.

In the bathroom, he stuck a toothbrush in his mouth, as questions bombarded his mind one after the other: Who would kill a man in Assistens during the worst riots in Copenhagen for several years? Who was the victim? Why had he been killed? And how?

It didn't sound like a normal murder. If one of his fellow cops was behind it, all hell would break loose. The tension between police and autonomists had been rising steadily in the many months leading up to this, and although it looked bad enough on the streets now, Axel was well aware that a story that the police had killed an activist would make everything explode.

But that wasn't his problem. He had to solve the case; it was up to others to clean up the public mess.

He went into the hallway and checked his jacket. Wallet? Voice recorder? Notepad? Then he picked up his phone, went down into the yard and got rid of a bag of rubbish. Through the gate to the side street where his car was parked.

He stepped over a half-eaten kebab; dressing, transparent lettuce and grey meat spread out on the cobblestones between bite marks in the bread.

The smell of burnt plastic and smoke hung between the houses. He checked that the suitcase with his equipment – gloves, thermometer, plastic tweezers and evidence bags – was in the boot.

It would normally have taken him two minutes to get to the scene of the crime, but the fires made it impossible. Instead of driving via Nørrebrogade directly to the cemetery, he had to leave the main artery and drive down the small side streets. As soon as he reached Jagtvej, he could see the circular Runddelen junction and, behind it, the police cordon by the Youth House, where police vans stood side by side blocking the whole road. It looked surreal in the fog of night. He turned left before reaching Runddelen and parked in Fyensgade, a small side street opposite the cemetery. There was plenty of space. Most people had moved their cars, afraid they'd be set on fire.

He took his case of equipment and threw his protective overalls over his shoulder. He stood on Nørrebrogade, a one-and-a-half-mile axis of asphalt stretching from the edge of the inner city by the lakes out to the border of Nordvest, the northwestern district. Two lanes, bike lanes and pavements: the busiest road in Denmark. Normally. But nothing was normal now. About 500 yards further in towards the city, a large crowd was setting about burning two cars. Axel hesitated. Would they come up here? If there was one thing he hated, it was being disturbed at a crime scene. He went diagonally across the street and started walking down towards the green gate into Assistens Cemetery.

Along the almost 250-year-old yellow wall surrounding the cemetery, there was graffiti – "Fuck The Police" – in many places.

A police van with seven officers in combat equipment was parked at an angle in front of the gateway. They looked sweaty and worn out.

Axel banged the window twice and showed his warrant card.

"DCI Axel Steen, Homicide. What the fuck are you doing here?"

"We've been told to stay here so that our people can come in without being hurt. There's a body behind the wall."

"You might just as well put a sign up saying: Come and stone us! Get out of here."

2

Axel Steen looked at the body sitting up against the ochre wall in Assistens Cemetery, surrounded by snowdrops. Balaclava over its head. Military boots. Dark clothing. Wet. The head was resting on one shoulder as if the man had fallen asleep. But you don't fall asleep with your eyes open and your hands behind your back. Especially not if they are tied up and totally blue.

He pulled on white protective overalls, shoe covers and hair net. Then he took a pair of rubber gloves out of the box in his bag, put them up to his mouth one at a time and blew them up, so that the fingers were distended with small pops. The smell of rubber and talc. He pulled them over his hands. Last, he put on a mask.

Despite only a few hours' sleep, the prospect of an investigation was like a spring being wound up inside him. The anxiety about his body was forgotten. His panic at the thought of his own death was matched only by his keen anticipation of a homicide investigation. It was a refuge from himself, a gateway that opened up into a part of life that he otherwise didn't have access to: into the darkness, where feelings, desires, longings and betrayal which no one knew about lay hidden.

He was restless to get started. But first he had to get through the discussion with the head of the Homicide Division, who was standing by an old oak with his back to the crime scene and talking on his mobile with a cigarette in his other hand. Corneliussen gestured to Axel to wait.

"Yes, yes, we're on top of it. Axel Steen's arrived… Sure. Yes, the man himself. If not, he'll just have to work with his mouth shut. Ha ha! No problem," said Corneliussen.

His eyes were two narrow black slits surrounded by folds of skin, and they didn't get any bigger when they fixed on Axel for a moment. His little compact body was trussed up inside a long, beige raincoat, his head resembling a bowling ball sticking up out of his collar, with a wreath of curly hair on the top. Fuck, he was ugly. The hair style had brought him the nicknames Cornelipussy, Hairy Bush or, pure and simple, the Bush.

The leader of the Homicide Division had inherited Axel from the former boss, Henriksen, who had followed Axel's turbulent career all the way back from the police academy but had now become the head of the Western District Police. Axel was alone. Under sufferance in his own department. And the shit had been raining down on him since Corneliussen had arrived.

He knew he was a troublemaker and took short cuts which had no basis in any code of law. There were complaints about his behaviour in his personnel file – both from criminals who claimed they had been threatened and from colleagues who had felt pressurised by him. He had twice been called in for a talk with HR, first because of an altercation with a colleague; the second time he had been given a warning for improper conduct after detaining a man who had used a dating site to trick a dozen women into meeting him, after which he had locked them inside his flat and raped them. The man had fallen twice and hit his head on the edge of a dining table when Axel was arresting him. Fancy that – the bastard.

Axel's obsession with murder inquiries and his workaholic frenzy constituted the lifebelt that held his head above water when Corneliussen tried to drown him in paper shuffling and strategic considerations. He got results for the department – one thing that was of infinite importance to the career-conscious Corneliussen. But not everything.

Now they stood at four o'clock in the morning with clouds of grey breath coming out of their mouths into the nocturnal darkness in Assistens Cemetery. Corneliussen's stank of rotten meat.

"It was beautifully done," he said conclusively and cast a satisfied look up at the Youth House. He put the phone in his pocket and turned to Axel.

"The Assistant Commissioner sends his regards. High priority, ultra-low spotlight. I don't want any bother. I don't want this murder linked to the Youth House. It has to be sorted calmly and quietly."

He went silent and looked anxiously up at the big four-storey building, where police in riot gear were keeping watch on the roof.

"Just think – if he's from in there, if he becomes a martyr or something even worse… Keep a lid on it," he said, turning his back on the cleared building.

"What if they do make a martyr of him? I haven't even seen the body yet. Are you asking me to rule something out already?"

"Of course not. I'm just asking you to keep the investigation quiet."

Axel held his gaze. Then he looked over at the Youth House. Beautifully done? That was the last thing he would call it.

"Task force, helicopters, sub-machine guns, tear gas. What the fuck's going on?" he hissed.

"What do you mean?"

"You know what I mean. There was nothing but a collection of snotty-nosed teenagers inside that building. And we go in as if it's fucking al-Qaeda."

"That's how the police work. Once we've been told to clear somewhere, we do it," said his boss defensively. "And besides, it was brimming with Molotov cocktails."

Five or six officers were tiptoeing around the crime scene. They had stretched out the plastic tape and been chatting with the doctor and the ambulance personnel. Now they had gone silent. They were all staring at Axel and his boss.

"It's your investigation now. I hope you've got the message. You'll be joined by some of your colleagues in about an hour."

"Who?"

"I've called John Darling."

Detective Chief Inspector John Darling, aka Mr Clean: the department's Administration of Justice Act incarnate, who always did things by the book and, besides that, was one of the few qualified policemen to have a university legal diploma to inform his work.

Even though Axel and Darling had the same rank, there was no doubt that Darling had a higher standing with the bosses. They had worked together many times and respected each other, but since patience was not one of Axel's strong points, they occasionally clashed, because Mr Clean didn't want any stains anywhere – certainly not on his CV.

"I've spoken to the DPP. He'll be there on the sidelines and must be kept informed if there's the least thing to indicate that we're involved in this. The Commissioner of Police and the Assistant Commissioner have also been informed, so no mistakes. If you blow this, you're finished!"

Corneliussen strode off through the gate.

Axel called over the divisional commander responsible for guarding the cemetery.

"Who found him?"

"In a way, we all did. We came by in the van along the wall at ten past three, and one of us noticed him."

"What did you do then?"

"We got out and shone a torch on him. He looked dead."

"Did you stomp around and tamper with him?"

"No, we went back to the van immediately and rang HQ."

"Did you see anyone?"

"No."

"How often were you patrolling here?"

"That's hard to say. Once an hour during the evening, but from 23:00 we had two men stationed here to keep an eye on the wall."

"So there's someone who's seen the perp and the victim?"

"None of my men have seen anything. Groes and Vang were responsible for this part of the path and they haven't seen anything. The street lights weren't working and there was a lot happening on Nørrebrogade."

"So what? Has that made your men blind?"

"No need to be sarcastic. We haven't seen him. Twice in the evening we had people over by the wall because there was chaos on the other side and we had to be ready to intervene if someone jumped over."

"And he wasn't here then?"

"No. The last patrol was 22:43."

"And since then, those two have been in charge?"

"Yes."

Axel looked over at the two uniformed officers. He raised his voice. "How the hell is it possible for a man to be killed right under your noses without you noticing it? What the fuck were you doing?"

"We haven't seen anything – we were on watch down there most of the night," replied the smaller of the two, a muscular guy with a crewcut and cold eyes. He pointed down to another gate less than 50 yards away.

"You will be questioned."

Axel turned to the divisional commander.

"What about the main entrances? Have they been guarded the whole time?"

"Not when it was at its roughest by the wall. We were asked by central command to provide assistance, so I sent everyone over here."

"Did you lock the gates?"

"I don't know. It was pretty chaotic. It's very confusing to be in here in the silence while the whole city's burning around you. I'll have to ask my people if they locked the gates."

"What about all the other gates – were they locked all night?"

"Yes."

"Is that something you know because you've checked it or is it just something you're standing here saying because you're afraid you've fucked up?"

"It's something I'm assuming."

"It sounds like you've all been sleeping on the job. When you've been told to guard the place, you should bloody guard it and lock it so no one can come in," said Axel, then softened up a little. "If not, the least you could've done was spot whoever killed him over there."

The last remark was said with a smile, but it just bounced off the officer.

"I don't report to you. We did what we were told to do."

Axel tried to imagine what it might have been like guarding the cemetery tonight. It was an enormous area. The two main entrances were 300 and 600 yards away. He went over to the paramedic and shook hands.

"Man in his forties. I think he's been strangled, but I'm not sure because his lips are bloody, as if he's been beaten. I can't say exactly what he died of. He's cold, but not totally cold," said the doctor.

"Have you taken his temperature?"

"No, I didn't want to touch anything."

"When did you get here?"

"Three twenty-two."

"Did he die here?"

"I don't know."

While they were speaking, Axel looked over at the dead man. He was slight and appeared to be dark-haired, with a narrow face and wide open, empty brown eyes. Axel took a few steps closer. The custom was to wait for the forensics team, let them do their work and afterwards hold a preliminary post-mortem with a forensic pathologist, but Axel always tried to read the crime scene right away. The first unconscious impression could be invaluable later.

There were traces of blood on the body's lips; not red, closer to black, the colour blood goes when oxygen has been working on it for a short time. The tongue was sticking out between them, thick and purple, as often seen in victims of strangling.

The earth around the body was heavy and black, with no grass. There were bottle tops, broken glass, a chipped cobblestone, wet branches and a pizza box between the white snowdrops. No particular signs of a fight, but on the wall about three feet above his head there were traces of a dried liquid, most likely blood. Maybe he had been killed right here?

Axel thought it through: was it one of the autonomists who, during the street fighting, had got into a scuffle with some officers, who had then overreacted? At the police academy in recent years, much had been done to ensure the mental health of the corps, but it didn't change the fact that many policemen hated the demonstrators in Nørrebro and their occasionally life-threatening actions. There weren't many who, like Axel, could remember as far back as May 18, 1993, when the police had found themselves forced to shoot at a group of demonstrators who were on the verge of killing them with cobblestones – but there were enough confrontations nowadays for the hatred to flare up again.

He had to swiftly get an overview of which police officers had been on guard duty in the cemetery. And if it turned out that they had nothing to do with the murder, who could have killed him and, moreover, dumped him in a place that was swarming with cops, while the rest of the city had been vacuumed clean of police?

Axel walked up to the wall and looked behind the dead man's back. His hands were bound with something that looked like strips – the modern plastic handcuffs that the police used. They had been pulled really tight and seemed to have cut into the skin on his wrist. He was wearing a pair of black military boots, black canvas trousers, a brown sweater and a black windcheater. He didn't look like a typical autonomist. Axel went over to him and bent down. The smell of death was mixed with the stench of urine. It could have been people who had pissed up against the wall, but it was more likely the victim who had wet himself during the treatment he had been subjected to. Axel carefully put his hand into the inside pocket of the jacket and fished around for a wallet or something else that could reveal who he was.

Nothing.

He called the divisional commander over.

"I'll need a list of the names and numbers of the men on duty in here last night, where they've been, when, and records of anyone else who's been in the area – personnel, people under arrest, press – with names and civil registration numbers. And then all of you will have to come into HQ to report what you've seen – or not seen."

"Isn't that a bit over the top? We've been on the go since eight o'clock yesterday evening."

"Nothing is over the top when it comes to murder." Axel looked down the path. "Do you have everything under control? Are you sure you haven't seen anyone here yesterday evening or tonight?"

He got an ice-cold, indignant look from his colleague.

"We've taken six people in total – four of them climbed over the wall during the street fighting outside and they were just thrown out again. Two were arrested. We hunted them down with dogs. They were stockpiling Molotov cocktails in here."

"No one else?"

"We haven't seen anyone. We've kept it completely closed."

Axel shook his head and nodded at a figure trudging towards them. "And what about him over there, you bloody amateur? Is he one of ours in civvies, maybe?"

3

Axel had seen him hundreds of times before. One of the city's originals, king of the cemetery, which he roamed all year round in a thin, long-sleeved blue jersey, torn at the back, dirty jeans and wellingtons. He would rummage in the rubbish bins, eat a packet of sliced bread or large bars of dark chocolate and wander about incessantly, gesticulating and talking to himself.

The divisional commander looked down the path, his face becoming more and more flushed as the man approached. He stopped in front of them, at first without saying anything, but looking inquisitively from one to the other.

"Mornin'," he said at last, with a deep and clear intonation, as if the greeting was so voluminous that it required great effort and care to get it out of his mouth. "You've closed down the finest park in town. I want to ask you to open it up again. It's not nice for people who live here. Not for the birds either," he said.

"Shall we arrest him?" asked the divisional commander brusquely.

"You're not arresting anyone."

Axel put a hand on the wandering man's shoulder and led him a little to one side, away from the body and the policemen. He had wild brown hair, full beard and pale blue eyes that looked without seeing anything.

"Aren't you freezing?" asked Axel.

"No. You could say I've got an inner warmth."

"How long have you been in here?"

"I've done my rounds. I've walked my paths. I have a system that I have to keep to."

"Have you met anyone in here?"

"I met lots of them over there," he said, pointing at the officers by the van. "But they didn't meet me," he sniggered.

"You have to tell me how long you've been here and what you've seen, or else I'll have to take you in to HQ."

"It isn't your cemetery, isn't theirs either – nor his," he said, pointing over at the wall where the body was sitting.

"Theirs? Who's 'theirs'?"

"People who come here. It's the dead who live here. It's their place."

"Have you seen that guy over there before?"

He turned his face and stared up at the sky with empty eyes.

"If you don't answer me, I'll take you down to HQ and throw you in a cell."

He looked at Axel as if he lived in a world where cells didn't exist.

"I haven't seen him. I haven't seen anybody. I heard them all over the place. Their screaming and yelling and lights and sirens. All night. Fires and bangs! I just walk around and look after the place. I've been keeping to Kierkegaard's end because them there've been up this end," he said, pointing at the officers. "But it's too bad for him that he's dead. Now he can live here. If he's allowed."

Axel got his name and the address of the hostel he was living in, and asked one of the uniforms to escort him out.

He heard the sound of a vehicle and saw a Ford Transit from forensics coming down the path. The driver, Brian Boldsen, never called anything but BB, was one of the department's veterans as far as murder was concerned, and Axel knew he couldn't have a better scene of crime officer. On the other hand, he was surprised there were only two of them.

He went over to the van and said hello to BB.

"Why aren't there more of you?"

"Why do you think?"

"I don't think anything, I just ask."

"The others are filming."

"Filming?"

"Yes, I assume they're all tucked up now, but we've had a handful of men allocated to filming the riots, so that we can get some proper evidence on everyone who's been arrested."

"Not you, too?" Axel shook his head. Even Homicide had had to allocate people to the clearing of the Youth House and the anticipated disturbances. Yesterday evening, Axel had seen three of his colleagues from his window in a group of six plain-clothes officers monitoring the riots in order to make targeted arrests. One of them had pulled two small young women off a bike because they were cycling without lights. Skilled murder investigators running around playing bogeymen towards punk girls with too much mascara and a whole iron foundry pierced in their faces.

He heard the sound of a helicopter and looked up at TV2 News' latest acquisition hovering above them.

There won't be any lack of television pictures of this show, he thought. He knew that would be an advantage. There would be recordings from the air, both from the police's own helicopter and from the TV2 News helicopter. And both TV stations had had numerous camera teams on the streets. Although they never handed over unedited tape from their broadcasts, Axel could draw on his contacts, and it had rarely been a problem to negotiate his way to some tapes with the journalists he knew. Axel would call a TV2 reporter he had been out with a few times and who, with some success, had tried to relieve his insomnia with sex and joints. In return, he had provided her with information on a few inquiries that were insignificant for him but interesting for her.

"Who's the victim?" asked BB.

"I don't know. He hasn't got a chassis number, nothing in his inside pocket, but he's been given a proper going over by whoever's sorted him. He's been beaten, probably strangled. His tongue's flopping out of his mouth."

"Have you been messing with him? You know I don't like that."

"Relax. He's as good as untouched."

BB gestured towards the path and the grass and the ground where the body was lying.

"All those tyre tracks, all of them, they must be covered now, so that we can get an impression before any other geniuses trudge around in them. Fetch the equipment and get going," he said to his colleague, whom Axel hadn't met before.

Axel left the dead man to BB and poured himself a cup of coffee from the big thermos forensics always had in the back of their van.

He looked up at the row of houses on the other side of the wall, mostly older residential properties, a five-storey red brick, and two properties on four floors, one ochre, the other peach-coloured and dull in the pale light of dawn. Between them, filling a gap, was a newer building in grey concrete with a flat roof and a balcony at the top. There was an owl on the railing. It was made of plastic and had been sitting looking out over the cemetery for as long as Axel could remember, but now he noticed it had company. A few feet further down the railing sat something that looked like a camcorder.

"What's that up there? Isn't that a camera?"

Axel waved the divisional commander over to him. He looked from Axel up to the roof.

"Maybe. Haven't seen it before."

"We have to get that down as soon as we're done here," said Axel.

BB was in the process of peeling the balaclava off the victim's head. A white plastic collar had been placed under his throat, like the ones dogs have put on them to stop them licking themselves, so everything that fell off him as the hood was rolled up was caught. Axel watched in fascination as the man's face came into view. His skin was white and stood out in stark contrast to the bloody mouth and purple tongue. Two abrasions at the temple and blue, swollen marks around both eyes. He looked Slavic.

"Any news on who he is?" Axel asked BB, who had left the body and had come over to the small gathering.

"Got nothing on him."

"What can you say about him for the description?"

"40-50 years old. Male. Between five-ten and about six-two. Black hair, moustache, brown eyes, thin but muscular, two tattoos, one on the chest, one on the forearm, one could be a prison tattoo. I need to transfer the photos to my laptop so we can get them sent in. That's our best chance of identifying him, along with the fingerprints."

"Can I see them?"

"Tread carefully and come here."

Axel followed BB over to the body. The forensics technician had opened the victim's jacket. He pulled up the left sleeve. On the forearm it said 'Louie' in childish writing. Was he gay? Or was it a girl's name? A son?

BB lifted up the sweater and the shirt underneath. There were bruises on the upper body, black hair on the flat, muscular chest, and two inches above the left nipple was a different, clean, clear tattoo. On the heart side. A black, two-headed eagle with the tongue sticking far out of the beak and the date 18.3.2001 underneath.

Axel thought he recognised it, but couldn't recall where from.

"If the fingerprints don't give us anything, we'll have to send the pictures out."

Axel was dying for a smoke. Four years without cigarettes hadn't driven out the craving in the pit of his stomach. He helped himself to another cup of coffee.

The light hadn't yet pierced through the clouds, but the day would soon be here. A squirrel ran over a path and shot up a tree trunk. The leafless crowns were stretching out like a forest of arms appealing to the morning sky. It was quiet now. The riots had stopped, the demonstrators and troublemakers had gone home to sleep, but Axel was sure they would return in numbers during the day.

He looked around. Murder and police-marking tape.

Assistens normally meant peace. He knew the cemetery from long summer afternoons in the sun with his daughter, on a blanket between the overturned headstones and old trees. There were no memories here of crime scenes or confrontations with suspects. The consecrated ground and its half-million dead had always been an oasis surrounded by crime on all sides. Now it had become part of the neighbourhood.

Axel didn't like it.

He stood in front of a large green steel noticeboard with the cemetery's rules of conduct printed in Danish, English, Arabic and Turkish – yet another expression of the municipality's abysmal ignorance of the composition of the population in the district. The Turks had long since left for suburban municipalities. The majority of the neighbourhood's current foreign inhabitants were war and poverty refugees with few possessions and a lot of trauma in tow.

Next to the rules there was another green plate with a map of the many noteworthy graves that lay spread out across the various sections of the cemetery. Hans Christian Andersen, Søren Kierkegaard, Dan Turèll, Michael Strunge, Hans Scherfig, Jens August Schade, and others from the Danish literary canon. In the old days, it was said that Nørrebro would be the cultural centre of the country if it was allowed to include its dead.

That was then.

4

A Volvo Estate rounded the corner of the path on crunching tyres and stopped two yards from Axel. The Swede and Mr Clean. Forensic Pathology and Moral Virtue got out and walked towards Axel, who, despite being almost six foot two, had to admit he was still two or three inches short of Darling's impressive height.

The detective chief inspector was the owner of the tightest trousers in the Danish police force. They sat so far up in his crotch that you'd expect him to break into castrato arias when he opened his mouth. The tight crotch was the subject of many whispered conversations – not least among the force's women – because you could see the bulge from his dick that lay like a crumpled, slumbering snake on the left side. It was no small boost for the interest in him that John Darling had the look of a clean-cut male fashion model. Tall, muscular, fair-haired, with friendly blue eyes, smiling and very serious at one and the same time. He was an able investigator, faultless and thorough, but those trousers? Bloody hell, they must be uncomfortable.

Axel spat sour coffee out on the path in front of the two men.

"Nice to see you two've come out of the closet and gone public," he said.

John Darling's lower lip curved a fraction and an indulgent smile blinked in his eyes; otherwise he kept a straight face. The Swede, whose proper name was Lennart Jönsson, laughed heartily and disarmingly.

"Philip Marlowe in all his glory, I'm honoured. I picked your colleague up at the gate. We didn't know if there'd be room for both cars. I can hear you're in a good mood as usual. Shall we drop the pre-school witticisms and get to the point, or is this just your way of sweating off all the weak beers you drank yesterday?"

"Bit bloody rich – it's you two staggering in late morning like you've been on the booze all night. I've been here since four."

"Shut up, Axel. What do you have for me?"

Axel gave him the details of the case.

"God, that balaclava – spells trouble. I'm glad it isn't me having to take it to the press," said the Swede.

The chief pathologist's hands had rummaged around in the cadaver of just about every murder victim in Copenhagen for the last fifteen years; he was a legend among murder investigators across the whole of Europe. The tsunami in Thailand; the bombings in Madrid; the ethnic cleansing in Kosovo, and before that in Bosnia – moreover, Lennart Jönsson was a frequently used media commentator in TV crime programmes because of his straightforward and jovial manner, always ready with an aphorism or a pithy quote. Tall, with a potbelly, a genial, impish smile in the eyes under his grey hair, bags and wrinkles in his entire face, forever chewing tobacco. And Axel's best friend.

They went over to the body where BB and his colleague were working.

"A body in a place like this – it's just too much," said Darling with disgust.

"What do you mean? There's nothing but bloody dead bodies here."

"Cemeteries just give me the creeps."

As the investigation was Axel's, it was his job to do the preliminary post-mortem with the Swede. They agreed that Darling should take care of interviewing witnesses and the residents of the houses opposite, as well as the police officers in the cemetery. In addition, he would investigate whether there were officers on the street who might have seen anything and would make contact with the video people and the police helicopter crew. He immediately got going with calling people in for door-to-door inquiries.

Before Axel began the post-mortem, he grabbed Darling's arm and pointed to the owl.

"What the hell? It's gone!"

"What's gone?" asked the tall, fair-haired policeman.

"The camera. There was a camera on the railing only an hour ago." Axel called the divisional commander over. "Tell him what you saw when we were standing here and I pointed up at the railing!"

"There was a camera up there. Looked like one, anyway."

Axel had already started walking before he had completed the sentence. Darling followed him out through the gate and across Nørrebrogade.

"Has the crime scene journal been started?" he said from behind Axel.

"No, I haven't had time. You're very welcome."

"You know it should be done from the start. You'll have problems with Corneliussen because of this. It isn't just a load of bullshit. It's important if something goes wrong or a lawyer tries to screw us in court."

Axel wasn't much for paperwork at this stage of a murder investigation – certainly not the journal, where you had to register who was at a crime scene, what they were doing and when they did it. It was usually done by a detective, but as Axel had been alone, he should have got one of the uniforms to do it. It was a mistake.

"I was alone. I was busy. We'll have to fix it when we've done this."

"If you do an overview for the first four hours, I'll take over. I'm just saying: Corneliussen is ready with the knife if you make the slightest slip-up. He asked me to keep an eye on you."

Axel wasn't in any doubt about that. Corneliussen was collecting mistakes until he had enough to get Axel out of the division and preferably right out of the police district or even the force. He shivered at the prospect of being condemned to a Jutland police district or stationed in the Europol mausoleum in The Hague.

Darling pressed on all the buttons to the entry phones at the front door and they waited until they were let into the hallway. Axel stopped at a noticeboard where there were various messages, including a phone number for the caretaker. He added it to his contacts and they started going up the stairs.

"OK. But he was right. You've already caught me out once. Why don't you just give him what he wants?"

"Because I respect you. You're a skilful investigator and a good colleague. You just don't know where the line is, so you step over it time and time again. Perhaps you do know, but you ignore it on purpose. And I don't like that."

They had reached the last floor. A steel staircase led up to the terrace. The door at the end was old and locked. Axel looked up the number of the caretaker and rang him. After four rings, it went to answerphone. He put his mobile in his inside pocket. Darling was about to say something when Axel grabbed the railing with both hands and kicked the door in. The lock splintered and the door flew open, split by the lower hinge.

"I have to live up to my rep," he said to the despairing John Darling.

Copenhagen is built up to the fifth floor throughout the city, broadly speaking. The five districts that surround the inner city – Nørrebro, Østerbro, Frederiksberg, Vesterbro and Amager – consist mainly of brick-built residential properties from the turn of the 20th century, with Dutch windows, bays, stairwells and sloping slate or red-tile roofs. Axel and Darling were on what corresponded to the sixth floor and thus had a view over the whole city: the City Hall tower, the Church of Our Lady, the two SAS hotels and the HC Ørsted power station with its gigantic pennants of white smoke against the dark, grey sky.

The plastic owl sat in pomp where it had always sat. Axel and John Darling went to the railing and studied the spot where Axel thought the camera had been located. There was an inch-long shiny new scratch. Axel stepped back and looked at the base of the terrace. Nothing. Or was that dust on the edge of one of the wooden sheets that served as a floor? It looked like plastic particles.

John Darling bent down and gently lifted the sheet next to the mark on the railing. There was a cracked camera foot lying under it. Axel called BB.

"We need you to get up here with fingerprint equipment, camera, evidence bags, the whole lot, right now."

He went over to the railing without touching it and looked straight down at the crime scene, which lay diagonally below them. BB was already on his way to the van for the equipment. Assistens Cemetery spread out beneath Axel and around it lay the rest of the neighbourhood he recognised as his own, for better or worse.

On one side, Kapelvej and Blågårds Plads, once a red and raw working-class quarter, later filled with left-wing pubs, third world solidarity associations, small revolutionary parties, eco shops and a favourite hang-out for squatters and autonomists. In the 80s, refugee families from the Middle East and North Africa moved into the plethora of municipally assigned housing. And some of their children now saw the neighbourhood as their only refuge in the middle of a country they felt had disowned them. That had given extra work to Axel's colleagues.

The gang from Blågårds Plads had appropriated Nørrebro's hash trade, which amounted to a double-digit million figure per year. The hard core had all of the serious crimes against the person on their criminal records: armed robberies, violence, knife attacks and murder – including that of an innocent Italian backpacker who had come to the neighbourhood late one night looking for a little hash and left it in an ambulance with six knife wounds in his body, two of them fatal.

If Axel looked the other way, he could see row after row of tenement houses from the turn of the 20th century. Here lay Jægersborggade, a city-renewal project without end, where some Hell's Angels lived and had their hash clubs. The Hell's Angels didn't get mixed up in the current conflict. With their Neanderthal ideals, they didn't harbour any sympathies for the Youth House and the alternative lifestyles of its users.

Axel turned to John Darling.

"Who would set a camera up here?" he asked, adding, before his colleague could answer, "and then remove it again?"

"Who says the person who set it up removed it?" asked Darling.

"It must be someone with access to the roof. We have to get the people in this stairwell out so we can check out the residents straight away. I have to do the post-mortem now, but I suggest you have the entrance guarded and keep everyone indoors so that we can interview them before they go to work. I'll be back when I've finished with the Swede."

Axel went back to the cemetery. His stomach was rumbling. He would have to eat something soon.

The whole area around the victim had been thoroughly photographed. Everything had been collected and packed in 172 evidence bags, which were in the back of the forensics van. There were soil samples from under the body, hair that had been sucked up with a special hand-held vacuum cleaner that picked up things so small they were hard to spot – fluff, dust and crumbs – a thread, six pieces of string of different sizes, a cigarette butt, four different bottle tops, a pizza box, three coke cans, 27 branches and a chipped cobblestone. The wall had been dusted with fingerprint powder, and various impressions of shoes and tyres had been marked, which the assistant was in the process of taking casts of. Axel knew it was just the beginning. BB would be dusting off around the cemetery for the next couple of days. But he was finished with the body for now. Two ambulance personnel were waiting to move it to the criminal forensics department when the Swede gave permission.

He sat in the front seat of his Volvo rummaging in his snuff box. Axel sat down beside him.

"You look a bit hangdog, Mr Steen," he said without looking up at Axel.

"I'm sleeping badly at night."

"We have remedies for that."

"I have the same dream over and over again. I'm having sex with Cecilie. Nice, but unbearable at the same time because I know she's not mine."

"Doesn't sound nice. Perhaps you're reading too much into it. You know, during sleep, blood runs into the genitals, so you get an erection.

In men, it happens a lot of times during the night, most strongly in the morning."

"Which means?"

"I'm just saying that it may not be as symbolic as you want to make it. It doesn't necessarily say anything about your relationship with Cecilie. She's just the person you last had a good, long sex life with; she's your unconscious frame of reference when it comes to screwing and being happy. I think you should drop all that dream analysis, take some good sleeping pills and drink a few large glasses of red wine so that you can get some peace at night."

Maybe he's right. Maybe I should replace the hash with pills and red wine, thought Axel.

The Swede put a twist of tobacco in his mouth, sat still for a while and stared out of the windscreen with his hands folded on his stomach and his chin resting on his chest.

"Succubus," he said.

"Suck you what?"

"Succubus, my dear Steen. A succubus is a female demon who visits men at night as they sleep, screws them and collects their semen so that they lose their power and wilt away. They were fashionable in the Middle Ages. Does your ex-wife come in the guise of a succubus?"

"What are you talking about?"

"Does she have small bat wings on her back, cat's eyes, furry tail or horns when she comes to you?"

"You're nuts."

The Swede picked his nose.

"Then it probably isn't a succubus," he said reluctantly. "Shame – that could've been fun. Perhaps you should consider following my advice. I can write you a prescription."

They sat a while and saw BB return from the roof terrace and start working around the body again. The Swede opened the car door, hawked and spat a clump of black slime out on the path.

"Wouldn't bloody mind actually having a visit from one of those succubuses at night," said Axel.

The Swede chuckled and opened his mouth, so that Axel could see straight into a rubbish dump of tobacco and silver fillings.

"Bloody hell, are you that desperate? Let's get started with the post-mortem before everything dissolves into medieval fantasies."

They got out and went over to the body.

"I haven't finished the temperature measurements, but off the bat I'd estimate he died between midnight and two, depending on whether he died here or was somewhere warmer first, but I can't answer that until I've done the autopsy."

Between midnight and two. They had to get a precise picture of what was happening on the street during that time – and quickly. Demonstrations, patrols, pedestrians, witnesses from the houses opposite. It was going to be a huge job.

"The cause of death is probably strangulation. There's clear point-shaped bleeding in the eyes, marks on the throat, and I think both the larynx and the thyroid cartilage have been crushed."

"Are you sure he's been strangled?"

"My dear Mr Steen. I can't rule out anything at this stage. I'm just saying, my bet is that someone's strangled him here with their hands and that he's been so debilitated by violence, the bound hands, alcohol, drugs – or whatever – that he hasn't been able to put up much resistance. The typical post-mortem findings in this kind of strangulation are very striking and they're all here. Do you want a medical examination?"

"No thanks."

"The victim has multiple lesions on the body and in the face from blows – blunt force trauma. An interesting case. Not least because of the plastic handcuffs around his wrists. The strip is really tight. He must've been completely numb. I'm looking forward to getting him opened up so we can get into the details."

"Is there anything else?"

"Yes, there's something rather strange. There are signs he's been electrocuted."

"Electrocuted?"

"Yes, I think so. Stun gun, you know. USA. That shit can be bought online. I can tell you what it is when we've examined it."

"Could it have been a woman?"

"Because of the stun gun? It only paralyses short-term. And he's been strangled very forcefully. So he would have to have been lying down or been anaesthetised otherwise. And she would have to be strong and have big hands. He isn't all that small, you know."

It was ten o'clock. He would soon have to go over to John Darling and see how it was going with the interviews.

"Once you're finished up here, come out to me after lunch – by then I'll be able to spell it out for you," said Lennart Jönsson.

Axel sat in the Swede's car with the preliminary post-mortem report. He knew perfectly well that he was playing with fire. As if it wasn't enough that for two years he had been finding it harder and harder to sleep at night, the sleeplessness had acquired a companion during the day, which made him go out like a light for a short time. A mixture of dizziness and a paralysing chill in the brain that, quick as lightning, slid into sleep – often combined with a rapid bombardment of dreams and visions that fed on the reality he had just left and from the sounds which still penetrated through the gauze of sleep. It didn't last much longer than a couple of minutes, but that was bad enough, he thought, because he had no control over it.

The only person who had caught him in it was the Swede. In some periods, it had occurred several times a month, most frequently as an investigation was coming to a head and his sleep deprivation was at its worst.

He knew that right now there was a risk he would slide into one of his short sleep breaks, but he had to sit a while and get some warmth and read. The preliminary post-mortem report was beautifully filled out, and he studied it, but he didn't get beyond the temperature notes before it came oozing in, the chill in the brain, the fatigue and the paralysis. The sight of the cemetery, the hard-working technical investigators and the Swede, who was crouched by the body, disappeared behind his heavy eyelids. He just managed the thought that it was impressive a man of Lennart Jönsson's age and weight could get up so nimbly from such a difficult kneeling position. The dream from last night came creeping back like a siren and devoured him whole: his longing was satiated with the taste of her skin, her smile releasing a surge of feeling within him. Velvet-soft sex without obstacles, the kind that reality never offered; creamy caramels, freedom, pussy.

His body gave a jerk. Then he was awake. Two or three minutes had elapsed. This time it hadn't been quite as painful as last night. The dream was mixed with the memory of Cecilie, her tenderness towards their daughter, Emma, a gentle, conciliatory caress for him, her empathetic listening to his problems. Axel surrendered to his memories of his time with her. Normally, he didn't dare see her like that; her good sides were hidden behind a screen of egoism and ruthlessness. Normally, he saw her only as the one who had left him, rejected him; he saw her wet vagina and her seductive smile as a mockery of his loneliness, but now he sat again in the middle of their everyday life two years ago and asked himself if he could have prevented it.

5

There was a café on the ground floor of the property where Darling and two other police officers were conducting door-to-door interviews. Axel ordered a cup of black filter coffee and sat facing the street.

'The only good cop is a dead cop' was written in big black letters on the yellow wall right opposite him.

He took out his mobile phone. Three text messages had arrived; the first was from Cecilie.

"Don't think Emma should go to yours during all this chaos. It'll frighten her. Cecilie."

It was his turn to have Emma this weekend. Right now, he was having difficulty figuring out how he was going to handle this investigation and be with her simultaneously, but he had no intention of forfeiting his time with her. Three days every fortnight was already little enough.

He opened the next message, also from Cecilie.

'Will you please answer? I have to send her to kindergarten now.'

The last text was from John Darling.

'We're on the third floor. Come up!'

Axel tapped the eight numbers he knew in his sleep.

"Hi," she said.

"Hi, I'll pick her up at four o'clock. There's nothing to worry about."

"Haven't you got a murder investigation?"

"Yes, but…"

"I won't have it, Axel."

"It's my weekend. I'll take care of her. I can't just move house because you're overprotective."

"I'm not being overprotective, I just know what you're like when you've got an investigation on your mind. Last time you left her alone at home for a full afternoon. I'm not having it."

"Relax. She sat watching Jungle Book while I was out for two hours. It's no worse than letting her watch TV while you do the shopping, is it? I'll take care of her."

"She watched Jungle Book twice. Promise you won't leave her alone. And you won't sit watching street battles on TV together. And you won't tell her about your new investigation. And you won't take her with you to forensics and other sick places like last time. I'm just not having it. She's only five years old, for God's sake."

"Can I talk to her? Is she with you now?"

"No, she's on her way to kindergarten."

"But aren't you at home?"

"Yes. Jens has taken her."

Axel took a deep breath.

"I'll pick her up at four o'clock."

He hung up without waiting for an answer.

Jens.

Jens has taken her.

That was the name he would have preferred not to hear. Axel didn't know him personally, but knew he was good. Good at his job in the pinstriped way: a bright, perfect smartarse on his way to the top of the PET hierarchy. He had previously been employed by the prosecutor's office at Copenhagen Police and for a number of years had been the person who decided whether charges should be brought in cases investigated by Axel and his colleagues. He wasn't interested in the actual cases, but in what results they could produce for him, and if there was the slightest doubt as to whether a case could lead to a conviction, he dropped it. That didn't make him popular with the police, but it had done wonders for his career. Like many of his fellow officers, Axel distrusted lawyers, not only because they had a longer education, earned more and were an arrogant bunch of know-it-alls, but also because, with all their pedantic rules on administering justice and their circular deliberations, they were grit in the machinery of a hard-working detective. Jens Jessen embodied everything that Axel loathed in police lawyers, and quite a lot more.

Following his period in the prosecutor's office, Jens Jessen was moved further up the rankings to the National Police's Operative Department, where he worked with Cecilie, a head clerk. This was two and a half years after Emma was born and their marriage was on the rocks. Axel worked in the Homicide Division and thought of nothing but pursuing the perpetrator of two unsolved murders of women. Cecilie was in the process of kick-starting her career again and Emma filled the rest of their lives. Five months later, Cecilie resigned and got a job with a hotshot lawyer specialising in criminal law.

On her first working day, Emma was deposited at her grandmother's, and Axel naively thought they were going to celebrate Cecilie's new job. For once he had come home early and discovered they were alone. Instead, it became a long, dark conversation about divorce, child arrangements, maintenance and Jens Jessen. The surprise and humiliation over not seeing it coming – that was the worst. He had nothing to contribute. It was all decided before he had said a word. He tried to convince her that it was wrong, both for them and for Emma. And that he would change and work less, be at home more, closeness, intimacy, he would do anything, but he knew it wasn't working. They were just words. And she was totally cold.

The less he thought about that day the better.

Axel emptied his cup of coffee, got up from the café chair, walked up to the bar and asked if they knew anything about a camera that had been set up on the roof terrace. No one knew anything about it. So he went out on the street. To his left was a bed showroom, which had had its windows smashed several times during previous disturbances, a newsagent, four kebab shops, two hairdressers, a bicycle mechanic and two greengrocers, most of the façades bearing both Danish and Arabic lettering. Two carpenters were boarding up the display windows of the bed showroom. Dream Sleep, it said on the façade, but the dreams lay broken on the pavement.

The boarding up of windows was routine on Nørrebro when disturbances were expected, or on New Year's Eve, when dozens of businesses would have their windows smashed. The vandalism wasn't arbitrary. There was a hierarchy. The banks were at the top, closely followed by McDonald's and 7-Eleven, because in the eyes of the hooligans they were in cahoots with the United States. The previous owner of the bed business had complained about the general squalidness of the district, which in his opinion was caused by people from the Youth House and, in particular, about their vandalisation of the listed wall around Assistens Cemetery. And the hooligans had never forgotten that. He had ended up moving to Østerbro.

Axel went into the bed showroom. The Pakistani owner came running out from a back room.

"Everything closed," he shouted.

"Axel Steen, CID, I have a few questions."

"Police? Ha ha! What use you to me, police? Everyone gone now. So you come. Ha ha! Police, you not good enough."

"Calm down. I understand your frustration, but a crime's been committed just over there on the other side of the wall, and I have some questions I'd like you to answer."

"Yes, you're right. Many crimes committed here, but you couldn't care less. Everything smashed and burned. So go away and take your crime with you, police."

"I saw a camera this morning on a railing on the roof of the house next door. Do you know anything about it?"

"I know. It's mine. Not illegal!"

"You set it up?"

"Yes, I set it up."

"It's very illegal, but that's not why I'm here. I want to hear about the camera."

"Yesterday, I couldn't get carpenter to come and board up, because too much unrest so they were scared, yes, everyone scared, so I set up camcorder to film them. Evidence, you understand? So I know who smashed. You don't come with help."

"Do you have the camera here?"

"I do not have camera. On the roof. You just said."

"It was up on the roof. Now it's gone."

The man ran out of the showroom with Axel on his heels.

"When did you last see it?"

"It's gone, that shit! Don't give me that shit, that Nørrebro shit, that police shit. Nothing working. You can smash it all. No one come and help. Police are busy. Police ask if I am in mortal danger when I call, or if I call from own number, or what number I live, or my civil registration number. They say I am not in system or on their screen. Can I call again later? What good is all that shit when they rob my business and burn my beds? I hate your police shit," shouted the owner.

Axel dragged him back in the showroom and shook him, making his head bobble back and forth.

"Calm down, for fuck's sake, and listen to me. You close your business and then we'll get the evidence together so that you can get everything you've lost replaced. Now tell me when you put that camera up."

The Pakistani's eyes were completely dead. They looked as if he had stopped in the middle of something and couldn't move on.

"Do you hear me? When did you put it up?" shouted Axel.

"Ten o'clock. Yesterday."

"And how long could it run without being changed?"

"36 hours."

"And now you don't know where it is?"

"No, I know nothing. Nothing."

He shook his head despondently. Axel got the make of the camcorder, left him and went into the house next door to find Darling.

The main door of the third-floor flat was plastered with stickers from autonomous meetings and festivals. "Capitalist scum out!" shouted a sticker bearing Nørrebro's postcode, 2200 N. The door was open, so Axel went into the flat and continued down a long passage, guided by the sound of voices.

John Darling was sitting with two young women in a kitchen overlooking the backyard. On the table between them was a lump of hash the size of a walnut, next to a wooden box with space for six bottles. There were only two in it, but they were both full of a clear liquid and had a cloth stuck in the neck. It was almost too good to be true.

"I don't know shit, man. I don't know where it came from. Get that into your head!" spluttered one of the girls as Axel came in. She was in her early 20s, blonde with purple stripes, large gilt hoop earrings, black leggings and a grey vest of fine-mesh net. She was smoking and looked extremely offended. The other girl was smaller and thinner, withdrawn under black hair and seemed younger, maybe. She seemed to be on the verge of a breakdown.

"Shall I take over here?" said Axel, pointing at the younger one.

Darling winked a yes.

"Do you live here?" Axel asked.

The girl nodded once.

"What's your name?"

"Rosa… Rosa Lux."

"Come on, what's your real name?"

The girl looked like she was going to cry.

"Rosa Jensen."

"You don't even have the right to be here, you fucking pigs. Do you have a search permit?" shouted the blonde.

Axel looked at her.

"What's your name?"

"Liz."

"Now listen, Liz. It's called a search warrant and you're partly right. We don't have one but we have you two, a lump of hash and two Molotov cocktails, ready for use. Outside there's several million kroner's worth of damage caused by these. And you probably had six, but four are gone. Perhaps you can only see the funny side and not the link, though you don't need much imagination to, but I can and I'm quite sure a judge will be able to. And he'll make sure we can investigate properly without you interrupting us, don't you think? Know what that means? That means that you two land in a cell straight away and sit there for two weeks with no one to talk to. If that's what you want, you can have it right now."

Liz shut up and looked away. The hate in her eyes had turned to defiance.

"I don't have time for any more of your crap. I need some answers. Now!"

Rosa was crying.

"How shall we do this? Are you going to answer our questions or should we call a police van?" said Axel.

The blonde bent her head in something that could be interpreted as a nod.

"Why don't you and I talk somewhere else. Where's your room?" he asked Rosa.

She showed him into a room where there were two mattresses on the floor around a low table with a block candle, which had melted over the table top.

The wall was covered in a large poster with the words "69 will never surrender": the house number of the Youth House, now transformed from something that, for the whole of Axel's adult life, had recalled childhood sniggers over a shorthand for mutual oral sex into a symbol of the struggle against him and all that the uniform stood for. A hatstand with riveted belts and leather cords hanging from it stood in the corner. From the window there was a clear view down to the crime scene. The body wasn't visible, but the officers, the projectors and the people in white overalls left no doubt that somebody was dead.

"Dry your eyes and sit down. Nothing's going to happen. I don't give a damn about the disturbances. I need information about a camera which was up on the roof and has been removed this morning.

Do you know anything about it?"

The girl sniffled and nodded.

"Where is it?"

"I don't know. Piver took it."

"Piver?"

"Yes, someone who lives here. This is actually his room, too."

Her eyes were wet, but she was beginning to get a grip on herself.

Axel looked around the room and noticed the big military boots, the skateboard behind the door and the pile of CDs in a corner.

"We were watching you from the window this morning and you pointed up to the roof several times."

"Then what happened?"

"Piver went down to the street to see what you were pointing at, and when he came back up he was completely off his head. He said there was a camera up there and that it had probably been filming everyone who'd been taking part in the demos down the street."

"So what? Why did he care about that?"

Now she started crying again and shook her head.

"What did he do next?"

"He ran up and fetched the camera and came down to the flat with it. Then that other officer banged on the door. And Piver disappeared down the back stairs."

"Taking the camera with him?"

"Yes." She was crying.

"Did you see what was on the camera?"

"No, Piver was about to switch it on when you came."

"Where's Piver now?"

"I don't know. He didn't say where he was going."

"Lend me your mobile."

She hesitated.

"It's important, for Christ's sake!"

He snatched it out of her hand. He ran through the contacts until he found Piver's name, then pressed on the details and took a note of the number before pressing call.

It was answered straightaway.

"Have the pigs gone?"

"Piver, you're speaking to Axel Steen from Copenhagen Police. It's very important that you don't destroy the camcorder you removed..."

The line went dead.

He rang again. Now the call didn't go through. He cursed his own stupidity.

"What does Piver look like and what was he wearing?" asked Axel.

The girl gave him a description that could apply to hundreds of young people on the street, but it would have to be enough for the time being. He took out his mobile and called the central communications service at HQ.

"I need tracking and tapping on a mobile number right away. A suspect in a murder investigation." He went out into the passage and gave the number of Piver's mobile.

The duty officer was sullen.

"It has to go by a judge and the prosecutor, you know."

"Yes, all right, for fuck's sake, but get going on it now. Call the telephone company and get it done under self-authorisation. We'll have to arrange the paperwork later. And get the conversations sent in to me and to Erna so that she can type them out."

All phone tapping had to be approved by a judge and, formally, it couldn't be put into effect until the judge had signed the warrant, but in urgent cases, the police could initiate the tapping at the telecommunications company "under self-authorisation" – in anticipation of the court's approval – and then had 24 hours to get it. And this was an urgent case.

Axel repeated the description of Piver and how he was dressed.

"Check him in criminal records. And send out an internal inquiry about him."

It made Rosa Jensen jump when Axel said the words "suspect in a murder investigation".

"A murder investigation? But… who's dead? Piver hasn't killed anybody."

"Maybe not, but if you want the best for him, get him to come in and hand the camcorder over to us, because it may well contain pictures of the murderer we're looking for."

"But what's happened?"

"I can't tell you that, but the camcorder is important to us. And in that context, it's completely uninteresting to me whether or not there are recordings of some autonomists smashing a window. Would you please tell him that when you make contact with him? And would you please give him my number? He can ring around the clock. I'm only interested in that recording. Tell him that."

6

Piver looked over his shoulder before getting on the bus. No one seemed to be watching him, but the intrusion by the police was still reverberating in his body. He pulled the cord on his hoodie tight around his head and sat down at the back after buying a ticket. Normally, he just showed a used one with an unclear date and time, but he didn't want any trouble over an illegal ticket today. The skin on his arms and legs was itching with a mixture of tiredness, excitement and withdrawal symptoms, and his pulse was still pumping with a wickedly heavy beat.

He had got away from the collective on Nørrebrogade to avoid the blue flashing lights. First through the backyard and the side streets, then venturing into the more crowded streets and finally out onto Nørrebrogade.

It was as if the city had been woken up too early. The colours from the night's bonfires were gone; the daylight seeped inexorably between the tenement blocks and revealed everything as a grey blotch of burned-out rubbish bins, burned-out cars and all-encompassing bleakness.

Nørrebro was under siege.

The police were driving round in their blue transits and stopping people in black clothes. A ring in the nose and a lilac tuft in the hair, and you were certain to be searched.

When he reached the Lakes, he began to panic. There were cops everywhere. And they were after him. He was sure of it. On Dronning Louises Bro, the bridge connecting Nørrebro to the inner city, they were spread over both pavements in small groups in riot gear – helmets with visors, pistols and handcuff strips hanging from their belts – leaning on motorcycles or police vans and guarding the crossing.

He had to get away, out of the district, relax the tension in his body and find a place where he could be alone and see what was on the tape. He felt in his rucksack again to where the camcorder was, as if it were a fragile treasure; but wasn't that exactly what it was when the cops were so anxious to get their hands on it?

This was worse than anything he had been involved in before. This was really fucking serious. Perhaps the others would take him seriously now. He was in a direct confrontation with the pigs. And he had crucial evidence of... yes, of what? They'd taken Rosa, hadn't they? How could that pig otherwise have rung him from Rosa's mobile just half an hour after he had split?

He tried to get a grip on the events of the previous night and the morning. He had just fetched the camcorder from the roof and found out how it worked when the cops hammered on the front door at the collective.

For seconds, as time stood still, they had stared at each other there in the kitchen, Rosa, Liz and him.

Rosa was the first to move. She shot up and ran up and down, her eyes flickering in panic.

"What are we going to do?"

Liz had dragged her back down on the chair and held a finger to her mouth. She whispered, "Stay calm!" but the look on her face was shouting the words. Then Liz pointed at him.

"What about the Molotovs?" she asked.

They had Germans from Kreuzberg living in one of the rooms. With two boxes of Molotovs. Piver had thought it was cool, but Liz had told them to get rid of them because of the fire hazard. The Germans hadn't returned after the night's demonstrations, and none of them were sure whether the bottles of petrol were still in the room. Liz had looked uneasy, more uneasy than he had ever seen the beautiful, confident punk.

"It'll be fucking expensive for us if they find them," she said despairingly.

Piver had felt his heart beating up in his throat like a hard drum that just became more and more insistent. Then he jumped up and grabbed Liz by the arm.

"Let me get out first," he said.

Liz was cool. She had let him go because of the camcorder. She had been through this many times in R3, where she had lived for a couple of years. But in the Box, as their collective was called because of the shape of the house, they weren't used to visits from the pigs from PET or the police. The Box wasn't really autonomous like the three rebel collectives in Nørrebro, that were just called R1, R2 and R3. Just like Piver. He wasn't an autonomist, even though he had been struggling to be accepted by them for almost two years. Perhaps this was finally his ticket to the inner circle?

The first time he visited R3, he had been reverential; he wanted to hide it, but he was in awe.

"You know what this means, right?" Liz said when they had been let in by the entry phone.

"Of course. Rebel collective 3."

"Good, you've done your homework. Don't embarrass me. These are my old friends."

Yes, you bet he had done his homework. This was where they lived, the people who had set fire to the Immigration Office in protest against the expulsion of a gay Iranian. And the rumours said that some of them had been involved in almost burning down the Integration Minister's house by throwing a Molotov cocktail into her garage some years ago. To be here was to become a part of all that. He had a sense, if not of history, then of cobblestones whistling through the air, and he had been completely electrified as they were let into R3 by a tall guy with short hair who gave Liz a hug and introduced himself as "Peter, but they call me Paris. Are you the guy who can edit and do layout?"

They needed that for AFA's magazine – that and someone who could help with the websites.

AFA – Antifascist Action – it was like being selected for the national football team after playing a youth match. Was it just because of Liz? No, she had taken him along because he had something to offer.

Feverish, muddled fantasies had swept through his mind. Himself being released and acclaimed on the steps of the city court, where he sang the International in front of several hundred autonomists and rolling television cameras. When he spoke at the collective meetings, they listened to him. He got straight to the point and told them where and how they should strike with maximum effect. And he always offered to take on the most dangerous tasks. Even though Liz's eyes begged him not to. He was on his way in. He had imagined.

But he couldn't follow the advice not to behave embarrassingly. In the middle of the bean pâté and lentil salad, he had asked if there was any exciting action in the pipeline.

Liz had rolled her eyes and a paralysed silence fell over the gathering, until Peter Paris looked coldly at him and asked where he came from.

"Aalborg," he had answered with his mouth full of brown rice.

So that was that.

"You have to do something about your bloody accent," Liz said later. "And learn to keep your mouth shut at the right times."

They had accepted his skills, but not him. For the first few months, he had thought it was a phase, but it just went on and on. He never got an admission card to the inner circle. Of course, he was there at the demos; it was hard to keep him away as he had personally done the layout for the flyer where they were announced. It had slowly dawned on him that the people he knew from the Youth House and these people had very little in common. For one group, 69 was a home; for the others it was a symbol of a war that had been waged long before he knew there was somewhere called Nørrebro. The people at R3 were inveterate warriors who didn't hesitate. They didn't snigger in the wrong places; they didn't steal bikes to get home from town in the morning; and you wouldn't find them sleeping on a staircase off their heads on hash and beer. On the other hand, it was them who went to prison, took part in all the major demos abroad and had friends in Kreuzberg and Milan.

Piver got off the bus at Christianshavns Torv on the other side of the inner city, crossed the street and tried not to look at the three police cars in the square and the crowd of cops standing around them. But he imagined he could feel them looking for him. Three streets, then he would be safe. His hands were tingling all the way out to his fingernails; he was craving a joint and desperate to see what the hell was on that tape. As he rounded the corner of Prinsessegade, the stench of burned rubbish bins filled his nose just as he made eye contact with a plain-clothes pig. He was standing in a group of three men on a corner at the intersection by the Church of Our Saviour. Piver was closer to Freetown Christiania than them, but the entrance was still 150 yards down the road. If he could get inside, they wouldn't have a chance of grabbing him. The police only went into the Freetown if there were a lot of them, and two or three plain-clothes pigs would be stoned out in no time. He looked away and walked faster. When he heard the steps behind him, he ran for his life, screaming for help.

"Stop him," roared the cops.

He could sense that everyone's attention was fixed on him and the police pursuing him. He felt them getting closer. The entrance to the Freetown was close now; he was hanging on to the rucksack with the camcorder in one hand while his legs whirred. He didn't have much left in him, but fear made his body stretch that bit extra, lift his legs faster, because soon he would be tackled and have his head smashed against the asphalt – goodbye camera, goodbye demos, goodbye Liz, goodbye everything. People were shouting "Police thugs" and "Fascist pigs", and Piver hoped all the Freetown guards would stop them. As he reached the entrance to Christiania by Bådmandsstræde, the sound of the storming footsteps disappeared behind him in a chorus of whistles and jeers from passers-by and people keeping guard at the entrance. He ran in along the path and looked back to make sure his pursuers had given up.

The plain-clothes officers who had tried to catch him had stopped at the junction and now retreated under scornful shouts and the odd stone from the group of 20 or thirty people hanging around at the entrance.

One had pulled out his baton and was waving it in the air; the other one, whom he had made eye contact with, shouted something that sounded like "We'll be back," and pointed at Piver, but his words were drowned by people shouting and dogs barking.

He was safe for now.

But not for long.

50 yards into the Freetown, he was approached by one of the guards from the entrance, who wanted to know what the hell he was up to. Crewcut, with two rings in his ear, a barbed wire tattoo around his neck and shining, cold eyes with a cruel gleam, he shoved him in the chest.

"What's going on, kid? Why were the police after you?"

He spun him a line that he had given them the finger and shouted pigs at them, so he was let go with a warning that he would get a hiding if he brought any trouble.

He had 97 kroner in his pocket. It was enough for a gram, but not for the couple of gold label beers at Woodstock or Nemoland, which he had been looking forward to. Maybe he could bum a drag or half a joint somewhere – then he would have the beers to fall back on. He walked down Pusher Street looking for someone he knew among the faces. But there wasn't anyone who could help him with money or a clean mobile phone. Although he felt safe here, he was still hyped up over the camcorder and the law coming to the flat. He had to know what had happened. He had to watch the whole recording.

7

Axel stepped out onto the street. Two pigeons were stuffing themselves on a pink puddle of vomit. The morning air was clear and slightly damp, but there was nothing that indicated rain. He looked up and down Nørrebrogade. On weekdays, an inferno of traffic and a shopping mecca where you could get everything from hookahs, driving lessons, Arabian wedding dresses and veils, halal lamb and plucked eyebrows to phone unlocking services, foreign currency exchange, counterfeit goods from China, Stieg Larsson's collected works, a single ticket to Pristina or just get drunk as a skunk.

Now the street looked like a building site. The city's refuse collectors were in the process of clearing the burned barricades and there were sounds of splintering, hammering and banging, of broken glass being knocked out of frames and massive chipboards being set up in the broken windows.

"Hey, Steen, Axel Steen!"

He turned towards the voice, which came from a man with a mobile in one hand, pen and notepad in the other, and a photo vest with a billion pockets over a blue thermal jacket. He knew the alert blue eyes in the big bony face. Jakob Sonne, journalist at the tabloid Ekstra Bladet, one of the city's most experienced crime reporters – with a photographer in tow.

"What's going on?"

Sonne swept aside the curtains of auburn hair that fell down on each side of his pointed granite face with his left hand, ran it through his locks and waited for Axel's reaction.

The photographer began snapping away.

Axel lifted his hand in front of the camera and closed it around the lens.

"Forget it. You don't take pictures of me here," said Axel.

"Hey, this is a public space…" began the photographer, but Jakob Sonne interrupted him.

"OK, wait a minute, leave him alone, let's just hear what's going on."

Axel crossed the street and began walking towards Assistens. He had often chatted with Sonne, an old-school reporter who sniffed around wherever the police were working and who had many sources internally in the force, right through the ranks. They weren't confidants, but Axel knew him as someone he could count on – if that was possible for a journalist, that is. He had given him information off the record several times, and Sonne had kept their agreements, which was crucial for Axel.

"What are you doing here?" asked Axel as Jakob Sonne loomed up alongside him.

"I was about to ask you the same thing. What does it look like? We're just out gauging the mood and doing a little reporting. Who's dead?"

Axel weighed up the pros and cons. Jakob Sonne wasn't enough of a fool not to figure out straight away that Axel was hardly out looking at burnt rubbish bins. And he might even have heard about the murder on the police radio, so it was no wonder he was here.

"I can't say very much, but it seems to be a man in his forties, and he's right there on the other side of the wall, but we don't know who he is. We have some clues though."

Jakob Sonne's eyes lit up.

"What clues?"

"It's too early to say. Let us work in peace, then you'll get something. And remember – I don't want to see myself in your newspaper, not in print or online. I'll come after you if you don't do as I say."

"Does it have any connection to the street battles? Is he an autonomist?"

Axel thought about the balaclava but held his tongue. He didn't have a problem with lying to the press if it was important for the investigation, but the question was whether revealing how the man was dressed would advance it. It would in any case mean that the whole division would be asked to investigate and exonerate their colleagues.

"Not sure yet, but we can't rule anything out."

"What does that mean?" said Jakob, screwing up his eyes. He had a little sheepish smile around his mouth, as if he knew very well how it all hung together. Sonne again ran his hand through his long hair.

"Piss off now and let me work in peace," said Axel.

At that moment, John Darling came out of the door of the property opposite. He went over to Axel, briefly acknowledging Sonne, who moved away a little and lit a cigarette. Axel felt the craving again.

"I've checked him out. Piver. His full name is Peter Smith, 22 years old, enrolled at DTU in Lyngby. An unknown among the autonomists, arrested during the trouble around YoHo in December. Released without charge. Under questioning, he mentioned he does layout on AFA's magazine," said Darling to Axel.

They knocked on the gate at the cemetery.

"What did *he* want?" Darling asked, pointing at Sonne, who was on his way into the property they had just left.

One of the uniforms let them in.

"He wanted to know what was going on. I gave him a little."

"He's gone into the house. I hate it when they run around in our footsteps and interview all our witnesses."

"Me too, but it could work to our advantage. Maybe we should let the information about Piver leak to them if we don't get hold of him soon. Then we can issue a description of him through the press."

"Should I take care of that?"

"I thought that'd be best. They love you, you know."

Axel had seen Darling being interviewed hundreds of times: stand-ups at crime scenes, intelligent commentary on crime programmes, expert adviser on numerous legal-ethical issues – usually wearing an immaculate uniform. He would probably go a long way. Expansion of the DNA register? John Darling could speak for and against. Relaxing of the rules for searching and phone tapping? Darling was even able to reassure the knights in shining armour who defend privacy and freedom. Increased powers for the intelligence services? Darling could build bridges between the hard-liners on the right wing and the hysterics at the centre for human rights.

Axel sat in his car and turned on the radio:

"Several people have contacted the media about a particularly heavy-handed arrest on Nørrebrogade yesterday. Three plain-clothes police officers allegedly arrested a young man without warning and beat him with a baton several times, even after he had been handcuffed."

Witness: "I've never seen anything like it. He was walking down the street quite peacefully, and then they came running over to him, hit out at him, lay him down and handcuffed him."

Reporter: "Was he behaving in a threatening manner towards the police?"

Witness: "He was just walking along, but the most shocking thing was that they lifted him up in their arms, and as they were dragging him over to a van, they beat him around the head. He was just hanging and dangling and couldn't protect himself. Then they threw him into the van and drove off. I felt like I was in a banana republic..."

Axel switched off. It was all beginning to boil over.

8

He steered his way through the Freetown's main thoroughfare, Pusher Street. Past the two pubs, Woodstock and Nemoland, and left at the Moonfisher, where he had been with Liz many times. He went down to the kiosk, bought two bottles of gold label, then went round the back and up onto the roof. Here he found a concrete ledge and sat down with a view of the water. He opened one of the beers with his lighter. There was a dead gull in the reeds. It was down there they hid the hash, or so he had heard. In vacuum packs lowered into the water. It wasn't a good idea to fish them up. Rumours said that a guy from Amager had once taken up a package from the muddy water and sold it on. He was found in his car repair shop with two fingers cut off.

The call from the cops had come as a shock. Piver had taken the battery out of his mobile, as the others at AFA had taught him to do. He didn't really know why, because if it was turned off, it couldn't be traced, but he had followed the rule just to be on the safe side. So far today in any case.

Now he put the battery back in the phone, waited for the signal, entered the code and called Liz. It was two hours since the police had hammered on the door. If they had taken Rosa, they would also have taken Liz, but he had to try.

"Piver, where the fuck are you?"

"That doesn't matter, Liz. What's happening, man?"

"Rosa told the cops about the camcorder, and then they went crazy about getting hold of you. What's all that about?"

"I don't know. I'll figure it out. What got into Rosa, for fuck's sake? How about you? Are you OK?"

"They've confiscated a box of molos, but they haven't charged us. I don't think they'll do anything before they've got hold of you or the camera. They told Rosa it's about a murder."

"What do you mean?"

"They aren't interested in anything else except that camera because it shows something about a murder that might've been committed in Assistens. Perhaps it's best that you contact them."

It was the last thing he had expected to hear from Liz. Now he had to hold his ground. He moved the phone away from his mouth and sank the last of the beer. One left.

"I'll check the tape first, then we'll see. I'm not in any danger, Liz, even if they're after me."

"It's not just you I'm thinking about. How much bloody fun do you think it is having them running around here? A journalist from Ekstra Bladet came up and interviewed us about the search, and Rosa said another one has called from Counterpress. He wanted to help you. Maybe you should call him. Rosa's texted you the number." She hesitated a moment. "Honestly, Piver, I think it may be a good idea to hand yourself in."

He could feel how tired she was. So close to being arrested last night; so close to getting her back again. If it hadn't been for Rosa. Fuck, he was so unlucky all the time.

"I have to go. I'm scared they'll trace me. Say hello to Rosa. And Liz…"

"Yes?"

"Thanks for helping. I've got hold of something important."

He checked his text messages and found the number of the guy from Counterpress. There was no name, but he knew Counterpress, the left-wing online portal. They were OK – the only media outlet that didn't let itself be controlled by capital and power.

He knew that several members of the editorial board had been there in the battles with the police on May 18, 1993. He had read about the rush they had felt; the power they had felt when they had forced the police back by raining stones on them. OK, that may well have been before he could even spell Nørrebro, but fucking hell, what they'd done was so cool. The pigs had been so under pressure that they could only react by shooting at people. They had showed their true face. The so-called guardians of the people were soldiers. Killing machines who weren't looking after the people, just power and capital. And afterwards, the system tried to shut down the whole inquiry. Not just the police, but the courts and lawyers: all the pigs protecting each other and attempting to hide the fact that the police had tried to kill people. Shoot at the stones, they claimed had been shouted, but it turned out to be, Shoot at the legs. If they could shoot at ordinary people, they themselves deserved to die.

Piver saved the number in his address book, turned off the mobile and took out the battery. Then he went back to Pusher Street and the pubs. No cars, a village community with its own rules, its own rhythm and pulse, in the midst of a stressed Copenhagen. Even though the police had cleared Pusher Street in a huge effort to stop the hash trade, there was still a lot of hash and pot on the tables, and the cops usually only raided if the press or the politicians had been making a fuss about the Freetown. He loved the place for its atmosphere and its tranquillity. But the tranquillity was gone now. There were many more people than usual, even though it was morning. The unrest from the city was like a virus that had infected Christiania.

Piver went into Nemoland. He felt safe enough in here to turn his attention back to the camcorder. He bought another gold label and settled in a dark corner on an old sofa and took out the camera.

A section of Nørrebrogade right next to the Box appeared on the screen. The full light of day. Pavement, cycle lane, road, cycle lane, pavement, wall and a section of the cemetery. He estimated that the camera covered 100 yards along the street and 50 yards wide. The time indicated that it was set up at 10.21 on Thursday morning. He spooled forward and saw the riots, demonstrators throwing stones, rubbish bins being pushed over, the police driving wildly after people in their transport vehicles. He relived the whole day.

At 15.23 he saw three plain-clothes officers chasing a man and smacking him up against the wall of the cemetery. There didn't appear to be any demonstrations at that point. Piver stopped, spooled back and tried to find a button he could use to zoom in. He couldn't, but there was no doubt what was happening on the small screen. The man had his hands twisted behind his back by two of the officers, while the third pressed his hand against his throat in a half stranglehold. The man's cry for help came through clear as a bell. The officer holding the man around his throat now began hitting his upper body with his baton. At the same time, the other two had put him in handcuffs, and now they lifted him up and began to drag him off. Both had their batons out and used them several times. They were really hitting him hard – on his back, neck and head, before throwing him into one of the police vans. The man didn't resist at any point.

Was that what they were afraid of? Was all that talk about a murder just a smokescreen to hide the fact that they were looking for some footage that clearly showed pure, unadulterated police violence?

Whatever – it looked completely crazy. Piver was agitated.

He carried on watching on fast forward. Yesterday's riots flowed across the screen like a surreal ballet with activists and uniformed officers in the leading roles and curious Copenhageners and the press as passive spectators. Occasionally, it went quiet, and the grey asphalt of the street lay bare like an abandoned stage. At one point, two containers were set on fire and the white light of the flames rose and disappeared at express speed. He kept an eye on the cemetery as it moved towards evening and darkness fell. He stopped the tape whenever he saw someone moving into the murk under the trees behind the yellow wall. There were uniformed police officers on patrol, plain-clothes police and individual citizens, but nothing that looked like a murder.

Until 01.33.

They came out from under the trees inside the cemetery just opposite the camera. One of them was wearing dark clothes and a cap pulled down over his head so that his face was obscured. The other was bareheaded with dark hair, but walking as if he were drunk or dizzy. The first one had an arm around him and it looked as though he was helping him along. They disappeared behind the wall exactly where the cops had been bustling about with their projectors all morning. A couple of minutes passed and the man with the cap appeared again. He stared at something that was hidden behind the wall. There was a white flash. He put something in his pocket, which Piver guessed was a camera or mobile, lifted his cap and first looked up, then to the sides before turning around and disappearing under the trees into the cemetery.

Piver's whole body went hot. His pulse was pumping so crazily that he got earache for a moment. Could it really be true? Here it was. The evidence the cops would do anything to get hold of. There was no doubt. Now he understood why it was crucial for them.

9

From the outside, Copenhagen Police Headquarters looks like a Nazi architect's wet dream, loved and hated for its monumental, fortress-like exterior. For criminals, a visit to the triangular grey colossus is the first step on their way to a stay in the shadow kingdom. For the many activists gathered in the city, it was a cold, dismissive symbol of the extended arm of the quasi-fascistic state.

For the people who worked there, it was HQ.

And HQ was Axel's second home. He loved the exterior of the building just as much as he loved the labyrinthine interior, where even seasoned policemen could get lost. It had been the architect's idea to turn the building inside out and let its beauty flourish on the inside. He had succeeded. The strict, cold exterior hid a beauty, insight, light and a wealth of small details that Axel enjoyed.

He walked through the main entrance, up the low staircase, showed his warrant card to the guard and entered the huge, round courtyard of columns, where all the live interviews with the bosses usually took place. Everything was chaos. In front of the colonnade, he saw the Commissioner of the Copenhagen Police, the head of the emergency call-out department, the press spokesman and the Assistant Commissioner in a clinch with various groups of journalists and television teams filming.

He walked diagonally across the tiles with their star motifs and cast a glance into the monumental memorial courtyard at the end, where the statue of the Snake Killer stood guarding Axel's fellow officers who had died in service, as a symbol of the struggle between good and evil. It had originally been the intention that Justitia – the goddess of justice – should stand there, but Axel was pleased that it wasn't the blind goddess of the judiciary who watched over the dead officers but instead a man prepared to kill to expel the wickedness of the world.

He looked back over his shoulder and made eye contact with the Assistant Commissioner who, at the moment their eyes met, signalled to him.

"Steen, I need you for two minutes."

There was only the Commissioner above Rosenkvist. Axel liked him as a boss, because he always spoke his mind within the walls of HQ and was able to escape from almost anything in front of the press. He was tall, balding, with a long black tongue of comb-over that went from one side of his skull to the other, serious, with brown eyes and a smile that seemed more like a friendly, disarming reflex than anything that could develop into laughter.

"Is there anything new on the victim?"

It wasn't usual for a man at Rosenkvist's level to ask about the investigation of specific cases.

"No, we don't know who he is, but despite the balaclava and combat boots, I don't think he looks particularly like an autonomist."

"There's little about this case that is how it appears. I assume you're aware that I don't want anything about this matter to slip out before we've got some of the facts straight."

"I've been told. Perhaps you could make sure that manpower is assigned to areas other than the Youth House, so that we can get enough technicians and investigators on the case."

"It's a question of how necessary it will be. That was precisely what I wanted to talk to you about. We've already had help from outside, you could say. Perhaps I should call it a visit. The public prosecutor's people are in the process of interrogating all the officers who were in the cemetery last night."

"What? Why hasn't anyone told me that?"

A reporter looked at them. The Assistant Commissioner ignored Axel's protest.

"It's a security measure. We have to cover ourselves. As far as I know, there are problems with two officers' explanations. They should've been keeping an eye on the spot where the victim was found but can't explain why they didn't see anything. From what I understand, he was probably lying there for a few hours."

Where the hell did he know that from? Axel was furious that other people were doing his job.

"If that's true, someone's been well and truly asleep on the job in there. Can I sit in at the interviews?"

"I can't see any problem with that, provided you know your place and let the DPP handle the show. The police federation has provided a legal representative. I'm sure you're well acquainted with him."

The smile again – this time with a touch of sarcasm. Axel had on several occasions needed one of the federation's lawyers in inquiries where he had been accused of having crossed the line and had had to be reviewed by the public prosecutor.

"I suggest you concentrate on the two officers who've screwed up: Kasper Vang and Jesper Groes. We also have two PET people in the building. They're looking for some foreigner. They're sitting up in your division and reviewing everyone arrested during last night's demonstrations."

The paperwork on the large numbers of people who had been arrested was with the Homicide Division, whose lawyers were in charge of the inquiries. The Assistant Commissioner straightened his uniform and prepared to leave.

"What's it about?"

"We don't know. They're from organised crime, so I doubt they'll find anything on – to put it bluntly – the bunch of arseholes we've brought in."

A journalist had come over to them.

"We're going live in three minutes, Assistant Commissioner."

The smile. And a calming hand in the air. He turned back to Axel.

"I'm warning you again. If this comes out before we have an outline of where the investigation is going and a suspect at the ready, it could have disastrous consequences in the circumstances. Ultra-radicals have been arriving in numbers from Germany, Spain and Italy all day. I don't want my city smashed up more than necessary."

He smiled in Axel's direction just for the benefit of the press, who were standing waving for Rosenkvist.

Then he went into the stairway entrance that led up through the emergency call-out department and one of the equipment sections to the Homicide Division. The events of the evening and the night had left their mark on the corridors. The emergency call-out department was cluttered with equipment, visors, shields, tear gas grenades in open packets, water bottles in large plastic pallets, boxes of energy bars, helmets and fireproof clothing. He looked out on the street that ran along the back of HQ. It was cordoned off from one end to the other. This was where the customers were being sluiced in. The duty magistrate, who was based in this part of the building, had been put in charge of processing the large number of arrests, and when they had been remanded in custody, some of them ended up in the Piss Hole, as the HQ's prison was called by the hardcore criminals who usually sat in there. The cordons were intended to prevent sympathisers from getting in and interfering. And they looked good on TV. Underlined the seriousness of the situation and were good to have in the memory the next time appropriations had to be discussed with the number punchers at the Ministry of Finance.

Up in Homicide it was packed. In the corridor outside sat a dozen officers wearing varying layers of riot gear, some with the suit pulled all the way down around their boots, sitting in their thermal underwear, while others were asleep in their uniforms. Axel recognised three or four of the faces from the crime scene at Assistens. They looked up, but none of them greeted him.

"Groes and Vang – is that any of you?"

They shook their heads.

The offices led off the corridor with a door to each one, connected by doors en suite. At the end was a meeting room and behind that was Corneliussen's corner office. Axel went in the third door on the left. His own office. At the desk sat a man in a suit interviewing a constable in riot gear. At the constable's side sat the police federation's lawyer, whom Axel knew from his own inquiries. The suit contained Jens Ellermann, DPP assessor. Axel recognised the officer from Assistens Cemetery, Jesper Groes, fair, greasy hair, sweaty face with a studied, casual look, contradicted by a worried wrinkle between the eyebrows.

"We were given permission to use your office. We'll take a short break," said Ellermann.

"That's absolutely fine with me. We met each other at the crime scene, but we weren't introduced," said Axel to Jesper Groes.

He offered his hand to the officer, who took it hesitantly. Groes' hand was red and swollen around the knuckles.

"Would you like something to drink?" asked Axel.

Groes shook his head.

Axel went into the office which belonged to John Darling. In here were a man and a woman bent over piles of reports with photos of arrested people. Neither of them looked up.

He went out on the corridor where he met Ellermann.

"How's it going with him?" he asked the lawyer.

"It's hard to say. He and a colleague had the task of keeping an eye on the exact 200-yard stretch where the body was found. And they haven't seen a thing."

"I've been given permission to sit in on the interview. I won't interrupt unless you want me to."

"That's fine with me. You can ask questions if you want. We'll take another round, but if he doesn't come up with anything else, we'll have to let him go."

"Have you noticed his hands?"

"No, I haven't."

"Then forget it and let me confront him with them. They have abrasions that could easily come from striking someone. And our victim has been hit repeatedly."

"OK. I'll go through everything with him again and then you can take over."

Ellermann went to the toilet.

As Axel came in, Jesper Groes was sitting bent forward, staring at the photos of three women under the glass plate on the desk. He looked shaky.

"I think I know one of them. Are they members of your family?"

"No, I wouldn't say that. They're three unsolved murders from recent years. Miranda. Stina. Rajan. Fredens Bro, Pisserenden and Rådmandsgade. Any of them ring a bell?"

"Were they your cases?"

"Not really. I was involved in one of them as a young officer."

"Why do you have them lying here then?"

"To remind me of why I'm here."

"OK. You take it very seriously, don't you?"

"And you should be doing that right now, my friend. You're up to your neck in shit."

The lawyer broke in.

"Come, come; language, my friend. You aren't conducting this interview."

"I will be in a moment. I'm going to assist the public prosecutor."

Axel went outside and waited for Ellermann.

He had a weird feeling about it all. He was in the process of an investigation and had only come into HQ to review the data received and, hey presto, he had a main suspect. Or two. But why would two young officers have beaten and strangled a middle-aged man dressed as an autonomist?

It didn't make sense.

His thoughts were interrupted by the sight of John Darling.

"You have very fine visitors in your office," said Axel.

"I could say the same thing to you. It's all taken a bit of a change of direction. What do you think about it?"

"I don't, pal. This is a waste of time. I want to be out there hearing what's happened at Assistens, and I want to go to the autopsy. Then I'd very much like to see those damned helicopter recordings, and get hold of that Piver and the camcorder."

Darling nodded.

"Who are those two in your office? Are they the ones from PET?" asked Axel.

"Yes, but they won't say anything, other than they're looking for a foreigner who's disappeared."

"Who they've got under surveillance?"

"I don't know."

"Don't you think it's a strange time to be coming in here?"

"What do you mean?"

"Have they said anything about this foreigner being connected to the disturbances?"

"Not a word. They're going through all the arrests hoping they'll find him. They think he ended up there by mistake."

"It sounds pretty far-fetched, unless they have nothing better to spend their time on. Who's the babe?"

"I don't know them personally, but he's supposed to be one of the top minds out there, and she's also very capable, they say. She's been in terror, security, drugs, but now it looks like she's in special operations."

"What?"

"You know – agents, informants, source protection. They have their own department in the bunker, where only a chosen few have access. There's nothing more hush-hush than that in hush-hush-land."

"So how come you know about it?"

"If anyone other than you said that to me, I'd take offence and break up with them straight away."

Ellermann came towards them.

"This is my caseworker from the DPP. As you probably know, we've been allowed to participate in the interviews. I'll take Jesper Groes. Don't you think it'd be a good idea if you sat in with his visually impaired comrade?"

A quarter of an hour later, Axel Steen wasn't any more convinced of Jesper Groes' guilt. But there was no doubt that he was hiding something. He had replied willingly but nervously to the prosecutor's questions, but it still didn't make any sense. After the worst of the clashes during the evening, he and Vang had been ordered to patrol the upper part of the cemetery bordering Nørrebrogade. For most of the evening, they had been standing 50 yards from the spot where the victim had been found, been on the usual small errands, gone into the bushes for a piss a few times, fetched extra water, and so on, but they hadn't seen anything from 23:00 to 03:00. They had been picked up by a police van, which had driven past the body soon after, and then the alarm had been raised.

"Do you know the victim?"

"No, not at all."

"Are you sure?"

"One hundred percent. I've never seen him before."

"Don't you think it's strange that you're telling us that you were on guard, smoking, talking and watching the path, when at the same time there's absolutely indisputable evidence that a man has been murdered and left by the wall during the exact same time period? Without you noticing anything at all?"

"Maybe it sounds strange, but not noticing him doesn't make me a murderer."

"No one's said you're a murderer. Why would you be? You aren't even a suspect, but we need to figure out what's happened. And you were nearby when the murder was committed or the body was thrown into the cemetery. You didn't see anything. And you can't explain why not. If you didn't see him, what were you up to?"

You would have expected it to be harder interviewing officers who knew all the interrogator's tricks, but it made no difference to Axel. When you first get people's consciousness working, when doubt takes small bites out of the dogged lie or distortion, most people react the same way, and then you know you are on to something. A wavering gaze, a nervous twitch of the eyes, wrinkles quickly smoothed out, a studied laid-back attitude, itching and restlessness in the body: all indications of a suspect who is searching for a new explanation.

Jesper Groes turned his gaze inward, looking for an exit. Without finding it.

"We didn't do anything. We were doing our job. There was a lot of noise. I can't explain why we didn't see him."

"Listen to me. I will do everything I can to clear you, but you have to give me something. Not this same old story that you haven't heard anything, haven't seen anything and you can't explain it. Because you can. You're hiding something and it's pretty stupid of you not to tell me what it is."

"I've nothing more to say beyond what I've already said."

Not being able to open him up tormented Axel. Jesper Groes was hiding something more important than getting himself out of the sticky situation he was in now. Something he wouldn't even give up to prove he wasn't negligent. Not even to escape a murder charge.

It didn't surprise Axel. Everybody lies. About something or other. Big as well as small. And once people have started, it is hard to get them back to the truth. Jesper Groes was no exception. No matter how vigorously Axel appealed to his common sense and his sense of duty, there was no hole in his story. But it would come. Time ate people's resilience. And Jesper Groes and his colleague would be isolated in the force when the rumour came out that they had been asleep on duty and afterwards had been given such a thorough grilling that they had had to have a representative from the police federation at their side.

Axel changed tactics.

"OK. Our victim's been beaten with clenched fists. And you have fresh wounds and abrasions on your knuckles and fingers. How do you explain that?"

"I got into several fights with demonstrators. I haven't hit anyone but we had to make a rather violent arrest of a demonstrator who climbed over the wall early in the evening."

"We'll check that out."

"Have you talked to Kasper?"

"There are others doing that now. Why? Are you nervous about what he might say?"

"No."

The answer was meek.

Axel got up.

"I don't have anything else. I can't see any basis for detention or suspension, but that isn't my decision. The lawyers from the DPP and the bosses will have to decide," he said, nodding to Ellermann.

Axel had to go in to Corneliussen and get him up to date with the latest development, although he always felt uncomfortable visiting his boss. He remembered the first day: Corneliussen had called him in to a meeting in his corner office at HQ, where he had been sitting in profile, staring out of the window, as Axel came in.

"Sit down," he had barked without turning, and Axel immediately realised that there was shit on its way down the shaft and it was heading for him.

He had sat in the chair on the other side of the Head of Homicide's desk, where he had often sat and discussed new clues or witness statements with his predecessor, Henriksen. The little smurf sat completely unaffected by Axel's presence with his hands folded on his stomach and his thumbs circling around each other.

Maybe he actually knew how ugly he was. And what people called him? Maybe he didn't give a damn. Maybe he knew, and maybe that was what drove him and had put him in this much sought-after chair as Head of Homicide in Copenhagen.

"I've heard a lot about you," Corneliussen had said. "A lot good, but mostly bad. You're a man of some notoriety, you know. Brutal arrests, harassment of witnesses and brother officers, a loner and a rule-breaker."

Axel had stayed silent.

"Do you know why I don't like your type?"

"No."

"Because you aren't a real politier. You're just an ego-tripper in a uniform, a freebooter who uses the warrant card to relieve your own frustrations. You aren't a team player and I can't accept that."

Even his language was old school. "Politier" was something officers called each other a lifetime ago – back when team spirit was the most important thing of all, and a cop used a baton without warning. Axel didn't give a damn about team spirit – and didn't have much time for old-school police officers with their mafia-like covering up for each other and their rigid understanding of what was needed to solve an investigation.

Corneliussen had looked disappointedly at Axel, as if he had expected one of his notorious outbursts, but Axel had held his tongue.

"Right now you're still in favour because of your track record and connections, but as soon as the reform's been implemented, I'll find a way of getting rid of you."

That's what the prophecy had been back then.

Now Corneliussen was sitting in exactly the same position, in profile, listening expressionlessly to Axel's account of the two officers. When Axel had finished, his superior spun round.

"The murder is already out on Ekstra Bladet's website," he hissed, "and the hyenas have started bombarding us with calls asking for comments. It's crucial that no one is told that the victim could be an autonomist. And as far as Vang and Groes are concerned, they must be kept out of the media."

"It'll come out sooner or later if they're brought before the duty magistrate," said Axel.

"You must get it under control before then. Now! Either you clear them or we'll have to charge them. Check their personnel files. Is there any Nazi hoo-ha or extremism on their files? It'll be a nightmare for the force if it turns out we're involved."

"I'll do what I can."

"What's your preliminary assessment of the perpetrator?"

"Whether you like it or not, there's a lot to suggest a man with access to the cemetery and a willingness to kill. This isn't an opportunist murder. Victim and perpetrator knew each other to some extent, I believe. It's someone who can get past the police cordon without being discovered, one of our own or… an inside job."

Corneliussen grunted.

"An insider? Is that what I should say to Rosenkvist and the Commissioner? I hope you bloody well come up with something better than that."

10

Piver went up to the bar. His hands were shaking as he lit a cigarette on a candle. The guy behind the counter had long hair and a look in his brown eyes as if nothing could surprise him.

"Do you have internet access? Can you check the phone number at Counterpress for me?"

The bartender looked reluctant, but there were no customers waiting.

"Please, it's important."

It took some time for him to find the website and even longer to find a phone number.

Piver went back to the old sofa in the corner and rang.

"Counterpress, Jeanette speaking."

"Hi, you're talking to Michael. I've been called by someone who says he works for you, but I just wanted to check the number. 20154495?"

"We don't give out phone numbers."

"I'm not asking you to either. I'm just asking if you recognise it. You don't have to say whose it is."

"2015. It sounds like one of ours. I can't see immediately who has it. We have a lot of stringers out in town, but all of our numbers start with 2015."

He took a deep drag on his cigarette with a feeling of triumph and unease. And fear. He needed help with this. So he tapped in the number of the reporter from Counterpress.

He was ready now. He knew he had something that could get him a long way. And he knew why the cops were after him. He thought about the recording he had just seen. It didn't matter that the murderer's face was unclear, nor that the actual murder couldn't be seen. Because as the man left the scene, six reflective letters stood out clearly on his back in the darkness: POLICE.

11

John Darling swung his car through the gateway into Assistens Cemetery, closely followed by Axel in his own. BB and his forensics team were in the process of fine-combing the area for the second time. Three men knelt with their heads close to the ground, rummaging around with small plastic tweezers.

"Let's get some food soon, but first let's find out how it's going with the fingerprints," said Axel.

BB got up and came to meet them.

"Fortunately for you, I have access to the only fingerprint scanner in the country. I've sent the deceased's prints, but there's a little glitch with communications, so I haven't had an answer yet. They're having problems because there've been loads of arrests and inquiries about fingerprints. Over 200 were brought in last night, apparently."

It was a police force with a collective hangover and chaos in the duty rosters. For security reasons, only a handful of people had been told about the action at the Youth House, so it hadn't been possible to deploy some of the 1,000-plus men who had to be stationed on the streets once the building had been secured. During the night, the men in transits and arrest vans had been told to get ready. All the officers had had their private mobile phones confiscated so that they couldn't pass on the message or tell their partners that they probably wouldn't be home for the next couple of days.

The Swede called.

"That tattoo. It's the Albanian eagle. Are you near a computer? Try googling it, then you'll understand what I mean."

Axel got into his car and switched on his PC. He googled eagle and Albania, and the animal's silhouette popped up, black on a blood-red background. A two-headed eagle with bristling claws and a thin tongue sticking out of its mouth, its impressive plumage opened out. The

Albanian flag. He would have to take a look at the tattoo again at the autopsy. He shut down the computer and went over to Darling.

"I know a place over in Jægersborggade where they make the best coffee in town," said Axel to his colleague.

"We have an autopsy to get to," replied Darling in a neutral tone.

Axel guessed that Darling had brought a packed lunch with him and had eaten his way through it long ago.

"If I don't get some food right now I won't be responsible for my actions. And you wouldn't like that," said Axel.

They walked up the path to Jagtvej, past the equipment yard, which lay behind a dilapidated building with four Doric columns.

"What's that?" Darling asked, pointing at the temple-like building as they walked across a lawn.

"It's an old chapel. We should have it checked. What about Piver?" asked Axel.

"I don't know. Could he have seen something on the video? Even if he has, that's no reason to run off."

"He's mixed up in circles that aren't exactly known for their warm feelings towards us."

They crossed Jagtvej and went into Jægersborggade. It wasn't a street where police in uniform were made welcome. But Axel, always in plain clothes, often walked it without being attacked or provoked by the young hash dealers who hung out with their mongrels on a couple of old sofas on the pavement. Muscular, crewcut young guys, their arms covered in tattoos, their eyes as small and aggressive as their dogs. The young dealers and their undisguised trade in hash were the cause of repeated clashes between rival gangs, because the trade represented a market of hundreds of millions of kroner at street level alone in Copenhagen.

Axel had never bought his hash here. It was far too dangerous for him if someone in his neighbourhood found out he smoked.

Opposite sat the local drunks with just as many dogs – though hardly as well-nourished – and kids, seven or eight-year-old girls growing up in a boozy environment where Mum got screwed for a bottle of schnapps and had done the rounds of most of the drinkers in the group.

In addition to the Hells Angels' hash clubs, there were a wealth of small workshops, dressmakers, fashion shops, a toffee shop, a book-café and lastly Katz Deli, right where the street joined Jagtvej on the right-hand side. They had to wait for two other customers in the spartan basement shop, but eventually they got their coffee in paper mugs and Axel's bagel with marinated chicken and chilli. He paid for both coffees.

They sat outside at a shining, silvery café table on the pavement, but Axel had to give up eating at it as it rocked too much. Darling looked at the table in disapproval, at the holed pavement, the eternal roadworks and from there along the whole street towards where the pushers sat.

"What a hole. Why don't we flush that scum out?"

"How the hell is that going to help? They'll just wash up on land further up the street." Axel had found a stone which he put under a table leg.

"Forget that crap. Let's discuss the investigation." Axel knew what was coming now. It was a ritual in murder inquiries with Darling.

"What do we have? Was he murdered by someone he knew or by a stranger? Was he killed because of who he was or because he was in the wrong place at the wrong time?"

The answer was crucial, he would give him that, but Axel didn't work according to schematic definitions when it came to people and murder, though they could be useful enough if you had nothing to go on. In the first scenario, the murderer would be from within the victim's circle of acquaintances. So they'd be looking for conflicts, rivalry, jealousy or financial disagreements. The personal trail should always be investigated. You should never underestimate the victim's behaviour and connections.

In the second scenario, victim and perpetrator would know nothing about each other. Was the man the random victim of a deranged, sadistic killer or an attempted robbery? There wasn't much to indicate that.

"I think the perp or perps wanted something out of him which he wouldn't give. That's why he got beaten up before he was killed," said Axel.

John Darling scratched his chin. He hadn't been allowed to hold the long version of his friend/stranger murder speech, and looked a bit miffed.

"I don't understand how he got there," continued Axel. "Could he have been thrown in from the street? That doesn't make any sense. So he must've already been in the cemetery or come in there during the last 24 hours. We must assume that the victim's gone in there under his own steam and maybe voluntarily met his murderer."

Darling nodded. "Agreed. Four priorities now: footage from the air, witness testimony, investigations in the cemetery and identifying the victim."

"Have you noticed we're constantly talking as if the perp being one of us is out of the question? But as soon as news gets out about the balaclava, that's what everyone will think."

John Darling looked unimpressed.

"One of us? Forget it. They may well have been fast asleep and overlooked a murderer, but let's not start accusing them of killing anyone before we've exhausted all other possibilities. Why would they strangle a demonstrator? They could get just as much satisfaction from bashing him around a bit and cuffing him," said Darling.

"Maybe they got carried away. We can't afford to exclude anyone just because they're in uniform."

"Do you think that's what happened?"

"Fuck knows, but it's strange – he doesn't look like an autonomist, does he? He's far too old, he doesn't look Danish – but foreign activists have been pouring in. Could he be one of them? Hard to believe that it doesn't have some connection to the Youth House. What about the crime scene? What does it tell us?"

"Hard to say. There aren't many leads. If he's been dragged there and then killed, it doesn't indicate an impulse killing – then again, it was clearly violent and that might suggest the perp just lost it."

"Or he may've done it to confuse us," said Axel. It seemed crystal clear to him that it was either a cover-up or something worse: an inside job. "What about the recordings from the police helicopter? Is there anything on them?"

"I haven't seen them, but Corneliussen says there's nothing. And that's a bummer," said Darling.

Axel had finished his bagel. His mobile rang. It was Jakob Sonne.

"Anything new in the investigation?"

Axel considered for a second and then hung up without answering. He got up from the table and walked off a little way. Then he looked up the number of Dorte Neergaard from TV2 and rang it. It was picked up immediately.

"Hi, Axel."

"Hi, Dorte. I need your help."

"What's up?"

"Can't say a lot right now, but I'll give you something later. I need to look through the footage from the area around Assistens close to Runddelen."

"Axel dearest, you know I can't give you that. I'd love to help, but if it comes out that we've given you pictures so you can bust people for street disturbances, they'll start attacking us on the streets and we'll never be allowed to come near a demonstration again."

"Listen. I don't give a shit about autonomists and drunks. I have a body in Assistens. Haven't you heard?"

"Yes, I was just about to ask."

"We found a dead man, murdered almost several times over and thrown up against the wall in the middle of the night while the fighting was at its peak right on the other side of the wall."

"While your colleagues were guarding the cemetery?"

"That's my Dorte. It's all a bit complicated, but I promise you'll get it if you let me see the footage from your helicopter, or if you have anything else around the crime scene."

"Wait a minute. Who's your suspect?"

"You get nothing else until we have a deal."

"I'll see what I can do. I don't even know if we were in the air at that point."

"You were in the air all night, for Christ's sake."

"Yes, but there was trouble at Christianshavn last night too. We may well have been out there. There were terrible fires."

"Never mind about that. Just get hold of those tapes and give me a chance to look through them, and I'll feed you along the way."

"Can I use what you've given me now?"

"Yes. Anonymously."

"And that he's been thrown in there while the police had the whole cemetery cordoned off?"

"Say what you want. I can't stop you thinking for yourself."

"I'll try to get hold of the tapes. When do you need them?"

"Five minutes ago."

"I can't let you see them here, you know."

"I have my daughter this weekend, so it's going to be tricky for me to get out, but how about you come to my place this evening once she's in bed?"

"Sounds like a good idea."

"Then we can watch them together."

"Sounds like an even better idea."

Dorte Neergaard, tomboy, adopted child from Korea, head and shoulders shorter than him, full of restless energy, extremely well-oriented. She had sources all over the place – police, hash dealers in the Freetown, major convicted criminals and street workers. She could talk her way into everyone. Including him.

Axel opened the boot of his car and took out his equipment. Gloves and evidence bags. The tracking division with the dog teams hadn't arrived yet. The front seat was tempting him, though he knew that sleep was just around the corner. He sat in the car and turned on the radio.

"One day after the clearance of the Youth House, Nørrebro and Christianshavn are completely calm… latest figures from the police are

219 arrested. The first 36 were brought to the magistrates' court for preliminary hearings on Thursday evening and last night. This morning, several preliminary hearings will begin for 25 to 40 arrestees… The Secretary of State for Justice Lene Espersen says, 'The continued use of violence and vandalism damages the young people's case. Dialogue and peaceful demonstrations are…'"

The familiar feel of the icy chill in the left side of his head above the hairline announced itself like a freezing fluid that filtered out into his brain and paralysed everything. He sat watching things around him stiffening and retreating: the distance to the dashboard, windscreen, bonnet, the path and the cemetery with the bare trees and shrubs without leaves, everything became dislocated. He managed to look up at the dizzy heights in the sky before his eyes slid shut.

The radio voice continued grinding inside him.

"… published a photo of a body… the police will not comment… press conference later in the day… three injured activists…"

He saw his ex-wife before him, but this time she was sitting up against the wall of Assistens, smiling at him with blood running like spring water from a hole where she used to have a mouth. She was laughing hideously, or was it crying, and slamming her hands down into the soft soil. The sound went on and on until Axel discovered it was Darling banging on the side window. He rubbed his eyes and opened the door.

"Time to get up."

Axel was blinking rapidly.

"Don't you sleep at night?"

"Yes, I do, but not very well. Insomnia. But it helps to close my eyes and sit for a bit," he lied.

"If that's closing your eyes, we'll need to use a roadside bomb to wake you when you're really asleep. Are you taking something for it?"

"No. Not crazy about that stuff."

"Maybe you should get something to help you fall asleep. The effect quickly disappears."

Maybe you should shut your mouth, thought Axel.

He called in to the central duty officer to hear if there was anything new about Piver. His girlfriend Rosa had helped put a description together and there was already a result. A group of plain-clothes officers had spotted him at Christiania and come close to arresting him, but had to let him go as they were confronted by a large crowd of stone-throwing troublemakers and were heavily outnumbered.

Piver's mobile was being tracked and tapped, but it had been dead since he had run off, except for two short spells. The telecoms company hadn't yet been able to provide mast information, so it was impossible to say where Piver had been holed up when he had used the phone, but the call must have been tapped and they had to have a log of telephone numbers at HQ. Based on the plain-clothes officers' information, Axel concluded that the young autonomist was hiding in the Freetown. They couldn't do much about it right now, but he could go out there later. Then he could buy some hash as part of his cover.

The hounds were baying in the dark blue vans that had arrived outside. It was the sound of the hunt, blood, scent. He got out of his car and saw the handlers steering them over to where the body had been lying. The dogs were allowed to sniff around a little and were then sent off with their handlers. At the same time, forty men began a thorough search of the entire cemetery from the opposite end. 10 yards apart, they walked from the wall on the other side of the cemetery towards Axel and his colleagues.

Darling came running over to him. His facial expression told Axel that something had happened.

"We have to leave right away. A photo of the body's been published online."

"Who took it?"

"The murderer."

12

Piver's hands were shaking as he put the phone to his ear. It was answered on the third ring and he thought he heard a man's voice whisper "Hello?" At the same time, in the background, someone was speaking as if from a television speaker, loud and official-sounding.

"Hello, it's Peter. Who am I talking to?"

"One moment, just leaving the room."

There was a crackling sound. Then the sounds disappeared and it went quiet. The voice came back. Piver was nervous.

"Who is it?"

"It's Piv… Peter. Someone gave me your number. What do you want with me?"

"Are you the guy living on Nørrebrogade in the collective?"

"Yes."

"…Who the police want to get their hands on?"

"Yes."

"I can help you. I know the police are looking for you because of a camcorder."

"I don't understand, man. Why do they want to get their hands on me?"

"There's something on that tape they want. They're trying to cover up their own brutality."

Piver felt like telling him about everything he had seen, but held back.

"I've watched the whole tape. There's crazy stuff on it. They beat up an activist."

"It has to come out. They mustn't get hold of that tape. We have to stop them putting a lid on it."

"There's something else on the tape."

"What's that?"

"You know someone was bumped off in Assistens?"

"Yes."

"I'm going to say something you mustn't tell anyone else."

"I'm with you. You can trust me completely."

"The police killed him."

The line went quiet. Then came what sounded like a laugh or a cough.

"What's up? Don't you believe me?"

"I believe you – I'm just shocked. It's crazy. This makes it all much more dangerous. You have to be very careful."

It was a completely different voice now. Quick talking, a tone higher, infected with Piver's excitement; it sounded almost happy. Piver had the sense that the other guy was having difficulty believing what he had told him, but Piver didn't care because he had the evidence in his hands. The video would speak for itself.

"I have the evidence. I'll show you."

"Excellent. You'll be a hero when this comes out. Where are you now?"

"I'm at Christiania. Should I come over to Counterpress?"

"Bad idea. The office is being watched. They'd get you right away. I can pick you up in my car and drive you somewhere safe. Once we have everything in place, we can hold a press conference with you at Counterpress. It'll be a fantastic scoop."

Piver chewed over it. It was almost too good to be true. And that made him even more nervous. Could he trust it was true?

"I don't know. I don't know you."

"Trust me. Show me the footage and we can make an agreement about everything. You decide where to meet, but it has to be soon. We need to get that recording out now, so the pressure on the cops doesn't let up. It can change the whole atmosphere. Maybe it can stop YoHo being pulled down."

Piver was ecstatic at everything he was hearing and everything he'd seen on the tape, but he didn't believe that anything could save the house.

"First you have to show me the footage," continued the voice when he didn't answer, "and then we'll decide how we're going to get it out. We'll have to get you a lawyer and hide you in a safe place. Let's meet – trust me, I can help you. We can find a hiding place and a lawyer."

"OK, but we have to meet up out here first. I'll show you the recording then." Piver gave him a time. "And something else. I'm flat broke. I need some dosh."

"No problem. How much do you want? A thousand, is that enough?"

Piver went dizzy. One thousand kroner? That was a hell of a lot.

"OK, but listen. It's not in payment for the tape. That's mine. Or, I mean, it's not actually mine, but I'm not in a position to sell it. It's just so I have enough for a couple of beers and… some cigarettes."

"No problem. I'll bring some money with me. How do I find you?"

"I'm sitting in front of the Moonfisher at some tables. I have a black rucksack with a red sticker. It says Ali's on it."

"OK, I'll find you. I'll be there soon."

"Hey, wait. What's your name?"

"Martin. Martin Lindberg from Counterpress."

Piver recognised the name. He was one of the veterans from May 18. Wasn't he one of the eleven who had been wounded by police bullets fourteen years ago?

13

The photo had arrived in Counterpress's inbox at 14:03. It came from a Hotmail address and wasn't noticed until 13 minutes later, but from there, things moved fast.

It took 20 minutes before the editorial team was ready to put it on the website as a lead story under the headline, "Autonomist killed at Youth House. Police cover-up."

The story of a body being discovered and the possible murder of an unidentified man at Assistens Cemetery was already on several of the major newspapers' websites because of Jakob Sonne's article in Ekstra Bladet's online newspaper, and it had been mentioned in DR's radio news bulletins and on TV2 News because of Dorte Neergaard. Nevertheless, Counterpress sent a man out on the street to check if it was true and, when it was confirmed, one of the editorial team's most experienced journalists, Martin Lindberg, rang the police and got hold of Corneliussen, who tried his luck with jovial crisis management.

"It's Martin Lindberg from Counterpress."

"Good afternoon, Counterpress. Who are you countering today?"

"Very funny. I'm ringing about a murder. Is it true that you found a body at Assistens Cemetery last night?"

"No comment."

"But isn't it true that right now there are forensics technicians at the cemetery wall close to the Youth House?"

"You're correct in saying that we have people at the cemetery. I can't tell you any more than that."

"Is it true the victim's an autonomist?"

"I don't know what you're talking about."

"But isn't it true that a dead autonomist wearing a balaclava was found near the Youth House last night?"

"That's incorrect. We don't know if he's an autonomist."

"But he's wearing a balaclava, isn't he?"

"Where do you know… He had some kind of headwear on, yes, but I don't know what kind."

"I do. Because I'm sitting in front of a photo of a dead man wearing combat boots and a balaclava with his hands tied with the strips you use when you arrest people. He's sitting – or sat – up against the wall in Assistens, and you currently have a forensics team combing the area. Can we agree that much?"

"I can't go into detail, but I can confirm that we've found a dead man out there. And that the Homicide Division is looking into the matter."

"Thanks."

He hung up. Corneliussen hadn't denied any of the information Lindberg had confronted him with, and that was enough. He had been caught out several times during the 102-second-long exchange. The Head of Homicide had refused to comment on the information about a dead man in Assistens, but he had confirmed that there was a body, that it was wearing headgear, and that the Homicide Division was looking at the case. Combined with the photo they had received and the fact that Assistens had been completely cordoned off and intensely guarded by the police in the last 24 hours, there was more than enough for the media to go into a breaking-news meltdown.

Corneliussen had been so flabbergasted by the call that he hadn't even managed to threaten the journalist about publishing the photo before he hung up. And repeated subsequent calls had no effect. Panic broke loose in HQ's executive offices.

Within six minutes, the photo had hit the Danish online media. CNN had the picture on their front page 37 minutes later.

An hour later, the Police Commissioner had to go on TV and promise an in-depth investigation. She stressed that there was nothing to indicate that the police were in any way responsible for the death of the person in question.

But before it had got that far, Axel and Darling were sitting in a police car heading towards Counterpress, which was housed at the back of a building just before Nørrebrogade opened out to Dronning Louises Bro. Axel slammed the light on the roof and Darling pressed the accelerator to the floor. The city court had been called and, according to the police lawyer, they could count on a search warrant within five minutes. Axel had asked for three manned police vans to be stationed by the Lakes, but first he wanted Darling and himself to go in alone to prevent anyone from deleting anything. Axel had been in the editorial office before to get hold of some photos that could shed light on an old rape case, but without success – the press defended its neutrality with a hysteria that bordered on the sectarian when it came to helping the police document illegal activity. And Counterpress was by no means an exception. Axel didn't have anything against the news portal's journalism, but he had a serious problem with one of its employees, a completely blind spot that he didn't intend to tell Darling about. One of the five editors was an old veteran from May 18, 1993 – the night when Axel lost his innocence as a young police officer. Martin Lindberg was part of the autonomist movement at that time, the ringleader and rabble-rouser who incited the demonstrators into showering the police with cobblestones. He had been hit by one of the live rounds fired by the police. It had come from Axel's gun, and he had had to serve as a witness opposite Lindberg in two court cases. Lindberg and his activist friends had brought one of them against the police; the police had brought the other one against Lindberg. Lindberg lost both cases and was sent to prison for nine months.

It wasn't so much what Lindberg had done that night. It was his behaviour in court, his attitude and his words. There was no understanding, no remorse, no doubt; just contempt and scorn for Axel and all the other police officers who had been close to losing their lives that crazy night. Every time Axel heard about Lindberg or saw a picture of him, hatred flared up. It hadn't diminished over time. Certainly not after his best friend and her boyfriend died. Nina, a recent graduate from the police academy in the same year as Axel, in the front ranks at the battle on Fælledvej, had had most of her jaw smashed by a cobblestone. Niels, her boyfriend, group leader responsible for some of the worst injured, only broke an arm, but was so devastated by the experience and the lack of support afterwards that he ended the lives of both of them three years later. He had drugged Nina, put a pillow over her face, shot her and then shot himself through his mouth with his service pistol.

Darling parked the car in Ravnsborggade, and they walked completely relaxed over the road and through the gate to number 5. Axel stopped Darling.

"I'll take the back stairs. You wait here until I'm in."

Axel doubled back and turned into Blågårdsgade and then down Baggesensgade. Here stood the first of the neighbourhood's many scabby-red public housing blocks, which had been built in the late 70s after a comprehensive clearance of the old tenements. The satellite dishes on the front of the building left no doubt that extravagant municipal dreams now lay in tatters. They had certainly succeeded in getting rid of the neighbourhood's former inhabitants, along with the old fire traps with toilets in the yard, but the most controversial and ugly city renewal in Copenhagen's recent history today only housed another underclass.

Axel went in quickly, took a shortcut over a playground and opened the back door, which he worked out led up to all four floors of the property. Once upon a time there had been small factories and workshops here, but now the building had been taken over by a photo agency specialising in the Third World, a left-wing printer and Counterpress.

The door to Counterpress on the first floor wasn't locked and he opened it silently and found himself in a kitchen where three young people sat bent over a laptop watching some footage of the night's disturbances. He walked swiftly past them and entered a large room where people were working at multiple computers. Eleven people and at least as many screens – any one of those computers could contain the photo of the body – all of them could for that matter. He didn't get further in his thoughts before the front door opened and Darling stepped in. Everybody's attention turned to the tall, handsome cop who was smiling broadly.

"It's the police," said one.

"What are you doing here?" asked a girl.

"We need to have all the information about the photo you've posted online. Where it was sent from, who sent it and when," Darling replied.

Axel broke in.

"We need access to your computers. Now. Leave them in the same state they are in now."

Everyone in the room suddenly looked at Axel.

"Fuck, it's him from the picture," said one of them, pointing to something on the wall right next to Axel.

The whispering became a murmur.

"That pig," said a crewcut girl, her eyes overflowing with disgust.

Axel turned round and cast a brief look at an enlarged, grainy photostat from May 18, 1993. It was a collage of pictures. On one of them, he recognised his own angry, shocked face as he and a colleague dragged an injured Nina down Blegdamsvej, away from the chain of his retreating colleagues. Her eyes were frozen in shock and her jaw hung crookedly in the bloodied underside of her face. He had his service pistol raised in one hand. For a brief moment, he heard the crashing of cobblestones hitting the asphalt, the cracks from the police pistols, and the raging of the crowd billowing back and forth in the smoke at Sankt Hans Torv. In another picture, Lindberg could be seen being carried away with the blood flowing from a bullet wound in the abdominal region. Axel felt the hate rumbling in his stomach.

Then the main door opened and Martin Lindberg entered the room. Slim, fair bristly hair, dark brown eyes. He went over to Darling with quick, silent steps – black tennis shoes, jeans, a T-shirt with the text "Stop trafficking!" underneath a leather jacket, a home-rolled cigarette clamped above his ear – and stood in front of him with a hand on his hip, a head shorter than the policeman, without it being noticeable in the physical power balance. Axel stayed where he was.

"What are you doing here? Fucking typical. You can't take to the streets for five minutes without you lot coming swarming in. You have no right to be here. At all. It's illegal entry if you don't have a search warrant."

"We have a search warrant and it's valid from now on. It's on its way here and you can see it in a few minutes," said Darling.

Lindberg looked at him and shook his head despairingly.

"That's not good enough. You think you can use all your new police state rules from the terror package against peaceful activists protesting about you wanting to demolish the Youth House, but you're not doing anything here before there's a judge's signature on a piece of paper."

Darling smiled disarmingly.

"We're here because of a murder. Don't mix things up."

Axel took a step forward.

"No one leaves the room!" he shouted.

The girl who had just called him a pig turned to her laptop and began to move the mouse around. Axel was behind her in a second, a hand on her arm.

"Nobody touches anything. Especially not your laptops. There'll be technicians here in a few minutes."

Axel kept an eye on them to make sure everyone was obeying his instructions. He signalled to Darling and went into an office with Lindberg's name on the door. There was a large computer on a desk. In the toolbar, he found Outlook and began reading emails while listening to Darling talking with Lindberg.

There were more than 200 emails from the last three hours alone, many of them with photos attached, so Axel had to open each one to see if it was where the picture came from. Pictures of burning cars with the text: "Is this what we are fighting for?" Policemen beating demonstrators; crying emojis by the Youth House. Finally, Axel found the photo of the body, sent from the email address 69forever@hotmail.com. He forwarded the message to his own email and to the technical department. Then he called BB.

"I've sent you an email with a photo taken of the body before we found it. It doesn't look like it was taken by a mobile because it's pretty sharp. It's from a Hotmail address, which you need to put everything into tracking now."

He checked the Counterpress website. 33 minutes had elapsed from the email being received to the photo being published with a brief factual article about the murder – and it was written in Lindberg's style.

Autonomist killed at Youth House. Police cover-up.

Have the police covered up the murder of a Youth House activist? A pertinent question after it emerged that an autonomist has been murdered close to the Youth House in an area that only the police had access to.

Counterpress has just received a photo of a dead man from an unknown source. The body was found just 100 yards from the Youth House. In the picture, you can see the man sitting up against the wall in Assistens Cemetery, wearing dark clothes, balaclava, combat boots and with his hands bound behind his back with police handcuff strips.

During the clearance of the Youth House, the cemetery was cordoned off at the request of the Copenhagen Police, which has had several police units guarding the area. The police would not initially admit that they had found a body there, but reluctantly confirmed it when confronted with the facts. Copenhagen Police will not comment on whether it is an activist, though evidence overwhelmingly suggests that it is.

This comes just a day after the police used unprecedented violence to move into the Youth House on Jagtvej, clear it of activists and arrest 39 people.

More to follow.

Lindberg

The headline was unfortunately true and Axel knew from experience that it would send shockwaves through the police hierarchy, the media and the entire judiciary. He went quickly to Ekstra Bladet's and

Jyllands-Posten's websites. Burning car wrecks in dark streets were no longer the top story. The picture of the dead man with the balaclava was everywhere.

Lindberg's high-pitched, agitated voice pierced through him.

"We don't help the police. It's a principle and it applies in all cases. It's about freedom of the press."

Axel had had enough. He went out into the large office where Darling was surrounded by Lindberg and a handful of indignant staff members.

"You don't understand, do you, you idiot? It's nothing to do with freedom of the press. This is about murder. And you've been sent a picture that might put us on the track of the murderer. This isn't a discussion on whether or not you're allowed to sit and fiddle with your website and your demonstrator info all day. I've seen the email now and copied it, but if we don't get access to the hard drive and the server it's on, we'll shut you down right now."

"We have to do something, Martin. It'll be a disaster if we have to shut down," said the girl who had looked at Axel with disgust. "If we can co-operate… if we can trust them…"

Turning to Axel, she continued, "If you can guarantee that you won't spoil anything."

Lindberg interrupted her.

"We can't trust them. We don't co-operate with the police. Ever. If you want to help them, I'm out. If they take everything with them, we might have to shut down for a few hours, but they can't close the website."

Everyone began talking at the same time. About emergency preparedness, the Youth House, the police state, searches and the spirit of May 18.

"If you think the murderer sent that email to us, he may well want to send us more. So you also have an interest in the communication channel staying open," said Lindberg to Axel.

"Common interests, Lindberg? Hell will freeze over before we get to that stage. I've got fuck all to talk to you about. Nothing, got that?"

He was annoyed that he couldn't stay cool, all the more so because he could see from Lindberg's smile that he had put his foot in it. Axel raised his voice.

"Our technical division is on its way upstairs, and more officers will be arriving. Anyone who doesn't have anything to do with this should leave now. Otherwise, you'll be taken to HQ and charged with hindering the police in connection with the investigation of a murder. And that'll mean the party's over for you for the next two weeks."

Mumbling disapproval, but he also sensed some uncertainty.

Axel went over to Darling.

"What about that Lindberg fucker? I think we should take him into HQ and question him."

Darling wrinkled his forehead.

"What's your problem with him?"

"Nothing!" said Axel. Too fast. "I just think he should be shaken down so that we can see what falls out of his pockets."

"He isn't a suspect, Axel. There are a lot more urgent things to be dealt with. So let me question him here and we'll see if it's necessary to talk more with him."

Axel let it lie. He didn't want to provoke Darling's interest in his relationship with Lindberg any further. He cast a glance at the former squatter, who must now be about 40. You could see it in the wrinkles around his eyes, the tobacco stains and the loose skin on his throat, but somehow he still looked the same as back then. He stood provocatively in front of the photocopies from May 18 with his arms folded, keeping an eye on them.

There was something itching on the inside of his brain, somewhere Axel couldn't reach, but it wouldn't disappear. There was something that escaped him just as he was about to put it into words, and he knew it was important – he knew it was about Lindberg. And the body.

14

Piver was sitting on a bench in front of the Moonfisher, smoking a joint. It calmed him down a little, but not enough to relax properly. There were 10 minutes to go until his meeting with Martin Lindberg. He was having second thoughts. Even though the hash was doing its job, he was still nervous all the way down into his belly. In his hand he had half a joint, which he had bummed from a group of Swedes hanging around a table. He took another hit and closed his eyes.

His mother's worried face popped up: the weekly calls to the halls of residence in Lyngby and her anxious voice. He had come a long way from fucking Aalborg and the provincial academic fug – they thought they knew it all, but they knew fuck all.

But Piver knew enough. About his mother's vermouth bottles, which stood spread around like secret provision depots throughout the home; her accident, which was how she referred to the cyst that had caused her to have her womb removed by mistake, thus ending the possibility of her having more children after he had been born. About his father and his old issues of *Private*, which he had hidden behind the books about fly fishing in the bookcase in his workroom after she had discovered them once and cried for two days. He knew the sound of the Thursday fuck's four-minute creaking of the floorboards on the first floor and the glasses with sleeping pills and nerve medicine. And he was never going to return to that tawdry half-life, where nothing was ever fulfilled and you made do with a little because you didn't dare aim for a lot.

He opened his eyes and looked around. Martin Lindberg. It was him he was going to meet – the hero from May 18. If anyone would be able to understand him, it was Lindberg; he was sure of that. And Liz – wouldn't she see him in another light, even though she sounded scared?

It was now half past two but no one had contacted him yet, even though Lindberg had sounded like nothing could stop him, as if he would do anything to see the video. Piver had felt he could trust him. He could really use the money right now. The more uncertain he became, the more he craved beer, cigarettes and hash. And pizza. Hunger had also started to grow in his stomach.

He lit a cigarette. He would give him 10 more minutes. He began preparing himself for what he would do if Lindberg didn't show up. The Box was a no-go area for him now, and there was no question of him going back to Nørrebro, not as long as it was daylight anyway. But he knew someone who lived out at Dyssen, further out in the Freetown; an older guy, a painter and weekend pusher who had come to the Box – someone Liz knew, an ex-boyfriend of hers. He could go out to him. He would ask him to hide the camcorder, and then he would go to Counterpress to hear if they wanted to make a story out of it. Or should he hang on to the story, so that they could dedicate an issue of AFA's magazine to it? A whole issue about police violence and the Youth House based on his own experience of the pigs hunting him throughout the city for the film? It wasn't such a bad idea, but he wasn't certain that he could get it past Peter Paris and the others in the inner circle.

He opened an elephant beer he had bought with the last of his money. The alcohol started working immediately because of his empty stomach and blended in a gentle anaesthetic with the aftermaths of the joint.

In front of the entrance to the Moonfisher, he caught sight of a man standing looking for someone. Piver was immediately on his guard. The guy stood 10 yards away from him with his hands in his pockets, swaying slightly, casting regular glances at the door to the Moonfisher, Pusher Street and the street that went around the back, as if he were waiting for someone. Piver had seen that face barely an hour earlier as he had bought a beer. It wasn't Lindberg – he knew that much. Probably one of the local dipsos from the shopping centre.

He came over to Piver with a fatuous expression on his face.

"How yer doing, mate? You my man?" he asked. His voice was croaky from cigarettes and weed.

Piver took a tighter grip on his rucksack with the camera.

"What do you mean?"

"Can I bum a cig?" coughed the drunk.

Piver felt in his back pocket. He had just started pulling the packet out when he saw a large pair of military boots just behind the drunk.

"Clear off," said a tough voice.

"Hang on, mate, I just want…"

The drunk didn't get to say anything else before he was swept aside, gently but firmly, by a man who then gave his full attention to Piver: a tall guy wearing a black hoodie, but too old to be from the local milieu. He was wearing worn-out army trousers and the collar of a sweater stuck up from under his black hoodie.

"Peter?"

"Yes, are you Martin?"

"No, Martin couldn't come. I'm here instead." His eyes rested on Piver the whole time, calm, inspiring confidence. And firm. He didn't look like a journalist. He looked like an old man who had got lost in a hoodie. Piver laughed inside at that thought, but he had to be on his guard.

"I'm not sure about this. Can I trust you?" Piver screwed up his eyes and looked at him. There was something familiar about the voice. He mostly felt like just going along and doing what the man wanted him to do. He wanted someone else to take responsibility because it had already been far too crazy a day.

"Yes, you can. I'm sorry about the delay. Lindberg's been prevented from coming, but he's asked me to come and meet you. And I can help you just as much as Martin. We have the same goal."

Do we really? Piver asked himself, trying to maintain critical awareness. The man glanced down at his bag.

"Do you have the tape?" he asked.

Piver nodded.

"Is there anything you need? Beer, cigarettes?"

"I've actually had nothing to eat all day. Maybe a pizza or something."

"I have a car parked out on Prinsessegade. We can pick up a pizza and drive to a safe place so that I can see what this gold is you have for us."

For us? It wasn't their gold; it was his story.

"It's my film. You're not just going to take it over. If that's what you want, collaboration stops here."

"Take it easy. You're the main man. I just meant it might be gold for the milieu, from what Martin's told me. If the pigs have killed one of us, it has to come out. And if they're trying to hide it, it'll change the whole atmosphere. But if they get hold of this recording, no doubt they'll wipe it. They want to cover their tracks. And they'll chuck you in a cell without telling anyone about it."

They were now out on Prinsessegade.

Piver's whole body felt sore, his high was fading, his hunger making him nauseous, and he was tired enough to fall asleep if he just closed his eyes. He felt his rucksack for the camcorder, heard the double beep from an electronic car lock and saw the lights on a Toyota Hiace with tinted windows flash briefly. His companion was waiting with the keys in his hand.

"Shall we go?"

They went over to the car. He opened the passenger seat door and, before getting in, cast a brief glance into the back seat, where there was a jacket and a computer bag.

15

The smell leaves no doubt.

While the eyes get used to the sight of dead, dissected and mutilated bodies, you never get thick skin in your nostrils. It is worse in the summer, as the heat concentrates the smell of the mortuary, which is never totally the same, but always consists of the same components: disinfectant, blood and putrefaction. Chemical, heavy and sweet.

For Axel, the season was neither here nor there. They could show him the most mutilated traffic victims and mangled bodies, if only they'd spare him the smell.

He had suspected Lennart Jönsson of feeling the same way, although you'd never get a forensic pathologist to admit it. Unlike all his staff and the former bosses who had offices on or above the autopsy corridor on the ground floor, the Swede had moved into the basement next to the morgue, where the bodies were stored in a refrigerator at five degrees and the atmosphere was clinical and gloomy, with neon lights and exposed piping in the ceiling above the long, tiled passages. But down here there was no smell.

He stepped into the office holding Emma's hand, threw his bag on one of the filing cabinets and sat his daughter in the big armchair in front of the computer. He found DR's website. It was Children's Hour, four programmes in a row, each lasting 30 minutes, so that he could manage the rest of the autopsy, even if it dragged on.

"When are we going home?" she asked.

He gave her a small carton of apple juice.

"I have to do a bit of work, then I'll be right back. Here's my mobile. And if you want me, press here and I'll be here right away."

He had put Lennart Jönsson's number on the display so that she could call the autopsy room and get hold of him if she needed him. It wasn't the best solution, but it had to be done.

Eight men and one woman stood around the steel table bathed in cold projector lights. The smell wasn't all that bad; a distinctive, cool waft of butcher. The body had been opened, the ribs cut and the viscera taken out. They lay neatly in a row on a table beside and shone in a wealth of indigo, brown and red shades with patterns from tissue and veins. As Axel entered, a post-mortem examiner was taking samples of the liver. He saw the needle slide into the soft brown mass.

In addition to Lennart Jönsson and the examiner, a forensics technician, a forensics chemist and an assistant, Darling, BB and his assistant were present. And Corneliussen. And that wasn't because he was interested, but because he wanted to be sure he had all the information about the investigation.

Axel squeezed in next to Lennart Jönsson's staff, so that he was facing the Swede. He looked down at the body. The skull had been opened and the brain lay in a bowl, shining like a huge, beige walnut. The blood channel around the steel table was full. There was a brief pause; the Swede fixed him with a serious look over his spectacles, and Corneliussen sighed.

"As I was just saying, he's been strangled. And it was done with considerable strength. Both the larynx and the thyroid cartilage have been crushed."

"Doesn't that take a long time?" asked Axel.

"Often, yes. The textbooks say four to five minutes, but there's a lot of individual variation. There are cases where death has occurred almost instantly and cases where the grip has been held for minutes without killing the victim. Crushing the thyroid cartilage doesn't in itself lead to death, but is an indication of a very strong grip around the throat. Someone has really held very firmly here."

"What does the body show about the course of events otherwise?"

"You'll have to wait for our final report, but I'll bet he's had prolonged exposure to various forms of pressure, blunt force trauma to the face, extremely tight binding of the wrists that must have been painful and restricted his blood circulation quite severely, and there's a lot to suggest that he's been electrocuted."

As he spoke, he pointed to the lesions on the face and on the wrists, and when making the last remark, his pen rested on a blue spot on the victim's upper body.

Axel looked at the dead man. His cheekbones were marked, a little moustache with half-twisted ends, small ears that lay flat against the head, a long neck; he was slim without much fat on his body, and his muscles, which had contracted after death, were stiff under the skin. His dissected upper body sent out a damp smell of decay, blood and intestines, which hung in the air between them like a foul-smelling ghost, asking them when they were going to find his murderer.

"Electrocuted? Does that mean he's been tortured?" Corneliussen asked in his self-cast role of the bright student, which once again confirmed he was far outside his compass.

The Swede made a disapproving pout.

"No, unlikely," he retorted drily. "He's been given a shock from what's called a taser. A popular pacification device in the United States. That's my guess, in any case."

Axel couldn't see the chest tattoo because the skin it was on had been cut up and folded to the side so that the examiners had been able to empty the torso of organs and intestines. Axel asked the Swede's assistant to turn the skin over so that he could see the eagle.

"Yes, that's probably the closest we are to an identification for the time being," said the Swede, pointing at the eagle. "Shqiptarë. The Albanian national symbol. A double-headed eagle, which according to legend always guarded the first Albanian king, who saved it from being killed by a snake. Hasn't watched over this guy."

Albania, Macedonia, Kosovo, Montenegro, Greece. There were

Albanians in many places.

"Do we know anything about that kind of tattoo?"

"No, not more than that it's the eagle on the Albanian flag, which is primarily used in Albania, but was also popular in Kosovo in the 90s as a symbol of resistance to Serbia," said the Swede.

"There are 8,000-10,000 Albanians in Denmark, 50,000 in Sweden," added Darling. "We have passed it on to those circles and to our brothers across the Sound. But there's nothing to confirm he was resident here."

"OK, if we have to make a guess about the course of events, the order, what would you say, Lennart?" asked Axel.

"Taser, plastic strips, blows to the face, strangle grip, maybe more blows, throttling, balaclava."

Corneliussen woke up.

"Does that mean we're certain the balaclava has been put on him last?"

The Swede sighed and looked indulgently at Corneliussen.

"Nothing is certain. But I was at the scene of the crime and saw the hood. It's totally unmarked and clean on the outside. And I therefore consider it unlikely that it was on the victim when he was being electrocuted, beaten and strangled."

"So it isn't even his?" asked Corneliussen, elated.

"We have no way of knowing. He could still have been a middle-aged squatter from Kreuzberg, who had the balaclava in his hands and has been subjected to police violence. It's your job to figure that out. But it smells like a bit of camouflage, doesn't it?"

"Deliberate attempt to mislead, I'd call it," interrupted Axel. "And it's nice to know, but it doesn't get us any further. We're still not one inch closer to the murderer because of that, let alone the victim's identity."

"No, but we may be closer to being able to say who it isn't," chomped a satisfied Corneliussen, turning on his heel with a "thank you for today" and a comment that it had been extremely educational and interesting.

The door had just closed when a breathless, fair-haired young man with a white coat and a bright-red face flung it open.

"There's a little girl opening the drawers with the cadavers down below," he said. "She's singing to herself. It's like Lars von Trier's The Kingdom."

Axel rushed out of the door with the Swede in tow.

Down in the basement, Emma was in the morgue in front of a refrigerated drawer with the body of an elderly man. She had pulled it out, so that he was visible from the chest upwards. His eyes were closed, his face white and thin around the cheeks and nose. She was patting him on the shoulder.

"Don't be afraid. You'll sleep well, I'm sure. I'll fetch my Daddy and ask if you can have some warm clothes so that you don't have to be so cold."

Axel called out and ran over to her in three light steps.

"Now, Emma, you're not allowed to be in here. You were to stay in the office and call me if there was anything, weren't you?"

The little girl looked up at him.

"But the film had finished and I was bored, Daddy."

The Swede closed the two drawers Emma had already opened, and went over to the next one she would have opened. He looked down in it and shook his head. Axel followed his gaze down to the totally smashed face of a traffic victim.

"Why aren't they sleeping in their beds, Daddy? I mean… why are they asleep?"

The Swede looked at Axel and tossed his head towards the thick steel door with the porthole in. Axel's brain was working at high pressure to find an answer.

"They're asleep because they're tired, sweetheart. You mustn't go in to them. What did you watch in Children's Hour on the computer?"

His daughter spread her hands and looked disbelievingly at him.

"But then… why are they so cold?"

"Because it's cold in this room."

He took her by the hand and led her into the Swede's office.

"But aren't they freezing?"

The Swede came to his rescue. He held two clenched hands up in front of Emma and asked her which hand she wanted. In one there was a little doll; in the other a lollipop. Whether it was because the girl could feel that they would very much like to change the subject or because she was genuinely happy with the little doll, she said, "I'll call it Sille. Like Mummy."

"Come now, sweetheart, it's time to go home. Do you have anything else for me?" This last was addressed to the Swede.

"Judging by the contents of the stomach, the victim has eaten a shawarma. No alcohol, lots of smoke, but that's no use to you until you know who he is. What did you miss up there?"

"Age?"

"I'd estimate he's between 40 and 45 years old."

"What does his body say?"

"Haven't we talked enough death now? There are long ears here. Let's take that later."

Axel tumbled out into the light holding his daughter's hand. Emma was chatting happily to the little doll and seemed completely unaffected by her visit to the morgue.

Which was more than you could say about her father.

16

Things were going the wrong way for Piver. He was sitting in a car with a man he didn't know. He had got a vegetarian pizza, which he had already eaten, a six-pack of canned beers and a packet of cigarettes, but he wasn't feeling comfortable. It wasn't the first time in his life that he was heading into an unpredictable situation. He recognised the feeling of going along with something he wasn't ready for, of sitting avoiding another person's gaze, someone he felt was stronger than himself.

When at one point he had taken his phone out to call Liz, the other guy had put his hand on his arm and said he shouldn't because he could be traced through it.

"Can't I borrow yours then?" he had asked.

"The battery's flat," was the answer. "You can call when we arrive."

"Where are we going?"

"I have a safe house out near the Nørrebro railway line, an old factory where you can stay completely unnoticed."

The guy from Counterpress was doing it his own way, and he seemed as if he was going to do so all the way, whether Piver wanted to follow along or not.

Now they were sitting in the car by an old warehouse in the industrial district at the railway yards in Outer Nørrebro, watching the footage through.

They were surrounded by ruin and decay; a jogger, a dog walker and a waiting truck were all he had seen as they had swung in here from Rovsingsgade. They were maybe 100 yards from the road, which was right up against the Aldersrogade ghetto. Piver had insisted they watch the recording in the car, so that he could get out if something went wrong. He had a strange feeling in his stomach, but he didn't know whether it was from tiredness, exhaustion or the burgeoning distrust he harboured for this man.

"Have you watched it all?" asked the man curiously.

"Yes, quickly. But enough to see two interesting things that will be a problem for the police."

"Tell me!"

"We can watch it, so you know I'm right, but I won't let you have it before I know and I'm sure about what will happen to it and to me."

The man wrinkled his brow and looked at him with an insulted expression, so Piver corrected himself.

"Not because of anything in particular, but it's my arse that's on the line if I'm arrested. After all, you have your press freedom to fall back on."

"That's absolutely fine. I understand your concern," replied the man.

Piver took the camera out and switched it on. The man leaned over him. Eager.

"Oh wow, man. It's really clear, isn't it? You can see everything that's going on."

Piver spooled forward to the place where the plain-clothes policemen attacked the lone demonstrator. His companion said nothing, not even when the episode was over and the police and the activist were out of the picture. That surprised Piver.

"Isn't it just sick?" he asked.

"Exciting stuff, really interesting. Can you find the place with the murder?"

He seemed unimpressed.

"But don't you think this proves they've gone way over their boundaries?"

"Yes, of course it does. A hundred per cent. But the other thing is the serious stuff, isn't it? Come on, let's see it. How far forward do you have to spool in time?"

Piver spooled the tape forward to 1:30.

At first, everything looked quiet in the cemetery, but then two people came walking out under the trees. Into the camera's main field. They watched the chain of events all the way through. Piver couldn't believe he was sitting there looking at pictures of a man who was about to die. In his neighbourhood. Less than a day ago. But not just that. The cap concealed a murderer.

The man reached out for the camera.

"Let's see it again," he said. "You can zoom in here. Let me show you."

The picture came much closer than Piver had been able to get it. The two men came out under the trees. He couldn't see their faces, but he was sure he would have been able to make them out clearly if they had looked up at the camera. It was only now that he realised that the bareheaded man had his hands tied behind his back.

"Look, he's handcuffed," said Piver.

"Have you shown this to anyone else?" asked the man.

"No, not yet."

A minute passed without anything happening. The two men were hidden behind the wall. Then one of them came in view again, the one who had POLICE written on his back. He took off his cap and looked up. Piver spooled back and zoomed in. He felt a hand on his shoulder and suddenly knew that something was really wrong, like he had just made a connection as the last escape route was closed off.

"Stop right there," said the man.

His voice sounded cold and black.

"Who are you really?"

"Don't worry about that now. Just sit completely still."

Piver slowly lifted his head and looked up at the man who had claimed he was a friend of Lindberg and a member of Counterpress's editorial team. A cold shiver went down his back as the man swept off his black cotton cap and revealed the same smile, the same hair, as Piver had just seen on the tape.

The thought of opening the door and jumping out of the car only managed to lightly skim through his mind before the man pressed something against his chest and everything went black.

17

Friday was deemed to be the peak of the unrest, but Axel hadn't imagined how bad it would be. He put Emma in bed in the children's room just after nine. She seemed to have quickly forgotten the sleeping men at forensics. They had talked about going to the cinema the next afternoon after coming back from the 24-hour nursery that Axel and his ex-wife had put her in because of their variable and long working days. Cinderella and pizza. But first Axel had to do some work. There were many disagreements between him and Cecilie, but it was rarely about how much they worked and how little they saw their daughter while she was with them. Some things are too painful to squabble about and, in this case, they both had bad consciences.

After they returned from forensics, Emma had watched children's TV while Axel made spaghetti carbonara and replied to text and phone messages. There were several messages from journalists which he ignored, except one from Dorte Neergaard, who asked if it was OK for her to come at 10pm if she could get off. Everything was fine as long as she had the footage with her.

Axel had a history with her, which included sex. One day she had suggested that they smoke a joint afterwards. "If you can't sleep, I promise you this cocktail will work." She had been right. He slept like a log for the first time for several weeks. Whether it was because of the sex or the weed, he didn't know, but when he had tried it without the sex a week later, it worked. He had been using it ever since.

They had been together in a kind of collective agreement, he had felt. They exchanged sex. He got his sleep and rest; she got information. That was OK. Dorte was challenging and direct, on the verge of teasing, but her lust was also hard in a way that frightened him. Nothing about love and relationship – she wasn't preparing the ground for that at all; and if he was honest, it confused him that it could be so simple: fuck, bodies, talk, gossip and a joint or three. With a month's interval or more.

He closed the door to Emma's room, which fortunately overlooked the rear courtyard so she wouldn't be woken up by the frequent sound of sirens prowling through the night. In the living room, he returned to his distracted switching of pastimes from zapping between the TV news channels and going to the bay window to see what was happening on the streets below. Nørrebro was still slumbering; there were cars driving up and down the street, the windows rattled when a lorry or a bus drove past, and everything looked familiar, but it surely wouldn't be long before it would change.

The entry phone rang at 22.30. She looked like a party for two and not a reporter who had been on the go for 12 hours. The perfume struck him as soon as he opened the door; the Asian tomboy was tucked away under fresh make-up – eyeliner, mascara, lipstick and foundation; her face came close and he bent down and gave her a hug. Her lips brushed his cheek, she closed her almond-shaped dark brown eyes, and he was in her helmet of lacquered black hair. My little China girl.

They had never met at his place before, so he briefly showed her round; she saw the sleeping Emma and sighed with something he interpreted as tenderness before he brought her into the living room where there were two glasses of wine, although Axel almost never drank.

She went over to the window and stood with her back to him. He turned off the Keith Jarrett CD, which had been playing in the background.

"Fuck, what a view! You must've been able to see everything last night."

"Yes, but I don't waste much time on that. That's not my department," he lied.

"But it's still crazy. You can see almost all the way into town. You're the only cop I know living in Nørrebro. Actually, why *do* you live here?"

"I feel settled here. I don't want to live anywhere else. Didn't you have a video tape we were going to watch?"

She walked over to him. Really close. As she usually did. She was one of those people who didn't respect other people's personal space; she always stood those two to three inches closer than she should. Although she was head and shoulders shorter than Axel and probably weighed half what he weighed, he felt pressed into a corner.

"Is that what we're going to do now?" she purred.

He tried to smile his way out of the physical encroachment.

"Isn't it? I thought we might just as well get the serious work out of the way."

It wasn't a total rejection, but she took it as such.

"So it's not me you want?"

He was having difficulty assessing whether she was hurt, or just being coquettish – probably both, but he had to pull himself together.

"You know me. You know how I am with work. Right now you have something I have to watch because there could be a lead on it. To a murderer. I can wait with the other stuff."

It worked.

She walked out into the hall and fetched her bag, a large, light-brown leather case that looked like it was well worn, but the shiny buckles testified that it was just the look and that it would probably have cost the earth. She pulled out a laptop in a red foam case, put it on her lap, rummaged in her bag and found a CD-ROM.

"There are six hours from the air on this, from 21 to 03. It's from all over the city so there's a lot to see… unfortunately."

As she was taking out the computer, opening it and putting the CD-ROM in, Axel looked at her knees, legs and the section of her thighs visible below the skirt, the black leather boots with high heels, the black tights. Her silk blouse over the completely flat breast. Was that what made her so arousing?

He looked at the screen.

The helicopter floated through the night sky like a purring moth. The footage was unedited and accompanied by crackling and fragments of sentences and messages between the pilot and the studio, but it was amazingly sharp, despite the fact that the camera was constantly in motion. The helicopter sailed around above a Copenhagen which seemed enormous in its extent and yet small, grey and anonymous in the dark. Even the city's spires, towers and high-rise blocks were miniature from the camera's position.

"How high up is it?" asked Axel.

"I don't know, but we can zoom in. What do you want to see?"

"I'd like to see footage from 23:00 above Assistens Cemetery, Runddelen, the Youth House, everything there is of Nørrebro."

The picture suddenly became very local, with chimneys, red roof ridges, slate, satellite dishes, old TV antennas and new mobile masts. It was difficult to see right away where they were, but then the Lakes and Dronning Louises Bro with its eight luminous globe lamps came into view. They stood out like yellow cats' eyes in the darkness. The helicopter continued beyond Nørrebrogade, past the bend at Griffenfeldsgade, and then he could see the cemetery and the stretch along Assistens until the picture froze at Runddelen and the Youth House.

"What are you looking for?"

"I'd like to tell you, but you must promise not to use it. Not until I say so."

She frowned, but agreed, and Axel told her about some of his suppositions and what they had found so far.

"I'm interested in seeing how the victim got there. I'm sure he must have met his murderer inside the cemetery. And there are a couple of our guys who should have been keeping an eye on the spot where the body was found and have been sleeping on the job."

She spooled forward while they were talking.

"What's happened to them?"

"This is also off the record. They've been questioned by the DPP today."

He could feel her focus moving away from the images on the screen and being directed 100 per cent to him.

"OK. Are they suspected of having anything to do with the murder?"

"No, not really, it's to cover every eventuality. If the shit starts flying later, no one can come and say that we didn't investigate our own ranks. I've questioned one of them myself, and he's a very unlikely murderer, but he hasn't been doing his job either, because the murder took place in the area they were supposed to be patrolling."

"So what happened?"

"I don't know, but if it weren't for the fact that they were two men, you'd think they'd been screwing in the bushes."

"Who says they haven't?"

At the top corner of the screen, Axel could follow the time whirling away on fast forward. The helicopter had been flying all over the city. The camera panned across the Lakes and on to Rådhuspladsen, the large square outside City Hall, where more than 1,000 people had gathered in a funeral procession with white coffins and flaming torches. They began moving up towards Nørrebro and Folkets Park, a polluted building site right in the heart of the district, mostly used by pushers from Blågårds Plads and drinkers from the soup kitchen on the corner. At 23.30, the demonstration began to fall apart in the area and from the air Axel was able to see the famous task force operation unfolding in full. Officers closed all the side streets with police vans and began pushing forward to occupy the park; people ran and leapt to all sides with groups of policemen after them.

"You really get stuck in, don't you?" said Dorte Neergaard, not usually known as a softy when it came to hooded demonstrators ravaging the streets, but Axel didn't fail to notice that batons were being swung without restraint.

The helicopter moved again towards the Youth House and she stopped the recording when it reached Runddelen. The time was 23.34 and Axel could see something that very much resembled two officers standing having a smoke by a gravestone in the shelter of the wall 50 yards from the upcoming crime scene.

He showed her the area that interested him and asked her to zoom in.

The body wasn't there and it gave Axel a shock to know that the dead man was probably still alive at this point and that he would perhaps get to see what had happened to him in a short space of time. He could see the two police vans parked at the main entrance far from the crime scene. And there was apparently another police transport van right opposite the Youth House, so there were a hell of a lot of his colleagues in the cemetery. Nothing was happening. Everyone was standing still and, on the street outside, the smoke from a burned-out rubbish bin was hanging in the air.

The two officers, whom Axel assumed were Kasper Vang and Jesper Groes, stood chatting with each other, or were they dancing? Axel could see their helmets lying on the ground next to them. One of them began to take off his one-piece suit. What the hell's going on? he thought.

"Hello – now he's doing a bloody striptease," sniggered Dorte Neergaard.

For a moment, Axel thought she was right, but the officer who had taken his suit off gave the other a pat on the shoulder, went over to the gate, pulled himself up, looked both ways, then jumped out into Nørrebrogade and began walking in towards town. The other one disappeared between a grave and a tree. At about the same time, Axel noticed something moving on the path a little way inside the cemetery. They spooled back and zoomed in. It looked like a man walking, but he was totally dark and only showed up in short flashes under the foliage.

At 00.55, the helicopter returned to Runddelen. Axel couldn't see the two police officers. They zoomed out a bit and saw that bonfires were being lit in two different places on the street, but they were 300-400 yards from the crime scene. The cemetery lay peacefully in the darkness.

At 1.33 there was movement near the crime scene. The helicopter was hovering over the Youth House, and the angle meant that the trees were concealing most of the view, but it didn't prevent Axel from seeing two men come walking under the trees by the wall. Five-six steps, then they disappeared behind a tree trunk.

"Stop there and zoom in," he said.

They were walking, one with an arm around the other, in the direction of the Youth House and the chapel, heading towards the wall where the body had been found – he counted seven steps and then they were gone. A minute and a half later a shadow seemed to fall under the street lighting over the ground where they had disappeared – or was it a man's back? Axel asked to see it again. Now he knew. It was a flash. The perpetrator had photographed his exploit. The Counterpress photo! Then one of the men came out on the path and walked into the cemetery. He was unrecognisable in the dark, compacted on the screen, but maybe the technicians could do something about the pictures. They watched the sequence through twice more, but Axel was none the wiser.

12 minutes later, one of the officers climbed over the wooden gate, and a couple of minutes later, the two men again stood smoking up against a gravestone.

It was surreal.

"It's a bloody good story, this," said Dorte Neergaard.

Axel had forgotten all about her, but now she was demanding his attention.

"Yeah, maybe, but what does it mean?"

"I don't know, but your colleagues have been totally asleep on the job. I don't know where they are or if they have anything to do with the murder, but a man's been murdered on their watch and they've seen fuck all because they're not doing their job. It's still a bloody good story."

She took the computer and made as if to get up.

"And I'm off back to work to write it right now."

Axel put a hand on her arm with a firm grip.

"We need to talk about this. When do you want to do that story? And what do you want to say in it?"

There wasn't the slightest residue of desire for him left in Dorte Neergaard's eyes. On the contrary – "ambitious journalist with the scent of a scoop" was flashing in capital letters in the look she sent him.

"Axel, this is my clip. I've shown you something, so you can't set conditions."

"I'm not either, we just need to discuss what's happening and what we can conclude based on your clip. It's my information that's made it possible for you to do this story, otherwise you'd have been at a total loss. One officer jumping over a gate and another disappearing under a tree means nothing. You don't know what they're up to, or why, or what their orders are. And you can't just use it."

"What do you suggest?"

"I want to talk to the two officers first, then you can do whatever you want with the footage. I'll do that tomorrow. As soon as I've spoken to them, you'll be notified, and you can go ahead with the story."

She held her hands up in the air, as though she was writing an invisible headline.

"'Demonstrator murdered under noses of sleeping officers'. Or what about: 'Police let demonstrator die while sleeping on the job'. I think the first one's best."

"Fuck, the idiots," groaned Axel. "But we don't know if your headlines are true, do we?"

"No, but you'll know tomorrow. I promise to hold back on the story, then you tell me everything you find out, so I can include it."

"Forget it. I can't do that when I'm the one who's questioned them. It would be as good as resigning," he said, thinking about it. "You don't need me. You can guess your way to the story yourself. One of them leaves his post, the other disappears, maybe he takes a nap, maybe he's out picking up pizzas, but one thing's certain: he's not where he should be. If there's a very good reason for their absence, I'll give it to you. But wait to run the story until I'm ready."

Axel got up. He was sure he had an agreement with her, which would let him use the pictures on the tape to break the two officers' story. Now he just needed the tape.

"I need that footage. Not to show to others, but to use it in interviewing those two."

She shook her head fiercely.

"You must be mad. If my bosses find out that I've given you the footage, it'll be me getting the bloody boot. No way."

"I won't tell anyone that it's press footage. I'll just say they're pictures from the police helicopter."

"What was on the police recordings?"

"Nothing connected with the murder."

"I can't give you that recording. If it goes further in your system and is used, everyone will see it comes from us."

"That footage is crucial not just for the two officers, but also for the actual murder investigation." He hesitated, but there was only one thing for it now. "If you don't give me it voluntarily, I'll arrest you here and now for obstructing a murder investigation."

"You're joking!" She laughed nervously. "You can't fucking do that, you can't!"

Axel looked at her.

"Yes, I can. Right now."

She looked at him, exploring his face, as if she couldn't understand what he was saying.

"Wait a minute… Is this some new dark side of you? Foreplay for a kinky sex game? If it is, you'd better stop it, because I don't find it very funny."

"It won't go further in the system, I promise you. I'll give you the story solo as soon as there is something."

"Kiss my arse, you arrogant bastard."

But she had lost and he had lost her for the time being. Five minutes and many insults later, she took the CD-ROM out of the bag and thrust it into his chest.

"You're the most fucking extra psycho pig I've ever met, you know that? Fuck you."

Axel looked at his watch as the front door slammed – it was nearly twelve. He fetched his laptop, connected it to the big screen and watched the clip twice more while trying to ignore all his thoughts about Dorte Neergaard and the angry exchange they had just had. The noise from the street confirmed the riots were in full flow. Shouts and commands rang between the houses, fire engine sirens blared incessantly, but after a while they were replaced by police sirens and Axel knew that the firemen had abandoned turning out to more fires in Nørrebro because they were being bombarded with missiles. The normal traffic was gone and it meant that, at times, there was an unusual stillness, a strange dreamlike silence in the street that was normally roaring. In one of the still periods around half past one, he suddenly became aware of the golden gleam dancing in through the windows from the junction right below him. Burning embers leapt up towards the sky in the air outside his windows, accompanied by the crackle of flames.

Axel lit a joint and inhaled the sight on the street, as if it were something happening in a completely different reality.

Sitting on the asphalt were 12 or 13 people around a bonfire made of bulky refuse – discarded beds, a couple of bikes and stacks of compacted advertising circulars which the flames were having difficulty spreading to. It would have looked just like any other drinking binge by very drunk men who only had their blood-alcohol level as a social binder, if it weren't for the stove being replaced by a street bonfire. Two of them got up and tried to kick the circulars that had fanned out over the asphalt back into the flames. Axel knew both of them. Bartenders from the local pub, too old for juvenile pranks, but forever young in the lurching locomotion of their intoxication, they looked more like babies who had just learnt to walk than men in their late 40s.

Tiredness began to creep into his eyes, which he closed without noticing. Now he could find peace.

18

Saturday, March 3

March is the worst month of the year in Denmark, dirty brown and grey, sandwiched between the white snow of February and April's heralding of spring. Neither here nor there, just a cold interval of hopelessness.

This year was no exception, thought Axel, with a cup of coffee in his hand as he looked out at a Nørrebro that made his heart sink. The sky was slate grey; the asphalt, coloured white by road salt in winter, now resembled skin on a scarred body, with large burn blotches after the night's riots, while the buildings stood like colourless walls around the city's grey-misted morning.

The hash had once again given him the sleep he usually struggled to get, so he felt ready and full of energy. He couldn't feel his heart at all unless he actually put a hand on his chest.

It was just gone seven, Emma was still asleep, and Axel was considering what to do about Kasper Vang and Jesper Groes. The public prosecutor had decided they didn't have enough on them to send them to the duty magistrate, but he might look at it differently if he saw the footage Axel had taken from Dorte Neergaard. The two officers had been taken out of the duty rosters until further notice. Axel wanted to have a go at them today, but only after he had checked their files from Human Resources.

He fetched the daily newspapers from the hallway. Sonne had been to the collective and done an interview with Piver's two girlfriends, who told readers about police violence and assault and about their missing friend who was being hunted by the police. It was heartbreaking and a pack of lies. The story from Counterpress about the murdered man with the balaclava had got legs, and since yesterday it had started to spread at something that could only be described as breakneck speed, or as the police press office would of course call it: an uncontrollable story that had to be stopped at once. It was the top story in all the newspapers – with the same angle – most sharply formulated on Ekstra Bladet's front page in monumental capitals: "Were police involved in autonomist murder?"

Axel knew exactly what colour Corneliussen's cheeks would be as he read that sentence, not to mention how Rosenkvist's comb-over would flap. And it wouldn't get any better when it came to light that two officers had been sleeping on the job when the murder took place. Sleeping? Was that all? Hadn't he seen one of them actually disappearing for the precise period when the murder was being committed?

He would have to plan how to handle this investigation thoroughly, because if it turned out one of them had something to do with the murder, uncontrollable wasn't the word. That would put a bomb under the force. And under peace in the city. At the same time, he would have to be careful about the recording, because if he was linked to Dorte Neergaard it could be costly for both of them. He intended to keep his promise to her that she could go ahead with the story about the officers. When he was ready.

The phone rang on his way in to wake Emma.

It was BB. Before he had finished his opening sentence, Axel knew there had been a breakthrough.

"We have a bite, Axel. The victim's paws are in the fingerprint register."

"Who is he?"

"He matches a Macedonian with the name Enver Davidi. Forty-eight years old."

Enver from Macedonia. The name was Albanian. It smelt of drugs, human trafficking, kingpins and concerns.

"Do we know him?"

"Yes, we have a small bookshelf on him."

"Is it drugs?"

"Yes, among other things."

"Have you got hold of his criminal record?"

"It's on its way, but they've had to pick it up manually and that's what's odd about it."

"What do you mean?"

"He doesn't have any papers with us any more, not officially, because he's out of the country."

"So what? There's loads more like him. Where does he live?"

"Well, that's my point. He doesn't exist any longer in Denmark because he was deported. Forever. He was nicked with 17 kilos of cocaine back in 1996 and got eight years for it. And then he got a deportation order on top, so he was chucked out after serving half his time."

"What's he doing here then?"

"Yes, that's a good question, Holmes. But it's your job to find the answer to that."

Without knowing anything specific about Enver from Macedonia, Axel's first thought was that he probably had to get help from Narcotics at HQ, because the victim's sentence for drug smuggling stank all the way from the Balkan route, along which heroin travelled from Afghanistan to Denmark. The Albanians in northern Macedonia had long ago moved in on that vein of gold and they had been sitting on a large part of the cake for decades, completely unaffected by whether their area was ruled by Tito, Slobodan Milosevic, changing Macedonian governments or NATO forces in Kosovo. Together with the Serbs, they were responsible for transporting the drugs into Kosovo and Montenegro through the high mountains north of Tetovo and, from here, onwards to the rest of Northern Europe, where the Balkan diaspora, in an ugly mix with local crooks, bikers and second-generation immigrants, were sitting on the distribution.

But who would have killed a drug offender so close to the Youth House the night after it was cleared? And who had dressed him up as a militant activist from Kreuzberg?

The drug trade could explain the violence and hardness associated with the murder. The bound hands, the blows to the face. It wasn't certain that they had been trying to get something out of Enver; it could just as well have been a way of setting an example.

On the other hand, it was difficult to understand what a deported drug felon was doing in Denmark.

"Where are you calling from?"

"The cemetery. The search produced new clues, and I'm in the process of investigating where the victim and the perpetrator have been besides the crime scene. I'll be here all day."

"New clues. What are they?"

"Nothing that could immediately be linked to the murder, but a couple of packets of hash, some drugs, a bundle of money – all hidden in different burial plots."

"Do you have a link to Criminal Records?" Axel asked.

BB was one of the few policemen who did everything online. Axel and most of his colleagues hadn't even had an email address until last year and there was no connection from their laptops to the database network with information on criminal records and wanted persons at various police stations.

"Yes, I do."

"Can you send me what you have on this guy Enver, now?"

"Yes, but you have to call in yourself and get someone to pull out his old case files."

Axel rang off and went in to Emma. She was lying on her back with her arms stretched over her head, her mouth wide open, so that the air was wheezing softly through the hole where her front teeth had been. Her lips were cracked and dry due to lack of moisture. He forgot the investigation and sat down for a while, filled with love for her, but the disquiet in his body made him put a hand on her shoulder and whisper her name.

"Emma, love, it's time to get up. We have to get you to kindergarten.

And Daddy has to go to work."

She needed 15 minutes to lie there and wake up, so Axel went into the living room and switched on his laptop to read the email from BB.

Enver Davidi, born in 1959 in the village of Shipkovitsa in the mountains three miles north of Tetovo in then Yugoslavia, now Macedonia. Arrived in Denmark in 1980 as a 21-year-old with his brother and father; the rest of the family stayed back home. Enver Davidi had earnt his living as a taxi driver. He had lived in a public housing flat in Korsgade in Inner Nørrebro with his father and brother: classic 70s guest worker set-up, where the men take two to three months summer holiday in their homeland and graft away the rest of the year to send money home to the family. The father died of cancer in 1989; the brother died in a traffic accident in 2005. Both buried in Tetovo. The brother had been suspected and held for several drug offences, but never formally charged. Enver had several flags in his criminal record: drink-driving, one conviction for violence, three for possession of euphoriant substances, one for disorderly conduct, a restraining order, and then the really big one, the drug smuggling case from 1996.

In 1995 he had married a Danish woman; they had had a child in 1996 and were divorced in 1997, the same year he was sentenced to eight years in prison. He had tried to get the deportation order rescinded by the Supreme Court, but was refused, and in 2000 he was expelled from the country after serving half his time, as was usual for deportees. In 2003, he was arrested in Malmö and sent back to Macedonia after the Swedish police asked the Danish police if they had anything on him. He had been arrested in Denmark in 2005 by a patrol in Nørrebro – it coincided with his brother's death. He had a return ticket and had been locked up and put on a plane six days later. He had since been spotted on two occasions in Copenhagen, when the police had been tipped off by witnesses who had recognised him on the street. It had been decided at the request of the prosecutor not to intervene and arrest him due to a pending investigation.

Axel wrote times, names, addresses and phone numbers in his

notebook and made a note to contact the Narcotics Division to hear what had been hidden behind the phrase "pending investigation".

These pieces of information – especially about the last visits – raised more questions than they answered. Why was Enver Davidi being subjected to special attention and from whom? And what was behind him not having been arrested and thrown out of the country when he had been seen several times?

On the other hand, it meant that somewhere in the police there was someone who knew more about the victim than Axel currently did.

He scrolled down through his phone contacts until he came to Frank Jensen, a former colleague, now posted abroad as a liaison officer for the Danish National Police in Skopje, Macedonia.

"Axel! Are you still rushing around chasing scumbags for Homicide in Copenhagen?"

"You bet I am. What about you? How are things in Skopje?"

"Nice, sociable, easy women, but there's fuck all to do if you mean real police work. It's networking and connections, all of it. Official dinners and all the unofficial business where anything goes."

"Then you might be able to help me with some unofficial information about a victim in an investigation I have."

Axel gave him Davidi's data. Frank asked him to wait.

"He's on my long list of deported drug felons who have settled down around Tetovo. There are so many of them that they almost have to bump each other off to pass the time – there isn't enough gear to go round."

"Is it normal for them to come up to Denmark to commit new crimes after they've been deported?"

"There's nothing you could call normal with these guys. Some develop into psycho-gangsters; most of them have lost contact with their wives and children after deportation, so they don't have much to lose. Others change their life completely and enter a monastery, but your friend certainly doesn't belong in that category."

"Do you know him?"

"No, but we've been collecting information on all of them, because they can be a problem for us and the Macedonians. His name came up in connection with an investigation into a dead Moldovan whore five or six years ago. I'll have to call some contacts to find out more about him."

"It's a murder, Frank. It's urgent."

"You don't sound like you've changed a bit. You'll be hearing from me."

After a quick goodbye, he rang off and called Erna in the Homicide Division.

"Have you found the old case files on Enver Davidi?"

"I've been in the archive. There are only a few small things, some violence and threats. The big drug case file has been borrowed. An H. Nielsen, Detective Inspector in the Flying Squad has signed off on it."

"What? It's 10 years old! Get hold of Nielsen's number and text it to me. I need to have a chat with him."

Emma was standing in the door with her polar bear in her hand. Axel rang off. He would have to sort it out later.

"It says troot troot troot," she said. "That means good morning in polar bear language."

"Good morning, sweetheart."

His mobile vibrated.

There was a text from Corneliussen: "You take the interview with Davidi's ex-wife. Darling takes the cemetery and the door-to-door. I've told him. We have to get things moving – now."

It was customary for two officers to go out and tell people that their nearest and dearest was dead, but Axel was fine about doing it alone. Meeting next of kin was always a critical moment, and every policeman knew it was often among them that the perpetrator was found. But it was unusual for Corneliussen to get involved at this stage. He was doing it in this case because of the photo of the body and the rumours flying around that the police were involved in Davidi's murder. Those rumours had been elevated to truth in activist circles. The riots of the night before had been the worst yet and were close to costing some policemen their lives at Sankt Hans Torv, where they had been trapped in their fireproof vans. These had proved to be not quite so fireproof after all when showered with missiles and Molotov cocktails. The smart café area with the expensive flats on the square had become a flaming torch during the night. Between 10 and 20 cars had been set on fire, and the fire brigade had been prevented from entering and extinguishing the fires. Axel was in no doubt that the photo sent to Counterpress had added more fuel to the hatred of the police and frustrations over the clearing of the Youth House. He had watched the TV clips, heard shouts of police murder and seen fragments of interviews with activists who accused the police of murder and violence.

"We have to get dressed. Let's see who's ready first."

Emma was in her room before he could say another word. Five minutes later, when Axel had pulled on his jeans and a shirt and came into the living room, she was already standing there in her pink princess dress with a fake crown dangling crookedly in her curls and sunglasses with lilac plastic frames and black glass.

"I'm ready to party," she said.

Once he had dropped Emma off, he drove in to HQ. Homicide was in overdrive. At least six of his colleagues led by Darling were in the process of reviewing witness statements and a host of tip-offs and calls that had come in since yesterday.

Axel called the police communications centre and checked the address of Enver's ex-wife, Laila Hansen. She lived on Rentemestervej in Nordvest. He took the car.

The wind had picked up and the small pennants on Dronning Louises Bro, which were meant to stop the swans from the Lakes flying into the power lines, were flapping and whipping in the wind. His fellow policemen stood around the transport vans on the bridge looking tired.

It only took him 15 minutes to get there because the city still hadn't got up. He heard on the radio that the number of arrests was now up to 273 after the night's disturbances.

Nordvest, unlike its big brother Nørrebro, isn't known for anything good. It doesn't attract any media attention; it is chock-full of pensioners, junkies in search of money and a fix, drunks on the street corners and big flashy cars with chrome wheel rims and gilt spoilers. Almost the entire district consists of old, dilapidated rental homes from the 50s and properties with assignment rights from the municipality. There are a lot of people on social security, unemployed immigrant families and white trash in a grey patchwork of abuse, trauma, emptiness, junk and booze.

Axel switched off the radio and turned into Rentemestervej. To his surprise, there was a row of detached houses at the end of the road that stretched out to Utterslev Torv. A small segment of brick-built idylls on the edge of supplementary payments country. Number 12 was a red house in the English style with a garage and a strip of grass in front. The time was 10.45. The street was almost deserted.

Axel rang the doorbell. There was a shout, and half a minute passed before the door opened.

The woman who opened the door was his own age, short with red hair, cut short at the neck, blue eyes and broad lips. He recognised her straightaway.

19

She looked startled. Then astonished. And a little afraid.

"Hello there," she said with an inquisitive look.

"Hi."

"What... erm?"

Hadn't she said she'd just broken up with someone?

"I'm sorry, but I'm from the police. I'm here because we found Enver Davidi dead yesterday. I understand he's your ex-husband and father to your child."

A lot of small, fine wrinkles welled up around her eyes, which suddenly looked transparent.

"This isn't a joke, is it? You're a police officer? That's..."

What had he said he was back then – a lawyer?

Then she started crying.

"I'm sorry, but I need to ask you some questions."

She shook her head.

"Come on in. Louie, my son, is at football. What should I say?"

Then she stopped and stared up at him. He could hardly hear the words as she spoke.

"But how did he die?"

She buckled and fell towards him. He put his arms around her. She smelt sweet, of sweat and suds, and Axel wondered if she had been cleaning when he rang the doorbell. She straightened up, dried her eyes with the heel of her hand, sniffed and took a short step away from him. She wore a light-coloured, short-sleeved cotton shirt buttoned up to the neck, white leather sandals and a pair of tight jeans, which she smoothed out mechanically.

He remembered how she had repeatedly put her hand on his thigh when they were around town together. She had had an almost gluttonous way of making contact with him. Back then.

"When did you last see him?"

"See him? But he was thrown out of the country seven years ago."

"And you haven't seen him since?"

She sat down on a natural white sofa and rubbed her hands around her face as if she had just woken up. Then she got up.

"I need something to dry my eyes with."

Axel looked around. What was it she said her job was? Nurse? Health visitor? Health care worker? He tried to remember her name. She hadn't called herself Laila back then.

When she came back, he went through the usual routine with her – enemies, debts, what about her? Was anybody pursuing her? She answered hesitantly and dismissively, and when he asked about contact with Enver, she closed off completely and maintained that she hadn't seen him since he had been deported.

Axel was sure she was lying – not only because of the information that Enver Davidi had been in the country on several occasions: what father wouldn't visit his child and its mother after so many years of separation? – but also because all the classic signs were there: avoiding eye contact, nervous twitches, distracted picking at her clothes, as if she were somewhere else all the time. Perhaps that place was sorrow over her ex-husband's death? Perhaps it was an escape from the truth, perhaps something else entirely – but instead of pressing ahead, he evaded the issue, fell silent and left her in peace. It shouldn't be now, while she was processing the news that her child had become fatherless, that Axel should be probing deeper, but he would get around to it at some point. And it would come sooner than he realised, because she suddenly sat up straight and looked at him as if she had made a decision.

"It doesn't really matter now, even though I promised not to tell anyone. He rang me on Tuesday and said that he was in Denmark and that he would come and visit me and the boy soon."

"Did he say anything about why he was here?"

"No, but he said that big things were about to happen. And that the future would be very different."

"Did you have any idea what he meant?"

"He was a dreamer, so I just thought it was the usual. I said that to him, too, but he wouldn't hear it. He was very eager to come and explain it to me."

She looked out of the window.

"What am I going to say to Louie?"

"How do you spell his name?"

She spelt it.

It matched the tattoo on Enver Davidi's body.

"What about the date 18.3.2001? Does it mean anything to you?"

"No, why?"

Axel didn't answer, but let her sit with the questions about her son's father, now dead.

"What happened to him? Where is he?" she asked.

"He's been killed. He was found the night before last in Assistens Cemetery. I'm sorry, but it's already out – not with his name, but you'd still be able to guess it was him, so I might as well prepare you."

She looked shocked, shook her head and began to cry again.

"Oh no."

"You say he called on Tuesday. What did he say?"

"He said he had come home. He just had to fix some things for some people, and he would come by soon. I said it would have to be when Louie was at school or he had to let me know in good time, so that I could get him taken care of. I have a surprise, he said. Everything's going to be all right."

"A surprise? For you?"

"I don't know."

"But what did he mean – that everything would be all right?"

"I don't know that either, but he always had loads of ideas and fantasies that the future could be different. They just never came to anything."

"Did he say anything about where he was living?"

"He said he could come at 10 minutes' notice because he was staying at a hotel in Nørrebro."

That was good news. Nørrebro had everything apart from street-walkers and hotels. Axel could only remember one, in the middle of Nørrebrogade, a transit camp for people from all over the world trying to find happiness in Denmark, or Danes on their way to the bottom, people who wanted to get away and not draw attention to themselves. He had been to the Hotel Continental for two murder inquiries over the last five years.

"What happened?" she asked.

"We don't know anything yet, but it's difficult not to believe it's connected with his past, his prison sentence, his life of crime. We know he's been in Denmark several times. And when you say he's contacted you, I get very curious because it's a pattern we often see in connection with deported drug offenders – not necessarily that they come back here again, but that they carry on in the trade and help manage the smuggling from abroad. So I need your help. Does that mean anything to you?"

"I don't know anything about his life now. We hardly had any contact at all, but I don't think David was controlling any drug trafficking. He was far too disorganised. He wasn't in the trade, as you say. I don't think so in any case."

"Did you call him David?"

"Yes."

"How was your relationship?"

"What am I supposed to say? You got him thrown out, so what do you mean by relationship? He wasn't allowed to stay here and see his son. I haven't had the money to send Louie down there, so we didn't have any relationship."

"I need to know something about what your life is like now."

"What do you mean?"

"Job, relationship, Louie's school. I need factual information."

"Why do you need that? Am I a suspect?"

"No, you're not, but I need to know where I can get hold of you if necessary. You're not a suspect, but you're not excluded either until I've checked you out."

"It must be strange to have a job where you can never trust people." She shook her head. "I work as a day nurse so that I can take care of Louie. I earn OK, make ends meet. Louie goes to Frederikssundsvej School. I'm single. I had a boyfriend for a year after David, but we broke up. Anything else?"

"Not right now. Can I have your mobile number?"

They exchanged numbers. He got up from the sofa and stood in front of her. She was very attractive, beautiful in a vulnerable, fragile way, the transparency in her eyes and the soft shape of her lips. That smell again – sweat and soft skin. Her hand was warm and damp as he said goodbye.

He stopped at the door and watched her clearing the cups.

"I don't remember your name being Laila when we met."

There was no warmth left in her eyes as she raised her head and looked at him.

"I don't remember yours being cop."

20

It was getting on for 12 o'clock and Axel turned on the car radio; there was nothing about the murder. On the other hand, all parties were out in force condemning the night's disturbances, and there was no end to the proposals to tighten legislation and give the police new resources. When he heard a centre-right law and order spokesperson demand that the police be equipped with water cannons, it reignited his loathing for politicians and he turned the radio off.

He drove into town along Nørrebrogade. There were a lot of people around the Youth House satisfying their curiosity, even more who were in mourning, and the remains of last night's fires were still visible, including some burned-out cars in the side streets, but otherwise the streets had returned to their everyday state. The colourful signs and street displays of the multi-ethnic shops were out on the pavements once again.

His mobile rang. It was from Skopje.

"Stanca Gutu, 21, Moldovan prostitute, found dead at the Hotel Macedonia in Tetovo one morning in March 2001. Strangled and beaten about the head. Murder never cleared up."

"What did Enver Davidi have to do with it?"

"He was questioned twice during the investigation and was linked with the clan leader, who was running the import and sale of girls from Moldova and Ukraine, weapons, drugs and other gear. A big shot down here who got involved and paid for the investigation to be shelved."

"What sort of nonsense is that? Explain!"

"As I understand it, this adorable Moldovan girl was found dead in the hotel after an all-night party, which Davidi was possibly involved in, but I suppose there was nothing to indicate that he had killed her. He was a regular customer of one of the other girls. And she gave him an alibi, but disappeared shortly afterwards. Was probably passed on to the West. That's the way it goes."

"What are they doing in Macedonia?"

"They're beaten and fucked before being sent up to us. Broken in. That's the way most of them become resigned to serving hordes of Western European men."

"What about Davidi? Is there anything else on him?"

"Not right now, but I have a good source in the Tetovo police, who I haven't been able to get hold of yet. I'll call as soon as I've heard from him."

A 21-year-old prostitute from Moldova and a 42-year-old drugs offender. Stanca Gutu. Enver Davidi. Both dead. Axel reminded himself that it would be better to get her case file up here if that could be done, or at least a picture of her. It could be relevant or it could be a blind alley.

He turned into Griffenfeldsgade and stopped just before the part of the street known as Little Mogadishu because of its numerous Somali clubs and shops. At number 13, he got out in front of a basement shop, where three very black and upright, veiled Somali women were sitting talking at the open door despite the cold. Hargeisa Beauty Parlor. The women pointed at him and sniggered and gradually their twittering increased, which he didn't understand any of. He waved to them and they exploded with laughter like little schoolgirls.

Axel looked up at the house in front of him. The memories came back right away. It had been one of his first watches after he had graduated from the police academy and been given a position in the uniformed police. He and a partner were driving round on patrol in Nørrebro when they got a call about a man who had rung and complained that there was a baby screaming in a neighbour's flat.

"It's probably just colic," his partner had said, so they had coasted quietly out there.

In the door to the stairwell, which he was standing in front of now, they had been greeted by a man in his 60s, dressed in vest, braces and worn-out trousers, with red eyes and a sweetish smell of booze around him.

"There's something totally wrong up there," he had said.

"Up there" was a two-room flat, inhabited by a young couple with two children, a five-year-old and a baby. They could hear the baby right down on the street. A summer afternoon, 28°C, closed windows. They went up to the door and Axel lifted the flap on the letter box. It smelt stuffy and of baby shit. The infant was screaming at the top of its voice, a sound which drilled right into his brain. His partner, who had two years' more experience on the street, said they should wait for a locksmith.

He took 15 minutes to arrive, and by then the baby had stopped screaming and just lay sobbing. The five-month-old girl's face was flushed and swollen, lubricated with all the body's secretions at the same time. She had shit and pissed so much that it had soaked through. Axel, who had never changed a nappy, asked his partner, who had two children, what they should do, and his partner replied that they should wait until social services sent a nurse.

"But for Christ's sake, we can't just bloody let her lie there, man. Can't you change a nappy?" he had yelled.

"If you want to change her, be my guest. I'm not having anything to do with it."

Axel searched the flat and eventually found some nappies in the kitchen. He took a tea towel and a kitchen roll and went in and dried her face, gave her water from a baby's bottle and took off her nappy. She was burning red on her bottom, her skin was cracked in several places, and she immediately started screaming again. Further up on her bottom, she had bruises. Axel tried to wipe the shit off her, but she was writhing in pain, so he got it over his uniform and hands.

"Ugh," was his partner's only comment.

After a while, a nurse arrived from the social services' 24-hour cover and took over. It was far from the first time she had been there.

"The eldest daughter is in kindergarten. And the parents… well, yeah… if you're lucky, you can pick them up down at the local. It's their watering hole."

"But what the hell is the baby doing here?" asked Axel.

"They're usually able to take good care of her. It's rare for it to be this bad. There has to be a little more than parents who drink for a forcible removal."

"You can't be serious. She's almost dying. She might easily have suffocated. And she's been beaten. How bad does it have to get before you do something?"

His partner had already gone out on the stairs. On the way down, he told Axel that he had to learn to take it easy and do something about the things they could do something about and leave the rest.

They had continued directly down to Café Nørrehus, the pub opposite. Axel had gone up to the waiter and had asked for Svenne and Lissi, and when he pointed them out, he had gone over to the table and had grabbed the beer glass, which Svenne, a long-haired alcoholic in his mid-20s, had just raised to his lips, and forced it down on the table again. Lissi was sitting dead-drunk next to him. Axel felt like slapping her face.

His partner had taken over.

"The party's over, Svenne lad. We've just had to let ourselves into your flat with a locksmith because your baby daughter was lying there suffocating in her own vomit. I hope she gets taken away from you fucking pigs but, unfortunately, I can't guarantee it. So why don't you take your charming wife home and sober up so that you can look after the children you've brought into this world, know what I mean?"

Svenne looked up at them as if he couldn't care less. "Oh no, little brat. Has she been making a fuss again? She was supposed to be having her afternoon nap."

The baby girl had been taken to hospital where they had kept her until the next day. The examination that was conducted couldn't conclusively show that the child's injuries came from violence, but it couldn't be excluded either.

Back then, he had made a mental note of his partner's words: do something about what you can, and leave the rest.

In the evening on his way home, he had driven past Griffenfeldsgade and had rung the entry phone of one of the other residents on the pretence of delivering a letter. When Svenne opened the door, he had barely managed to utter a word before Axel had pushed him into the flat and locked the door behind him.

Axel had grabbed him between the jaw and the larynx and pressed, so that Svenne didn't resist. Then he pulled out his gun, held it up in front of Svenne's panicked face for a brief moment, so that he was sure that the drunken bum saw it and understood what was happening before pressing it against his temple.

"Where's your wife?" he hissed.

"She's asleep," said Svenne.

"Good for her. I feel like killing you right here and now for being such a bastard towards your child. In fact, I feel like doing it so fucking much that I think I will."

Click.

Svenne had wet himself, shaken, and Axel had been full of glee.

"Now listen: If you ever leave your baby alone in the flat, if you ever hit her, as I can see you've been doing…"

"I haven't…"

"Shut your mouth, pig. I've seen the bruises. If you ever hit her again, or leave her alone or get totally pissed when you should be looking after her, I'll hear about it. And when I hear about it, I'll come round and sort you out. Are you with me? I'll come and kill you and your piss-head wife, so you'll never be able to fuck it up for any kids ever again, do you understand? I'll come with this," Axel pressed the gun against Svenne's temple. "And blow your brains out."

Axel had learnt several things that day. It was the last time he would wait for a locksmith. It was the last time he would take the advice of an older colleague instead of following his instincts. And it was the last time he would give his inner Clint Eastwood free rein without carefully considering the consequences. Two days later, Svenne and

Lissi had moved – not only out of Nørrebro but also out of the police district, Copenhagen and Zealand, and had settled in an outskirts municipality where there were no psychopathic cops and meddling social workers on their heels. Axel had indirectly heard about the continuation of the little abusive family's life. And it had convinced him he should have worked soberly to get the children forcibly removed instead of frightening the life out of the father, so that he managed to hide from the authorities for three more years before it eventually happened.

Axel switched off his memories of Griffenfeldsgade and rounded the corner to Nørrebrogade, seething with Saturday traffic, walked past the supermarket and his favourite music store, and in through the glass door of the Hotel Continental. In the hallway in front of reception, the wall on the left was covered with post boxes that didn't seem to be in use. On several of them, the flaps were broken off and others were full of old advertising circulars.

"I Love New York" was on the chest of the smiling woman standing behind the counter. There was a Polish calendar on the wall and a Modigliani poster. The poster made Axel feel sad.

"Yes?" said the woman, with a distinct Eastern European accent.

There was a man standing at the counter next to Axel, and in an armchair by the metal winding staircase leading up to the first floor, another man was sitting in a leather jacket, cleaning his nails with his nails. He looked lazily at Axel and said something in Polish to the woman, who smiled even more mechanically at Axel.

"Can I help you?" she said.

She had got the message.

"How much for a room?"

"4,000 a month."

"Is that with a bathroom?"

"The bathroom is… er…"

The woman turned to the man and asked something.

"…on the street."

The man fired a few words at her.

"Sorry, in corridor."

"Do you want to see any ID, passport or any identification?"

"No, you just have to pay in advance."

Axel pulled out his ID and showed it to the woman. The man in the leather jacket didn't look at him at all.

"I'm not here to rent a room, but to see one. I'm investigating a murder."

"Yes, of course…" she began.

Axel interrupted her and spoke to the man in the chair.

"You there in the leather jacket. Do you speak Danish?"

He looked up as if he didn't understand, but Axel could see that he understood every word he said.

"English maybe? Better than New York here?" said Axel.

"New York, yes, yes," said the woman, smiling a little nervously.

"You're a long way from your dreams," said Axel, pointing at the T-shirt.

"Maybe, but I'm closer than when I lived in Warsaw," she said.

Axel doubted it. The Hotel Continental on Nørrebrogade was a hole in the ground, a place where people were so heavily weighed down by their pasts that they couldn't drag themselves on in their lives. It was a state of being, a stopover where you had been dropped off against your will and were rarely picked up again.

The first time Axel had visited the hotel was five years ago. Lucky Yusul was a 17-year-old Gambian who owed money for poker and heroin to some Yugoslavs in the South Harbour area. He had just needed a place to keep a low profile until he made enough money to go over to his big brother in London. He had borrowed the room in the Continental from a mate. Lucky lost his life in room 232 at the hotel on the boulevard of broken dreams in a one-and-a-half-hour orgy of violence, where someone had tried to strangle him, beaten him with a crowbar and a chair, kicked and stabbed him again and again with a paring knife and a pair of scissors. It hadn't been the Yugoslavs killing him because of gambling debts, but a couple of Poles in their 20s who killed him for a joint and 172 kroner.

The man in the chair got to his feet and came over to the counter.

Axel had his laptop with him. He slammed it down on the counter, pulled up the picture of Enver Davidi and turned it towards them. Both the woman and the man looked at the screen and Axel could see recognition in their eyes. They again exchanged a couple of fragments in Polish.

"Is this man staying at the hotel?"

"There are so many people staying here. What's his name?"

It was the man who had answered, in flawless English.

"His name's Enver Davidi, but he's probably not staying here under that name."

"He looks like someone staying here. What's it about?"

"You've seen my warrant card. That's what it's about. I need to know if this man has rented a room here or if someone has rented a room for him."

"He's staying in number 408."

"How was the booking made?"

"It was paid for him before he arrived. A man delivered an envelope with four thousand kroner in it and a note with his name and the date he would arrive."

"When was that?"

"A week ago. The man arrived last Tuesday."

"How long is he staying?"

"He's rented the room for the whole month."

Axel held his gaze and stayed silent. The leather jacket sighed and took out a passport, as well as a copy of a hotel receipt.

"It's this guy. Ismet Takidi. He checked in on Tuesday. I don't know how long he wants to stay. I've only seen him a few times."

"I want to see his room."

The leather jacket looked doubtful, but at that moment, an older Pole with a bushy grey moustache came in through a back door. A latter-day Lech Walesa. Axel thought he recognised him from some of his previous visits to the hotel. He smiled in spite of the tense atmosphere.

"You call these people your staff?" Axel asked him.

"Take it easy now, my friend. We'll sort this out. If you say somebody's dead and you'll produce a search warrant later, you're welcome to look now. We don't have to come and keep an eye on you, do we?"

"No. Do you only have Poles staying here now?"

"It's mostly Poles nowadays. You know, the craftsmen, they're cheap, much cheaper than the Danish, so they rent the rooms together, but there are still some of the old clientele left, Danes on their uppers, refugees, people from all over the world," said the man with the moustache.

He walked in behind the counter and took a key which he handed to Axel.

"The passport. I need the passport," said Axel.

He weighed it in his hand. It felt too light. He took out an evidence bag and put the passport and hotel receipt into it.

"I'll find my own way," he said, starting to go up the spiral staircase. A dusty, sour smell greeted him on the first floor, where there had obviously once been a kind of lobby, now empty, brown and shadowy. He continued up the worn linoleum of the main stairs. On the second floor, it smelt of cabbage, the floor creaked, and there were voices and TV-speak in Polish coming from the rooms. On the fourth floor, some of the carpet was missing. A fire here a couple of years ago had cost the lives of two Romanian women and the 12-year-old daughter of one of them, because a neighbour had left his room and forgotten to blow out a block candle on a wooden table. They had actually had enough time to get out, but had been suffocated by the smoke because they had tried to pack their suitcases.

The door to room 408 was scratched. Axel took out his mobile and put it on silent. He bent down to see if the occupant of the room had put something in the door jamb to reveal uninvited guests. Either it had been removed or Davidi hadn't been paranoid. He put the key in the lock and opened up.

He immediately got the sense that the room had been searched. He couldn't say why; it was just a feeling that someone had stirred the air, as though an energy had been triggered before he arrived.

Now he had to look for two things. Leads on Enver Davidi, and clues confirming that he wasn't the first person to search the room. He knew that Enver had spent many years inside, and he knew he was probably a drug user. The combination of these two facts would have made him an expert in hiding things – prisoners were capable of hiding their stash in the most unlikely places.

The room was fairly large and dismal. The sound of buses and cars came in through the dusty windows from Nørrebrogade, but otherwise it was quiet. A dry, dead smell of ash and synthetic fabrics, along with the static electricity from the faded, large-check curtains and the carpet, gave a feeling of being in a kind of time pocket, as if the world was outside and irrelevant. On the double bed was an open suitcase with a Caravelle brand mark on it – not much bigger than an enlarged attaché case. Axel bent over and looked under the bed. Nothing. He lifted up the folded clothes in the suitcase, but there was nothing but a belt, a car magazine and a paperback entitled The Concrete Blonde. Next to the suitcase was a sweater and a pair of jeans. On a small dark chest of drawers made of imitation mahogany there was a framed photo beside a TV. Even though it was fifteen feet away, it wasn't hard to see that it was of Laila and a boy who had to be Louie. Axel went over and picked it up. It was old – the boy appeared to be around three or four.

He looked round the room; apart from the suitcase, the sweater and the framed photo, there was no trace of Enver Davidi.

The fridge was empty. He bent down and saw that there were deep marks from its feet in the thick, dark-blue synthetic carpet and that they were now visible because it had been moved. Most likely pulled out from the wall to check if there was something underneath. Axel put his head all the way in against the white, wood-chip wallpaper and looked down behind the fridge. There was nothing but the cooling element.

Toilet bag? Where was that? There was a cooking island with an electric kettle, a thermos and two small hotplates in an alcove into the neighbouring room, but there was no glass and toothbrush. Apart from the chest of drawers and the bed, which in fact was two beds placed side-by-side, there was a white wardrobe, two wooden armchairs with check upholstery and an old coffee table with white and black rings in the wood from bottles or glasses that had once stood on it. On the wall was a poster with Monet's Water Lilies from the garden in Giverny, a blue implosion of chaotic colour, which once again gave Axel a stab in the chest – what was beauty like that doing in this hole?

He looked behind all the furniture without finding anything. Then he lifted the edges of the carpet and checked if there were signs in the dust that someone had been there before him. He rummaged through the bed, but found nothing under the box mattresses. Going over to the window, he checked the curtains, which gave off a sour smell of cigarettes; a cloud of dust fell on him when he lifted them and he looked up at the pelmet near the ceiling. There were numerous flats opposite. They would have to question the residents – something that would really suit Darling's aptitude for accuracy and meticulousness.

He was about to turn round and leave the room when he caught sight of a small piece of string. It ran out over the eight-inch-wide window ledge on the façade under the window. Axel opened the window and stuck his head out. The string was fixed to a metal eye bolt and disappeared under the sill. He followed it with his fingers and got hold of something. A small plastic case closed with gaffer tape so that it was waterproof. It had sat tight under the sill. He closed the window again and sat down in one of the armchairs. Then he opened the bag. There was a passport with a pile of banknotes inside. 20 thousand in fresh Danish 1,000 kroner banknotes. The passport was issued to a Fadil Osmani, who had all of Enver's data, and was equipped with a brand-new photo, in which the passport holder was smiling.

What's hiding behind those eyes? Axel asked himself. Who are you and what were you doing here, Enver, David, Ismet, Fadil – the man with four names? Who did you cross? Why did you have to die?

Axel weighed the passport in his hands and looked at its texture, the beetroot-coloured imitation leather cover, the plastic laminate, the photo, the watermarks. It was such good work that he couldn't distinguish between this and a real one. Maybe it was a real one?

He put it in an evidence bag, together with the string and stuck it in his jacket pocket.

Then he called BB and left a message on his answer phone.

"I have a hotel room on Nørrebrogade, where the deceased has been living for three days. Hotel Continental. Room 408. You should vacuum it from top to toe. I get the strong sense it's been searched. Apart from a passport that I'm taking with me, I haven't really found anything."

21

Axel saw them before they caught sight of him as he came down the stairs to reception. His instinct told him to turn around, but he knew he wouldn't make it in time.

Axel had several gripes about PET, the Police Intelligence Service. His ex-wife's new guy was a constant thorn in his side, and every time he met people from PET – even old colleagues – he had a strange feeling that they knew about his shipwrecked marriage and that that bastard Jens Jessen had taken his place. And it filled him with shame and anger. As if everyone knew he wasn't good enough.

He thought he noticed a blink of recognition in the eyes of the woman as she lifted her head and caught sight of him.

She poked her colleague in the side. His eyes were hidden behind a pair of mirrored sunglasses, which for Axel were the epitome of bad taste.

The bleached Polish receptionist, who had been in conversation with them, now looked up too.

"That's the man," she said.

Five steps down the stairs and Blank Face took off his glasses. Axel went over and stood in front of them.

"Axel Steen, Copenhagen Police Homicide Division. How can I help you?"

The man tossed his head.

"Let's go outside."

Axel stayed where he was and threw his hands out to the side as a sign that they had to introduce themselves.

"Kristian Kettler, Centre for Organised Crime, PET Operations Department." He nodded towards the woman. "This is my colleague, Henriette Nielsen."

Axel couldn't hide his surprise. H Nielsen from the Flying Squad, who had Enver Davidi's old drugs case file, was not a man. That was something Axel had assumed because 99 per cent of the staff in the former Flying Squad had been men. H was for Henriette, and she had apparently been transferred with the part of the Flying Squad that had ended up in PET.

"Just because you've become operational doesn't mean you can act off your own bat, does it? And this is my police district and my murder investigation and I haven't asked for your assistance. So what are you doing here?"

"We're interested in the case you're investigating and we'd like to discuss it with you, but not here. Could we have a meeting out at our place?"

The change that had taken place in the Danish police in recent years was by no means small, though most of it was only restructuring and overblown action plans to satisfy politicians' eternal pursuit of the thousands of voters who had been alarmed by the media's reports of extortion, biker and immigrant gangs, terrorists and young men armed with knives at night. Fear ruled as always. One of the things that had provoked little debate in the press, but many raised eyebrows in the police, was that the elite investigation team, the Flying Squad, had been shut down and divided between the Forensics Department, the National Investigations Centre and PET, as part of a trade-off between the National Police Commissioner and the Ministry. A number of experienced investigators thus suddenly found themselves in PET, thrown together with all the young spies, the paper tigers and the counter-terrorism officers who worked by a completely different set of rules than the rest of the police. Two of these investigators now stood before him wanting to meddle in his case.

"Whenever I see a pair like you I think of a saying about the FBI's suit-and-tie boys that an old street cop in New York told me when I was on a course in the US. 'They took the suits, we got the streets,' he said."

Axel thought he could see the shadow of a smile slide over the woman's face, but maybe he'd just imagined it.

"In case English isn't your strong point, it means you always come waltzing in when we've done the groundwork, but when there's tidying up to be done, it's beneath you."

"We shouldn't be talking here," said her partner, who looked as if he had been cut straight out of a recruitment campaign for the US Marines and stuffed into his expensive suit. Crewcut, blue eyes, broad chin, humourless face.

"We know you've been up searching Enver Davidi's room without a search warrant. I suggest we carry on this chat at our place."

Axel hated being given lessons about rules and regulations, and he had no intention of letting them in on his investigation, but there was something that told him that they had information that he could use. He held up a hand and took a deep breath.

"I'm investigating a case of murder and don't have time for cosy chats with you in your bunker in Søborg."

Kettler gestured towards the street, but Axel opened the doorway to the passage, so that they had to go out in front of him. The woman was almost as tall as him, but the last two inches were heels. Her hair was dark brown and fell down to her shoulders in a soft perm, and she walked in long strides, broad-shouldered and straight-backed. She turned towards him. Her blue eyes were so bright that they would have made Michelle Pfeiffer envious; her nose was large, her face broad and tanned, and her voice deep and sharp, as if she had spent her entire childhood in the asphalt jungle.

"You have to co-operate with us. This is bigger than a murder investigation. We can help each other," she said.

The man opened the door out to the street and held it for Axel.

"You have no choice. It's already been discussed at the top level, as I'm sure your boss will tell you very soon."

Corneliussen, he thought. He would jump at the chance to stick his tongue right the way up the PET people's rectums, in the hope that they would remember him at the next reshuffle and he could be bumped up and sit around all day sharpening pencils.

"Top level, what do you mean by that?"

"You wouldn't want them to think you're planning to cause trouble, so it might be time to put on the velvet gloves and work as a team," said Kettler.

Axel's mobile began to ring. Teamwork – now he'd even heard it from a PET officer. They were usually so tight-lipped about their sources that it was impossible to get the full picture of an investigation based on their information, which couldn't be verified properly and which they were reluctant to share.

"Someone's learnt a new word. You can't come here with your PET crap and think you can take over my murder investigation, no matter what the hell you're up to with your secret operations. This is a murder and it will be investigated as such. I'll find the person or people who killed Enver Davidi and hand the investigation over to the DPP, and then you'll have to see what deals you can stitch together afterwards."

Kettler looked as if he was on the verge of tearing into Axel. Just you try, you muppet, he thought. Henriette Nielsen laid a hand on her colleague's arm and turned to Axel.

"Let's all just take it easy. We're on the same team, right? We have to prevent and solve crimes and you have a murder investigation that we won't interfere with, but your victim is part of… how shall I put it… of a bigger puzzle and the pieces don't fit together yet, and we're sitting at the table too watching it all. Which means that we want to know what you find, and you obviously have an interest in getting to know more about Davidi. We have a lot on him. Doesn't that make sense?"

Axel didn't say anything.

"And we're interested, of course, in what you found up in that hotel room. Drugs, money, a passport maybe?" she said with a smile.

He ignored Kettler and looked her in the eye. Should he tell them about his feeling that someone had been in the room after Davidi? Not until he had investigated it further.

"There actually was a passport."

Axel put his hand in his pocket and handed her the passport he had been given by the Pole at the reception desk.

"There you are, my friends. Have a nice day. It's been fascinating talking to you, but I have a lot to do."

He walked swiftly past them, brushing past Kettler, who grunted in protest but didn't seem keen on laying hands on Axel. Unfortunately.

When he was back in his car, he took out his mobile. There were four missed calls. One from Rosenkvist. One from Sonne. One from Dorte Neergaard. One from his ex-wife. And two text messages.

The latest was from Darling: 'PET have announced their arrival. Call me. JD.'

Corneliussen: 'Meeting with AssCom. Come to HQ. Now. Urgent.'

Then he called voicemail and heard the Assistant Commissioner's familiar voice.

"Rosenkvist. I'd like to see you in my office as soon as possible. We have something we need to clarify. Now."

The Assistant Commissioner's voice had been completely neutral, firm in the restrained manner that came naturally in his position of power. Axel thought he had enough problems with Corneliussen, and now he had to go for an additional walk on the carpet in Rosenkvist's office. Be taken to task and forced to collaborate with PET. But why were they having to join the party? It had to mean that they had been monitoring Enver Davidi and that he was part of a major drug-trafficking complex, with all the ties to cross-border organised crime and collaboration with foreign intelligence services that involved. The Copenhagen Police had their own narcotics department, which looked after the inquiries in the capital, while PET assisted around the country. Perhaps he should ask Narcotics at HQ if they could explain what was going on.

Then there were two messages from the press.

"It's Jakob Sonne. I just wanted to hear if there's anything new about the murder victim. I have some information about the investigation that might interest you. Call when you have a moment."

"It's Dorte Neergaard. What's happened to those two officers? I'd like to run the story soon. Call me. You owe me BIG TIME after yesterday… you shit."

The last one was from Cecilie.

"Hi, Axel. Would you please call so we can talk about yesterday? I don't want to have a row with you, but I just don't think it's good for Emma if you're not there at all. I'd like to come by with her new wellies today or tomorrow if that's convenient."

Axel put the phone in its holder and drove out onto Nørrebrogade.

It was both convenient and inconvenient. He wasn't used to having visits from Cecilie – they had had as little contact as possible after she had moved in with Jens Jessen. Axel would rather forget her, but the prospect of a visit created expectation. Of what? he asked himself. Of being able to talk, work things out, maybe make love. You're a ridiculous person, Axel Steen.

Axel drove back to the hotel and parked in front of it. In reception, the bleached blonde was gone. Only the leather jacket was left with the same indifferent, dopey look as before.

"How long do you spend sitting here?"

"I do my job. I don't get hung up on hours."

Axel assumed there were no surveillance cameras anywhere at the Continental. The last thing the guests wanted at such an establishment was to be kept an eye on.

"The man in 408. Did he ever have any visitors?"

"I don't know."

"How long have you been here today?"

"Since morning. Six-seven, I think."

"And who else has been here in reception?"

"No one before me. People use their keys at night. We don't have a reception desk like a regular hotel."

"But have you been sitting here the whole morning?"

"Almost. Me and Svetlana."

"Someone came and searched the room before me. Do you know anything about that?"

"As I said, I haven't seen anyone."

"Just try and listen. We can do this two ways. The fast and friendly way: I ask questions, you answer them and tell me what you've seen. If you keep lying, it'll be a lot worse. And then we'll be seeing an awful lot of each other in the immediate future."

"What do you mean by that?"

"You don't get it, do you? The man is dead. Murdered, for Christ's sake. And the people who did it may have come here and dusted down his room. Maybe they'll come back and talk to you. But of course you haven't seen anything, have you? Perhaps they even told you straight out that you haven't seen anything, right? I'm sick and tired of your shit. I want to know what's happened and if you don't tell me, I'll make life really fucking difficult for you. Every day. I'll come by as often as I can, I'll get my colleagues from the licence section and the Immigration Department and foreign police onto you and you'll eventually get so tired of running a hotel that you'll wish you ran a fucking shawarma bar instead. Either you tell me who's been here or I'll piss off and come back with a search warrant that applies to the whole building for the next 14 days, and then I'll be back again to make life so bloody uncomfortable for your guests that they'll get tired of it and all move out. What do you say?"

The leather jacket looked very offended by the prospect of having to run a shawarma bar. The door to the back room opened and Lech Walesa came out.

"Are you still here?" he said with his trouble-shooter smile. "I thought your colleagues had taken over the investigation. That's what they told us. They said we should call them if something happened or someone came to ask for the man in room 408. Should we call them to say you're here?"

Axel shook his head.

"You're far too smart to call the police to complain about the police, aren't you? Too smart to complain that the police are doing their job while one of your employees is standing there lying to my face."

There was a brief exchange in Polish, with gestures flying through the air, and the leather jacket appealing to his boss.

"He's had some visitors. We don't remember exactly when and who, but there have been some."

"While he was in the room?"

"We don't keep a check on when people are in their rooms."

Axel got a description of the guests they could remember – one was a tall woman with long brown hair, her surname was Nielsen. And she had visited the hotel the evening before Enver Davidi was killed. And five minutes ago.

22

Out on the street, Axel called Darling.

"What the hell's going on?"

"Are you on your way? Your presence is sorely missed."

"But what's up, John? Surely you know."

"I can't say. But the word is that we've got babysitters from PET on the Davidi case."

"I've met them. What's that all about?"

"Just a second."

Axel could hear Darling walking around.

"I'm not going to have my arse on the line because of you, so I don't want to be quoted for this, but they've had me in twice and they want you here now."

"What's happening?"

"We've been called for a meeting with Rosenkvist. The two PET people from yesterday are here. The lanky woman and the guy in the suit. Just get yourself here so we can see where we stand."

Next, Axel called Dorte Neergaard, but he got her answering machine.

"Hi, Dorte. Sorry about yesterday. I haven't got any further yet, but if you promise to wait a bit longer, I'll have something else for you. Talk to you later."

Sonne would have to wait. All journalists had information that they thought was interesting, otherwise they wouldn't be bloody journalists. But that old trick wouldn't get him to ring back.

He ended up by writing to Cecilie that he was going to the cinema and out to eat with Emma, but that he would call.

She answered immediately. She wanted to come tomorrow evening, if convenient.

Up in Homicide, Axel dumped his bag and his coat before going up to the executive offices, but two coats on the chairs by his desk stopped him in his tracks.

He put a hand in the inner pocket of the dark raincoat and fished out a wallet. With Kettler's ID card and police badge. Born in 1969. Employed by PET. In the women's jacket, a North Face Gore-Tex, there was only a lighter, a packet of cigarettes and two sets of keys.

He walked into Rosenkvist's office. It was located a couple of offices away from the Police Commissioner's in the curved passage overlooking the square and was just a rectangular office with a desk, a desktop PC on a small table behind, and four chairs. Darling was sitting in one, Kettler and Henriette Nielsen in the other two.

Everyone turned to look at Axel. He felt like a schoolboy arriving late for an exam.

"As last to arrive, you'll have to stand, Steen. I understand that you've already met, so no further introductions are necessary."

Rosenkvist's eyes drilled into the two PET people.

"I was PET Operations Director for a number of years – admittedly before you became as operational as you are now – and I fully understand that you're working on matters that can't be shared with us. I understand from your boss that the murdered Enver Davidi and people in his circle have been attracting your attention for a long time, to such an extent that you need to be involved in this investigation, but not just that: you will also have the option to veto certain investigative measures if it appears to create conflict with your operation. Have I understood correctly?"

The two PET people nodded.

"That, of course, isn't ideal for us, but your operation is obviously so important that we have to co-operate and we can't be taking action that gets in the way of what you're doing. And I'm fully prepared for that. And so are my staff, of course." He looked briefly at Darling, who nodded, and then at Axel with a raised eyebrow. "Isn't that right, Axel?"

"Yes."

"Having said that, I'd like to make it clear that murder is still the worst crime we can be confronted with and it makes no difference whether the victim is a law-abiding citizen, a homeless person or a drug addict. The case has to be solved and the same applies to the murder of this Macedonian, and not even a whole raft of undercover operations can change that, so I would urge you to co-operate on both sides of the table. Is that understood?"

Everyone agreed.

"To be specific, the investigation will continue as follows: Darling will gather all the information that we have on the investigation, giving us an overview and managing our investigation, and Kettler will do the same for PET, managing all your current operations. Axel, you'll be partnered with Henriette Nielsen. You're still responsible for the murder investigation, and you make the decisions about the investigation together with Darling, but you inform Henriette Nielsen about everything. And if she wants to join you in interviews, autopsies and the like, you take her with you. Without resistance. You are to share all of our material on the investigation with her, understand?"

"I understand, but what's she going to be sharing with me?"

"Whatever she considers necessary. I know it will be difficult for you and if you can't handle it, Corneliussen already has a replacement in the wings."

The two PET people looked at him, Kettler with an ironic smile.

"That won't be necessary."

"Excellent. I'm sure you'll work well together."

The other three made to get up, but Rosenkvist raised his hand.

"Lastly, I'd like to emphasise that, with an investigation like this that is so delicately structured, I want minimal press coverage. We live in a small country with one police force, and if I find myself reading stories about splits and disagreement between PET and the Copenhagen Police, I'm going to be bloody furious. Any disagreements must stay behind closed doors. If not, I promise you it will be resolved quickly and I will remove you from the investigation if necessary. You reply 'no comment' to all press inquiries, understand?" His voice had gone up a notch. "Are there any questions?" He looked around at them and answered himself. "No. Then I'll just say thank you for an excellent meeting. I look forward to hearing from you when the case has been solved. Not before."

Axel was the last one on his way out of the door when he heard his boss's voice.

"Steen, could you just stay for two minutes?"

He went over to the desk and sat down.

"I want this investigation delivered without any problems, and if there are any doubts along the way – about your PET friends' methods and actions, for example – I want to be notified immediately before anything's put in writing. Before anyone gets to know about it. If they've been messing things up, you come to me. Understood?"

"Yes."

Axel felt depressed. Was that really all his boss had to say? He just wanted to protect his career by collecting dirt on other departments.

"You've created problems before and you're on your last warning. So I assume we're clear on this? No doubt about the instructions?"

He had to try to get something out of him.

"I understand the instructions. You don't want any problems and everything has to be cleared up without any bother, but I don't understand why I have to hold hands with the lanky lady from hell during my investigations and why Crewcut should sit out at PET and read all my interview reports and approve every new step in the investigation."

The Assistant Commissioner gave Axel a completely dead, mechanical smile.

"You aren't exactly a beginner at this, are you, Steen? I'm sure you've already figured out some of the context. Your victim was involved in their investigation. I can't say how, but it's delicate. So you should tread carefully – there are several interests involved here."

Axel had a pretty good idea what it was all about. PET had had contact with Enver Davidi in a way that made his death a big problem for them, because it could reasonably be assumed that it was precisely this contact that had caused it. And the interests the boss had mentioned were of course about the force, which didn't exactly need negative press coverage on the merger of the central investigation departments and the major reform. He decided to raise the stakes.

"But what have they been using him for? Have they brought him up here as an agent?"

"That isn't relevant to your investigation."

"You know as well as I do that it may turn out to be extremely relevant – otherwise I wouldn't have had those two arrogant arseholes foisted on me. If you weren't all shitting yourselves over the possibility that we pushed Davidi to his death with some kind of amateur undercover crap, I would've been allowed to carry out my investigation in peace."

"You don't know what you're talking about, Steen. It's nothing like that, I promise you. But for your part you must promise to do what I've asked. It'll work in your favour in future. That isn't an empty promise. Thanks for now."

When Axel came down to Homicide, there was no sign of the two PET people. So much for collaboration. He checked their phone numbers on the intranet and called Henriette Nielsen. He left a message.

Then he went to the comms centre all the way up under the roof at HQ to find out if any new information had come in about Piver.

This was the force's nerve centre – all the officers and patrol cars were directed from here. Axel almost always stuck his head in to get an idea of the tension level. Right now it was low; a handful of uniformed radio operators with headsets sitting around the monitors and phones, fragments from the radio breaking the silence.

"Over... beep... 1-207 reporting, come... beep... come in, over."

The central watch leader was talking on the phone. Axel positioned himself behind one of the radio operators. Green, yellow and red dots were flashing on a large electronic map – the green were available patrol cars, and there were only a few of them; the yellow were cars on a break, and there were just as few of them; the red were in action.

The radio operator switched between different conversations while checking online addresses and criminal records. In the midst of all the cables and lights there was a small yellow sticker with the text: think – type – think – speak.

Axel liked that a lot. Think. Before anything else. It was good advice that maybe he ought to follow a little more often himself. At the police academy it was a mantra, and for the radio operators it was a credo. They were crucial to the officers on the streets, and when communicating over the radio, there was no time for yackety-yak. On the streets, an incorrect or ambiguous message could be the difference between life and death.

The central watch leader had finished his conversation, but it took a while before he understood what Axel was asking for. There were 11 reports about people who had seen Piver since he escaped from the plain-clothes officers at Christiania the previous day. And that was a fairly small figure, bearing in mind that his description would fit several hundred young people who were permanent fixtures at the demonstrations against the clearance of the Youth House. Seven of them had been stopped and investigated and had ID showing that they weren't Piver; the others had run off at four totally different locations in the city. Axel made a note of the locations.

"Something's come in from the telecommunications company. His mobile has been switched on and there are two conversations. We haven't received them yet, but we can see where he's called from."

"Where?"

"It looks like it's from Christiania. Let me just check."

The coordinates, determined by the broadcasting mast, came in code, so they had to decipher them before matching them with their own map. It was Christiania.

Axel went back down to Homicide to get hold of Erna, who

would have to type out the interceptions. He wanted to check the mobile numbers right away in the hope that he could get hold of the young autonomist from the people he'd called. The knowledge that he was walking around with a recording that was probably much more precisely and sharply focused on the crime scene than the one Dorte had shown him yesterday made it even more important to arrest him.

Axel checked the two numbers he had been given. One belonged to Liz, the girl from the collective, the other was unregistered.

When Liz answered Axel's call, she insisted that when she had been called by Piver she had told him to give himself up to the police because of the murder investigation, but that he had been sceptical about it and had said that he had something important. Axel was unable to learn from her where Piver was.

He called the unregistered number.

"Yes?" said a voice.

"This is Axel Steen from Copenhagen Police. Who am I talking to?"

There was some static on the line and then the connection was terminated.

23

Piver had woken up on a hard metal floor with his hands bound tightly behind his back. He assumed it was with a police strip. It was dark and he was lying on his stomach. He tried to get up by pulling his lower body underneath him. He got up on his knees, but when he tried to lift his upper body, he lost his balance and tipped over onto his side.

His sense of time was completely gone. It could be evening, night, the next day, and what was the next day? Was it Saturday? Or had even more time passed? At first he had been hungry and thirsty, but now only thirst remained. And aches and pains in his whole body.

He thought about the man in the hoodie. Where was he now? And what was he doing here? He remembered the voice, which he thought had sounded familiar. It was the same as Lindberg's on the phone. It was just that this guy wasn't Lindberg. Or was he? It wasn't absolutely clear to him what the journalist looked like. He remembered having seen pictures of him in the media, but that was years ago.

Piver's head was spinning. He tried to shout. It was now he realised that his mouth was sealed with gaffer tape. The floor was icy cold, sending a shiver right into his bones. He was scared.

Why the hell had he gone along with it? He had sensed there was something not quite right about it. Fuck, he was naive! Don't you ever learn? Liz had said to him. You should keep your mouth shut and trust your instincts; never show your cards to people you don't trust 100 per cent.

But what was going on? Why was he lying here, bound and gagged?

Had the police caught him? Was the man a pig? He had heard all the stories of plain-clothes patrols that didn't officially exist. They nabbed people on the street and drove them around, threatened them, or took them out into Hare Forest and gave them a good going over.

Was the man in the hoodie one of them?

He heard the sound of a car outside. The door opened and it dawned on Piver that he was in a transport container, and the light shining in came from one of the gates, which had been thrown open. His eyes were completely dazzled. He closed them quickly and then opened them again, blinking to try and regain his sight.

A pair of big black boots.

A mobile rang. The man turned side-on to him and put it to his ear.

"Yes?" he said. He listened briefly, took it from his ear again and rang off. He opened the back of the mobile, ripped the battery out and threw it on what looked like an old carpenter's workbench. Piver still couldn't see his face in the light. The man pulled the container door shut and hit a switch, and everything was bathed in a white neon light so sharp that Piver had to close his eyes again. But he had seen his face.

24

Axel called the Copenhagen Police Human Resources department. There was an answering machine giving the private number of an office manager called Erik Frandsen, if urgent.

It was urgent, but Frandsen, who was in a summer cottage up on the coast, was dismissive until Axel asked for discretion and stoked his fear of his superiors.

"It's rather delicate. It's about two young colleagues of mine and the murder at Assistens on Thursday night. I can't say more than that, but you're welcome to call Assistant Commissioner Rosenkvist… although he may have a lot of other things on his plate right now."

Frandsen instructed a guard to let Axel into the department where access was otherwise prohibited. He walked along the rows of filing cabinets, the guard following him, and found Groes' and Vang's personnel files from their service numbers, signed for them and went back to his office.

He rang Henriette Nielsen again, then Kettler. Without success. He was pissed off. There was no doubt that they had much more on Davidi than they were telling him, and even though he hated the idea of collaborating with the arrogant scumbags, he needed them even more than before – and apparently more than they needed him.

It was nearly three; Emma had been in kindergarten since nine o'clock. Axel packed the personnel files in his briefcase. He would read them this evening when Emma had gone to bed and get himself up to speed on the investigation.

On his way down to his car, he took a look into KSN – the special command centre, which was in charge of major accidents, riots, street battles or visits from the American president. It was still fully manned, even though the street parties hadn't got going yet.

The general perception was that the evacuation of the Youth House itself had been successful, because it had happened without anyone dying and without any police officers getting injured, but the rest of the process was not a success. In the end, 2,000 officers had been brought in to keep control of the city, and even though training and planning had taken place, no one had expected the disturbances to spread so explosively and break out in so many different places. While his fellow officers had been busy clearing barricades in Nørrebrogade, small groups of mobile activists dressed in black had set cars on fire and started fires in twelve different streets in the Nørrebro area, and at the same time a small crowd had forced their way into a high school at Christianshavn and smashed teaching equipment, computers and televisions worth many millions of kroner – all without prior warning.

It was the people who owned the streets.

It was half past three when he fetched Emma, with the same twinge of conscience about working so much that he had never managed to do anything about. It didn't get any better when the deputy leader pulled him aside and asked for five minutes, which she used to share her concern with him: his daughter was tired and talked a lot about death and about people being killed. Could it have anything to do with his work? She hoped he understood that such a little girl couldn't handle the sort of things that adults could. He promised to talk to his ex-wife about it, which apparently satisfied the woman. Was he number one on the top 10 list of shitty dads? Maybe.

Then he went in to fetch Emma. It wasn't exactly what he wanted, but it was his only way to avoid giving her back to Cecilie for the rest of the weekend – just the thought filled him with a highly explosive combination of guilty conscience about his daughter and rage towards her mother because he had seen Emma so little since they got divorced. And now she wanted to come and visit tomorrow. Axel knew he couldn't just take it at face value: delivering a new pair of wellies. He thought up all kinds of possible reasons for it, unconvincing though they were. What if she had changed her mind? What if she now…

He caught sight of Emma in the back room, sitting drawing at a table with two other girls.

Axel went over to the table and Emma looked up.

"Daddy! You're here!" Her eyes shone. "I've drawn a squirrel for you."

He crouched behind her chair and stuck his head all the way over one of her shoulders, so that his nose ended up in her hair. He wanted to stay in that smell forever.

In the drawing, a little squirrel was on his way up a tree trunk.

"This is a squirrel on the way up the tree in the cemetery. Just like last time we were there."

The image of Enver Davidi's body flashed through Axel's mind, before he remembered their last walk in Assistens Cemetery, when Emma had seen and counted 23 squirrels.

Emma didn't seem at all tired. On the contrary, she was happy and expectant at the prospect of a trip to the cinema and a pizza, but first they had to go to the cemetery – "Shall we play hide and seek again, Daddy?" – to see and hear what BB had discovered. They passed Rådhuspladsen as another demonstration was taking shape, like a snake behind an open trailer with loudspeakers pumping out music. The number of people arrested during the last two and a half days had now passed 500, but Axel was expecting it all to calm down a bit, because large units had been out most of Saturday morning arresting foreigners in the autonomist collectives and in the People's House.

"Perhaps we'll have some time to play hide and seek, but Daddy has to talk to someone first. It won't take long, sweetheart."

He drove out along Åboulevarden's polluted grand slalom and swung right at Jagtvej, flashed his warrant card at the entrance to the cemetery and got them to open the gate so that he could drive in along the path leading to the chapel where he knew BB was working. Now I'll get my breakthrough, he thought, opening the door to get out.

"I want to go with you, Daddy. I don't want to sit here, it's boring," shouted Emma.

Fuck, he had completely forgotten her again.

Axel smiled and let her out of the child seat.

"OK. Come along, we have to go over here and talk to that man."

He pointed towards BB, who was investigating some hatches that led down into the ground 10 yards from the chapel.

"Can't I stay here and count the squirrels?"

Axel looked around. He wasn't usually afraid of letting Emma go exploring on her own, but this was a crime scene and the murderer was still at large.

"Yes sweetheart, but you mustn't run off."

"No, no," she answered with a drawling resignation in her voice. "But where shall I start, do you think?"

Axel looked up at the crown of a century-old sycamore.

"Here, I think."

Then he went over to BB, while the sound of his daughter whispering, "Squirrel, squirrel, come out now, or I'm going home" faded away behind him.

"What have you got for me?"

BB lifted his head and looked up at him with a pair of huge, blurry, water-blue eyes that – shut in as they were behind two layers of spectacles, one ordinary and one magnifying – vainly tried to focus until he lifted the outer layer up and smiled.

"I've been waiting for you. I think I can chart most of the course of events before the murder. I've had help from the tracker dogs and I'm sure the victim and the perpetrator have been down here." He opened one of the hatches, so that Axel could see a small staircase that led down to a five-foot-deep passage. Then he straightened up. "And over there." His index finger was pointing at the chapel. "There are traces of them in both places. Blood traces, boot prints that look like ones we have found around the crime scene, and other stuff that may well turn out to contain traces of their DNA. Just let me finish here and I'll show you everything."

Axel was restless. He needed to know something *now*. He looked around. There were uniformed officers to the right of him, at the crime scene, and to the left, by the wall opposite the Youth House, but where was Emma? He was about to go and look for her when he heard her light voice ringing out among the trees a little way off, completely out of place in the heavy afternoon atmosphere, with the white-coated forensics team, the candy-striped tape and the numerous combat-clad officers.

"Aaaaaaaall animals come ou-out, or eeeelse I'm going ho-ome."

Axel went over to the chapel with the four columns, a 25-foot-high building in an advanced state of decay. The walls had once been white, but now they were speckled with grey and green stains, and the outer layers of paint were peeling off. There must once have been a door between the columns, but it had been walled up, and instead there was a small wooden door on the right, which had been kicked in. On the wall to his left was written, "69 Will Never Surrender". He stuck his head through the splintered wooden door and could faintly see a workshop that hadn't been used for many years, but there were footprints on the floor.

"It's actually a residence for the gravedigger," said BB, who had followed him over.

"It was built in 1805 by Jens Bang, who had great plans for the cemetery. He wanted to transform it into a romantic garden, but a stop was soon put to that. It turned into a bit of a disaster. The columns were too close together for two men to get through with a coffin."

"What about our victim – has he been in there?"

"I'm not sure, but there were fibres from his jacket on the splintered wood."

Axel looked at the smashed door; the wood was old, but the splintering was completely fresh. With all the noise from the street, it might have been possible to have kicked the door in without anyone hearing.

"But if he hasn't been in there, how do you explain the fibres from his jacket?"

"Maybe he was just as curious as you and stuck his head in to have a look." BB pointed to the wall. "There are clear traces here."

A brown smudge, which Axel immediately knew was congealed blood. At head height. He could hear a hollow sound far off, the sound of danger, he thought.

"I haven't been able to find any trace of him inside, but I'm sure this is him here." BB pointed to marks on the worn wall, the rough surface of which could have had a face pushed or pressed against it for 12 to 15 inches across the plastering.

"But they must have met somewhere. Could it have been here?"

"Yes, why not? My guess is that he's been overpowered here, perhaps while he was looking into the house, he's had strips put around his wrists and may at the same time have been pushed hard against the wall."

"And he hasn't tried to get away from his attacker, because there were police all over the place. Or he was paralysed by a shock from the taser."

"Yes, that tends to make people incredibly compliant. And then our perpetrator may have dragged him to the underground passage over there. They may have hidden there, but that's just my guess. Afterwards, he's dragged him over to the wall and strangled him."

Emma looked out from behind one of the columns.

"Hi, Daddy, I've found three squirrels. One, two, three, where have you got to, number four?"

She tiptoed away again.

"Pretty girl, looks like her mother," said BB.

It had been coolly executed. It had required planning and local knowledge; they must have known each other, but Axel just didn't understand why Davidi had come in here – the risk of discovery would have been huge.

"Are there any traces of drugs?"

"No, but it doesn't have to have been a trade. He could have been holding a meeting about delivery here."

Axel looked up at the little verdigris-coloured roof that hung out above the columns. The sound from earlier had become stronger, and now he could hear that it was a drum, and along with it, the battle cries from the demonstration he had passed half an hour ago at Rådhuspladsen.

"The passport I mentioned on the phone – I'd like you to examine it for me."

"Where's that from?"

"I found it in Davidi's hotel room today and it looks genuine, so I'd like you to check it out before my new friends from PET get their paws on it."

BB shook his head disapprovingly.

"I heard you've got babysitters. You know I don't like going behind people's backs, but go on, give it here!"

Axel took it out from the pocket where he'd been keeping it since he found it that morning – which would be called careless handling of evidence if anyone were to find out about it, but they wouldn't. BB weighed it up in the evidence bag before putting on a pair of clean gloves and taking it out. He flicked through the pages.

"It looks like the real thing, but you never know. I can check the number when I get to the office, but it could of course be from an unknown series."

"What does that mean?"

"Military Intelligence, witness protection, PET, Foreign Office, all that secret stuff. They have to have passports that are genuine, but which can't be traced and are none of our business. It could easily be such an undercover passport." BB weighed the passport in his hand, examined it again. "If this is a fake, it's been done by a damn magician."

Axel thought about what BB had said. It confirmed the feeling he had had all along. He looked up. The sky was milky white and the clouds were floating so low that it felt as if he could reach out and taste them. The air was cool and dry.

"Aaaaaaaall animals come ou-out, or eeeelse I'm going ho…."

The sound of her voice stopped suddenly. Axel froze, stood still and listened. Then he ran. As fast as he could.

"What's up?" exclaimed BB behind him.

But he didn't have time to explain, he just had to find his daughter.

Axel rounded a group of conifers, which he was sure she was behind, but Emma was nowhere to be seen. He stopped and listened. Shouted her name. Further on past two burial mounds, low, shaped hedges with little obelisks around gravel and large stones, he checked round to see if she was there. He stumbled along a fence by the equipment yard, ran round a corner and bumped into a uniformed officer who tried to grab him and shouted, "What the hell?"

"Have you seen a little girl here?" Axel roared into his face.

He shook his head and Axel ran on, shouting Emma's name.

No reply. He had now come round the chapel and the equipment yard, so the buildings were between him and BB. He ran back up the opposite road, asphalt, a thuja, ivy, a bed of rose bushes, moss-grey, toppled gravestones, cracked stone plinths and broken crosses, shouting her name over and over again.

BB came towards him.

"Have you found her?" he asked before Axel could ask the same question.

Axel shook his head and ran back and out to the gate to Nørrebrogade, but it was closed and locked. He was now on the asphalt path; he turned round and could see 100 yards of the path that led further into the cemetery. He started running again, as fast as he could. The officer from before came towards him. Axel described Emma and got him to continue along the path into the cemetery. Axel reached a junction and could now see a long way in between the trees. He stopped and listened intently. There was hardly any wind; he could only hear the monotonous sound of hate-filled battle cries, the drum and the yelling.

What had happened? She had walked past barely two or three minutes ago, and then he had heard her calling but it had been shut off in the middle of the sentence, as if someone had put a hand over her mouth. Was he paranoid, or was he going mad?

His heart was beating so hard that it felt like it was about to burst out of his chest. It would be so apt if his blood clotted in his veins right now and shut his entire system down. He hated himself for his self-indulgent thinking. He was scared; screaming, hammering fear, for once not about his own death, but his daughter's life. The only thing more important than himself.

Emma was nowhere to be seen. The noise from the demonstration out on Nørrebrogade was massive; the shouts sounded like war had broken out.

He shouted as loudly as he could, over and over again, and ran a little way down the path while cursing himself and his irresponsibility.

What would Cecilie say if Emma had disappeared? What would he say to her? How was he going to explain it?

Then he stopped; he thought he saw something red visible between the tree trunks 150 yards away.

He ran like a madman, then slowed down when he saw Emma tiptoeing after a squirrel which was blithely hopping around. As he caught her eye, she held her finger up in front of her mouth.

"You mustn't shout like that, Daddy – you'll scare them away!"

25

When darkness settled over Nørrebro on Saturday evening, it wasn't quiet in the streets, but it felt like it. The street lamps threw a cautious yellow gleam down onto the asphalt, people were out walking, bike lights were blinking everywhere, and even cars and buses were gradually venturing into the neighbourhood. There was a tangible, if tentative, optimism in the air, which had wiped the dampness off itself and was now clear and cold. Out to the west, the sun had set over Brønshøj in a bloodbath of red nuances like a promise of what the night would bring.

Emma was tired, so he carried her up the stairs. He had deliberately parked his car in a side road three streets away from Nørrebrogade to try and avoid it being set on fire. After the cinema, pizza and ice-cream with flake, whipped cream and chocolate hundreds-and-thousands at the Italian Quattro Fontane restaurant on Sankt Hans Torv – which, with its solid, rustic eighties interpretation of Italian cuisine, had the nickname The Four Containers – they had driven home, snug and satisfied.

He had listened to a long report on the car radio from the evening's demonstration, which had concluded in Nørrebro Park only 100 yards from his flat. It had come from both Vesterbro and Christianshavn, the two other districts in Copenhagen where people didn't just spend their time looking after their equity and to hell with everything else: there were several thousand people, lots of them peaceful but many others furious about all the arrests over the past few days – especially about the alleged maltreatment of the young man on Nørrebrogade, which was beginning to grow into a big story. Several politicians were now demanding an inquiry. But it wasn't all an easy ride for the demonstrators – there were interviews with residents who were tired and frustrated because of the fires and the vandalism. Here too the police were in the firing line for not having taken control of the situation.

Emma listened too, and once again Axel had to try to explain to her what was happening. It was hard enough to explain to an adult why everything was in chaos, and not least why it had got that far, but the absurdity of it all was crying to the heavens as he heard himself talk and saw the puzzled frowns and the questions they raised in his five-year-old daughter's face. Maybe that proves it, he thought – if you can't explain it clearly to a small child, it's because you have a crap case.

It had been a good day and Axel felt justified that he had done the right thing by insisting on holding on to Emma, even though he felt guilty about it. Maybe it was precisely that which had persuaded Cecilie she had to come by tomorrow? Wasn't that why she had given him an opening? For him to show her that his daughter meant everything to him?

His daughter, not Jens Jessen's.

When he had brushed Emma's teeth and she was on the toilet in her nightdress, he took out his mobile and started to scroll through the missed calls and messages. There were lots of them as he had had it on silent since they went to the cinema four hours ago. He saw there were several from both Sonne and Dorte Neergaard, as well as other journalists and John Darling, but he skipped past them and immediately opened a text from BB.

It said that he was 99.9 per cent certain that the passport was real enough, "otherwise it has been made by someone who is employed at the printers, and that's impossible", but it didn't exist in the passport database. Axel wanted to ring back immediately, but Emma called him.

Once she was in bed with her soft polar bear – "Can they swim, Daddy?" – she couldn't get to sleep. They talked first about the cemetery, about all the squirrels she had counted, and then she changed the subject to something Axel had hoped she had forgotten: the cold old men who didn't want to sleep, lying in the drawers with their eyes shut. The questions bubbled out of her mouth with little pauses in between, as he sat in the darkness at her bedside after they had read and sung, and he had made up two stories and told them to her.

"But how do the men get out of the drawers?"

"Does God come and help them? Even if he doesn't exist?"

"But Daaaddy, how do they get warm again, the men?"

He stroked her on the stomach and gradually there were longer and longer pauses between the words. Her eyelids slid shut.

BB picked up right away.

"Bad news. I've had a call from PET, a guy named Kettler, who wanted to know why I'd searched for that passport number."

"How did he know that?"

"Computers, pal, they see everything we do. We don't just keep an eye on the people, we also keep an eye on each other, and if they're on red alert about this case, I'd think everything through very thoroughly before doing anything online if I were you. They're probably already keeping tabs on you."

Axel thought briefly about it, but he hadn't sent anything by email or visited any websites that he couldn't answer for. The only thing was the TV2 footage he had received from Dorte Neergaard, but he hadn't sent it to anyone, so PET couldn't know anything about it.

"But what did he want from you?"

"What do you think? He wanted the damned passport. And he's got it. They've already taken it."

"What did you say to him?"

"I played dumb and said you'd asked me to search the hotel room and that I'd found it under the window ledge – just like you told me. And then I'd taken it with me, but forgotten to enter it in the log, which was why they hadn't heard about it."

"Did he fall for it?"

"I don't think so, but he pissed off and took the passport with him."

"Thanks, BB. I'll remember this."

"You'd better. You owe me one, and not a small one at that, but you know nothing about this, because if you let on, the hammer falls on me."

Axel sat on the sofa with his laptop and replayed the film that Dorte Neergaard had so reluctantly given him. His heart started beating away in his chest again like a frightened bird. He tried to ignore it. What would happen if he collapsed with a heart attack now? What about Emma? Would she come into the living room tomorrow morning and find him out cold on the floor? Would that be her last memory of him?

He rang Dorte Neergaard, who answered the call immediately. He was afraid she wouldn't want to talk to him at all, but her voice sounded unaffected by yesterday's row.

"I'm sorry about what happened yesterday, but I'll make sure you're not involved."

"What do you have for me? You said you had something."

"The murdered man isn't an autonomist. He's a deported drug offender, 48 years old, Albanian from Macedonia. His name's Enver Davidi and he was arrested with 17 kilos of cocaine in 1996 and got eight years for it."

"I just have to write this down."

In the silence of the flat, Axel noticed that the sounds from the street had disappeared. Yellow light flashed across walls and ceilings; he could hear the crowd way off.

"Is this a joke – or an attempt to wipe yourselves clean?"

"It's the truth, Dorte. We'll release it tomorrow. You can run it now. Just don't quote me."

"Don't worry about me not quoting you. No fucking way do I want to be linked with you publicly. Or privately for that matter. In any way ever again."

Axel got up from the sofa and walked over to the window. A column of transport vans with call-out lamps flashing was going past in the street below.

"What about the two officers? Have you got any further with them?"

From the window he could see past the church opposite and down along the streets that ended at Nørrebro Park. It was full of lamps, torches and people. The noise penetrated clearly through to him.

"No, but I'll deal with them tomorrow. I don't know what it is. On the surface, it looks bad for them. When I've talked to them, I'll call you and you'll be able to run the story."

"OK. Hang on a minute." She sounded excited. The job came before everything else.

The police were driving up and down the surrounding streets and had a cohort of twelve vans parked from Axel's building along Nørrebrogade towards the city. Groups of hooded youths broke out of the park and threw stones and bottles at the officers in the vans. He saw the gold of the Molotov cocktails flooding out across the road, sucking in oxygen, and flames several feet high in the still evening air.

"Where are you? It sounds like you're in the middle of a street fight," said Dorte Neergaard.

He watched the huge demonstration, now crossing Nørrebrogade further up and apparently surrounded by police vans on both sides.

"I'm at home. Nørrebro. Business as usual."

"Will it never stop?"

"Not as long as they have something to be angry about. And you lot are contributing splendidly to that."

Axel said a brief goodbye and sat down with the personnel files. He skimmed through them. Vang had a single case of violence against a man during the demonstrations around Denmark's EU Presidency. It hadn't led to anything, but according to the case notes, he had knocked a demonstrator down with his baton, handcuffed him, hit him twice more and said that if he didn't stop screaming, he would make sure he would go the same way as Benjamin – the innocent young man whom some fellow officers put in handcuffs during the New Year celebrations in Rådhuspladsen before they lay into his back so much that he had become a vegetable.

The case against Vang had collapsed due to contradictory witness statements. Groes had testified in Vang's favour. Otherwise there wasn't anything. He watched the film all the way through again. It didn't give any answer as to what the two officers had been doing instead of their job.

Axel was sure that Vang was the one who had climbed over the wall and been away from the cemetery for about two hours. He had left his post – that was unforgivable and could easily cost him his job. What his companion had been doing all that time was still a mystery to Axel. He was holding firm to his insider theory and that wasn't good news for them. They had at the very least given the murderer a free space to work in and, in a worst-case scenario, they were getting close to a charge of murder or aiding and abetting. Could one of them be the man in the dark who came walking up with Enver Davidi? Why hadn't they just admitted that one of them had been sleeping on the job and the other had left his post? He still didn't get that, when half the police force all the way up to the Assistant Commissioner was breathing down their necks and their future careers were in tatters. They would be lucky if there would even be a job for them in passport control at Kastrup Airport.

The street was deserted now. His heartbeat reminded him that he was still alive; but not so alive that he couldn't die, too.

Axel fetched a joint, sat on the sofa and smoked it slowly, while his body sank into itself and calmness reigned. He floated in and glanced at Emma before returning to the sofa and crashing out. Vang and Groes. First thing in the morning, he thought.

26

Sunday, March 4

Axel had called Kasper Vang and Jesper Groes and asked them to come in to HQ on Sunday morning. Groes had sighed and said he couldn't help any more than he already had. Vang was more hostile and had asked what the point was. Axel had responded obligingly that there were just a few details he had to get clear in order to close that part of the investigation. He had had to reason with him for five minutes before he agreed. It was incomprehensible to him that Vang didn't realise what his future was looking like.

They were told to show up at nine o'clock, which gave him time to drop Emma off at the kindergarten. He had promised himself that she wouldn't be there all day.

HQ was almost deserted when he arrived. Murder or the worst street riots in recent times – it would take more than that to interfere with a policeman's sacred Sunday morning with the family. It suited Axel just fine to conduct the two interviews in peace, without interference from higher powers and nosy colleagues who would do everything they could to wipe the stains off the force's reputation – and he was sure that there would be plenty of stains to wipe off by the time he had finished with Groes and Vang.

He took Groes in first; he seemed to be the weaker link.

Axel asked if he had been thinking about what they were doing.

"We were doing our job. We didn't see anything. That's not a crime."

"It isn't if you're doing your job, but were you actually doing it?" Axel raised a hand as a sign that he didn't have to answer. "Or were you taking a good old-fashioned forty winks? You wouldn't have been doing that, would you? You've both done a first-class job of neglecting your duties. While you were doing God knows what, your buddy left his post for two hours."

"I don't know anything about that."

"You will do pretty soon."

Axel turned his computer round so that Groes could see the film. He sat glued to the screen and saw the pictures of himself and Vang, who was smoking, before Vang slipped out of his combat-suit, climbed over the wall and disappeared.

Axel could smell Groes' discomfort. It was seeping from every pore in his body, but he still tried to rescue the situation.

"He went to get some water."

"Where? In fucking Frederikssund? He didn't get back until two hours later."

Groes went pale.

"I didn't leave. I stayed at my post."

"OK, but you didn't see anything. You didn't see the murderer walking by with the victim, even though they would have been right in your line of sight. Less than 50 yards away, an unobstructed view."

He was finished. Axel could see it.

"No. I fell asleep. I'm really sorry."

"What about your buddy? What was he up to?"

"He…" Groes hesitated and looked like a little boy who was now beyond anybody's help. "He had some business to see to. He wouldn't say what it was. He was going to visit someone."

Axel didn't get any more out of him, but he was more than satisfied. Just like anybody who made a blunder, whether it was dereliction of duty, petty theft or full-blown murder, the young officer was mostly preoccupied by the consequences for himself.

"What'll happen to me? Will I get the sack?"

"I don't know. And to be honest, I don't care. But I'm not finished with you yet. Wait outside while I talk to your colleague. And then we'll have your full explanation afterwards."

Axel was in a bubbly mood as he pulled in the next one.

Kasper Vang was not.

"Is this an interview? Because if so, I want a lawyer present. You're spending your time hunting down your colleagues when the whole city's full of criminals and autonomists – unbelievable!" he blurted out.

"Are the autonomists criminals?" Axel asked tonelessly after waiting a whole minute. He had been studying Vang on the quiet before he started talking; arranging papers and opening his laptop again, examining the CD-ROM with the film and he was now sitting pretending that it took some time to set up. Vang seemed hard in a streetwise way, or at least that was the aura he was trying to project: stubble, a mark from a needle in his left ear, sunburned, muscular in the steroid class, tattoos with Nordic motifs on his arm. A tough guy who could only just have passed the height requirements for the police academy.

"You know what I mean. There are disturbances everywhere and you're just after us because we didn't see a murder. We're the foot soldiers. It's not our job to solve murders, that's yours."

"Are you a local?" asked Axel, as if he hadn't heard what Vang had been saying.

"What do you mean by that?"

"Where are you from?"

"Amager," he replied.

"When you say you don't have to solve murders, it's only partly true, right?"

Axel knew that Vang would be as limp as a rag when he had finished with him, and he was tempted to make a full show out of it, but he had a lot to get through.

"What do you mean?"

"The task of all police officers is surely to solve crimes and prevent them being committed, right?"

Vang was about to answer, but Axel turned up the volume and the tempo.

"But it's hard to solve something or prevent something when you leave your post, right?"

"I don't know what you're talking about. I didn't leave my post."

Axel got up.

"What do you think the helicopters are doing? Do you think they're just there for fun? Or do you think they're watching what's happening down on the street so we have evidence against people who commit vandalism or violence against the police?"

Vang was silent.

"I have proof that you left the cemetery just before twelve and didn't come back until two hours later."

Axel turned the computer round so that Vang could watch.

"Surely it's not against the rules to climb out and fetch something to drink?"

"We-ell, I'd say it is. It's dereliction of duty at the very least – not of a serious kind, no, but I think we can agree that it's verging on grounds for dismissal to leave your post for two hours. No, no, don't say anything stupid before I'm finished. On this recording, you can be seen crawling out of your protective suit before jumping over the gate. And unfortunately we can't see what happens next, but your suit can be seen lying in the grass in the cemetery for the entire time you're gone. And that's two hours. Two hours too long to be fetching something to drink, which you incidentally had plenty of in there. So now I'd bloody well like to know what happened. Where you were. And what your buddy was doing in the meantime."

Vang's brain was now working at full speed. He was weighing up the pros and cons and looking for an escape route. Axel gave it to him.

"This is my film. No one else has seen it, but it's embarrassing for both of you – embarrassing and revealing. I'm only interested in one thing and that's the murder. If you have anything at all to do with it, I promise you that I'll have you out of the force in disgrace, without a pension, all the way down in the shit. But if you don't have anything to do with it, I don't give a damn about what else you've been up to. So right now, you have your chance. Not in five minutes, but now.

Otherwise, this footage will go further through the system, and you're both finished as police officers. But you probably are anyway, what with all the lies you've been telling."

"I have nothing to say."

But he did anyway.

"I went and fetched some water. That's all. Then I went back again. I climbed over another place and sat down in shelter under a tree and smoked."

"Together with your buddy? That's what he said."

Vang smiled. He had suddenly seen the light, he thought, but Axel was ready to turn it off completely and leave him in the dark if he said yes.

"Yes that's right. I'm sorry we didn't see the murder, but it's like my mate says."

"No it isn't, you bloody amateur. I can see you didn't come back until two hours later and your partner's confirmed that."

"I have nothing more to say."

Axel shook his head.

"That's up to you. Then I have to tell you that you're being formally charged with murder. You're under arrest."

"But I didn't kill that geezer."

"You'd better call your lawyer."

Vang looked unable to process what Axel was saying.

"My lawyer can't help me. I'm fucked. Completely fucked."

Axel opened the door to the other offices. Darling had just arrived.

"Can you take care of this guy? Get him to give a full explanation. He was away from his post during the period that Davidi was killed and he cannot or will not explain what he was doing. I've charged him with the murder. His colleague has confirmed he was gone for two hours."

Darling looked completely confused. He had questioned the same man two days ago, and there hadn't been anything at all to go on.

"I'll take his colleague now," said Axel.

He called Groes in, went through his explanation and got him to sign it. Then he sent him home with advice to contact the Police Association lawyer.

"You're going to need him," said Axel.

He sat down and surfed through the online news. Dorte Neergaard hadn't wasted any time since their conversation yesterday. Enver Davidi's name was featured in all the news media with TV2 as the source.

He called Rosenkvist to update him on the latest development.

"Come up to my office," came the order as soon as Axel told him what had happened.

Rosenkvist was standing with his back to the door, looking out over the harbour entrance, when Axel came in.

"An insider. Weren't you the first to come up with that theory?"

"Yes, I was."

"A murderer in my police force."

"A possible murderer. I suggest we keep him in here and go out and search his residence."

Rosenkvist turned round. There was none of the disarming, smiling manner to trace in his face. Rows of wrinkles lay under his comb-over hair.

"Yes, it has to be done." He sat down in his chair. "And we keep a low profile. Nothing must come out about Vang, nothing."

"On the other hand, the fact that Davidi's identity and history is now known shows the victim isn't an autonomist, so that takes the pressure off us a bit."

"A bit. But we don't need another trip through the media mill."

Axel thought about the footage, which he had promised Dorte Neergaard she could use. He had bought himself some time by giving her just the victim's identity, but she'd soon be snapping at his heels to run a story about dereliction of duty and incompetent police officers. And if it came out that one of them had been charged with the murder, all hell would break loose.

"You can go now, but keep me updated."

On the way down to Homicide, Axel called Dorte Neergaard. She didn't pick up the phone, but he left a message that she was welcome to release the recording and there was apparently nothing else in it than that they had been negligent. A deal was a deal. The force's reputation wasn't his responsibility.

In his office there was a distinguished visitor. Henriette Nielsen sat with her legs crossed in the chair in front of his desk, talking on her mobile with a naturalness that made him furious. On the desk in front of her, Enver Davidi's criminal case files, which he had ordered, lay in a pile and he noticed that the elastic around the top one was missing. He took the pile and threw it in his bag.

Henriette Nielsen looked up at him while continuing her conversation unruffled.

"We must get everything translated quickly… Then you'll have to ring around and call people in… Good. See you."

She looked up at him when she had finished the conversation. Then she stood up, so that they were facing each other with the desk between them.

Her smile could be seen in her eyes.

"Thanks for all the calls. We were busy yesterday. I figured we should meet up and exchange information. I'm anxious to hear what you got out of Davidi's ex."

He didn't move.

"Has the collaboration begun?" said Axel ironically.

"Yes, exactly."

"Since you found it necessary to go through the files on my desk."

Her look froze to ice.

"I haven't touched your files. I would never think of doing that."

He looked her in the eyes. She was completely dismissive.

"You must think I was born yesterday."

"I haven't touched your files."

He looked at her for a long time.

"But you've at least touched the file I'm looking for, right? Because it's gone, lent to H. Nielsen for a long time. And that's you. In my ears, it sounds like you know quite a lot about my victim and now I want to know what it's all about."

"Fine by me. I suggest that we all hold a meeting out at our place so that we can share what we know."

Axel took his jacket.

He hadn't asked her to come with him or, for that matter, invited her into his car, but she sat down beside him in the front seat.

"I've heard a lot about you," she said.

"Is there anything I need to respond to?"

"No, but you've just confirmed part of it."

"Which part?"

She looked straight ahead.

"The part that says you're an arrogant, sour-arsed bastard," she said.

He couldn't help smiling. A little.

"One nil. And I've heard bugger-all about you, but maybe you could explain what you're actually doing?"

"It's not exactly a mystery. I'm in the branch of the Flying Squad that deals with organised crime. Before that I've been around a little. Anti-terror. Protection officer for three years."

There were very few female protection officers.

"Why did you leave?"

"I was too tall."

"Too tall?"

"There are far too many VIPs who don't like having a woman four inches taller than them as a bodyguard, so there was only Maggie left for me and there was competition for her."

The Queen was almost six foot tall.

"You're kidding?"

"No, you'd be amazed how many men get turned on by tall women. Not all, but many. I'm six foot one."

He held his tongue, but would have liked to say he didn't think it was a problem.

"So now you're in narcotics and organised crime."

"Yes, that's where I've ended up. For the time being."

"But why?"

"Why not? It's just as interesting as rotting corpses and spouse murders. I know very well that you homicide guys consider murder the only way to salvation, but it's not so clear-cut for me. You unravel while we spin webs. It's exciting. And just as important."

"But why PET?"

"They don't throw money at the other departments, do they? We get the best deal. And more new departments, positions and leader jobs are set up every year than there have been in the rest of the police for the past decade."

"So what?"

"It's not just that. There are good working conditions, good colleagues. And you can get pay in lieu of time off without any problems."

"Exciting," said Axel, without hiding that he meant the opposite.

He stayed silent. He thought about Kettler. Was he the sort of person he could ever call a good colleague? Hardly. She was clearly the more forthcoming of the two and Axel sensed that they might actually be interested in what he had, and perhaps in what he thought. And there was no doubt that they knew all sorts of things that could benefit him.

He put his foot down on Øster Søgade beside the municipal hospital. The sun was reflecting from the windows of the mansion flats opposite Sortedams Lake. They drove across Fredens Bro, where the naked body of Miranda, a 17-year-old girl of Chilean descent, had been found in a thicket twelve years earlier. Raped and strangled. And unsolved. He couldn't drive this way without getting flashbacks to the crime scene, details of the autopsy and the parents' grief when he had to break the news that their daughter would never be coming home. Where were they now? Had they moved on in their lives?

"Did you find anything in that hotel room?" she asked.

He would rather not lie to her, but there was a small shift in tone that made him hesitate.

"Nothing we can use, I don't think. Why? What are you looking for?"

"You'll hear the whole story when we're at our place. Kettler will be briefing you, but I can tell you now that we're in the process of unravelling a large narcotics chain. The Blågårds Plads gang is involved and they're having their phones tapped and are under surveillance. There are connections to groups in northern Macedonia, Kosovo and Albania, and that's why we've been keeping an eye on Davidi."

Keeping an eye on! That was a bit of a bloody understatement, if things hung together the way Axel figured they did.

"But where does he come into the picture?"

She hesitated, as if she were searching for words.

"He's got a conviction for a serious drugs offence. He's been deported. He comes from down in the main transit area where it all enters the EU, and he suddenly turns up here. Isn't that enough?"

"Maybe. Maybe he just wanted to see his son. There's no death penalty for that. Yet."

"Maybe I've overestimated you, Axel Steen. I didn't think there was room for sentimental naivety in the 100 kilos of cynicism you're carrying around."

"Ninety-eight kilos, if you don't mind. What's being smuggled?"

"It's not just a couple of hash clubs. Coke and heroin in large quantities. We're talking 50, 100, 200 kilos. One kilo is worth between a half and one and a half million kroner on the street depending on purity, so you can see there's big money involved."

"But what's Enver Davidi's connection to it?"

"He has a conviction for drug smuggling. He knows many of the people involved because he's grown up in the neighbourhood. His brother was a major gangster, and he travels the same route as all the drugs. Doesn't that make him interesting?"

"Not to me. You haven't explained what it has to do with his murder. Where's the connection between Davidi and the gangsters?"

"You'll get more information when we get to our place."

"But does that mean you think the cause of the murder is going to be found in the drug scene?"

"It certainly can't be ruled out."

He was silent a while.

"Can it be ruled out that you lot fucked it up?"

"What do you mean by that?"

"I mean this whole charade. Haven't you tried to recruit Davidi and use him to get someone on the inside with the ringleaders, and now he's dead and you're pissing your pants that it's because his contact with you was discovered and that it's going to come out? Isn't that why you're sticking to me like flies to a wet turd? You want to make sure no one finds out?"

She didn't bite, but she didn't reject it either. She ran her hand through her hair and sighed. Nothing he had said seemed to have had any serious effect on her, but maybe she was just cooler than her accommodating attitude immediately radiated.

Her voice sounded tired.

"I can't be bothered to argue with you. You'll wise up. And if you think I'm sitting here filled with joy at the prospect of being showered with abuse, you've got another think coming. I look forward as much as you to this collaboration being over."

"What can you actually do?"

"What do you mean?"

"You must be able to do something special, since you're in organised crime and narcotics. There aren't many women in there."

"It doesn't have a damn thing to do with being a woman, you chauvinist. I can investigate. And I know how to use the net. Six months with the FBI in Quantico and plenty of continuing education courses at Bramshill and elsewhere. I can track people online – even when they think they've deleted all their tracks and made themselves invisible."

"That will probably solve the case. Shall we just get on with it instead of all this personal blather?"

Henriette Nielsen put on her sunglasses.

"You're the one who asked, for Christ's sake."

They hadn't got any closer to a partnership.

27

"Who's going to be at the meeting?" asked Axel as they left the motorway and swung into the car park in front of PET's headquarters in Søborg.

"Besides Darling, you, me and Kettler, there will be my boss, a lawyer. You might know him – Jens Jessen?"

Was there a teasing note in her question? Or was Axel just paranoid? He certainly was, but the prospect of a meeting with Jens Jessen involved gave him an acute pain on the left side of his chest, from where it shot down his arm and stretched all the way over the elbow cavity to the wrist. A sure symptom of a heart attack on the way, as he knew from his countless studies of web pages about heart disease. What would he do if he had a heart attack up here? In front of that fool? He swallowed a couple of times, leaned his head back and pressed his hands on his thighs, so that the seat creaked and the headrest cracked.

"Are you ill?"

Axel took a deep breath and breathed out.

"No, I'm fine. Why do you need to have a lawyer present?"

"We always have a lawyer present in cases where there are several interested parties and where doubt could arise about who's entitled to what."

It came rolling up from his stomach.

"But for Christ's sake, that's not the case here. We have to solve a crime together, not play cat and mouse with information like you usually do. It's bloody absurd."

Axel shouted the last words in frustration as he got out of the car and slammed the door. He struck the roof with the palm of his hand.

Henriette Nielsen's mouth was wide open in astonishment.

"What's the matter with you? What the hell have I done? I've been trying to be nice and talk properly to you and you still act like a son of a bitch. I don't decide what you're allowed to know. I'm just as interested in solving the murder as you are – I just don't want to risk it fucking up our operation. If you carry on like this, we'll have to investigate it in parallel, without any collaboration, because I'm not having you pissing on me."

Axel had calmed down.

"OK, OK, I'm sorry. I just want to keep my investigation moving. And I'm having trouble seeing any conflicts of interest between your investigation and mine."

She said nothing but began to walk towards the anonymous office building built of yellow bricks, steel and concrete. Until a few years ago, it had been the headquarters of Denmark's largest laundry company, which was one of the reasons that the local police, housed in an eight-storey unmodernised monster of a sixties high-rise on the other side of the motorway, called it the Washbasin. But it was just as much because the building's current residents were always queueing up with ready-soaped hands when the shit hit the fan. And they usually got off scot-free. The shit fell down the line and landed in the lap of the ordinary police, who couldn't hide behind such formulations as 'consideration towards foreign powers', 'confidential', 'classified', 'no further comment', or the trump card, 'a threat to national security' – a poker hand that no one in police and press circles could beat.

They went into reception, where she arranged for him to be issued with a pass, and then they went down the big hall to the lift. On top of his heart rumbling, he was feeling nauseous. Could he sneak into the toilet on the way and throw up? Would they be able to smell it?

Axel had been to a lot of meetings in his career, both in the old headquarters at Bellahøj and in the Washbasin, in connection with inquiries where PET possessed information in the form of wiretaps or intelligence from sources or foreign services. When it was the latter, it could never be used for anything because it couldn't be made public out of consideration for the source's security and confidentiality with other services. It was of vital importance for PET and, basically, fair enough, Axel thought, but it was nevertheless an extreme nuisance for an investigator to hear about crucial details in an investigation that one couldn't see the documentation for and that therefore couldn't be used in court.

PET had got better over the years, Axel had to admit that, even though Jens Jessen working there had made him feel on show every time he was in contact with the service and its staff.

With the onset of terrorist threats, the intelligence service had begun to open up to society because it was dependent to a greater extent on information and tips from ordinary people, and co-operation with the police was now more the rule than the exception.

Henriette Nielsen led Axel up to the top floor and into an elongated and more than spacious meeting room, where Montana shelving in cherry wood holding PET's annual report and other ministerial books and reports flanked a large TV screen on one wall and a window looked out onto Søborg's flat suburban idyll on the other.

Two men sat on the side of the table with the view while Darling was sitting alone on the other. They all got up as Axel and Henriette entered. Axel shook hands with Kettler, and then hesitantly with Jens Jessen, who sent him a little confidential nod, and to Axel's disgust, patted his hand, as if they had something together and everything would surely work out fine. Jens Jessen sat down again and signalled that the others should take their seats. Axel noticed how calm Jens was: controlled, well trained, his gaze radiating overview and interest. He had tics from his eye to his nose, and his hair was one of the strangest things Axel had ever seen. Afro-white, something that must have been really tight curls, cut down to a length of less than half an inch, so that they lay like an ornamental helmet around his skull.

Axel got the feeling that everyone was staring at him and Jessen, as if they were just waiting for all hell to break loose. His heart was pounding up in his throat and drawing black dots in front of his eyes, and the burning feeling in the skin on his face was painful.

Jens Jessen spread his arms out wide with open hands and smiled.

"OK, welcome to our little headquarters. We know each other, so I'm looking forward to this, Axel, John Darling. We have a major operation in progress involving cross-border international drug trafficking, which includes liaison officers from the intelligence services and police forces of several countries, as well as Europol. For that reason, we're very committed to making a good start."

Axel had heard it a hundred times before. International cross-border crime was the mantra of the new era. When Europol was mixed into it too, the only certainty was that some magnificent reports would be produced full of fine intentions, but the criminals would be long gone before the numerous different services could make up their minds to work together. But for police officers who wanted to rise through the system, it was open sesame.

"Now is the time for us to share what we know, and since you're our guests, we'll start. I'm sure we'll solve this case quickly. You'll be working with two of my most skilled and experienced staff, both of whom have worked in a wide variety of roles, but who also possess special skills that you can't find everywhere in the police force. Yes..."

He paused for effect and brought his fingertips together. Axel was fidgeting in his chair, sweat dripping from his armpits and trickling down the side of his body.

"... You have a murder; we have a complicated investigation with branches abroad, involving drug crimes, money laundering, and if I may say so, even worse things."

"What things?" wheezed Axel.

Jessen looked at him with a cheerful expression, a cliquish smile, and opened up slightly for a little laugh, which at the same time served to indicate that it was he who decided what would be said.

"I'll come to that later... actually no, I won't." He sniggered. "Even worse things – you'll have to guess what they might be. The point is that we're going to help each other and we would like to give you everything we have, but as you've probably heard before, there are certain considerations that prevent us from doing so."

Axel felt faint. He tried to calm his breathing, but his heart was like a kettledrum on which Jens Jessen was hammering a rhythm that was far too fast. He stood up to the great amazement of the others.

"I… sorry… but is there a toilet?" he stammered. "I have to…"

"Is something wrong? Are you feeling ill?" asked Henriette Nielsen, getting up and showing him out to the corridor.

Axel heard Jens Jessen say something about "a short break", before reaching the toilet where he loosened his tie and his collar and splashed water in his face. Then he went into a toilet stall and knelt down in order to throw up. But nothing came.

This was what absolutely mustn't happen. He felt his chest and counted; it was the same as it usually was – his fucking heart was beating exactly as it usually did. He had panicked because of that impossible idiot; all his puerile friendliness coupled with his power.

Axel got to his feet, put his tie in his pocket, thought of his daughter and walked out of the door and back into the meeting room.

Jens Jessen looked at him with some concern.

"Is everything OK?"

Axel nodded, and the PET boss paused, throwing out his hands as if he had just presented a good offer.

"We have a group of criminals known under the names of the Blågårds Plads gang, Pladsen or BGP under surveillance because we suspect them of extensive drug offences, and the same applies to their connections with several different people resident here but originally from the Balkans. We've been investigating this connection and the trail has led us to Kosovo and northern Macedonia. And this is where Enver Davidi comes into the picture. We followed him on his way up here and were tailing him."

Axel was clear in the head again and interrupted immediately, making everyone look at him in surprise.

"But then everything's all set, surely? You must know who killed him?"

"We don't," Kettler said dismissively.

"Let's get to the point. He's been spotted in this country twice by witnesses during the past few years, without us having picked him up and sent him home. Is that your doing?"

Henriette Nielsen looked first at Kettler, then at Jens Jessen, who nodded.

"Yes, we flagged him in the records and we were keeping him under observation both times so that we could step in and warn the ordinary police – your people – to keep their hands off."

"What do you suspect he's been up to?"

"We suspect he's brought drugs with him every time. He has nothing to lose after all."

Except for his son, thought Axel, but he has already lost him once. And now he has lost his life.

"What about his wife? Have you been keeping her under observation too?"

"No. We regard her as irrelevant," said Henriette Nielsen.

Jens Jessen took over.

"Yes, that's how it is. Shall we get started? Kettler, would you like to give us some background?"

"Enver Davidi was born in 1959 in the village of Shipkovitsa in northern Macedonia. An Albanian, arrived here in 1980 with his brother and father. Settled in Inner Nørrebro, the rest of the family stayed in Macedonia…"

Axel broke in.

"Thanks. We've read his criminal record. Skip the history lesson and tell us when and how many times he's been here since he was deported!"

Kettler looked as if he was about to lose his cool, but Jessen nodded to him.

"He's been to Denmark several times since his deportation. We became aware of him in 2005, when he was picked up by a patrol, allegedly in connection with his brother's death, but we think he was here as a courier or to negotiate agreements for the delivery of drugs. We've seen him three times in Copenhagen and tailed him every time, and we monitored his mobile contacts as far as we could."

That explained why the case file had been taken and why no one had arrested Davidi when he had been spotted by the police. But it didn't explain why Henriette Nielsen had visited Enver Davidi at the Hotel Continental the evening before he was murdered. Axel decided to save that information for later.

"What did you get from the phone taps? Who was he in contact with?"

Kettler looked at Jessen, who nodded.

"His wife and old acquaintances from the Blågårds Plads area, but also – and this is what really matters – Moussa, the leader of the gang, who runs a large proportion of the trade in hard drugs and hash in Nørrebro and elsewhere – a not inconsiderable business after you people shut down the market at Christiania."

Axel didn't understand a thing.

"But why are you messing about with this? It's a case for the Copenhagen police, isn't it?"

Jessen broke in.

"There's more to it than just the trade with a few kilos of hard drugs – that goes without saying – but the nature of the case means that I'm unable to elaborate."

Axel looked appealingly at Darling, who was hiding behind his perfect cop smile and didn't give any indication of noticing Axel's look. He didn't want to get wound up and expose himself in front of Jens Jessen with so many other people present. Axel shook his head and looked at Henriette Nielsen, who was sitting on nails, while Kettler was twisting in his chair, as if he had a shit his pants. Only Jessen was totally calm. Was it him they were ill at ease about? Was it because everyone knew about the situation with Cecilie?

"But what's your theory about the murder, if you have one?" Darling asked.

Both the PET officers were about to say something, but Jessen got in first.

"We don't have a theory about the murder. We've been monitoring the entire milieu for the past six months and Davidi's just one piece in the puzzle. Our goal is to get them all behind bars. For a very long time. And in that respect, it's clear that a murder helps. So we'll be very happy if there's a connection to Moussa and the others in the gang. We listen in to mobiles, we have informants and we have cameras installed at several places, including the café down there... what's the name of it?"

Axel knew which one he meant before the answer came. Escobar, a café with outdoor seating in the square, was the gang's hangout. It was here the leaders came rolling up in their four-wheel-drives or Audis and flashed their power in front of the others. Several of them knew Axel directly from his work, after they had been pulled in for questioning in connection with murders and two of them had been convicted of more or less random knife murders in the nightlife. The absolute leader, Moussa, was feared for his brutality and the stories about his punishments of people who didn't pay on time were legendary.

"But we aren't ready to go to court yet," said Jessen, emphasising his words by spreading his arms once more and saying, "It would ruin everything. To put it simply. Do you understand?"

His facial expressions were incredible: a bit like a cold, experienced killer trapped in a five-year-old boy's manically happy body language.

"What have you found out? What do you have on them?"

Kettler took over again. It was clear that Jens Jessen made the decisions and Kettler was in charge of the investigation, but what was Henriette Nielsen's actual role? If Axel was right in his hunch that there was a closer connection between Davidi and PET, and if the Pole had told the truth and she had visited Davidi at the Hotel Continental, Axel was well aware that she was the key – the lead officer who had had the direct contact with the agent. And the agent was dead.

"We have a lot on them, threats, violence, agreements on deliveries and money transfers. And we've combined that with banking and tax information, so that it paints a clear picture of organised crime, which will double the sentence. There's enough to lock them away for a long time."

"Do you have enough on the leaders too?"

"We have something, but not enough yet."

"And what role does Enver Davidi play in all this?"

Both men looked at Henriette Nielsen and Axel's suspicions were confirmed. She looked uneasy but straightened up.

"OK. BGP has respect for Enver. He took his sentence without singing and that means something to them. And he can deliver the goods from his home district, which is the transit area for hash, drugs, weapons and women."

How did she know that Enver Davidi could deliver the goods without having talked to him herself? As each minute passed, Axel was becoming firmer in his belief that they were hiding something from him.

"But what was Enver Davidi doing here?"

Kettler looked at Henriette Nielsen.

"Enver Davidi came up here on Tuesday as a courier in a major drugs operation, which we've been following since he left Tetovo on Monday so that he could get here without being stopped. We didn't want to pick him up until he delivered the drugs."

"Who was he delivering them to?"

"He had contact with Moussa via a guy called Kamal, a fixer. Davidi stayed at the hotel for three days and we kept him under observation throughout the period. During that time he had several conversations with Kamal and they had agreed on a meeting on Friday at Escobar, but Davidi didn't show up for obvious reasons."

"You've been keeping him under observation, you say. Then you must have been following him on the night of the murder!"

Henriette Nielsen looked uncomfortable.

"He left the hotel without us noticing, down a rear staircase because he didn't want to be seen. So we weren't keeping that good an eye on him."

"What do you think happened?"

"It's reasonable to assume that there's a connection to the milieu; that he was killed as part of a deal that was screwed up and then they tried to conceal it."

"With autonomist camouflage? Those thugs aren't that sophisticated," said Axel.

"What have you got from the wiretaps in the time up to the murder and afterwards?" asked Darling.

"That's the strange bit. There's nothing. You might think that's normal, but these arseholes aren't usually so quiet. They babble and brag every time they've cut a finger off a debtor or beat the living daylights out of someone, but there's not a word about Davidi."

"Not even about the picture that Counterpress published?"

"Yes, of course, but only something like: 'Have you seen that geezer on the net, man? Isn't he Salki's brother?' It's remarkable they haven't reacted at all."

"Moussa and his mob," interrupted Darling, "I can't avoid the thought they must now be number one on the list of main suspects in this investigation. How much drugs are we talking?"

"Fifteen kilos of cocaine. That's between seven and twenty-two million kroner on the street, depending on the purity."

Axel couldn't keep his mouth shut any longer.

"And I can't avoid the thought that this entire investigation stinks to high heaven of an undercover operation with Davidi as the bait. What did you promise him in exchange for Moussa? And what went wrong?"

Henriette Nielsen stiffened and looked at her boss, who was smiling and trying once more to give the impression of being calm and collected, but Axel thought he could trace a flicker of irritation in his indulgent smile.

"Axel, this isn't conducive to our collaboration. Your comments are crossing the line. You have to work with us on the murder investigation and only the murder investigation, not the drugs operation, and you shouldn't be implying that we have anything to do with his death."

"Don't you?"

"Enver Davidi disappeared from our surveillance the evening before he was killed," answered Henriette Nielsen. "That'll have to be enough of an answer."

"Not for me. You could easily have provoked him into a situation where he ended up being killed. This investigation is all smoke and mirrors. Who was Enver Davidi? Is he a small fish or a major player with connections to the Balkan mafia? Is there anything to indicate he's smuggled drugs before? Evidence? You say you've followed him on several other deliveries. Prove it! And why does he go and risk years of imprisonment by coming up here with such a large delivery? It seems idiotic, right? And it seems strange that you don't have any answers to such basic questions."

He decided to raise the stakes.

"But it seems even stranger that your lead investigator visited our victim less than six hours before he was murdered and you don't mention it."

Mr Perfect immediately woke up out of his trance.

"What's that?" asked Darling. "Why haven't I been told about that?"

Kettler looked at Henriette Nielsen.

"It's true that I visited the hotel on Thursday evening," she said, "but I was only there to check if we could bug the room. I had no contact with Davidi whatsoever."

She gave Axel a look that could freeze. Happy now? asked the look.

"If we're going to work together, I want all the information. I don't want to be fobbed off with you calling it irrelevant who the victim saw the evening before he was murdered. Just as I don't want to be fobbed of with all sorts of incoherent rubbish about there being worse things to concentrate on. We're police officers, for fuck's sake, and we're working towards the same goal. Why not just say it's terror so we can move on?"

Jens Jessen was smiling and blinking. He spread his hands again and paused for effect once more. How can she stand this idiot? And what about my daughter? Should she really have goodnight stories read to her by a man who looks like a clown on speed?

"But that's it – yes, that's it," he said, looking at them with wide, serious eyes, as if he was going to burst into tears at any moment. Then the smile broke through. "Yes, the cat's out of the bag. As you know, if you've been keeping up, there are lots of links from Bosnia to al-Qaeda. The Mujahideen helped the Muslims during the Balkan War, and some of them are still living and hiding in the Muslim part of Bosnia. Just a year ago, we had a terrorist case involving Danes. Although the Albanians in northern Macedonia work with all types of criminals, they are Muslims, and most of these guys from Blågårds Plads are too. And it's well known that many of them flirt with Hizb Ut Tahrir, who want a violent overthrow of Western society; they've been convicted of saying as much. We have good reason to believe that some of the drug trafficking revenue helps to fund international terrorism via Bosnia, and that's what we're trying to chart in collaboration with our overseas intelligence partners."

It was the most ludicrous paranoid bullshit Axel had heard since the Homicide Division, on PET's orders, was forced to arrest a notorious Muslim agitator from Brønshøj for planning an attack on the Oslo ferry and ended up having to settle for charges of bike theft and possession of a weapon because he owned an ancient Persian sword from 300 BC. The bastards at Blågårds Plads were criminals of the worst order. Their codes of honour were medieval and they were happy to express their hatred of Denmark, but it didn't go any deeper than that Denmark just happened to be the country that was trying to prevent them from carrying out their violent, criminal behaviour. But terrorism – he didn't believe that for a second.

"Is there anything to indicate that the murder investigation has links to terror in Denmark?"

"I'd really like to answer that, but I can't. It's confidential. And now I've said enough. And, unfortunately, I have to leave this meeting now as I'm going on an official trip this afternoon. I trust you'll take all necessary steps for us to solve this case quickly. And I trust that you'll maintain confidentiality."

He got up and took the yellow manila folder that had been in front of him throughout the meeting, gave a big smile, then lifted his left hand in a Roman salute, but stopped in the middle of it.

"Axel Steen, could I just borrow you for two seconds before you go?"

He pointed at him with one finger like a pistol barrel and flashed a roguish smile.

Axel got up, watched Jens Jessen wink with both eyebrows to the others and followed him out of the room.

He stood with the folder under his arm and smiled mechanically but looked directly at Axel in a way that seemed both challenging and innocent.

"Good questions, really, really good. Now that we're sort of family… I thought…"

"We're not family."

"Oh."

"And never will be."

"No… ah, well… but I just thought I'd say that I hope of course that there's nothing personal between us because I'm now… yes, I mean I have nothing against you, I've only heard good things about you, not least from Sille, but also from others. I just wanted to make that point."

"And now you've done it, but it doesn't alter the fact that I have my murder investigation and I won't be cut out of any information that can help clear it up."

Jens Jessen smiled and held one hand up in a conciliatory gesture.

"No, I'm sure no one's in any doubt about that. I'm sorry if it was a little weird in there, but I'm sure we'll tackle it like grown-ups. I must run."

He turned to go and stopped as if something had come to mind.

"You're OK, aren't you? You aren't ill or something? You're OK with it?"

Axel didn't know which of the questions he was supposed to answer. So he stayed silent and went back into the meeting room.

28

Piver had taken a battering. Several batterings. He had tried to buy some time by telling the man that he had made a copy of the video recording, that he had hidden it with a friend in the Freetown and that his kidnapper wouldn't be able to find it himself so he would have to take Piver along as a guide.

But it had all gone wrong. The man had no intention of using Piver as a guide. He intended to beat the truth out of him.

Now he was lying on the floor of the container with the taste of blood in his mouth and the man towering over him.

The light pounded down from two fluorescent tubes in the ceiling.

Then came another kick. Piver was surprised how clearly he saw it. The man stared down at him with a malicious smile; it was like a bad movie, and then he pulled his leg back as though he was going to boot a football and followed through, his boot hammering into Piver's stomach, one more, another, and finally one which caught him in the ribs. He was screaming with pain, but nothing came through the gaffer tape; the dumb roar died in his mouth. They're broken, he thought, and watched the man bend over him and reach towards his face. I'm going to die now, I'm going to die now – but instead the gaffer tape was ripped off.

He screamed for help as loud as he could.

"Scream as much as you like. No one can hear you."

The foam rubber on the walls swallowed everything.

He screamed even louder, but the boot came whistling through the air again and this time it hit him in the mouth. The pain wasn't as bad as the blow to the stomach, but the shock was paralysing; he was bleeding and his lip was split – he could feel it as he ran his tongue over it. His front tooth was loose.

I'm going to die. He's going to fucking kill me.

It wasn't a realisation that arose in his mind, not a thought, but something his whole body instantaneously knew, and it reacted by going into complete panic. It felt as if he had been recharged in a split second, the pain disappeared, and all his muscles filled with blood, his consciousness was close to bursting with alertness; he had to find a way out of this vicious, hellish darkness.

"Where's that recording?" shouted the man angrily, grabbing his hair and twisting his face so that he could look him in the eyes. "I'll fucking kill you. Do you understand? Tell me now."

"I lied – it was all a lie. I haven't made a copy."

The man looked coldly at him.

"I don't believe you. I'll get it out of you. I'm going to put you up on the chair and tie you to it and then I'm going to start beating the daylights out of you. You'll tell me what I want to know."

"I haven't made a copy. You must be able to see that from the camera. I don't know how to do it. Stop, for Christ's sake."

At the same time, he thought that it was the only thing keeping him alive. The copy.

The man pulled some gloves on. They looked like synthetic leather. Then he lifted Piver up from the floor.

"Why are you doing this to me? I haven't done anything to you."

"No, you haven't really, have you? But you've got yourself into something you should have stayed out of, and now you're paying the price," he said, winking knowingly at Piver.

Then he was sat on the chair. The man raised Piver's bound arms up over the backrest and Piver screamed with pain. The man snapped them in place at a totally crazy angle, so that Piver thought they were going to break.

"Sit still, you insect, or I'll break your neck."

He began to lash Piver tightly to the chair with gaffer tape; first his upper body, and then his legs, each of which was tightly bound to a chair leg.

Piver sobbed and moaned; his arms were hurting in a way he had never known before, uninterrupted, as if his bones were slowly being broken.

"Jesus Christ, man – listen to me. I haven't taken a copy. This is crazy, I haven't done anything."

"Sit still, for fuck's sake."

Then he tried to stay quiet and bit into his split lower lip, but silence had never been his strong point.

"Nobody knows about that tape. I won't tell anyone. I won't say anything to anyone about it. Let me go. Please."

The man grabbed hold of his hair and lifted his head. Slapped his face. And again. Piver registered in shock how the man's hand moved from side to side, only slowed down by the contact with his cheeks. His ears were ringing and it felt as though his head was about to burst. His brain was boiling and swollen and wrapping a strange ecstasy of pain around him, and then he must have fainted… and yet, he woke up with the next blow, and the next, next, next and next again.

Then the man let go, straightened up and took a step back. He began taking the gloves off, finger by finger, carefully and methodically.

"Are you going to tell me what you've done with that copy?"

His tone was ingratiating in a twisted way.

Piver groaned and whimpered, "I don't have any copy, there isn't any…"

The man raised a hand in warning. The gaffer tape went back on; Piver's nose was so blocked that it was hard to breathe and he sniffed with the full force of his lungs to make a hole.

The man looked at him with cold eyes. He was putting the gloves back on.

29

When Axel re-entered the meeting room after his little exchange with Jens Jessen, they stared at him as if he had the plague. For once he was perfectly calm and behaved as if nothing had happened. He pulled out Jens Jessen's chair, sat down and looked at Henriette Nielsen.

"What about the drugs consignment?" he asked. "Where is it?"

There was silence. Confusion.

"Hello, anybody there? Don't we have a case to solve?"

"We don't know. The drugs have vanished."

"And the man is dead," added her colleague.

"What do you suggest we do now?"

"Maybe you could start by telling us what you know?"

John Darling began and told them about Groes and Vang.

The atmosphere had changed after Jessen had disappeared. True, there weren't exactly waves of warmth between Axel and Kettler, but now the four police officers were sitting around a table, exchanging information and looking at the case from different angles. And they were playing open hands – sort of.

"We've questioned all our people on duty at the cemetery – a total of forty-two men and senior officers, including Groes and Vang. It wasn't impossible to get in there, either over the wall or through the gates, which were unmanned on two occasions. And the question is whether Davidi has gone into the cemetery voluntarily. That someone could have forced a man into a place swarming with cops, without being seen, seems completely crazy."

"What about the witness statements from the houses opposite? Have they given anything?"

"Not really. We've been in forty-three flats and spoken with fifty-two residents and business people. Everybody's seen something, but no one's seen enough."

"What does that mean?"

"They've seen a hell of a lot during the evening and night, but no one's seen anything other than what I assume is our people in the cemetery."

"How can they know it's us?"

"Equipment, vans, helmets, uniforms, reflective letters on their backs. Even though they haven't been able to see if it was a police officer, they have assumed it was because of the different markings," said Darling. He looked up at them. "OK, shouldn't we try to make a guess where the victim has come from and how he got to the crime scene… if it is a crime scene?"

Axel interrupted.

"It is. One hundred per cent certain."

Everyone looked at him in surprise.

"I've watched footage from the air over Assistens. Both our own and a recording that I've got hold of on the quiet."

"O-kay," said Henriette Nielsen, raising her eyebrows and stressing the last syllable, while Kettler smiled, as if nothing could surprise him.

"But I have to be sure that no one outside these doors will find out I've got it, because if that happens, it will be a serious matter for the person who provided it. Agreed? None of all that 'you just have to hear…' stuff to your colleagues in the lunch break."

He took out his laptop and the disk with the TV2 recording and connected it to the projector. First he showed them the clip where an indistinct man could be seen walking along the path towards the crime scene after midnight. Then he spooled forward and showed them the clip with the two men who came walking under the trees heading for the crime scene. The questions came gushing out.

"Is that a policeman?"

"Is that Davidi?"

"Are they holding each other?"

"Is he wearing a balaclava?"

As Axel played it for the second time, there were no questions. The room went totally still while Enver Davidi was being murdered. Now everyone knew what had happened in the 90 seconds that passed before one of the men appeared again, looked at his work, took a photo, turned round and walked into the cemetery. They had been witnesses to a murder, and death made the gravity of the situation tower up between them like a wall of silence.

"Enver Davidi walked under his own steam with his murderer to the scene of the crime where he was strangled before the murderer disappeared. It took 90 seconds. There's no way you can beat a man in the face repeatedly, strangle him and clothe him in military boots and balaclava in 90 seconds. I'm sure Davidi was handcuffed. I'm sure he already had the boots on, and I'm sure nothing else happens other than him being strangled and getting the balaclava pulled over his head before the perp leaves the scene. And that means they've been holed up somewhere in the cemetery before this, somewhere where everything else has happened. They walked from the Youth House down to the scene of the crime. BB's fine-combed the area to see if there are any traces of the two of them, and there are. Two places. They met at the chapel, went down through a hatch to an underground passage, perhaps to stay in hiding, and it's probably here that Davidi's been beaten up and had the handcuffs and boots put on him. According to Lennart Jönsson, it's not impossible to strangle a human being in as short a time as 60 to 80 seconds. Davidi hasn't had his neck broken, but not far from it. His larynx and thyroid cartilage are almost crushed and he's been deprived of oxygen by an intense and massive pressure all around his neck. Davidi's almost six foot tall. He's been strangled standing up – it's the work of a man, or an unusually strong and very tall woman."

He looked at Henriette Nielsen, whose face was furrowed in thought.

"But why kill him at the cemetery? It makes no damn sense," she said.

"No, we've been thinking about that too, but maybe it's perfectly obvious. Either it's an insider, or the whole intention is to make it look like a police murder or a murder related to the Youth House."

"How organised is he?" asked Henriette Nielsen. "Can we rule out spontaneous murder, an argument which got out of hand?"

"That could fit the police theory – that is, an autonomist killed by a pair of over-eager, beat-the-bastard cops. But I don't think so. I think this has been very carefully planned; the perp's known that he was going to kill Davidi, but there may have been changes of plan along the way. He wanted to disguise it as a Youth House murder. And he's had a lot of help from Counterpress, who published the picture of the dead man – the picture he himself took and sent to them – it tells me all I need to know about how cynical he is. It's a planned murder carried out by a man able to get into one of the best-guarded places in Copenhagen at the time and get away again – without anyone noticing him. And the question is, how was that possible?"

"It could easily be one of Moussa's people," said Kettler.

"Are they that smart?" Axel asked. "I mean, they may be drug peddlers, but they're not magicians. And they're not exactly high-school graduates, are they?"

"No, but they've still dished out quite a few punishments, revenge raids and liquidations in recent years; they've been up in another league a long time," said Henriette Nielsen.

"Then we have to look at them. And we have to look at the police theory, even if we don't want to. We have Vang, and I'll be interrogating him once more either today or tomorrow. But we also have to look for a new perpetrator – we have to consider all possibilities," said Axel, pausing to give it time to sink in. "A young autonomist, Peter Smith, Piver, has a recording taken from a rooftop opposite the crime scene. It's hardly likely to show the actual murder, because the crime scene is sheltered by the wall, and the angle would be too oblique, but it may show the victim and perpetrator more clearly than the footage we've got here. Unfortunately, Piver disappeared into the Freetown when we last saw him."

Kettler brightened up.

"The Freetown – that's your patch, isn't it, Steen?"

"What do you mean?"

"I just thought you were out there quite often, a little random checking?"

Had they seen him buying hash? Axel ignored him.

"We're monitoring his mobile, but it's been dead since Friday afternoon, when two short conversations took place, which we're in the process of having transcribed. One call was to one of the girls from the collective, the other number's unknown. We'll follow that up."

"Where does it all leave us?" said Darling.

"Nowhere yet. I'd like to get on with Vang. I think I can break him today. And then there's Davidi's ex-wife, who I visited without getting a lot out of her. What do you know about her?"

Henriette Nielsen rummaged through her papers.

"Not very much. We have a sheet on her somewhere from when she was being wire-tapped before the trial against Davidi, but she was completely clean. Hard upbringing with foster families in Nørrebro, as far as I remember."

Darling broke in.

"Could there be anything with her? I'd like to know everything about her. What she's been doing, who she's been with, who she's been screwing. What do you say, Axel? Will you take that?"

Yes, that's right up my street. I know everything about that, he thought.

"Yes. That sounds logical," he said out loud.

Darling puffed out his chest.

"Then there's the narcotics theory. Isn't it best that you continue down that track – Moussa and his gang?"

Darling looked at Henriette Nielsen and Kettler. Neither of them protested.

"There are many other things to be checked. I'll make a list that'll be sent to you during the afternoon. The good news is that, as of tomorrow, we'll have help from six men from the division."

It didn't seem to please Henriette Nielsen and Kristian Kettler that they would be collaborating with a further six ordinary homicide detectives, but they smiled politely and gathered up their papers.

30

His mobile was full of messages. One of them was from Enver's ex-wife, Laila.

"Hi, it's Laila. I'm sorry I was so angry and took it out on you. I was upset about David's death. I'd like to help if there's anything I can do. Call me. Bye."

They had met one another a year and a half ago via the internet. It had developed into an evening at Pussy Galore, the Beer Bar, Osbourne, his bed, sex of the unrestrained kind that follows a lot of red wine and even more beer. Two bodies in the night, full of need. Nervous, almost desperate hours, where they were both too eager and more preoccupied with satisfying the other than enjoying themselves, because that wasn't why they were there. It was physical closeness they were longing for. Reflected by lust and longing. And that was what they got. She had such a firm grip on his upper arms while they were fucking that he still had the bruises a week later. Momentary relief. But nothing more. Sometimes you wake up the day afterwards and look the need you were trying to escape from straight in the eyes. There were no harsh words, coldness or regret. He had just taken the wrong medicine. Neither of them had felt the need to resume the contact.

Axel pressed the number. The phone was picked up after two rings.

"Laila."

"Hi, it's Axel Steen from Copenhagen Police."

"Hi."

"Thanks for your message. I actually have a number of questions that I have to ask you about Enver Davidi. Can you come into HQ or shall I come by?"

"It's a bit difficult for me to come to HQ. My son isn't very fond of police stations and prisons. He visited David of course in Vestre and in

Vridsløse for some years. And they aren't good memories. If it has to be now, you can come here."

"That's fine, but I don't think it's a good idea for him to overhear our conversation."

"No problem. He's good at amusing himself."

He rang off and switched on his PC. Frank Jensen had sent him a summary of his information about Davidi from Skopje, but most of it was about the drugs case and his deportation and there was nothing that was new to him. There was a document about the murder of Stanca Gutu, and two photos were attached of the young Moldovan woman, both before and after she had been killed. Right now, he couldn't see what use he had for it, but who knows?

He pulled up Frank Jensen's number and called. There was no reply, but Axel left a long message, thanking him for the attachments and asking if he had had contact with PET about Enver Davidi – calls, mails, visits, any contact at all. If it all hung together as he thought it did, Frank would have something for him.

Then he called Dorte Neergaard.

She hadn't hung about.

"I don't have time right now. I have to interview your boss about those two officers in two minutes. It's breaking news for us. But you still owe me. Call me when you have an explanation from them."

20 minutes later, he drove into Rentemestervej – relieved to have got out of the PET fortress in Søborg without too many scratches.

Laila Hansen opened the door before he rang the bell. She looked different – a red dress with tiny little white polka dots on it and a pair of black, cotton tights. Her face was serene, clearer and more focused than the day before. Her short, red hair was sticking up; Axel felt like running his hand through it.

"Come in," she said. "Louie's glued to the PlayStation upstairs."

They sat on the sofa; she had made coffee. He could sense that she was prepared, but for what? What would she tell him now? Which version of reality had she prepared for him?

"I don't know why I've been trying to hide it. It doesn't really matter much now that he's dead, but he's been here several times since he was deported."

"When was he last here?"

Now he suddenly saw her as a piece of the puzzle he had to solve and he noted the details of the home: the framed Japanese characters, the yoga books in the box shelves, three orchids on the window sill, a bonsai tree, the absence of a television, but also a banana palm, a poster from an Egon Schiele exhibition in Louisiana, a small black compact music system, and the natural white Ikea sofa in which he was sitting.

"He was here last Wednesday. He was waiting for me when I got home from work. He looked different, as if he really believed he'd get another chance."

"What do you mean?"

"He said that big things were going to happen. And that things would be very different in future, but I didn't believe him."

She got up and went through to the kitchen for milk.

"Did he mean another chance with you?"

"Maybe. Right when he said it, I thought he meant me, but maybe he thought he could have another chance in Denmark, but that was impossible. So I laughed in frustration, and he got angry and said he'd come back and explain everything to me, explain it to Louie, but I didn't want that."

"Did he see Louie?"

"No, he was at the after-school club."

"But did he ever see Louie when he was here?"

"He did see him at first, but Louie just couldn't handle it, so I stopped letting him, but I got the feeling he's been seeing him anyway. At a distance. That he's been waiting outside the school and watching him leave. Just to see him. Or seen him over at the club."

"Why?"

"Because Louie has said there was a man who looked like his Dad outside the school. The next time I heard from him, I asked him to stop. Or at least make sure he wasn't seen." She was far away. "He was a good father. Or would have been. He's never been there, but he loved Louie very much. Occasionally, I got the feeling that it was the only thing that meant anything to him. It was just that there wasn't much he could do in Macedonia without a job or money. But he tried. He sent small amounts when he got some money. For a while he worked as an interpreter and he earned a little from that."

She suddenly looked completely lost. And afraid.

"Can you try to tell me about him right from the start? How you met him. What he was like. I know it's a lot to ask, but it's my only chance of building a picture of him."

"I don't know if I feel like talking to you about it. You come here and we have…"

Fucked, he thought. She didn't finish the sentence, but wasn't that what they had done that time? Or was it something purer? Something halfway between fuck and make love? It had meant something, but it didn't mean anything right now.

"And you come and tell me that my son's father has been murdered. I'm still bitter at you and the system that took Louie's father from him. Even though he was a drug offender, as you put it, he was a good enough man, or he meant well. Yes, he was sentenced for the stupidest thing he ever did, but he wasn't that type at all. He was a happy, funny, positive man, who was put under pressure by some people."

"Who?"

"His brother and his crowd. Now he's dead, so it doesn't really matter, but David wasn't like them. He was actually a decent guy, even though he was easy to trap and didn't really know how to do things in moderation."

There was some French music playing from a speaker in the kitchen. Édith Piaf, he realised. *Non, je ne regrette rien.*

"How did it start?"

"I met him in a taxi. He drove me home from the airport after I landed from a holiday in Malta with an idiot who hadn't told me he was married. That was about thirteen-fourteen years ago. We got married in '95 and I'd known him for just over a year, so it must have been the spring of 1994. He was a handsome man, sweet and funny, and he loved to go out dancing and was fond of children."

It sounded like a fucking contact ad.

"But how did you get from the taxi to..."

"Bed? It actually took a while, though you might not believe it," she said, looking coldly at him. "But to be perfectly honest, what business is it of yours? What relevance does it have to your work if he screwed me in the back of his cab or bombarded me with flowers and short letters for three months?"

He was going off-topic. He had to try to straighten things out and get her more immersed in the past. He gave her some space.

"How's your heart doing?" she said, looking up at him with a little smile.

"My heart? What do you mean?"

"You know very well. You had two large hairless spots on your chest the last time we saw each other."

"That wasn't anything. I was taking part in a trial."

"Oh yeah. That's what you said back then too. Remember though – I'm a nurse. I know how you look when you've had an ECG."

"I'm sorry if I'm being clumsy, but I just want to get a better sense of him. That's why I'm asking you to give me the whole story."

"I knew him a bit from Korsgade, where I lived for some years in the 80s. He lived with his father and big brother up the next stairwell. David was the funny one who knew all the kids in the neighbourhood. He fitted in easily and wasn't as serious as his father or as arrogant as his brother. He was a very handsome young man back then. And when I saw it was him who was going to drive us home from the airport, I was happy. I happened to say I'd spent a week with an idiot who was unfaithful to his wife while the idiot was sitting next to me. Shouldn't we drop him off now then? said David. We were in the middle of the motorway on Amager. Deal, I said. So we drove off, leaving him standing there with his suitcase on the hard shoulder, the arsehole. David gave me his number. Call me anytime if you need help or just feel like a cup of coffee. It was an offer I didn't want to refuse. A couple of weeks later we met at the Café Blågårds Apotek. There was live music, a blues band, and David wanted me to get up and dance. There was no one else on the floor, and I was shy, but he convinced me. So we danced – wildly and intimately, following our instincts."

She went silent.

"There isn't much more to tell about him. I fell in love with him. He was easy to be with. I got pregnant. We bought this house with the money we had each saved up and moved in together. Although it wasn't planned, we were looking forward to having the baby. David drove the taxi. His father had had two cars and the brother and David had taken them over, so now they were cab owners. I didn't know anything about what the brother was up to, but I wasn't crazy about him. He looked down on me, not because I was Danish, but because I'd taken his little brother from him. He told me that to my face once. He had a wife and three children. They lived in Macedonia, where they went every summer. But after David got to know me, he didn't want to go home any more, and his brother didn't like that. It was difficult for David, because he was a boy inside in many ways. And his brother became a kind of father to him when their father died. So he was split. I had no idea that his brother was involved in all this drug trafficking. I first found that out when David went to prison."

"What happened?"

"Louie was born in the spring. It was a crap summer, it rained almost the whole time. In August, your colleagues came one night and knocked the door down and turned the whole house upside down. They wouldn't tell me what had happened. Only that David had been remanded for four weeks. 'It'll be the new millennium before you see him again,' one of them said to me mockingly. It was like a bad dream. So I called Salki, his brother, and asked what was going on. He refused to talk to me while the police were here. I had a little screaming boy in my arms, the house full of aggressive cops, and no one would tell me anything. After a couple of hours, a detective superintendent arrived and explained that David had been arrested with 17 kilos of cocaine in his car and that he was being questioned and would be remanded for four weeks. It's a lie, I screamed. You're lying. That's not my David."

She paused for a moment. Axel thought how he would have reacted if he had been in charge. Would he have allowed himself to be swayed by the fact she was holding a little baby? He would probably have requisitioned a female colleague and the social authorities, but only after trying to pressure her.

"They wanted to have me in for interview right away. What about my child? I asked. You're not taking my child from me, I screamed. I broke down. I tried to explain to them that I knew nothing about it, that I had no idea what was going on. I think the superintendent believed me, because he said it would be all right. But that they had to interview me about my husband's movements, his trips, phone calls, our finances, the house, the car, everything. I was allowed to keep Louie with me. It took all night. Eventually, they drove me home to a life I hadn't imagined in my worst nightmares. The one who followed me back into the house said that if I hadn't been such a little drugs whore, he might have felt like fucking me."

Could he have said the same thing? Had he said that in other situations? No, maybe not, but he had said worse things to provoke suspects or get information out of people. When he had done it, there had been a purpose, he thought; this was just petty malice. The little French sparrow ground on about need and longing from the kitchen. Axel had a stomach ache.

"We had fitted out a children's room with a changing table, big red and yellow flowers glued on the wall, a rattle and a wooden mobile with clowns and balloons, new red curtains and a cradle where Louie used to sleep. When I got home, it had all been ripped apart. All the flowers on the walls had been torn down, the wallpaper had been ripped off, and there were nappies all over the floor with a crushed bottle of baby oil on top. Even though I was shaken, I had my child with me, and I couldn't really feel anything, I was only thinking about Louie's welfare."

She wasn't allowed to visit Enver Davidi during the first few days because he was in isolation in the interests of the investigation. No one gave her any details about the investigation or what would happen. Axel understood it all very well. She was the drug bastard's wife! If they had to be caring and understanding towards her, before long everyone would have to have a social worker up their arse 24/7.

"I remember the weather changing. It was suddenly a proper summer again and everything in our garden turned green and lush. The year before, we had always sat outside on some small chairs and smoked cigarettes and drank coffee, and I thought it was a shame that he wasn't here, because now our time had finally come. Summer was here. But he was gone."

She scratched her forehead, pushing away a lock of hair that didn't exist.

"After a while, I was allowed to visit him in prison. David wept. He was afraid, he said. Afraid he'd never come out again. Afraid of what would happen to me and Louie. Back then, I thought it would all be fine, that we'd get our old life back, that I had a husband, and my son had a father who could take care of him, but it never worked out like that."

"What about Salki? Didn't you ever hear anything from him?"

"Well, yes, he came by one day and said that his little brother had done something stupid and that he would pay dearly for it. Him? I asked. What about us? What about his new-born son? Salki said that we should enjoy our freedom. There were others who had it worse. Until David was released, he would help us as much as he could. I had figured out that Salki had something to do with the case, so I asked him what he knew. He signalled to me that we were probably being listened to and said that he had had no idea about David's drug smuggling. He gave me an envelope with 10,000 kroner in it while holding a finger in front of his mouth. I don't want your dirty drug money, I said. I can look after myself. Get out of my house! It was the last I heard from him."

"Have you seen him since?"

"No, never."

"I can see you got divorced. Why?"

"Neither of us thought David would be deported. Even the lawyer said that they didn't do that when there was a child in Denmark with a Danish woman. But it didn't work out like that." She looked angry. "Yes, I'm sorry, but it still pisses me off that my son's had to pay the price for this. David got eight years and was deported 'in perpetuity', as it's called in that sterile language, after four years. We visited him in prison, but I couldn't see the point in it any longer. Why should we be married? After all, we'd never be able to live together again."

"But you could have moved down there to be with him, couldn't you?"

She looked as if she was considering hitting him.

"Do you have children yourself? Can't you just shut your face? You might not know anything about Macedonia, but surely you can imagine how it is? Unemployment, no education, no opportunities. David was an Albanian – they're a minority – there's money to be earnt from drugs, whores and weapons. Was that where Louie should grow up?"

Maybe not, but all children and fathers have a right to see each other, thought Axel. He looked down at a fingernail, picked at it a little and shuffled around on the sofa.

"I don't know, but he needed a father, surely?"

"So I should move to Macedonia? After what he had subjected us to? I'd rather he'd cheated on me a hundred times. He said he'd done it for our sake, so that we could have a better life and be financially secure, but I just wanted to have my family in peace. I was furious with him."

"Did you carry on visiting him while he was inside?"

"Yes. I did it for Louie's sake. I didn't know what was going to happen, although I could see it'd be completely impossible, but I still wanted to try to create a relationship between them."

Axel knew the visiting cells in Vestre and some of the other prisons around the country. And he remembered them as impersonal and dank spaces where the inmates either screwed their wives, lovers or whores to bits for a couple of hours or sat together with their children and built houses with the prison's dirty Lego bricks before returning to their small cells.

"Prison left its mark on David. He lost weight, looked worn out, but when Louie came to visit him, he brightened up. Every time, he had made something new for him in the prison workshop. I took Louie out there and handed him over and sat waiting outside until the time had passed. The first few times, Louie would cry when he was going to visit him, but it got better and eventually he would cry when he had to go home. It helped that David could send him away every time with a present he had personally made for him."

"What happened when he was released?"

"They threw him out. Your colleagues put him on a scheduled flight to Skopje, and that was that. We weren't allowed to say goodbye in any other way than by a regular visit to the prison."

"That was in 2000. When did you hear from him after that?"

"He called several times, but I didn't want to talk to him. What use was his longing to me? In the spring of 2001, there was violent fighting where he lived, and I was rung up by a journalist David had been an interpreter for. He came out here and delivered some money David had earnt. There were actually more people who did the same thing."

"When did you hear from David again?"

"One year later, when he was suddenly in Copenhagen. Incognito, he said and laughed. He wanted to see Louie. I let him. He kept saying that the most important thing for him was that we were well. He spent some time with Louie here one afternoon and Louie was happy afterwards. He could remember him quite well and missed having a father. It quickly turned to despair though – but he still adores him. He has all the things he made for him in prison on a shelf in his room. And he tells everyone who will listen that his father has a very important job abroad and that he doesn't have time to come and visit us. The next few times he came, I turned him away, saying he wasn't allowed to see Louie because the boy couldn't handle it. David didn't argue. I'd also met someone who Louie was beginning to like. I had to think of my son."

And yourself, thought Axel, who felt as if he was walking on hot coals every time the subject came up.

"The one doesn't exclude the other. Sons have a right to know the truth about their fathers. How else are they going to build their lives?"

"Louie's built well on the image he had of his father. And he's well on his way, without knowing that his father was deported because of a drug offence."

"Have you ever heard the name Stanca Gutu?"

"No, who's that?"

"I have to ask you where you were Thursday night between midnight and two o'clock in the morning."

"You're joking!"

"No, I'm afraid not."

She shook her head.

"You're bloody incredible."

"If you knew how often the perpetrator in a murder investigation turns out to be one of the victim's nearest and dearest, you wouldn't be so surprised."

"I'm not one of his nearest and dearest. I haven't had anything to do with David for almost 10 years. I was here. With my son."

"Was he asleep?"

"What do you mean? Of course he was asleep."

"So you could have gone out for a couple of hours without him having noticed it."

"What the hell are you talking about? You don't leave your child alone at night. Even if he's asleep. If you do, you're a colossal idiot. What if something happened?"

She looked exhausted.

"Is that all?" she asked, sending him a look full of both anxiety and hurt feelings, but also pleading.

"How are you feeling?"

"I'm angry, sad and confused. Why did he have to die? He didn't deserve that."

Axel had worked with crime and murder for long enough to know that death wasn't usually fair, so he said nothing.

She ran her hands down over her dress and bit her lower lip.

"Is there something you're frightened about?" he asked.

"No, it's OK. It's somehow so tragic, but it's also a kind of closure over something that never stopped gnawing at both Louie and me. What could have been, but never was."

Axel got up and went over to the window. What was she singing? *Je me fous du passé!* I don't give a damn about the past. Not exactly my middle name.

"It won't stop because he's dead," he said, just to say something.

"It's going to."

The conversation was over. He said thanks, went out into the hallway, took his jacket and turned to her.

"Don't misunderstand me. It's invasive, I know, but I have to ask these questions."

She nodded with a resigned smile. They said goodbye on the doorstep. She shook his hand, squeezed it almost. Hers was hot and dry, the sweaty smell from yesterday's visit replaced by something indefinably floral – Axel wasn't sure which smell he liked more. She folded her arms under her breasts, her hands rubbing up and down her forearms as if she was freezing.

"Ring if there's anything," she said.

There was. But it didn't have anything to do with the investigation.

I don't regret anything either, he said to himself as he got into the car.

31

How about those breasts – and that look? Why am I so weak? Fuck it, said Axel, giving the steering wheel two almighty thumps when he got back into the car. It didn't have a damn thing to do with breasts; her story had touched him somewhere else completely.

The lost child. Betrayed. No matter how furious he became at reports of women who in some way or another cut fathers off from seeing their children, this one had hit him deeper. The child having to suffer inhuman deprivation because of adults.

He tried to pull himself together; the pulse in his temples was uncomfortable.

But what have I got from her? That Enver Davidi was more a human being than he was a drug addict, a scumbag and a liar? They were always human beings when you got into the case, both the victims and the perpetrators, and the solution to the mystery was usually hidden in what drove them.

And what drove Davidi? Maybe he wanted to make a packet on a drug deal. Maybe he wanted to see his child again. Maybe it was his love for Louie that drove him – the strongest bond of all, but what sort of person would leave his children in the lurch?

He thought of his own parents, of his mother who, one milky-white foggy morning in March 1977, left the family home and was picked up by another man, whom Axel got to know as Leif. Every other weekend.

He had stood in the window of the villa on Fortebakken and watched her getting into a Ford Taunus, which then disappeared into the white nothingness. No one had said anything. He didn't cry until many months later when he realised one night that she was never going to come back, that he would never again experience her coming into his room, putting a hand on his brow and asking if he had had a bad dream, while the muted sound of the traffic on Grenaavejen rumbled in the background. She was twenty-one years younger than the old patriarch and she had come close to death giving birth to Axel. A fragile soul, his aunt had said about her. He thought of his father, the elegant, well-dressed *bon vivant* with his fixed routines and very firm hand; a consultant surgeon at Risskov Hospital specialising in lobotomy and a member of the city council for the Conservatives. He had never really known what to talk to him about. When he realised that some children actually talked to their parents as equals, he was shocked – they were like two planets each in their own solar system. The old fellow had drowned his sorrows with a new woman just three months after Axel's mother had disappeared, but it hadn't lasted; then there was another and another, and eventually Mona had arrived. And she was still there in the house in Risskov, but his father was gone. He had never really got the colour back in his cheeks again after the divorce, that glow in his eyes, that spark of joy or celebration that was his driving force; even his long tirades and speeches had something monotonous and joyless about them as the years went by and, in the end, cancer had eaten him up. He had never forgiven Axel's mother. She had had three more children with Leif, and Axel had always felt like a second-grade son, a memory of something she would rather have forgotten. A boy who came to visit and had to bring his own toys with him. Every time.

Axel had moved to Copenhagen as soon as he had finished high school and was left with Mona, whom he visited once, at the most twice, a year. They performed their one-act play around Christmas and in the children's school holidays; they knew their roles inside out. Only when Emma came along and suddenly started voicing awkward questions did they get thrown a little off track.

His mobile vibrated. Axel shook himself back to the present. He checked his laptop first. It contained several emails from Darling, witness statements, interview reports, declarations from PET's technical department that both passports were forged, and an analysis of hair and secretions from the balaclava.

A team from Homicide had been to Brøndby Strand and upended Kasper Vang's two-room flat, which contained an impressive collection of steroids but nothing that linked him to the murder of Enver Davidi.

There were several text messages. Cecilie asked if she should bring anything. Expectation, faith, hope, your naked body, your desire. Come to me, love me, he wanted to answer, but he snapped the mobile shut and opened the document on the laptop with the individual interviews of the officers in the cemetery.

In his summary, Darling mentioned that three of them had seen some of their colleagues at a distance whom they couldn't immediately identify. He would have to remember to read those explanations and possibly get hold of the three officers again, but he remembered nothing more, because the paralysis seeped into his consciousness like a poison gas, closing it down in a cold mist. Then came the darkness. He was alone in the cold, with no feeling in his body, just alone. With a heart that swelled and swelled until there was no room for it in his chest and exploded like a star in an orgy of yellow, orange and blood-red liquids. Then it became dark and chilly. He wasn't dead. But it felt like that.

He was woken up by the sound of a car door slamming across the road right outside Laila Hansen's house. Jakob Sonne had got out. Had he just arrived? Axel honked, rolled the window down and waved him over.

"Hey, where have you been? I've tried to get hold of you loads of times in the last few days, man. Why don't you answer my calls?"

His long fringe was swinging from side to side.

"We're busy, Sonne. You've been doing this a long time, you know the score: when a murder investigation like this gets rolling, we're on the job 35 hours a day. We don't know what's going on. And there are constantly new developments in the case. I don't have time to keep the press updated individually over the phone."

"That's something I've often thought about. Our work is similar in many ways, Axel. When I get to work in the morning, I don't know what I'm coming in to either, or where I'll be going and when I'll get off again."

Axel didn't like Sonne addressing him by his first name.

"I clear up and you smear. Our work isn't similar in the fucking slightest. When I'm working, you and the rest of the press are nothing but haemorrhoids up my arse. What are you doing here?"

Sonne tried to look hard, tilting his head to one side.

"I could just as well ask you the same question."

"Don't. If it's the ex you're going for, then show a little tact. She's upset by what's happened."

"Is she? I thought they didn't have anything to do with each other?"

"I can't say any more. What was that information you said you had?"

"Information? What are you talking about?"

"Stop playing hard to get. You won't get anything out of it. You left a message on my mobile saying that you had information about the case, right? Was that just a lie?"

"Oh yeah – no, it wasn't. Martin Lindberg, do you know him?"

Axel didn't turn a hair, but his whole body was listening.

"There are rumours that he's after that young autonomist you say you're looking for."

"After?"

"Yes, wants to get hold of."

"We haven't said we're looking for anyone."

"No, but you've put out a search for a Piller or something like that on police radio. Everyone knows that. We police reporters, those of us covering the disturbances, are one big family and Lindberg – even though he belongs to a rather special section of the press – is part of that family. And he's been asking about the guy."

Maybe it was just a coincidence; maybe it was too good to be true.

"OK, thanks for the information. I don't quite know what to use it for. I guess you're all interested in getting hold of Piver?"

"Some more than others. Do you have anything for me?"

"No, we're working on several different possibilities, but I can't say anything yet."

"Not even off the record? What about the autonomist angle? Has that been ditched? Are you sure it's not one of your own? What about those two officers that News is running all the time now?"

Axel saluted in the naval fashion and rolled up the window to take shelter from a shower of questions he didn't want to answer. Then he turned the ignition key and headed for Emma's kindergarten. It had been a good day so far. He liked Laila Hansen. He had to pick up his daughter and later he would be having a visit from his ex-wife. Maybe it would get even better.

He bawled Edith Piaf's melodramatic classic all the way into town.

32

The electronic chimes of the doorbell brought Axel to his feet. He was nervous. Cecilie's "Hi" crackled faintly through the entry phone as if it was coming from the other side of the globe. He pressed to let her in and she was totally real to look at as her face came floating up in small jerks between the bars of the bannisters. She stood in front of him. There was a smile on her face and a pair of red Hello Kitty wellies under one arm.

They couldn't shake hands, that would be too ridiculous, but the last time they had seen each other, there hadn't been the right atmosphere for any other bodily contact, so Axel didn't know what to do. She reached out to him and gave his upper arm a squeeze.

"May I come in?"

"Yes, of course. She's just fallen asleep."

"That's late. Have the pair of you had a good evening?"

Axel vacuumed her tone of voice to find a shadow of reproach, but it seemed perfectly sincere.

He told her what they had been doing, opened the door a little to Emma's room, so that she could see her sleeping daughter, and then invited her into the living room, where he left her and went out to the kitchen. There was more than half a bottle of red wine left from the other day, a bowl of olives, a lighter. He walked silently back to the living room and got a brief glimpse of how she was walking and looking around the flat, as if it was a woman who had stolen her husband. She also had memories here, even though it had been his private mausoleum of their love for a long time.

It was almost two years since she had last been here.

"It's just the same as ever, though a bit sparsely furnished, or should I say…" she said, looking as if she was sorry about the last bit.

"Would you like a glass of wine?"

She said thank you and sat in the sofa. Axel filled the glasses.

Her gaze was clear and vulnerable, like he hadn't seen it for a long time; her brown eyes with the yellow droplets looked up at him and the slight squint made her more beautiful than anything he had ever seen. She was wearing a grey skirt that fitted tightly around her hips, a checked shirt and a grey jacket, which was more fashionable than business-like. Her hair was gathered at the neck with a cheap, screaming-green, towelling elastic band.

He bent over the table to light the candle and got a whiff of a perfume he didn't recognise – smoke, cinnamon, golden tones.

"How is she?" she asked.

Axel told her about the last few days, but left out the details about the visits to the morgue and the cemetery. They talked a while about how happy they were for Emma and how happy their daughter was for life. There were many sentences, expressions and faces that they could share with each other, and for once it was joy and laughter that accompanied them.

They sat a while without saying anything. She sipped at the wine. Silence reigned between them. From the street came sounds of the buses' diesel engines and the whispers of car tyres on the rainy asphalt.

Cecilie got up and went over to the window.

"How quiet it is here," she said.

"Yes, it's the first time for four days," he replied, getting to his feet and joining her.

The coloured light chains in the window of the Pizzeria Pronto opposite were blinking reassuringly; the door of the church was open and they could hear the sound of a gospel choir. Axel looked at the rain that was like a mist over the street and was splashing out of the drainpipes, through the gutters in the pavements and down the drains.

"Axel?"

He felt her hand on his upper arm, shoulder; she tugged him a little to turn him round and he knew what was about to happen, but couldn't quite believe it. Then she was in his arms and his confusion and nervousness stopped for a second. She turned her face towards him; her lips were soft, familiar yet strange at the same time as he kissed them. She opened her mouth and he threw himself into the opening she was offering him and disappeared. As she slid completely into his embrace and bound her arms around his upper body, he began to weep.

"What's the matter?" she said.

What wasn't the matter? he thought, breathing deeply into his stomach to stop the weeping.

"Should I leave?"

Axel drew her against him.

"No, I want you to stay, it's just… overwhelming."

He immediately regretted the last sentence. He was afraid of giving her any hint of his vulnerability.

Even though she smelt different to how he remembered and dreamt of her, there was still a nuance beneath the perfume, a scent of something that was his, something dry and soft and pure and safe; it smelt like coming home. He had forgotten how slender and fine she was; the bones just beneath her skin, her wrists and calves, the collar bones that emerged as she unbuttoned her shirt and took it off. Her bra and knickers were next to come off; she was slim, her breasts had collapsed a little, her life had left its mark, but she was divine to look at.

He couldn't get out of his clothes; his trousers got stuck and he felt naked before he was. But she moved in to him. And held him. Her hands caused small shocks in his skin as they moved up over his back; he wanted to touch her properly, but was unsure until she took hold of his dick, felt it, testing.

"I'm freezing in here. Can't we go into the bedroom?" she said.

What's happening here?

Axel lay awake by her side. The venetian blinds cut the street lighting into slices on the wall above his bed. He looked at her naked body in the semi-darkness: her pussy, freshly shaved around the dark brown labia, the greasy pubic hair above it, her white skin, her hip sockets framing the skin on her stomach with the two stretch marks like barcodes on each side of her navel, which had turned outwards since Emma was born. Up and down went her breast in a calm rhythm; her nipples had crawled in on themselves. Her lips slightly separated in deep sleep, a secure contour around her mouth, her hair all over the place.

What's happening here?

Cecilie in a backlight on the beach at Naxos with fluttering eyes and freckles from the sun: "Would you like to have a little child with me, Axel Steen?"

What's happening?

Her big eyes filling with tears as he told her how his mother had moved out when he was eight years old and the darkness that came afterwards because he was sure it was his fault that his parents had separated.

What's happening to me?

She loved churches because of their peace and beauty, so he proposed to her in Sainte-Chapelle, certain that it was her greatest wish, and she would be his. When he went down on one knee, she was completely unprepared and began to cry as soon as she understood what he wanted and said "yesyesyes" before an officious French verger came running up and chucked them out to wide grins on the square in front and nervous, interrupted kisses because he was stumbling on the steps.

What's happening?

They used to sneak out of HQ the first few months. He was in Homicide, she was in the DPP and at lunch time they sometimes met down at the harbour or in Tivoli, where they used his warrant card to enter. Once he had picked her up in a patrol car by the central station a block away from HQ and they had driven down to the south harbour. "Isn't this where the whores bring their customers?" she asked him as she pulled up her skirt and crawled up on him, while he struggled with her shirt and bra – "Don't break it, for Christ's sake, I don't have anything else to put on" – and didn't get to answer that the outdoor brothel was actually further along – "fuckme fuckme fuckme". That same evening, they were at a farewell party at Pinden next to the central station for two colleagues who were going to Iraq and she was radiant in a way that had everyone flocking around her, her flushed cheeks, her strapless, red, frilly blouse, her eyes exuding love and joy. He had watched his colleagues' looks and desire and became jealous until he embarrassingly realised that the measure of his jealousy was his own secret infatuation.

What's happening? What's happening? What's happening to me?

His longing for her in the past two years was like a coat he couldn't take off without feeling completely naked. Now she was lying here. But why? He didn't know how to embrace this happiness. Right now she was his, but for how long?

Before she had smelt unfamiliar; now the perfume was just in the background of a mixture of sex and sweat.

She opened her eyes.

"What are you thinking about?"

"I'm thinking about us, about why it all went wrong."

"What do you think?"

"Is there a chance for us? I could cut back on work."

"Do you think you could?"

"Yes, I hope so."

She moved in against him.

"What made you come?" he asked a little later.

"Impulse. I was alone. You never really give up on the person you've had a child with, do you?"

Then sleep took hold of him and laid him down at the bottom of a sea where dreams couldn't reach him.

33

Monday, March 5

It wasn't a dream. She was actually lying beside him and he could touch her; he reached out and grasped her bare shoulder under the duvet, felt her warm skin, and she opened her eyes. It was seven o'clock and Emma would be awake in an hour at the latest. Axel had to decide if Cecilie should be here in bed or if it would be better for her to be sitting dressed in the living room, so that her daughter wouldn't be able to guess she had spent the night there.

She looked at him with that look he knew so well from the old days when she was dragged unwillingly out of sleep: Who are you? What am I doing here? For once, there might be reason to ask the last question.

"What's the time?"

She rolled herself up in the duvet. Axel held her tight and spoke her name.

"Yes, yes, I will" she said, stretching, lying and staring a little up at the ceiling.

"What a… what a mess."

But she smiled as she said it.

She stood up with the duvet around her, went in and fetched her clothes, then sat down at the foot of the bed.

"Wouldn't it just be enough if I'm out of bed by the time she wakes up, so that it looks like I've just come by with the boots?"

Axel told her that he was counting on having a free day, even though the investigation was new. She asked about it and he told her about Enver Davidi, the hotel, the footage from TV2, without telling her how he had got his fingers on it, and he jumped over the autopsy, the meeting at PET and the passport. And he didn't tell her about his past history with Enver

Davidi's ex-wife either, but Cecilie had fastened on her in the story.

"You sound as if you're attracted to her."

"What do you mean?"

"You sound like you're completely fascinated with her."

"Not at all. Not with her, with the investigation."

"Oh yes, of course," she said.

Her irony was the kind you wrap murder weapons in. She got out of bed and started putting on her knickers and bra.

Axel felt annoyed; it was as if it were doomed to fail.

Cecilie sneaked out to the bathroom with the rest of her clothes in her arms. Did she regret it? Jens Jessen hadn't disappeared, nor had their withered past. And what was he going to do now? After two years struggling to get free, had he let it all go again in one night with her? He had a bad feeling in his gut.

He could hear sounds from Emma's room. At the same time, the door to the bathroom slammed open and Cecilie came stamping through the hallway, the living room and into the bedroom with a lump of hash in her hand. She held it as if she were a football referee with a red card. But the look on her face showed she was really mad. Before she had time to start yelling at him, Emma was standing by her side.

"Mummy! You're here," she shouted.

And threw herself into Cecilie's arms, while she flung the little slab in Axel's face over her daughter's shoulder and gave him a black look full of anger.

What fucking business is it of hers if I smoke hash? He tried to take courage from the question, but knew very well that the last residue of their togetherness the night before was gone. The respectable lawyer with a hash-smoking cop from the lower ranks – it was a doomed pairing.

Emma had torn herself away and was telling her mother everything she had done in one long mishmash.

"We were in the cinema and saw Cinderella and we ate pizza and I was at the cemetery counting squirrels and there were a lot of policemen and I tried to wake up the old men lying asleep in the drawers over at the Swede…"

"What did you do?"

Cecilie's smile was totally mechanical; she screwed up her eyes and they shone as if it was impossible for her to understand what her daughter had just said.

"Why are you looking at me so strangely, Mummy?"

"Where were you, did you say?"

Emma looked at Axel, who nodded resignedly.

"Tell Mummy, sweetheart."

"We were over at the Swede's and I saw a film on his computer, but then I got bored and went for a walk. Inside a room there were a lot of old men in some drawers sleeping and they were cold and I tried to wake them up but they wouldn't get up…"

"That's fine, my love, now just go and watch a cartoon while I talk to Daddy, and then we're going for a drive."

Axel crawled out of bed and started to put on his clothes, but he had only got as far as his underpants when he was hit by a tidal wave of white hatred.

"What are you thinking, you great dolt? You're a drug addict and you take your daughter with you to an autopsy and leave her in the mortuary where she can go poking around among dead bodies."

"Cecilie, it was an accident – nothing happened."

"I'm taking her with me now! You damn well bet I am! How could you be so utterly irresponsible? You drag my daughter along to a murder scene and then down to a corpse cellar."

She stomped around the bedroom with tears tumbling down her cheeks and tugged at the duvets and the sheet.

"Where the hell is my watch? Help me, for goodness' sake!"

Axel knelt down and looked under the bed at a snowy landscape of dust and fluff balls. The tears weren't for Emma, he could feel that much.

"I don't understand…" She shook her head. "… how I could ever…"

She found her watch.

"What do you think you're doing, Axel? Are you smoking hash? Are you an addict? I don't understand you."

"I'm not an addict," he said, knowing very well it was a lie. "I use it to help me sleep," he continued, at the same time knowing that she wouldn't believe him for a second. "I can't sleep at night."

She looked at him with her eyes wide open; they seemed even wilder because of her little squint.

"You're crazy, man. Whatever will it be next? I'm taking Emma with me. Right now. And then I'll have to reconsider whether this is the right arrangement."

Her talent as a lawyer was indisputable as she struck the final blow.

"And if you think I could ever dream of coming back to you, then forget it. You're insane – I will never live with a man who makes such insane choices."

She went into the living room.

"Emma, darling…"

"Why are you shouting at each other?"

"Come, sweetheart, it's nothing. You're coming with Mummy now. You're going to have a day off from kindergarten. We can visit Grandma and play with Frida," she said in a sugar-sweet voice that didn't fool Emma one bit.

"But I want to stay here with Daddy."

"Don't you want to visit Grandma and go for a walk with Frida?"

Frida weighed 15 kilos more than Axel and had four legs.

"Can I hold Frida myself?"

The prospect took hold of the little girl's feelings.

Axel stood in the door. Now he just wanted peace, to have them out.

"Of course, Emma. Just go with Mummy. We'll see each other again soon."

In your dreams, said Cecilie's face as she took her daughter's hand and left.

34

Axel lay completely still on the sofa trying to gain control over his body. He thought he felt pains in his stomach and back, and when he looked at the hairs on his chest – or what was left of them after the last ECG shave – they were vibrating like the bass at a heavy-metal concert. He closed his eyes and breathed deeply. He couldn't find any peace of mind. He felt the blood flowing through his veins, the thick, poisoned, tar-like blood that roared along like a tsunami, dragging everything with it on its way to the heart, where it would aggregate and make the chambers finally give up the ghost with a disappointed glug, an old man's bloody cough, a final belch of life.

He was ready to go down to the emergency ward and have himself admitted, but a call came from HQ that Kasper Vang wanted to talk to him.

For a moment, it suppressed the imminent heart attack and all the memories of the morning with Cecilie.

Axel biked in to HQ, where he called the Police Headquarters' prison and asked them to bring Vang down.

While he was waiting, he called Henriette Nielsen.

"Is there anything new from BGP?"

"There's a lot of unease around a consignment of cocaine. They're talking about fifteen boxes of coke that have vanished. I'll email you the audio files, but it doesn't seem to be something they've had their hands on, more like something they've heard about or been offered. And it's very likely it can be linked to Davidi's death."

"Why?"

"Because he's mentioned in one of the conversations as the Albanian who had contacted Moussa's henchman."

"So you think that strengthens the likelihood of it being a drugs-related murder?"

"I don't know, but it's worth following up on. In a conversation earlier today, they talked about his ex-wife."

"What did they say?"

"They talked about there being some Danish whore that he'd been married to and if she knew anything about it. One of them would try to find out."

"Maybe we should warn her."

"Already done. We've given her personal protection."

Kasper Vang looked serious; gone was all that boastful pugnacity. Axel asked him to sit down.

"You two are out in all the media now. Your bunking-off is running on a continuous loop on TV2 News. Is there something you want to get off your chest?"

"Yes, there is. As I said before, it doesn't have anything to do with the murder. I have a lady friend who lives nearby. I went over to her."

"Hang on a minute. Slow down. You were on guard duty with your old friend, Jesper Groes. You'd been told to patrol along the wall from 23:00. What happened there?"

"We'd nicked three autonomists earlier in the evening. They tried to climb over as they were being pursued by some officers outside. We handed them over. The rest of the evening and night, we stood in the same place, smoked, chatted to each other – there was fuck-all going on. So I texted a lady I know. And she gradually got me warmed up."

"So what happened?"

"She suggested that I came by. She was home alone."

"What did your partner say to that?"

"He was against it. But I didn't tell him who she was. In the end, I convinced him to let me go."

"Why did you take off your combat uniform?"

"I wasn't going to go through the streets of Nørrebro alone in that get-up."

Axel looked at him, waited, and when nothing happened, he gestured for him to continue.

"So, yes, then I went over to her. An hour and a half."

Axel groaned.

"What's her number?"

"I don't want her mixed up in this."

"What kind of idiot are you? Do you think you've been sitting in here all night just for fun? Don't you think I have something else to do other than talk to an idiot like you? What's her number?"

"She's married."

"I couldn't fucking care less. Give me her name and number."

Axel thought he recognised the surname and called the number immediately.

"Hello, this is Axel Steen from Copenhagen Police Homicide Division. I'm sitting here with Kasper Vang, who's in serious trouble because he disappeared for two hours from his guard duty the night between Thursday and Friday. He says he was with you. Is that true?"

Axel listened to the woman and then hung up. He shook his head. It was farcical, but could well be true, unfortunately.

"Will it come out? Will he find out?"

"Of course it'll come out, you dumbo, of course he'll find out. You get off a murder charge, but I seriously hope he gives you a bloody good hiding. Get out of my office. Now!"

He called Rosenkvist and left a message on his answering machine – it would certainly make him happy. A rank-and-file cop skipping off from guard duty to screw his division leader's wife.

35

Axel threw himself into the reports covering the previous day and night's work. The best undercover man in Copenhagen Police, Bjarne from Narcotics, had been to Christiania and shown round pictures of Piver. Several people had seen him during the Friday. One of the local drinkers, Black Arne, had been trying to bum a cigarette off the young autonomist when he had been chased away by a man. He had been too out of it to describe him. It wasn't much, but it was worth a follow-up. Maybe he would be clearer now and might remember more.

He found his bike and rode up to Langebro. A cop would never arrive on an old man's bike and, besides, his clothes were civilian enough for him not to look like an agitator in a stage-managed disguise – woolly ski hat, hoodie, big duvet jacket, sports shoes and jeans or combat trousers – that the pushers and their guards could spot at 100 yards. After Langebro he swung down on the footpath by the ramparts. He stopped at a bench and took out his mobile. He had once sat here with Cecilie on a summer's afternoon that became night without them noticing, and smoked cigarettes and drank cold beers and chatted and kissed; that was when they had just got to know each other. The memories didn't tug at him, they were very far away, he realised.

There were no messages from Cecilie. He was missing his daughter. Had Emma been very affected by the quarrel? He tried to convince himself that it didn't matter, but he knew that was a lie; she walked around both of them like a mouse whenever there was an argument, so as not to risk hurting anyone. Five years old! Fuck you, Axel Steen. A child's loyalty is boundless. Emma was no exception. Adults who constantly put that loyalty to the test were the worst of the worst in his book.

Axel got back on his bike, rode out along the ramparts, crossed Torvegade and continued across Prinsessegade to the old main entrance.

Here he got off and walked the bike past three guards, nodding to one of them as if they knew each other, quelling all scepticism.

The booths on Pusher Street were illuminated, and the plates of hash lay there alongside the chillums and all kinds of ganja symbols and rastafari knick-knacks. He was sure that one of the police cameras was in a flat somewhere in the block opposite, so he chose a booth that was hidden behind the trees and the Loppen music venue. 10 grams and three joints cost him 700 kroner – it was enough to keep him going for a couple of weeks. Then he asked around for Black Arne, who featured in their reports as a homeless person who had lived more or less on the streets for 20 years, but Axel immediately got a suspicious counter-question which he parried with a story that he was his cousin and that their grandmother was dead.

"Arne is everywhere, man," was the answer.

"But where is he now?"

"Is there any inheritance in it?"

"Sadly not."

"He could bloody well use it, the way he goes around begging."

The man looked over at a tree trunk that lay like a kind of fence at the entrance to Pusher Street.

"Sometimes he sits over there, other times he tries to bum dog-ends off us, but most of the time he vegges out down at Woodstock, or if the weather's good, in the sun down at the shopping centre."

Axel said thanks, locked his bike to a drainpipe and walked towards the Woodstock, Christiania's oldest pub, always packed with regulars hanging over the tables from the early morning, drinking coffee and beer and smoking cigarettes and joints. The air was thick with smoke from the wood-burning stove and the hash and tobacco fumes, but if you could blend in here, you would get information quickly. In these surroundings, it was one thing to sit down at a table with Greenlanders or the old pushers with a beer or smoking a joint, but another thing completely to start asking for a particular person – it could quickly lead to trouble. Axel hoped he would be able to spot Black Arne based on the picture he had seen of him.

He walked in through the broken door, bought a beer and stood by the bar. Then he took out a joint; he knew it was his admission ticket. A cop would never go that far to disguise himself.

He lit it at a candle on the bar.

"Hey you, none of that; put it out or take it outside now," said the bartender.

Axel couldn't believe his ears but obliged by nipping the lighted end off in an ashtray.

"What's that all about?"

"We'll be shut down by the filth if people smoke joints in here."

"Fuck's sake," said Axel. "Then give me two gold labels."

Axel paid. And looked around the foggy room.

"Have you seen Black Arne?"

"Who's asking?"

"I'm his cousin."

"Yeah, and I'm Father Christmas. He's sitting over there. The hat with a feather in it."

Axel said thanks and walked down the row of mismatched benches and black-holed tables which people were sitting at or lying slumped over.

He put a gold label in front of Black Arne, sat down and said cheers.

The face under the hat looked like a lunar landscape; eyes like two oily puddles and a nose like a small tuber between them. There were so many craters that you could play Kalaha in them.

"To what do I owe the honour?" said Arne with a nasal twang.

"I'm looking for a guy you met on Friday. He disturbed you as you were trying to bum a cigarette off a young autonomist."

"You're not a cop, are you? In here?"

Arne wasn't so far off in his own fog not to know that that didn't follow. Maybe he would be able to remember more after all.

"No, cops don't give free beers. Who are you then?"

The man next to him, a Greenlander with a completely closed face, slumped against Arne, who pushed him back over the table.

"I'm a journalist. I've been looking for that young guy and trying to figure out what's happened to him."

"Journalist? I've met a lot of journalists. They want to follow me around the city – once there was even one who wanted to walk with me for several days, but he wasn't up to it. He said he was freezing! Ha! Are you freezing too?"

"No, I'm never freezing, but how about you emptying that beer, and we go outside and talk and smoke this?"

Axel took the stubbed joint out of his pocket.

"Yessir, now you're talking," said Arne, getting to his feet.

They went outside and sat on a box under a roof overhang.

"He reminds me a lot of you, big bastard, who doesn't fit in here, but has dressed the part a bit. Journalist, ha!" said Arne.

"What do you mean?"

"Yeah, you're all bloody journalists, aren't you? Or are you? Maybe you're just cops in disguise."

Black Arne was totally clear. Axel laughed, counting on the homeless man not caring whether he was one or the other as long as there was beer, cigarettes and a joint in the offing and no risk of trouble.

"You're not quite as stoned as you make out. What did he say to you?"

"He said I should get lost and then he pushed me away. He wasn't all that pleasant, I can tell you – just his look was enough to make me leave."

"How do you mean?"

"He looked at me as if to say it would be painful if I didn't do what I was told."

"What did he look like?"

Black Arne described a man about the same height as Axel, wearing a hoodie, sweater, black military boots, beard stubble. It was impossible to say whether he had short or long hair, but Arne thought he had hair on his head.

"I heard a name as I walked away. The young guy asked if the other one was Martin."

On his way into town, his mobile rang. It was Frank Jensen, his old colleague, calling from Skopje.

"I got your message. I do have something for you, but it mustn't go any further."

"Of course not."

"I was asked to find accommodation and a car, and brief two PET people when they were down here back in the autumn. The first time for four days, second time for one, but that was in January."

"Let me guess! Kettler and Henriette Nielsen."

"Yes, well done – though the second time there were three of them. There was a slick legal type with them, who blinked all the time as if he had something in his eye."

"His name's Jens Jessen. It's just tics."

"Exactly. I couldn't get anything out of them about why they were here. But they were staying at the Eurohotel outside Skopje and they used the car quite a lot – back and forth to Tetovo every day, I'd think."

"Why do you think that?"

"Because the local police up there were after them a couple of times and checked their papers, I was contacted without them knowing about it."

"What about Enver Davidi – did the police ask about him?"

"No, they were very secretive, but maybe they should have asked."

"Yes, maybe. How did the PET people behave?"

"Behave? They behaved just like those guys do: confident in a rather comical way, completely lacking any sense for where they were. But her, Henriette Nielsen…"

"What about her?"

"She's visited me many times since."

"What?"

"In my dreams. Wet dreams. I love tall women. And she was definitely the most appealing of the three."

"You haven't changed a bit. What do you think they were up to?"

"I think they were trying to recruit an agent to infiltrate the Danish drug market. And, after what you've told me, he may very well have been called Enver Davidi."

36

Darkness had fallen as he rode out towards Rentemestervej. It was actually quickest to ride out along Åboulevarden, but Axel had to pick up his car on the way, and he always liked to approach Nørrebro over Dronning Louises Bro. The eight large glass globes illuminated the bridge and the pennants were snapping crisply in the wind. He looked up at the advertising. The Irma hen logo was dropping its nostalgic neon eggs down the façade above Sortedamsdosseringen. Green, red, white.

In front of him lay Nørrebrogade like a hole in the row of houses, an opening into a massive body of stone and steel, asphalt and houses, backyards and hiding places. His town. Life and light.

He trod on the pedals and allowed himself to be sucked onto the sparkling strip: dazzling headlights, illuminated buses, emergency call-out lamps and hundreds of small flashes from the diode bike lights, all surrounded by the colourful signs from the 24-hour mini-markets, bars and pubs. The stench of petrol blended with the scent of cinnamon, cumin, meat and deep fat fryers from the many shawarma bars.

When he had put the bike in the yard, he went up to his flat and changed into some warmer clothes. The two red wine glasses from last night were still in the living room. It felt like a hundred years ago that they had been drinking from them.

He drove past his colleagues in the civilian car and parked 20 yards from the house. There was a light on in the living room. He slammed the car door and went over and knocked on his two colleagues' window; when one of them rolled it down, he suggested they take a break and get something to eat. They were supposed to be finishing in three hours and he was letting them off early.

Then he got back in his car. And was out like a light straight away.

He was out hunting. In the cemetery. He was walking down the path from Jens Bang's gravedigger house. There was a man in full police uniform walking in front of him. He could hear his daughter singing *The sun it is so red, Ma* a little further down, and he was on his way to her. He knew she was sitting on a gravestone in her princess dress with innocence shining out of her completely open blue eyes, but he couldn't reach her. He had to get past the man, he had to get alongside him and see his face. The closer he came to him, the fainter his daughter's song sounded. But he didn't give up, he ran, his heart burning through his transparent chest. He could see it pumping blood through veins and arteries, the muscles around it trembling. He reached out for the man and threw him to the ground, and just as he saw his face, he heard his daughter scream.

Axel was woken up by the sound of a purring engine. A car was driving slowly past; the driver was wearing a hoodie and slowed down outside Laila Hansen's house. He looked towards the glowing windows, then accelerated and drove off.

Axel took a note of the number, called the car registry and was told that the car had been stolen in Hundige yesterday. There was good reason to go inside now.

She opened the door quickly, as if she were expecting someone, but this time she didn't look frightened when she saw him; she smiled. The dress had been replaced by a big sailor's sweater and jeans. She wasn't wearing makeup, which made her eyes lighter and her face younger and more vulnerable than the last time he had seen her.

"Hi. Do you want to come in?"

"Yes. Thanks."

Axel was still shaken by his dream.

"Louie's just on his way to bed; you can say hello to him if you want."

Axel was self-conscious about having to say hello to the boy. Did he know that his Dad was dead?

He followed her into the kitchen where the 11-year-old boy was sitting with a cup of milk and a biscuit. A blue wax cloth on the table, two small tealight candles in glass bowls. He was slight, freckled, with delicate sweeping lips and a Cupid's bow, an almost female mouth. His features were dark, but he had his mother's eyes. They were red and swollen.

Axel shook hands and Louie cast small glances at him, while Laila Hansen told him to take a seat and asked if he would like some coffee.

"Is there anything new?" she said.

Axel sent her a look intended to show that there was, but that it wasn't something the boy should hear.

"Louie knows what's happened to his father so you're welcome to say whatever it is."

Axel had sat with relatives a hundred times and knew that the only way was to say things as they were, but how was he going to tell them they had suspected a police officer but that he was now cleared and they were starting again from scratch? To an 11-year-old boy who had just lost his father?

"We're getting closer, but not close enough."

The boy looked at Axel as if he didn't understand him.

Laila Hansen looked expectantly at him.

"I'll certainly tell you something as soon as I can."

He thought she looked disappointed.

Louie looked from one to the other.

"Do you want to see my new gun?" he said, the worried expression evaporating and being replaced by excitement.

"Come on, Louie, upstairs with you now," said Laila.

"Do you?" asked the boy again, as if he were willing to make Axel privy to a big secret.

"Yes, I'd like that."

He ran into the living room and came back with a faithful copy of Axel's service pistol, a soft-gun version of the Heckler & Koch USP Compact.

"Do you have one like this… a real one?" asked the boy.

"Yes."

"May I see it?"

"I don't have it with me."
"Have you shot anyone with it?"
"Yes."
"Did they die?"
Axel lied.
"No."
"My friend has an AK-47 – it's so cool."

Laila went out into the hallway with her son.
Axel watched her.
She turned before taking the first step up the stairs.
"Will you stay a while?"
"Yes. I'll stay."
He walked into the living room that overlooked the front garden and looked out of the window. The street lights were shining through a weak evening mist; the road was still. There were movements and shadows from candles in the yellow windows of the house opposite.

Did she know how attracted he was to her? She was beautiful in a really simple and sensuous, sincere way, spoke her mind and looked him in the eye in a way that made him want to throw himself at her. And he thought there was something about the way she expressed herself that he recognised. He saw in her something of his own sorrow, he recognised the pain, the longing to belong. At the same time, she was carrying the whole case within her. He couldn't get rid of the feeling that, in some way or another, she was holding the key to it in her hand, whether she knew it or not. He had to try and hold back on her until he knew what was going on. He made that promise to himself.

When she came down the stairs to the hallway, he was still standing by the window and looking out onto the street, lying there in the pale, yellow light of the street lamps. She had taken off her sweater, even though it was slightly chilly. A white cotton T-shirt, a light brown leather belt with small rivets and scratches, a little bit of her midriff crawling over the edge.

"Are you looking after me now?" she said, searchingly.

"Yes, aren't you happy with that?"

"Yes. Very."

Her face opened like a hand, the blue eyes were so dark that he could hardly hold their gaze. It seemed that she couldn't either; she put a hand to her brow and let out a sound like a cross between a sigh and a snigger. Axel suddenly felt his tiredness all the way down in his legs, as though everything in his body was seeping downwards because, for a moment, he had relaxed and was giving his all to something other than the investigation.

She rescued him when she nodded towards the window.

"Is someone after me?"

"Not at present. The street's completely empty. But I wouldn't be too sure with Moussa's boys. They're crazy."

"It's funny, I've known them since they were really small. I lived in the neighbourhood for years, you know. And David and his brother probably played with them."

"Yes, exactly. And that's why they think you may have something to do with the consignment that Davidi allegedly had with him up here."

"It sounds so unlikely. I thought he was finished with that shit."

"To be honest, I don't think there's much in it either."

"What do you mean?"

"I don't believe he's come through customs with 15 kilos of cocaine, but the people from Pladsen may still believe it. And they'll do anything to get their hands on it if they think it's somewhere out here."

"Should I be afraid?"

She didn't look in the least afraid, but she was asking anyway, and Axel got the feeling that the conversation was now following an ancient track that only led to one place, so he had to try to get it back on course.

"Not at present. Not while I'm here."

"But what are you actually doing here? I thought you were in charge of the whole investigation."

"I am. So much so that I could send those two guys home and take over."

"So it's not a kind of punishment to be here?"

"I don't see it as a punishment."

"That's good. I'll do my best to stop it feeling like one."

She smiled and held his gaze so that a crater of desire opened up in his stomach. Then she came towards him. There were barely four inches between them. It was wrong, but it was too good to be true. What was it his old boss had said? "We beat up the suspects; we comfort the relatives; we fuck the witnesses." Laila Hansen belonged to at least two of the three categories, but Axel couldn't really decide which.

She looked at his chest, cast a shy look up at him, and stroked him on the outside of his shirt with her palm.

"You're afraid of dying, aren't you?"

"Maybe – aren't we all?"

Her fingers slid over the shirt.

"Not so much…" back and forth, where there were now small stiff bristles, "… that we get our hearts tested all the time."

"It's a coincidence that you just…"

"Shhhh, it doesn't matter. You're alive, you know. You're alive. I can feel it."

He looked down into her eyes and kissed her quickly with an open mouth; her tongue was hard and greedy, she tasted slightly sweet, of bolognese or ketchup, but it disappeared in the scent of flowers and sweat from her neck, which he pressed his lips against and bit as she stretched it and ran her hands through his hair.

He fumbled with her clothes while she held his shoulder with one hand and grasped his neck with the other. He couldn't get her buttons undone; she was trying his trousers – it was ridiculous. She giggled.

"Come on," she said, tugging at his belt. "I want you now."

Then she tried his shirt. She had more luck with that. She went totally still when she had undone three buttons and had one hand on his chest. She looked up at him while her hands slid over the hairless skin.

Exposed.

She opened his shirt completely and kissed him there.

"You're alive," she whispered.

He drew her face to his mouth, kissed her, and opened her bra. Her breasts flowed out into his hands. What was that Love Shop line? "My Masterpiece". He kissed them.

Her jeans were already down around her ankles, but as he knelt down and started pulling her knickers off, relishing the smell of her vagina and looking forward to drilling his tongue into her, he heard the sound of a car stopping, the engine continuing a while and then shutting down. He hesitated, but it wasn't until he heard the three beats from car doors slamming that he knew something bad was on its way. He threw her down on the sofa.

"What the hell…?"

"There's someone coming," he whispered.

He crawled out into the hallway, went through to the kitchen and took Louie's gun down from the table while assessing the height of the house. Could they see them through the windows? No, they would have to be six foot six tall and none of the boys from Pladsen were. He took out his mobile and found the emergency number. Should he ask for help now? He had an idea, thought it through once more and then put the mobile back in his pocket. Meanwhile, Laila was back on her feet with her trousers on and now stood in the door out to the hallway looking at him. Not frightened or at a loss, as many others would have been.

The doorbell rang. She shrugged her shoulders and turned her hands outwards, as if asking him what to do. There was some muttering outside. Hammering on the door.

"Open up, lady. We've seen you. We have to talk."

Axel crawled over to her. Whispered.

"Is there a way into the garden?"

"Yes, through the kitchen, three steps down to the back door, it's not locked."

"Count to 30, before opening. Keep them out until then. Shout to them that you're coming but don't stand behind the door when you shout."

"But…"

37

Axel was outside before Laila had time to protest any further. Out through the kitchen door to the backyard.

"Open up, you dirty whore, or we'll smash the door in!" he heard one of them shout.

Then he was in the yard, in darkness, where they couldn't see him. He retreated into the shadow of a black-stained board fence that separated Laila's plot from the neighbour's.

Three young guys, baggy jeans, duvet jackets, fur-lined hoods, Canadian Goose and Timberland boots or Nike trainers. All three with closely shaved heads, apart from a four to five-inch-wide strip from neck to forehead, just a couple of millimetres long. Tribal cut 2200 N, his hairdresser had called it.

The guy at the front who had just hammered on the door looked familiar.

"Come on, we're going in," he said, taking hold of the door. At that moment, Laila opened it.

Axel was only fifteen feet from them now.

"You're going nowhere. Put your hands in the air, all three of you, or I'll shoot your legs off."

They froze. The one who had been doing the talking glanced over his shoulder.

"Fuck, it's akrash," he said.

"Don't make a move! Lie down with your hands over your head. Take it slow. All three of you. Now!"

Axel found a Walther pistol and a jack-knife on one of them and a flick-knife on another.

Laila Hansen's face came into sight in front of them. She had put her sweater back on, her arms folded under her breasts.

"Should I call the police?" she said.

"Go back inside. I am the police," he said to her.

Then he turned to the one who seemed to be the leader.

"I recognise you. What's your name?"

"Fuck you, akrash, we ain't done nothing, why you waving a gun at us?"

Where was it he had met him before? In his memory, he swung down Vester Voldgade to the place on the green central verge where a Latvian au pair girl had been raped by a lowlife from Amager three years earlier, softened up on a cocktail of Bacardi breezers, speed and coke. He had asked for her help to get a car unlocked, after which he had knocked her down with a half-bottle of Smirnoff and raped her in the grass at three o'clock in the morning. For the next two hours, he had dragged her through the Inner City. After fifteen years working on murder and rape cases, Axel knew the crime scenes like little black pinheads on the map of perverted lust that was etched into his consciousness. Nikolaj Church, where he had ripped all her clothes off and tried to fuck her up against the church wall, but had been disturbed by heckling from other people on their way home from the city, not angry heckling, but a group of young men egging him on and one who wanted to join in. And later, a kindergarten playground in the Inner City, where he had forced her over a five-foot-high fence and fucked her in all her holes before leaving her with the unoriginal but effective closing remark: I'll kill you if you say anything!

Linda Ulmanis was 19 years old. She had been paralysed with fear from the start. Running away or shouting for help was impossible for her on a two-hour rape tour in the morning hours, where they had been seen by hundreds of people who didn't lift a finger.

The perpetrator had threatened her, but he had taken off his shirt during the rape and revealed a medium-sized tattoo of some runes that stretched from his collarbone down over his arm to his biceps. Ulmanis could give a precise description of him and with the aid of a police artist they made a sketch of the tattoo, which was immediately sent out to the press. Axel had known that somewhere in Greater Copenhagen the man was sweating, fully aware that it was only a matter of time.

Axel remembered the expression in the eyes of the man when he opened the door to the little two-room flat on Amager. As if there was no one home behind the forehead, no hint of recognition, just an inane smile. A baby had been crying in the background.

He had felt the twitch in his muscles, the urge to grab hold of him and wipe that inane smile away with blood. But it disappeared the more he looked into those eyes.

"You don't think it's me, surely?"

"I don't think anything. I just want to see your tattoo."

The guy had lifted up his shirt, some cheap polyester stuff, and there it was. It looked exactly like it, but there were some others which did too. They photographed him and the tattoo and took a mouth swab.

Ulmanis could identify him. The DNA matched. Four days later they went out and picked him up.

"Now I'm going to have those pakis after me too," he said in the car on the way in to HQ. His voice was thick with defeat and hash abuse.

"What do you mean?" asked Axel.

"Yeah, well, she was a paki or something like that, wasn't she?"

This sentence had been included in the police report; it was mentioned at the preliminary hearing; it was quoted in the newspapers; and it cost him two teeth and a broken jaw three days later in detention, when he was caught by a one-and-a-half-kilo dumb-bell in the weight training room in Vestre Prison, where the prison staff had let his identity slip. The young guy who had swung the weight was now lying on the ground in front of Axel and panicking. Kamal was his name.

"I don't know what the fuck you're talking about, man. We were lost and we just wanted to ask the lady here for directions and then you come and you're fucking akrash and now we're lying here. I don't get a thing. This is police violence."

Axel bent down and pressed a knee in his back.

"Do you want to feel some real police violence?"

"You're sick in the head, akrash."

Axel put strips on Kamal behind his back and did the same with the other two. Then he took the phone out of Kamal's jacket pocket and ran through the address book.

"Which one is Moussa? Is it M or Morten or Big M? Let me guess! Fantasy lost out to deference, and it became Big M."

"What are you doing, akrash, I don't know any Moussa."

"No, of course you don't know Moussa, because you're the thickest paki in Nørrebro, right? Everybody knows who Moussa is, even those two morons you've got with you, but you don't know him. Let's hope the Mouse knows you, so you get some help when you're inside serving your couple of years for threatening behaviour and attempted violence towards a witness in a murder case. You're going to need it."

"Go fuck your mother, akrash, I haven't threatened that bitch with shit."

"Yeah, well you won't be fucking your mother for a long time, you little shithead. The closest you're going to get to sex is being buggered by a 25-stone Hell's Angel with a nail in his dick."

According to PET, Kamal was Enver Davidi's contact with Moussa and, although Axel had promised not to approach Moussa and his crowd, Kamal had fallen as if from heaven, and now he was lying here waiting to be squeezed like a ripe orange.

Once again, he dug his knee into the young man's back. And pressed the toy pistol into his cheek.

"I need to know something now. From you. There's no one here to help you and if you don't tell me what I want to know, I'll shoot you in the leg. Both legs, then you'll be an invalid in a wheelchair for the rest of your life. I know you've spoken on the phone with Enver Davidi."

"You're sick, man, I have witnesses if you hurt me."

"Then I'll hurt them afterwards, you little shit. Do you think their words will be worth more than a policeman's?"

"Let me go, man. I don't know anyone with that name."

Axel could hear his fear in the first syllable.

"You might not know him by that name, but he's Salki's little brother, he was from Macedonia, Albanian, and he brought some drugs with him up here, which he was going to sell to you, coke, fifteen big ones. Now he's dead. Who killed him? Why?"

"I don't know what you're talking about…"

Axel released the safety catch on Louie's gun. It was a sound from the film world that had no basis in reality, but he knew that it would work on this guy.

"Your time's running out."

He moved the gun down to the back of his thigh and pressed the muzzle as hard as he could into the muscle. Then he fired.

Kamal screamed. More from shock than pain, as the little plastic ball slammed against his thigh.

"Hey, take it easy, man, wait a minute. I spoke to him, but he didn't say nothing about no coke, he wanted a meeting."

He hesitated.

"With you?"

"Yeah, but nothing came of it. He said he had something that would interest us. I didn't know what it was all about. We only found out about the snow after he died."

"What do you mean?"

"I don't know. Everyone's chasing some snow that's disappeared. There's rumours about another seller."

"Who is it?"

"I don't know, man."

Axel was satisfied. He relaxed the pressure and stood up. Kamal was lying on a wet patch.

Axel dialled the number for Big M. It was picked up immediately.

"What's up?"

"You're speaking to Axel Steen from Copenhagen Police. Don't hang up. This will only take 30 seconds. Your errand boy Kamal is here at my feet chewing the asphalt with his two friends. And in a short while, a van will be coming to drive them down to HQ. They're in line for a couple of years in the can for threatening behaviour and possession of weapons, but that's not why I'm calling. I'm calling to say that I know what you're looking for and I know something that you'd like to know. We should have a meeting."

"I don't know what you're talking about."

"I'll be sitting in Apoteket tonight at midnight. Meet me there."

The line cut off.

"You idiot, akrash, you don't talk to Moussa like that. He'll crush you," wheezed Kamal.

"I thought you didn't know him."

Axel took out his own mobile and called the duty officer.

"I have three rotten bananas lying on their stomachs at Rentemestervej 24. They're some of Moussa's boys from Pladsen and they need to be picked up now. They've threatened a woman we have under protection. And possession of weapons. We need a new observation team out here."

Laila Hansen appeared in the door.

"Louie is awake. I'm going up to him. Do you need me for anything else?"

He looked at her. She didn't mean what he hoped. The distance was back.

"No, I'll be back tomorrow. There are several things I'd like to talk to you about. They'll provide more security tonight."

The first police cars arrived in the space of two minutes, the blue flashes bringing people flocking out of their houses. Axel knew it wasn't good for Laila to be in the spotlight; it never would be in a small residential neighbourhood like this, but he couldn't do anything about it now. He waited for the transport van and the operations chief and briefed them on the situation before going back to his own car.

His whole body was tense and looking forward to the meeting with Moussa. It was 21:15. He would be meeting him in just under three hours. There was only one thing he needed, and the only person who could help him with that was a lanky woman from the intelligence service, who, from the first moment he saw her, had looked like bad conscience was about to break her. That needed to be addressed now.

He called Henriette Nielsen and agreed to pick her up in front of her flat in Frederiksberg.

38

If Axel had thought that Henriette Nielsen would break down in tears and reveal PET's game plan with Enver Davidi, he quickly had to think again.

"What the hell's this all about? Blågårds Plads is my territory. And the same goes for Moussa and his people… Meeting with Moussa! You must be crazy. I'm ringing Kettler now."

She was angry, smelt of wine, and Axel wondered if she had been drinking alone or if he had ruined a romantic evening.

"You're not ringing anyone."

"What do you mean?"

"Or you'd have done that already. Stay here and listen to what I have to say and then you can do what you want afterwards, but I doubt it will be Kettler you'll be calling."

"I think you're making a big mistake," she said tiredly. She rubbed her face with both hands and stroked a lock of hair away from her brow. "So what do you think is going on?"

"I know you've been to Macedonia and visited Enver Davidi."

She shook her head.

"And so what if we've been to Macedonia? We're perfectly entitled to do that. We're PET, for Christ's sake. We don't have to tell you and everyone else what we're doing. That doesn't connect us to Davidi's murder."

Axel hadn't said anything about that, but he was beginning to fear how deep this went.

"No, it doesn't, but it connects you to his presence in Denmark and thereby to his death. He was killed because he came up here, wasn't he? If he'd stayed in Macedonia, nothing would have happened to him."

"We don't know that. This is all pure conjecture."

But Axel knew he was right and he could sense it from her. The glow in her voice was gone, as were the protests.

"I know you've been down there and negotiated a deal with him. And I know that as part of that deal you equipped him with a secret passport and at least 20,000 kroner."

"How do you know that?"

"I found the passport and the money when I checked the hotel room."

"But wasn't that the passport you gave me?"

"No, why would I do that? I had no reason to trust you at that point. And I still don't."

"It's a forged passport – our technicians have examined it."

"I have stood with that passport in my hand. I have examined it. It's not forged. And you know it."

"That isn't good enough. You can't know the difference between a genuine one and a forged one."

"Not good enough for what? Just listen to yourself. Either you're involved, or you're not."

"How do you know it isn't a forged passport?"

"Henriette, I can't be bothered with all these bloody mind games. It may well be that it's all about what you have on each other and what can be proved in your world, but you're not a damn lawyer. You're a cop. Don't you care about right and wrong? That's all we have to go by. And then it doesn't fucking matter how I found out about it. I'm telling you what I know, and I know that that passport belongs to a special series that's used for diplomats, MI people, agents, and other dickheads. And you know I'm right. So let's move on. Let's solve this case together. I promise not to fuck with your surveillance, but in return you have to promise to tell me what you're up to."

"I'll never promise anything like that."

"I know about the passport, and I know about your trips down there with Kettler and Jessen. October and January. Tetovo. It fits all too well with Davidi. So well that I can work out the rest for myself."

She sighed.

"I'm afraid you can't."

For the next 20 minutes, Axel listened to a story that he had sensed and feared since his first meeting with the two PET people, but the number of fuck-ups was far more than he had thought. Kristian Kettler had been controlling the operation with blinkers on. He had either been asked, or he himself had requested, with typical eagerness and ambition, to review Albanians and Macedonians sentenced to deportation, in order to find people who could be hired undercover in drug cases. They had ended up with three potential agents, all of whom had a peripheral relationship with BGP and Moussa or his accomplices. Enver Davidi had been top of the list for further investigation and they had gone down to visit him because they knew he was interested in seeing his son. He had tried to have his deportation order revoked three times.

His connections down there were OK. He knew the Albanian gangs who smuggled drugs over the mountain passes to Kosovo, but on the occasions he had been seen in Denmark, PET hadn't been watching him and they had no knowledge of him coming home to smuggle drugs as they had claimed. On the contrary, he had been here twice, once to bury his brother, the other time to see his son – or that was what he had personally told Henriette Nielsen and Kristian Kettler when they visited him for the first time. And all the information about his contacts within the Albanian mafia in Tetovo came from him.

But Davidi was interested. And he had made contact with Moussa and his men – the PET people were sure of that. He had offered them 15 kilos of cocaine.

"Is that something you have on tape, or is it something you've got from Davidi?"

"That's something we've got from him."

"But that means you don't know anything about the deal?"

"We know that Davidi was very much on for it. He wanted to come home at all costs so that he could be with his son again."

"But it could all just be a wild goose chase. There's no certainty that he had any contact with Moussa about drugs." Axel put a hand to his head. "So what did you promise him?"

Henriette Nielsen looked uncomfortable.

"We gave him a new passport and talked to him about getting him a new identity."

"Talked to him?"

"Yes, we talked to him, persuaded him. He was well aware of the risk, but I don't think he quite understood the consequences."

"What does that mean?"

"If he was going to have a new identity, his family would have to have them too, and that meant he had to deliver something very big – not just hand over some drugs with a microphone on his body, but take the whole organisation down and dare to testify about it afterwards."

"So he thought it was a one-off deal, but you were trying to plant him as an undercover agent for an extended period?"

"I wasn't, but that's what the others wanted. Witness protection isn't something we throw around willy-nilly. If he would testify against BGP, we would consider it, but not just for one delivery and that's what he thought."

"Use and throw away – is that what you do?"

"What are you getting all holy about? You're notorious for solving your cases by any means possible, aren't you?"

"Not if it means that innocent people lose their lives."

"Enver Davidi was a convicted drug smuggler – he wasn't exactly innocence personified."

"No, maybe he wasn't, but he'd paid the price. He'd served his time and lost his family too."

She shook her head.

"I'm not proud of this case, but it's not our fault he's dead."

Axel was far from convinced.

"What about the hotel and the drugs?"

"We rented the room for him through a front man – a Serb we often use. He didn't bring any drugs from Tetovo – it would have been far too dangerous if he accidentally got nicked."

"So there aren't any drugs?"

"Yes, I'm afraid there are, but unfortunately they've disappeared."

"What?"

"I handed them over to him in the hotel room on Thursday evening."

"But yesterday you claimed you were there to see if you could set up listening devices. You said you didn't have any contact with him."

"I did. He got 15 kilos of cocaine which we had confiscated elsewhere."

"You're bloody having me on!"

"No… afraid not."

"And who's taken them?"

"We don't know."

"But you were watching the hotel?"

"Yes, but this was during the worst of the disturbances and our man had to move several times during the evening and night. There were fires and smoke on the streets, masses of people rushing around, and at some point, some of the demonstrators ran into reception at the Hotel Continental."

"Jesus, what a bunch of amateurs."

She went silent. Axel had to think through the whole case again. What did this mean in relation to BGP? They obviously didn't have the stuff, but was that the same as them not having killed Enver Davidi? Most likely. On the other hand, they could have discovered his double-dealing.

"What happened when you visited him at the hotel?"

"I've had quite a bit of contact with him, more than you've been told. We felt he was about to back out. He wasn't exactly unaware that the whole operation was dangerous. And he wasn't crazy about walking around Copenhagen, which suited us very well. In fact, he was pretty anxious about leaving his hotel room. But suddenly we couldn't get hold of him. He didn't answer the phone we'd given him. We couldn't make contact and he didn't come to the meeting place we had agreed for Tuesday evening, so I went there Wednesday morning to see what was wrong."

"And what was wrong?"

"It's hard to say, but he seemed downhearted, as if he were about to give up, as if he didn't believe it would work."

"What didn't he believe?"

"That he'd make a deal with Moussa and have a new life in Denmark. I talked it all through with him."

"But he was right, wasn't he? You weren't going to look after him?"

She hesitated before answering.

"I actually thought we did for a long time, but it turned out that no programme had been put in place."

"What does that mean?"

"Witness protection is very extensive. Setting it up is a long process. It takes several people working over a long period to implement it."

"How do you know that?"

"Because I'm one of the people responsible for it. Kettler wasn't planning to give him a new life – that was agreed with Jessen. They had no intention of doing anything. But I didn't know that before yesterday."

"But you can't do that. You're risking people's lives, for goodness' sake. You were so careless with his information and his safety because Kettler expected him to be sacrificed anyway."

"No, we don't work like that. I'm sure we'd have done something for him if he'd helped us with Moussa – it's just not certain it would have been in Denmark."

"Then you're just a bunch of bloody amateurs. Once he'd helped you with Moussa, he was finished. Not just in Denmark, but also among his own people in Macedonia and everywhere else for that matter. The only thing that could have saved him was a new identity. What about his family?"

"There was no deal for them."

"Does his ex know anything about this?"

"I don't think so. And I don't get the impression she's interested in having him back."

Axel agreed with that, but how did PET know?

"We sent someone out to interview her about being divorced from a deportee, supposedly for an anthropological research project, and we got a clear impression that she wasn't interested in having him back."

"There isn't much chance of that now, is there?"

Henriette Nielsen didn't answer.

"But then his mood had completely changed when I went in and delivered the drugs on Thursday evening. 'I'm on top again, Henry,' he said. 'Don't take any notice of me, it's just paki-blues. I've been away too long. Now I believe it. I'll bust Moussa for you.'"

"God, this is ludicrous. You all deserve to get a real fucking hiding for this."

Axel swung from Nørrebrogade in along Peblinge Dossering and parked the car in Wesselsgade. It was 100 yards up to Apoteket through a backyard. 100 yards and 25 minutes to decide what he was going to use to put pressure on Nørrebro's most dangerous gangster. If he turned up. They had agreed that Henriette would follow in the car and park in Blågårds Plads while Axel was in the pub.

"What will you say to him?" asked Henriette Nielsen.

It only took them two minutes to agree that Axel would play high stakes and try to shake the tree as much as possible.

39

Blågårds Plads. Feared by apprentice journalists and provincial newspaper readers, perhaps not entirely without foundation if they only get their information from the media. Axel slowed down as he approached the square. A small BMW with sideskirts and lots of bling was parked in front of Escobar, two men in the front seats, one on a lady's bike next to it with one arm on the roof. The conversation stopped and their eyes followed him as he walked across the square and stood five yards away looking in the window of Bønne's Antiquarian Bookshop. He could see the rest of the square reflected in the windowpane. It seemed abandoned, so he reckoned that Moussa was sitting in a car not far from here. The air was cool and wet; Axel had butterflies in his stomach as he walked towards Café Apoteket, the gravel making a hollow crunch under his feet and the asphalt sticky from the rain.

Apoteket was an old left-wing pub, located on the corner of Blågårds Plads. This was where tear gas had been washed down with cold draught beer after slum storming and squatter actions in the seventies and eighties, and the most popular drink after beer was Havana Club, because many of the regular guests had been on solidarity sojourns in Central America. Axel liked Apoteket because they left you in peace and the atmosphere was local and free and easy. In the summer months, it was like having a seat in the front stalls to watch life on the square among Kai Nielsen's primeval, heavy granite sculptures, the big lime trees, the cafés where women with prams drank morning tea and ate cakes, the alkies on the benches, a stream of students and young people walking and cycling and Moussa and his acolytes, hanging out at Escobar or cruising around in black Audis like little poisonous bugs spoiling the idyllic scene.

There were a lot of people at the bar, but plenty of tables free in the three rooms. Axel sat down with a cup of coffee in the room right at the back. And waited.

10 minutes later he heard footsteps and a pair of white Nike trainers stopped in front of him. Axel's gaze moved slowly upwards, but he knew this was a city boy before he got to his face. The legs were clad in black jogging bottoms, an open duvet jacket revealed a red sports sweater with a gang tag printed on the stomach, a gold chain, a head shaven apart from the edge of the brow to the neck, beautiful dark eyes; the look wasn't so much hard as tense under the studied veneer of indifference.

"You akrash?"

"Yes."

He rocked his head towards the door. "There's someone wants to talk, man. Out on Pladsen."

"Why doesn't he come in here?"

"Was you wanted to talk, innit? So Pladsen it is."

Axel stood up and followed the guy, who could hardly have been more than 16-17 years old. He walked with short, hectic steps through the premises, where the eyes of several regulars and the woman behind the bar followed them all the way to the door. There was no bad feeling between Apoteket and Moussa and his boys, but there was a distance.

He could see his car on the corner of Blågårdsgade and Pladsen, so Henriette Nielsen had to be somewhere.

They crossed the cobbled street and turned right under the lime trees along the low granite border that surrounded the tiled, sunken space. It was completely open, with no sculptures or fountains, a stage where lads played football in the summer and skated in the winter, but it was a completely different show in the offing now. The lad went down three steps. There was no one else to be seen. Axel followed him but stopped as soon as he came out onto the square. Next to him a dais reared up with a granite tree filled with small chubby climbing children.

"What you doing, man?"

"I'm waiting here. Tell him that."

"Come on. He said you should come with me. He'll be pissed off if you don't come."

"I'm waiting here. Five minutes. Otherwise I'm buggering off. Tell him."

"It ain't certain that he come, man."

The young lad shook his head, continued diagonally across Pladsen and disappeared into the darkness in a corner where there was a passageway to Korsgade through the concrete buildings. Axel leant up against the granite, lay his palms on two round children's heads, felt the cool, smooth, worn stone in his hands and looked up; the clouds were close, surfing along the bottom of the sky. The wind was ripping at the trees. He breathed deeply and closed his eyes; sleep reared up like dark breakers, waiting to gobble him up as soon as he relaxed. Not now. He tensed his muscles, which were tingling with unease and expectation.

When he opened his eyes again, he saw Moussa coming towards him surrounded by three men, one in front, two behind him on each side. It was time.

Axel pushed himself away from the stone and took three steps into the square.

"What do you think you're doing?" he spat. "It looks like a fucking bodyguard course. Why have you taught them to walk like that?"

Moussa spread his arms and signalled to his people to stop.

"If you're afraid of being shot down, walking like that won't fucking help. You look like a flock of ducklings that have shit their pants."

Moussa said something Axel couldn't hear so he went closer.

"Cop joker, yeah? Comedian. But you're the one who asked me to come, so I don't understand why you're wasting your time trying to be funny."

Moussa spoke Danish without the slightest accent or the small, aggressive inflections that characterised the immigrant slang of the ghettos. Everyone on the square and all the police in Copenhagen knew of him, but his appearance didn't live up to the pre-conceived ideas of a dangerous gang leader. Loose-cut black curls over an inquisitive, slightly podgy face with thick glasses, large, studious brown eyes, stocky body that looked a bit out of shape – but Axel knew about his convictions and reputation, and knew that, in that flabby body, there had once been enough power to break both the forearms of a pusher over the back of a chair with his bare hands when he caught him selling hash without paying Moussa his cut.

"Are you miked, cop?"

"No."

"What have you got then?"

The guy who had been walking in front came up to frisk Axel.

Axel lifted his arms. He was surprised at their amateurism. Microphones could be so small that a body search was completely pointless. But they carried on. Then the guy felt Louis's toy pistol, which Axel still had in his pocket.

"What the fuck? He's got a gun!"

"Of course he's got a gun, he's a cop. That's enough."

Axel had maintained eye contact with Moussa the whole time. Now he lowered his arms.

"So what do you want?"

"You're looking for 15 kilos of cocaine."

"I don't know what you're talking about, cop."

"You can't find it, I can't either, isn't there something wrong?"

Moussa lifted his eyebrows as if he didn't understand a thing.

"Fifteen kilos of coke. From the Balkans. Have you gone soft in the head?" Axel laughed scornfully at him.

"What the fuck are you talking about?"

"Ever heard of fucking cocaine from the Balkans? Somebody's trying to con you. I promise you."

Moussa spat in the gravel.

"Or do you really know fuck all about coke? Are you just a bunch of grubby hash boys running errands for the Hell's Angels?"

Moussa's boys were beginning to get restless. They wanted to sort Axel out, but Moussa raised his arms and told them to shut up.

"What is all this, cop? You ask for a meeting and then you just stand there insulting us. I know very well your bitch is close by. You won't get my boys to take the bait and start messing with you. But I still got no fucking clue what you're talking about. And if I don't find out right now, I'm off."

"You're looking for some gear. You sent your boys out to Rentemestervej for it earlier today. And now they're banged up at HQ. Fifteen kilos of high-quality cocaine – not some cut shit. No icing sugar or creatine."

"Icing sugar?" said one of the lads.

"Shut up," said Moussa brusquely.

"I know about the Albanian. I know about the gear. He came up here to sell you fifteen kilos of cocaine. And now he's dead and the gear's vanished. And the people he got it from are very upset and would very much like to have a little chat with whoever killed the Albanian and took the gear. Might be a group you'd like to stay friends with."

"Why are you here? Why do you come here and tell me all this shit, you ridiculous whitey?"

"Because I want to give you the drugs."

Moussa looked incredulously at him.

"You're sick, cop."

Axel knew he had got him. Moussa now knew there was neither a microphone on Axel nor a sound scanner nearby – nothing was being recorded here. It could totally fuck up Axel's career and would certainly cause a stir in court if a cop tried to make a deal to deliver fifteen kilos of cocaine to one of the most wanted gang leaders in Copenhagen.

"I don't give a fuck about the gear. You can keep it and do whatever the hell you want with it. You can give it to the South Americans, you can flush it down the loo, you can stick it up your arse, but I want the delivery man, you hear me? I want him. Alive."

Moussa was silent and lit a cigarette. He was cool in a screwed-up way.

"What's the seller done to you?"

"Drop the business school chat. You know what he's done. He's not a fucking seller – he's a murderer. And it's a one-night stand you have with him. He doesn't have any more gear for you. If you don't fix it and hand him over, the South Americans will take everything over and you'll have been conned out of the drugs for the second time."

"What do you mean?"

"The coke was for you. The Albanian tried to sell it to you – don't you get that?"

Moussa took a long, calm drag on his cigarette and exhaled the smoke into the black night, a smile creasing his face.

"I don't know what the fuck you're talking about. No one's tried to sell me anything. And why the fuck did you think I was just going to hand him over?"

Axel had just about run out of patience.

"Find a way, Moussa. And then let me know."

"And then you can come and bust me for fifteen kilos of coke – you must be crazy. Fuck you, cop!"

"I won't bust you for anything. I just need the man."

Moussa shook his head, turned around and walked away.

"You're sick coming here with your traps. You just talk shit like all the pigs."

Axel didn't have a deal, but he had got what he'd come for. Now they would have to wait. The price of cocaine had fallen to 500 kroner per gram as it became readily available over the decade, but it was usually cut. So 15 kilos of pure uncut cocaine could bring in twice as much, and would be worth at least 15 million. That and the chance to impress some fictional South American drug connections would probably get some action out of Moussa.

Axel went over to Henriette, who was leaning against his car smoking. The worried frown hadn't gone.

"Did it go well?"

"Maybe – in any case, he got really pissed off and scarpered. Have you called extra people in to listen and keep them under surveillance?"

"Yes, there are people working around the clock now. They'll call as soon as they get anything."

She threw the cigarette in the gravel.

"What are you going to do with what I told you about our operation with Davidi?"

"Nothing. For the time being. I want his murderer. And despite everything, it's not one of your lot, so shall we move on?"

The frown didn't disappear.

Axel dropped her off and drove home through the empty streets. He turned on the car radio and listened to the latest bulletins about the Youth House, as Jagtvej's wet asphalt, yellow in the reflection from the street lights, disappeared under his car.

The house had been almost completely demolished now and was being driven away by masked construction workers afraid of reprisals from the former house users.

"And now a curious story that places the police's efforts around the murder at Assistens Cemetery on Thursday night in a rather strange light. As previously reported, one of the officers left his post while the murder was committed. There has been speculation about whether he could have had anything to do with the crime. According to TV2 News, the man was held in detention for 24 hours charged with murder, but has now been released. It has emerged that he had nothing to do with the killing of the 48-year-old deported drug dealer. We have been unable to get any information as to why the police kept the charge under wraps. The officer left the cemetery for two hours, and the murder took place in the same period, but according to TV2, it appears that the officer in question left his post in order to spend some time with his superior's wife. We have tried to reach Copenhagen Police for comment about the case, but without success. According to TV2 News, the two officers have both been suspended.

Tomorrow the weather will be clear…"

Axel switched off. Dorte Neergaard was good, very good, and she had made the most of that story. He had given her the beginning and others had fed her with the rest. The affair was what it was, but the information that one officer had been charged with murder was something of a mischief to leak to the press. And it hadn't come from him. Though that is what everyone would believe because he had got hold of the recording, and he had been running the investigation. There were a lot of leaks in the police. They were rarely revealed, but when it happened, heads rolled. And Axel knew that someone had put out a silver platter for his.

40

Tuesday, March 6

Axel's mobile had run out of juice during the evening, but when he woke up and recharged it, messages poured in. The first one was from Darling and had been sent last night.

"We've arrested Martin Lindberg. He's had contact with Peter Smith, that is, Piver, but denies it. Major explanation problems. Continuing the interview early tomorrow."

Darling's text got him out of bed in a hurry; he quickly changed into shirt and suit and rushed down the back stairs. He went down to the courtyard, took his bike and pedalled in to Headquarters. On the way in, he took out his mobile and called Darling, but it went to answerphone.

Lindberg! That was an interview he didn't want to miss for anything in the world. Fuck, he'd love to bust the holy shit who'd played such a big part in driving his colleague to murder and suicide after the disturbances in Nørrebro 14 years ago.

Axel listened to the messages on the mobile as he cycled in. Darling had been busy. On a phone message from the same morning, he asked agitatedly where Axel was, so he couldn't be accused of going solo. The phone Lindberg had used to call Piver had been found by the Lakes near the Counterpress offices. The transcript of the conversation between them showed they had agreed to meet at Christiania and that Lindberg was very eager to get hold of the video recording that Piver had run off with.

What did that mean? Had the left-wing activist lost his head? Did he really have something to do with the murder and was the drug case a red herring? Had Lindberg staged a police murder to shift the focus from himself and take revenge on them? It was too good to be true. Suddenly it occurred to Axel what had been wrong with the article Lindberg had written about the murder. The very first story about the mysterious photo of Enver contained information that only the murderer and people who had seen the body close up could know at that point. The photo of the body didn't show the victim's hands bound behind his back. Even so, he had written that Davidi had been handcuffed with strips.

And Black Arne had heard a name. Piver had asked the man if he was Martin.

He locked his bike outside HQ and went up to Homicide. He had only just managed to take off his jacket when Corneliussen strode in. He stood by Axel's desk with his arms folded. There was a stench of old cigarette smoke around him that must have taken up residence in his unwashed clothes, because smoking at HQ wasn't allowed.

"It looks like a breakthrough, but not for you. I'd like to take you off the case right here and now, but I can't prove that the press leak about our two colleagues is your work. But when I can, you're done and then you'll spend your time sitting in a car on surveillance duty or writing transcripts of wiretaps."

Axel looked at him. He wanted to crush the incompetent fool.

"I don't know what you're talking about."

"But Rosenkvist certainly will. Everyone knows that you have a working relationship with that little Thai girl at TV2, and now they're running a story about one of our men having been charged and him having screwed a colleague's wife. It's the top story in BT and Ekstra Bladet today."

"I have nothing to do with that and I have an interview with our main suspect. Would it be OK if I get on with my work?"

Corneliussen's eyes were almost completely hidden behind the bags of skin.

"I've decided that Darling will handle the interview because we haven't been able to get hold of you for half a day. He's on his way down with the suspect. Maybe you can write it up for him."

"But I'm here now."

"It's not up for discussion."

Corneliussen stormed out of the office.

Axel walked through the doors linking the numerous offices until he reached John Darling's office, a room almost clinically vacuumed of anything personal and always pristinely tidy. He opened his laptop and prepared himself for the role of note-taking assistant allowing Darling to run the interview.

Shortly afterwards, the door to the corridor opened and Darling came in with Lindberg.

"Not him!" he said with a groan when he saw Axel.

Axel smiled back at him.

"Please take a seat."

Lindberg looked depleted, as all people do when they have been prised out of their own reality and locked up at Headquarters without warning. They would sit in there along with a small group of the capital's most dangerous and unruly remanded prisoners, and there was no soundproofing. So even though Lindberg had only spent one night in there, he had hardly been able to close an eye. What a big difference it makes being home or away, thought Axel as Darling pulled out the chair for Lindberg. At Counterpress four days ago, he had owned the whole room, defiant, dismissive and offensive. Now he sat, a glassy expression betraying his lack of sleep, as if he didn't quite understand what he was doing here, morning-glossy tufts of hair sticking out in all directions, the bordeaux sweatshirt and jeans seeming rather tatty and grubby.

He looked up at the two detectives and was suddenly on full alert.

"Shall we get this over and done with?"

"We'll take it slowly and calmly," began Darling. "We need a fairly long explanation from you about your last few days and we have plenty of time."

"I don't have to explain a damn thing to you. I've already said I don't know anyone called Piver, I don't know who he is, and I've never met him or talked to him on the phone. I have a lot to get done today and

I'm not going to let you sabotage my work."

Axel doubted that Darling would be allowed to plough on with his cognitive interview technique. This was largely about letting the suspect talk away and following him blindly around through the story, but it was rarely much use if people wouldn't talk at all. And Lindberg already seemed to have regained some of his fighting spirit.

"Ask me what you want to know and tell me what I'm doing here. You've charged me with withholding information from the police in a murder case – what's that all about? If you don't make it clear to me, I'm not saying anything more until my lawyer is here."

"Let's just call your lawyer then," said Darling. "Would you take care of that, Axel? And then we'll take a break until he comes. Or shall we continue the interview? I should make it very clear that whatever prejudices and ideas you may have about what we spend the day doing, it's not our choice to sit around here talking to people like you. We're not out to inconvenience you or harass you. We're investigating a murder and you're here because you're a person of serious interest in our case, as you well know. This isn't about your past and it has nothing to do with May 18, 1993 or your political point of view, much as you might want to believe that. We don't know what your connection is to our investigation, but we have to clarify what you've been doing at some specific times, who's seen you and who you've talked to. If you won't co-operate, it will be difficult. And prolonged. As I'm sure your lawyer will explain to you when he comes."

It seemed to make an impression on Lindberg, who was certainly an experienced activist and had been imprisoned because of street riots on several occasions, but it was one thing to be a revolutionary hero in activist circles and another thing entirely to be a suspect in a murder investigation.

"The sooner we can get you cleared, the better for all parties. What do you say?" asked Darling.

"I want my lawyer, but you're welcome to start."

"I'd like to know where you were on Friday."

"I was at Counterpress and on the street pretty much all day."

"What does on the street mean?"

"Around Nørrebro following the action."

"Were you anywhere else?"

He hesitated.

"Yes, in the afternoon I was at Stop Trafficking in Christianshavn."

"Why?"

"I volunteer to stop the trafficking of Eastern European and African women. I went in to fetch the post and respond to emails."

"When?"

"Around three o'clock, maybe. I was there for around an hour."

Christianshavn, where Christiania is – it fitted with the time that Piver had been in the Freetown. Axel went out and asked a colleague to call Lindberg's lawyer. When he came back, Darling had started from scratch.

"Why don't you take it from the beginning and tell us everything you did?"

Martin Lindberg told them about a busy day following the clearance of the Youth House. As unofficial editor-in-chief, he had to make a lot of decisions about directing the volunteer journalists and activists around the city, to the magistrates' court, to the Youth House and Runddelen, to the People's House; there was also a group following the demonstrations. Meetings had been held every three hours for anyone who had time to come in to the editorial office on Nørrebrogade, and Martin Lindberg had led the meetings, except in the afternoon when he was on the streets for a long period and at Stop Trafficking at Christianshavn. That was before Axel and Darling had been in to search the office and it fitted perfectly with the time that Piver had called Lindberg's phone.

"Were you with anyone from 13:30 to 16:00?"

"I was at Counterpress along with at least 20 other people who will be able to confirm. A little after two, we got the email with the photo of the body at Assistens. I wrote the article. Afterwards I went into town and followed all your dirty work on the street. Then I went to

Stop Trafficking."

"Why did you leave Counterpress?"

"I needed some fresh air."

"Did anyone call you?"

He hesitated.

"Of course, I got several calls, but there was a lot of noise, so someone could have rung without me hearing it."

"Try and remember. Was it only people you knew?"

"Yes, I think so. Colleagues from Counterpress. Why is that important?"

"It's not all that certain it is important. What's your phone number?"

He gave a different number to the one Piver had called.

"How many phones do you have?"

"I only have one."

"20154495. Is that a number you recognise?"

"Not at all."

"But it belongs to Counterpress?"

"We have invested in 25 mobile phones, so that we have some to lend to people in major crisis situations like YoHo or summit meetings. That number sounds like one of them."

"You've never had it or used it?"

"No."

"I'm asking because it was found in a rubbish bin by Peblinge Lake just 100 yards from your workplace. Do you know anything about that?"

Axel wondered if Darling was going to play his trump so soon. It wasn't like him.

"I haven't used it. Why's it important?"

"We'll come back to it."

The interview was being recorded. Axel was making notes, but during the conversation he had had time to read the transcript of the telephone conversation between Piver and Lindberg twice, and he had no doubt it was genuine. The whole them-and-us rhetoric was something he knew all too well. He had heard Lindberg fire it off fourteen years ago at the trial, just like now, when he had taken every opportunity to chip in that the police were just dogs you couldn't trust. But with the conversation they now had on the tape, the tables had been turned. It was Lindberg who had a serious credibility problem. On the other hand, the information that Piver had a video recording showing that the police killed Enver Davidi played the ball right back into their court. What the hell did it mean? It wasn't Groes and Vang, so who the hell could it have been? Axel was beyond confused. It was crucial to get hold of Piver and the recording, but right now Lindberg seemed to be the only person who had made contact with the missing autonomist, and he was therefore a reasonable person to suspect, too, until he had given a coherent explanation of the conversation and his meeting with Piver.

"Where were you Thursday night, Friday morning?"

"You can't be serious. You don't think I killed him, do you?"

"Who?"

"That's ridiculous, man."

"We don't think anything at all; we just have to ask you these questions. If you don't want to answer, that's OK. Then we'll wait for your lawyer to arrive or for you to come before a magistrate. If you want to get it over and done with, then I think you need to come up with some answers that we can use."

Lindberg sighed.

"I was at Counterpress and on the street. I would think I was home by three o'clock."

"Where were you between half-past twelve and two?"

"I was out reporting on the demonstrations."

"Were you with anyone? Is there anyone who can confirm that?"

"I was with most of the assembled Danish press corps plus several hundred activists. I'm sure some of them can give me an alibi if you really think that's necessary."

"Who can confirm that?"

"There were representatives from television and the big newspapers."

He mentioned a wealth of names, including Dorte Neergaard and Sonne.

"Were they with you all the time?"

"No, it doesn't work like that. After all, we're competitors of a kind. I walked or cycled around for most of the time, took pictures, recorded sound and film and took notes. Alone. But we crossed paths several times."

"That means no one was with you the whole time?"

"No, there was no one with me the whole time," he said in a tired voice.

Axel made a sign to Darling and was allowed to interrupt.

"How much do you actually know about how we work?"

"What do you mean?"

"How much do you know about police methods and possibilities for investigating a crime? You're someone who boasts about keeping an eye on the law-enforcement authorities and investigating if we've broken the rules. But how much do you really know about what we can do with modern telecommunications?"

"I have a good sense of it and I know the rules, but I have no illusions about you complying with them."

"We've had enough of your shit, Lindberg. If you know so much about it, you must also know that we can do more or less anything. You can't do anything with your mobile phone without us tracing it. We can see where you are, where you've been, who you've called and texted. And if you call a man we're looking for, we will obviously listen to him as well. And then we'll have a recording of your entire conversation."

"I don't know what you're talking about."

"You will – all in good time. And it will cost you four weeks on remand when you're brought before a magistrate in a couple of hours unless you have a very good explanation."

The door of the office opened and Corneliussen came in with a man who would aggravate the interview quite substantially.

41

Lindberg's lawyer was in full uniform: briefcase, raincoat, freshly ironed white shirt that probably cost him an arm and a leg, beer belly hanging over a leather belt, black Hugo Boss shoes and red-flecked tie that matched the French red-wine colour of his face.

"I hope you gentlemen haven't begun interviewing my client without my presence. Steen, Darling."

He nodded to them and shook Lindberg's hand.

"I'll get you out of here, Martin."

"He consented to us starting the interview. We've just been talking facts," said Darling.

"May I have a couple of minutes with the two gentlemen alone? If that's OK, Martin?"

Axel knew him all too well. He wasn't a lawyer he would have chosen to have sitting in on an interview because he was very experienced, razor-sharp, and the Administration of Justice Act and its one thousand plus paragraphs were written on the underside of his tongue.

Axel asked a colleague to keep an eye on Lindberg and then went out into the corridor with the lawyer and Darling.

"What's all this about?"

"We've charged him with obstructing a murder investigation, but we're ready to charge him with murder if he doesn't come up with some satisfactory answers."

"On what basis?"

"We have a recording of your client in which he's talking to a young autonomist who's disappeared, and whom we've been looking for since Friday in connection with the murder investigation from Assistens Cemetery. During that conversation, your client says that they should meet because the young man has a recording which shows the actual murder being committed."

"Do you have a copy of that conversation?"

Darling handed it to him. He skimmed through the two pages, muttering to himself.

"Interesting, interesting. Not least for you. He singles out one of your colleagues as the murderer and claims that the recording contains footage of a police violation. Is it my client or the recording you're after? Perhaps you're not too keen on that recording being released?"

He smiled ironically.

"We're looking for a murderer," spat Axel, "so drop the bullshit. There's a lot to indicate that Lindberg tries to fool Peter Smith into meeting him and giving him the recording, perhaps because he's involved in the murder. If your client doesn't have anything to do with the case, he'll be allowed to leave."

"How noble. I assume you haven't confronted him with the recording yet, but just lured him so far out on the ice that there's no way back?"

That was precisely what they had done. They had got him to say that he hadn't been to Christiania and that he hadn't been called by a stranger, so now it would be interesting to hear how he would explain the conversation.

"I just want to make it clear that if my client has said anything to incriminate himself, there will be a complaint on the prosecutor's desk tomorrow morning and I will ensure that the information you received from my client cannot be used in any legal proceedings. I am usually co-operative, but I could spoil your little plan by going in and advising him to refuse to comment. What will you have then?"

"We'll almost certainly be able to hold him. You can take that for granted. I don't know any magistrate who will let him go as things stand right now."

"No, you're probably right. Besides, Martin will certainly want to return to his work, so I'm sure he'll be willing to help clarify the matter. No more traps, please! Otherwise I'll be interrupting you constantly."

They went back into Darling's office.

Darling explained who Peter Smith was, what he was in possession of and what the police knew about him.

"At 13.32 on Friday, he called this phone number because he'd heard that someone wanted to get in touch with him. And that someone was you."

"Absolute rubbish. I haven't spoken to him."

Lindberg's lawyer put his hand on his client's arm.

"Remember what I usually say, Martin; let the nice men do their piece and think before you answer – then everything will be all right."

"We've been listening to Peter Smith's phone since he ran off," said John Darling.

He paused for effect. Lindberg responded by raising his shoulders and turning his palms out.

"Here's a transcript of the conversation."

John Darling handed the two A4 sheets to Lindberg. He let him read them.

"You've just told us that you were in Nørrebro and Christianshavn during this time and that you didn't call anyone or receive any calls at the time Peter Smith called this number. As we said, we've found the phone in a rubbish bin by the Lakes – it was switched on. And there is DNA on it, so in that respect we'd like to have a mouth swab from you to compare it with. And if you've ever held this phone, it'll come out, I promise you."

"This whole conversation you've listened to is a farce. I've never talked to the guy. I don't know who he is."

"Who has access to the phones?"

Lindberg was still reading the transcript, shaking his head and snorting and chuckling to himself.

"Fuck, this guy has totally had you."

Then he fell silent. He looked at them.

"Try to answer the question."

"You've got to play this recording to me, so you can hear it's not me."

The lawyer broke in.

"I think my client has a good point. Why don't we just listen to the recording?"

Axel broke in.

"We'll get round to that when we've reviewed it. There's more than just the recording that points to your client, so it's not that simple."

Lindberg sighed.

"Kafka would envy you."

"The phones?"

"They're meant to be locked in our safe in the editorial office, but often they're just lying in a box. Some of them have disappeared, others are probably lying around somewhere in the office."

"Look at the transcript. Haven't you heard anything at all about the video?"

"I've heard that you're looking for a young activist, but I didn't take note of his name. And I have NOT contacted him. I did not take part in that conversation."

"And it's not you stirring up Peter Smith? And calling him a hero?"

"No, for Christ's sake."

"And wanting to hold a press conference with him at Counterpress? And getting him to believe that it's a matter of life or death and that it can save the Youth House?"

"That's ridiculous. I'm not that bloody naive."

"You could easily make that stuff up," said Axel in a low voice.

"I'll ignore that, Axel Steen," said the lawyer.

"Let's just say that it isn't you. Who do you think it could it be?"

"It could be someone who'd just escaped from a blue van, or someone on a bad acid trip."

"Funny. But it appears to be someone with a thorough knowledge not only of the case but also of Counterpress. He talks about the editorial office as a familiar place he knows we've searched."

Lindberg looked down at the transcript.

"There's nothing here about the search. It says that he says we're being watched. I certainly wouldn't rule out you or the pigs at PET doing that, but it's not something anyone would know for certain, so where has he got that from?"

"My client has a good point. The wire-tap also shows that the young man singles out the police as responsible for the murder at Assistens. Shouldn't you be looking a little closer at that? And can it be ruled out that this man who is pretending to be my client is the perpetrator? If that is the case, you're wasting very precious time harassing my client."

Axel broke in.

"We're not idiots, you know. We have people investigating that possibility."

He looked at Lindberg.

"But we've also been talking to people who've heard you asking about Piver on the street. That doesn't exactly fit with your claim not to know his name."

"That's a lie. I've never asked about him. Why would I be asking about someone I don't know?"

"And then there's the article about the murder and the picture you received. Was it you who wrote the first version?"

"Yes."

"You wrote that the dead man was bound behind his back with the type of strips the police use as handcuffs."

"He was."

"Yes, he was, but you couldn't see that in the picture."

"Of course I could."

Axel showed him the picture of Enver Davidi sitting with his back up against the wall of Assistens.

"How did you know that?"

He hesitated for the first time in the interview. Lindberg lowered his voice.

"I don't know, I don't remember why. I guess I wrote it because I assumed that's how it was. Everyone can see that his arms are tied behind his back."

"So you made it up?"

"I never make things up. I drew a hasty conclusion – maybe I was wrong."

The door was opened and Corneliussen stuck his head in.

"Darling, can I talk to you a moment?"

Axel tackled Lindberg's alibi again. Martin Lindberg came up with a handful of names of people who would have seen him during the relevant time periods, but he couldn't be sure of specific times.

"Isn't it about time we listened to that recording?" asked the lawyer.

It was in Axel's mailbox; he started it and leaned back in the chair.

ML: *Hello?*

There was noise from a television in the background, but it sounded like Lindberg's voice, and Axel could see him lower his eyebrows, so that three wrinkles appeared between them.

PS: *Hello, it's Peter. Who am I talking to?*

ML: *One moment, just leaving the room.*

Clattering and silence.

ML: *Who is it?*

PS: *It's Piv… Peter. Someone gave me your number. What do you want with me?*

ML: *Are you the guy living on Nørrebrogade in the collective?*

The voice seemed a bit distorted, so it sounded like it could be Lindberg's, but it could also be an imitation. Lindberg looked as though his innocence had been proven, but Axel thought it was far from it. The voice was slurred; there were similarities and distortions – it could be him. They listened to it right through to the end.

PS: *I'm sitting in front of the Moonfisher at some tables. I have a black rucksack with a red sticker. It says Ali's on it.*

ML: *OK, I'll find you. I'll be there soon.*

PS: *Hey, wait. What's your name?*

ML: *Martin. Martin Lindberg from Counterpress.*

Lindberg had been sitting with his hands behind his head during the whole playback; now he slapped them down on the desk with a smile.

"Believe me now? It isn't me! Anyone can hear that!"

"Then I'm not anyone. I think that voice is close to yours, easily close enough for it to be you."

Axel had been watching Lindberg's lawyer during the playback. His brow had wrinkled several times, but now he came out all guns blazing.

"I wouldn't go to court with that recording if I were you. If you continue along this path, I will demand that it's played to a judge."

Axel knew that technicians were in full swing turning both Counterpress and Martin Lindberg's apartment upside down. They needed more time.

"I disagree. I'm not the least bit convinced that it's not your client. There are big problems with his alibi, and his explanation as to why he wrote that Enver Davidi was cuffed behind his back isn't very good. I can't see that we can release him now."

"But it's ludicrous," exclaimed Lindberg.

Darling had come back into the office. He looked shaken.

"What do you intend to charge my client with?" asked the lawyer.

"Provisionally, he's been charged with obstructing the investigation of a murder."

"Not any more," said Darling.

Everyone looked at him. The big blonde policeman's face was locked in an expression Axel had seen many times before.

"Now he's being charged with murder."

He paused and looked at Lindberg as he pronounced the last two words.

"Two murders."

42

They drove out in Darling's car. Lindberg had been sent back to his cell, but they would resume the interview later. Meanwhile, the public prosecutor had to decide if they had enough on him to bring him before a magistrate and have him placed on remand. Axel was doubtful, but Darling was surer of his case.

"It may not have sounded one hundred per cent like his voice, but there could be several explanations for that. He doesn't have an alibi, he can't explain why someone else should have used his name and, as you pointed out, he messed up in that article."

"What about a motive?"

"That'll come, I'm sure. Corneliussen and Rosenkvist are extremely satisfied. They see this as a breakthrough. And getting hold of that video recording is our top priority. Let's follow that trail for now and see what it brings. And stop making such a fuss, Axel, because it'll get you into trouble."

They drove out along Åboulevard's curved multi-lane highway; everything was grey, the traffic was heavy. They turned down Lundtoftegade, past Lunden, as the twelve-storey-high ghetto slum was popularly called, and came to Nørrebro Station, a greyish-green functional building with a clocktower and a concourse arching over the raised railway line like an overturned cylinder. They passed under the railway and out along Frederikssundsvej to Nordvest with all its early retirees, Arab greengrocers, dog owners, Turkish kebabs, video rentals, Thai brothels and businesses where you could get a mobile phone unlocked. Past endless rows of tenements containing small flats, interspersed with industrial parks that had seen better days a long time back and forgotten all about them. Bispevej was located in a deserted industrial district surrounded by three massive, depressing, red and yellow public housing blocks from the thirties and, to the north, the neighbourhood where Laila Hansen had her little red-brick detached house up at Utterslev Torv.

It was easy to spot where the body had been found.

Piver had been thrown onto a building site of about 40 by 60 yards surrounded by a steel fence on one side and the graffiti-covered, dilapidated wall of a house and the black concrete wall of an office building on the other two sides. At the roadside there were a number of large concrete blocks to prevent people from driving into the site. It hadn't stopped them dumping all kinds of crap though: a giant spaghetti of rusty pipes, rubble, builders' waste, an old sofa with springs sticking out through the upholstery and a cracked porcelain sink were lying among the leafless bushes and reeds around a small waterhole containing bluish-green splashes of oil. Axel remembered that, in the old days, the site had housed a rather suspicious car workshop, which in the end was forcibly demolished.

50 yards from the body there were already so many police officers that the entrance was blocked. Not only rank-and-file officers, technicians, paramedics and the forensic pathologist, but also Rosenkvist, Corneliussen, the public prosecutor and the PET people had arrived and were standing around in a more or less unified troop, looking like what they were: foreign elements in a form of police work which risked them getting their hands dirty from something other than sending shit down through the system themselves. The only person not standing there with them was Henriette Nielsen, whom Axel spotted in conversation with the forensic technicians and the Swede over by what he assumed was the body. She nodded to him and he got the sense yet again that she had a slightly worried expression on her face, which he interpreted as a sign that she wasn't exactly overjoyed with the investigation and its developments.

Axel went over to her and looked down at the body.

Whoever it was who had murdered Enver Davidi had gone up a notch in the severity of violence in murdering Piver. That is, assuming it was the same perpetrator.

Piver's face was battered not quite enough for him to be unrecognisable, but close on. He had been tied with strips around his wrists and gaffer tape around his legs, bound up like a pig, with a strip of tape from his hands tied behind his back down to his feet, which had been taped together. In addition, he had gaffer tape on his mouth; his nose was broken; most of his face was beaten black and blue, and the whites of his eyes had a deathly gleam under the eyelashes and the swollen brows.

Henriette Nielsen, dressed in gloves and overalls, was asking about his eyes and the mark on his throat that the Swede was in the process of examining.

"Yes, he's been strangled, but before that he's had a really heavy going-over. He's pretty cold, but I don't think he can have been here for long, is that right?"

Henriette Nielsen nodded.

"No, it's too open. Too many dog walkers. He's visible from the street."

Axel turned to Darling.

"How far from here does Lindberg live?"

"300 yards."

"What about forensics – have they found anything in his flat?"

"I haven't heard anything from them yet, but we can go over there once we're done here."

Axel felt a tap on his shoulder, turned around and looked straight into the black pores in Rosenkvist's chin and the little crater in the middle of it. Behind him stood Corneliussen smirking.

"I thought we had an understanding, Axel."

"We still do. What's wrong?"

"The press. I thought I expressed myself very clearly when I said we weren't keen to let any information about this case out into the press."

He couldn't believe this was happening. Henriette Nielsen and Kettler were close enough to hear what was being said. The others around them had gone quiet.

"I don't know what you're talking about."

"I'm talking about switching on TV2 News to hear what the two officers you've been interviewing did on Thursday night. There are a handful of us who know, but only one of us who struck a deal with Dorte Neergaard about TV2's helicopter footage from Assistens. And that would be you."

How the hell did he know that?

"I haven't leaked anything. I haven't told anyone that one of them was held on remand. Or that he's been screwing his superior's wife. Anyone who watches the recording can see that they weren't doing their job."

"I can assure you that I intend to investigate everything and if you've had anything to do with it, I will not spare you."

Axel was alone. No one came to his rescue. And he had been grassed up by someone who, at the same time, had fed Dorte Neergaard with all the juicy details. Everybody would assume he was the source.

"I want a verbal account from you later today. And let's hope you're on the right track with Lindberg."

Rosenkvist strode off down the street with Corneliussen after him. The first TV vans had arrived.

"Sounds like you're under a bit of pressure, Steen," teased Kettler.

Axel spun round furiously to face him.

Henriette Nielsen stepped in between them.

"You haven't got many friends," she said, but there was no trace of the malicious pleasure that Kettler so arrogantly directed at him.

"He's got some down there among the vultures," said Kettler, jerking his head towards the press people, where Dorte Neergaard had just got out of a broadcasting truck.

Axel watched Rosenkvist walking towards them with his arms spread. His broad smile fluttered to meet them. He laid an avuncular hand on Dorte Neergaard and pulled her to one side. There were several Axel knew, including Jakob Sonne, who waved to him, but Axel ignored him.

He turned to Darling and the Swede, who straightened up from the dead body.

"Like your Albanian friend, he's had his thyroid cartilage almost crushed – at least, that's how it looks and feels from the outside, but he has many more injuries than Davidi, just look at his cheeks."

Axel looked at the dark blue skin that showed no sign of external wounds.

"It could be slaps, a lot of them. No rupture, but massive blood aggregation under the skin. He's been tortured by someone who enjoyed it. It's pretty nauseating. You should get hold of this bastard before he does any more damage."

Martin Lindberg's flat was a loft over an old carpenter's workshop on Blytækkervej, a little further down Frederikssundsvej towards the city.

Axel knew that the body had been transported from the crime scene to the building site, so now it was important to find the murderer's car. Perhaps it belonged to Lindberg, if he even had one. The million-dollar question was why he had chosen to get rid of the body so close to his flat if he had anything at all to do with it.

When they got into the apartment via a steel staircase on the outside of the building, they found three technicians at work in white one-piece suits.

The flat was one large room with a built-in kitchen in one corner and stairs out to a toilet. A large poster with a red stop sign and the text 'Stop human trafficking' hung on the back of the door. Otherwise it was surprisingly trendy, spacious and stylish, with abstract art on the walls, Eames chairs around a modern dining table in pale wood, and a window frieze of small square stained-glass panes. The only pieces of furniture were an Arne Jakobsen Egg chair in worn dark-brown leather and a small table next to it.

They looked around and it soon became apparent that Piver hadn't been killed here. That hadn't prevented the technicians from dusting the entire apartment for fingerprints. Now they were turning out the contents of shelves, drawers and cupboards. Axel and Darling gave them a hand. After half an hour they had been through everything. There was nothing directly related to Piver's murder, but they had collected three boxes of mixed content: library books that should have been handed over a long time ago; bills for mobile phones; a car insurance policy; a passport and a bundle of bank statements; two cudgels; an antique pistol; comprehensive correspondence with left-wing radical groups in Hamburg; a very old joint, as Axel observed when he touched the dry paper and felt the tobacco crackling and disintegrating under his fingers; the hard drive of a desktop computer; three mobile phones and various letters and personal papers.

The technicians left the flat and let Axel and Darling keep the box with the personal papers.

They had to go back to HQ, but Axel had agreed to meet Henriette Nielsen to discuss reactions in the milieu around Blågårds Plads. That irritated Darling.

"Why do that now? Let them rummage through their drug dealers on their own."

Should he tell Darling about the meeting with Moussa? No, that would have to wait until he knew more.

"Because it could be important."

"Why not leave it to PET? We're focusing on Lindberg now. We have to find out where Piver was killed and where the recording is. That's top priority. You of all people have been so set on busting Lindberg."

"I wouldn't mind that, true."

Axel bit a nail and leafed through Lindberg's papers.

"So what's the problem?"

"I have a bad feeling about this. It's just a feeling."

"But this is where the trail's hot right now and I want you to come in and be there while we finish the interview."

"Later. I want to check the crime scene and do a bit of work with forensics. We need to get hold of everyone who was close to Piver and question them – he may have made contact with them before he was killed."

Darling shook his head.

"Bloody hell – you're just impossible to work with."

Axel was unable to see it in his mind's eye. Martin Lindberg could possibly have murdered Enver Davidi, but not the young autonomist – it didn't make sense. What was more, the violence suggested it was a man of a slightly different stature.

A key slipped into the lock, the door of the apartment opened and revealed Liz, the tall blonde girl from the collective on Nørrebrogade, whom Darling had questioned. She was wearing a screaming-red rubber raincoat, with the hood pulled down over her face, and she didn't notice them until she pulled it back.

"What the he…?"

She dumped the shopping bag she had in her hand, turned as if she were going to run off, but then her shoulders sank. She noticed that the door and the wall around it were sprinkled with fingerprint powder.

"What are you doing here?" she moaned.

Darling went over to her.

"We were just talking about you, actually, but we could very well ask you the same question."

"I have a meeting with Martin."

"And you have your own key?"

"Yes."

"You'll have to explain that further."

"What do you mean?"

"Are you in a relationship?"

"What the hell are you doing here? What's this all about?"

"Martin Lindberg is being held at Police Headquarters and is having a hard time explaining his movements in the last four to five days at some quite crucial times in a murder investigation. The same murder we were investigating when we encountered you four days ago. And now you come here. I think you should sit down and explain what's going on."

"I have no idea what you're talking about. Martin and I are working together on a project about trafficked women from Eastern Europe. He doesn't have anything to do with the murder. He really wants to help people in need."

"What are you doing here?"

"We agreed a while ago that I would come here today and cook a meal with him, talk strategy, not least in relation to you pigs, who just arrest girls and send them out of the country."

Darling ignored the indignation about police operations against trafficked women.

"So you haven't been with him in the last few days?"

"No, not at all."

Axel broke in.

"Does he know Piver?"

"I don't think so. He may have met him but only once. Do you know anything about Piver?"

They exchanged brief glances.

"When did you last talk to him?" asked Darling.

"I've already told you that. I called him after you came to the collective on Friday and asked him to call, and he did."

"Why did you call him?"

"To say he should turn himself in, that you were after him, and that it wasn't about YoHo, it was about a murder."

"What else did you tell him?"

"I told him that the press wanted to get hold of him. We had a visit from a journalist from Ekstra Bladet, who was keen to talk to him, and later several journalists called us to ask what had happened."

"Who?"

"I can't remember the names, but Rosa said someone from Counterpress called and wanted to meet Piver. We had lots of journalists coming by during the day and several of them got his number. You lot also called us up twice wanting to make sure that he didn't have any other numbers, as you were trying to trace him."

Axel looked at Darling, who shrugged. The field was growing steadily.

"Where is he? Have you found him?"

There is no easy way to deliver the message that your husband, wife, lover or friend is dead. There are no shortcuts. Axel took a step towards her and immediately he could see that she knew.

He looked her in the eyes and put a hand on her shoulder.

"He's dead. I'm sorry. We just found him."

Liz doubled up. Axel bent down and took hold of her.

"Come over here, sit down, and I'll tell you what we know."

Darling drove him back to the factory site. Henriette Nielsen was still there. She had been informed of the meeting with Liz and asked Axel a number of follow-up questions. On the one hand, she was far from convinced that Lindberg had killed Davidi, let alone Piver; on the other hand, she seemed relieved that there was a suspect in the spotlight – it shifted the focus from her own, and PET's, role in Davidi's murder. There were still a number of investigators, forensic technicians and rank-and-file police officers on the site, so Axel suggested that they take a walk up the street.

"Do you think there's a connection between the two murders? Is it the same perpetrator?" she asked.

"It's a very reasonable assumption, isn't it? They're very close, both in method and in execution. Both of them have been very violently strangled, both have been beaten up, and we're talking about a perpetrator who doesn't feel limited to one type of violence. He strikes in different ways – beating, torturing, tying up and killing his victims with great strength. I'm sure the recording that the last victim got hold of will help us, otherwise he wouldn't have been killed."

They had reached a crossroads and Axel had seen something on the way that had struck him. They turned around.

"And what about witnesses from the blocks over there?" Axel asked, pointing towards Frederiksborgvej.

"No one's seen anything."

"Maybe it doesn't matter. Perhaps we can manage without witnesses and Piver's video tape."

"What do you mean?"

They stopped opposite the spot where the body had been found. In the last 10 minutes, they had passed Nybolig Business Real Estate, Copenhagen Business Academy, the Danish headquarters of the international Islamic organisation Minhaj-ul-Quran, a car rental firm, a company that made plastic containers for the pharmaceutical industry, and Peugeot's Copenhagen workshop. They hadn't met a single person.

"In the 75 yards we've just walked, there are six surveillance cameras. And three of them are turned right towards that rubbish dump over there. We're going to have to be really bloody unlucky if we don't get anything on him here."

They agreed that Henriette Nielsen would get hold of the surveillance material, while Axel would check all the call information on Piver's phone, his friends' and Martin Lindberg's. He had to return to HQ soon to sit in on his old arch enemy's interview; it had to be in its final phase if they were to convince the public prosecutor's office to bring him before a magistrate.

His mobile rang. He wanted to turn it off but could see that it was Rosenkvist.

"You will come to my office immediately," was the short message before the caller hung up.

43

The echo of Axel's heels on the black stone floor was cold and hollow as it rebounded off the white walls of the executive corridor. As in the rest of the building, there are connections between the offices, so the outer corridor is almost always deserted, but while down in the departments the corridor seems like a peaceful spot overlooking the inner courtyard, there is a more intimidating atmosphere in the star corridor, as it is known by ordinary officers – not because they are fans of the occupants, but because officers with the most stars on their shoulders have their offices there.

First and foremost, the Police Commissioner in her dark-brown renaissance mausoleum lined with pine and hung with portraits of all her predecessors since 1682, staring at you from the walls with paralysing severity. Then there were the smaller offices: the Chief Prosecutor, the Deputy Commissioners and Assistant Commissioner Rosenkvist, the only one who didn't have a legal education and therefore enjoyed a totally different level of respect among police officers from the others.

He was standing by the window as Axel came in, but immediately turned round and asked him to take a seat.

"Lindberg's arrest has been leaked," he said, looking at Axel with raised eyebrows in a face whose tiredness seemed to be that of experience rather than exhaustion. "But not only that. Ekstra Bladet has a story online that Lindberg has been arrested because he's been trying to get hold of a film showing that the murder of Enver Davidi was committed by a policeman."

Axel was shaken. Of course, things leaked from HQ, but this information was hardly known by anyone other than himself, Darling, Corneliussen, Rosenkvist, the PET people, Lindberg's lawyer and the prosecutor who would be trying to get Lindberg remanded in custody. And by the perpetrator. If it wasn't Lindberg.

"We have to call a press conference on the matter soon and I have to deny the story," said Rosenkvist.

"Where did they get it from?"

"We're working on that now. We're listening in on journalists' telephones but nothing has come up so far that we can use."

"Could it be PET?"

He laughed, but there was neither warmth nor humour in his grimace.

"In your dreams. From the first second of this case, I've been emphasising the importance of keeping things close to us. And you're the first one to have leaked. Without telling us how, you've got your hands on a TV2 recording and shown it to the two officer suspects without clearing it with me, even though I explicitly requested it. Since then, the recording has been used by television to humiliate us and demonstrate our incompetence, aided by you explaining to them what's happening on the tape."

He saw no need to lie about his actions – they had got results.

"I moved the investigation on, didn't I? Unlike everyone else. We'd still be sitting chopping at Vang and Groes if I hadn't got hold of that clip. And it wasn't me who leaked why Vang actually disappeared."

"We're under pressure. Everyone knows that you got hold of that recording. And I have to act, even though I acknowledge that you got things moving. But you've had a run-in with Lindberg before, which could harm our investigation if a smart defence lawyer wants to use it in court. And when you don't tell me or your immediate superior such crucial details, I begin to wonder what else you're hiding. Or what you've been saying. Have you leaked Lindberg's arrest and the contents of his telephone conversation with the latest victim to Ekstra Bladet?"

"I'd never even think of doing that."

"I'm glad to hear it, because if that were the case, I'd have to send you home without pay. I'm removing you as a central investigator. You've got off lightly. You'll have yet another mark on your personnel file, and I'll remember this, Steen. I've instructed Darling to use you for various outstanding tasks, surveillance, reviews of witness statements and telephone information, but you do nothing on your own initiative from now on. And you keep away from Lindberg."

Axel didn't understand what was happening.

"Why don't you just remove me from the investigation?"

"Because you're loyal, aren't you? Even though you do everything you can to ruin things for yourself, you only have one goal: to solve the case."

"Yes – so what?"

Rosenkvist eyed him with an ironic smile, let his fingertips do their power dance against each other and looked as if he were making the decision that Axel was sure he'd already made before the meeting.

"There are many people interested in this case and things are going on which not even I – with all my years of experience in PET – know about. That's why you're not being demoted to the traffic division."

"So I should blab to you if the big boys in PET are taking the piss out of us?"

"Don't be naive. I saw through you a long time ago. You do things your own way, but if they were taking the piss out of us, you'd be even more upset than me, and where would you get help from then?" He lifted a hand and read an email. "This conversation is over, Steen. We continue with Lindberg at full speed – I will make the story public soon. It strikes me as significant that we're investigating a murder which the perpetrator has tried to disguise as part of the conflict between us and the autonomists, and that we have a suspect in our custody who has made hatred of the police his mission in life."

This last bit applied to a lot of people.

"What if it's not him?" asked Axel.

"Fortunately, you won't have to rack your brains about that now. It's no longer your problem."

Out in the corridor it was as quiet as the tomb in which Axel felt he had been locked. He started walking. Outside the Commissioner's office, there was a packet of cigarettes on the windowsill. He stopped and looked at it, picked it up, pulled one out and considered it, while looking at the peculiar swastika terrazzo floor with its large greyish-white spots that looked like a mixture of wear and excess detergent. The myth went that the architect didn't like his sketch and, during a drinking bout, smudged the charcoal drawing, which was later followed in every particular when the floor was laid.

"Have we booked time with the duty magistrate?" shouted Darling from the neighbouring office as Axel entered his own. He was bent over a transcript of the Lindberg interview, along with the chief prosecutor. Axel could read in their eyes that they both knew he had been sidelined and the humiliation stung. Was it one of those two arseholes who had grassed him up?

"Can you get it done now? We only have him for four hours."

One of the younger investigators stuck his head in.

"When for?"

"In three hours. We need to get him back for questioning again."

Axel broke in.

"Are you sure you should be taking him to the duty magistrate just with that?"

"New stuff has turned up. I've questioned Sonne, who maintains that Lindberg has been asking around for Piver – it confirms the suspicion. I'm sure we'll get him."

Axel shook his head and went into his office. What the hell was he going to do now? Was it him barking up the wrong tree? Could Lindberg be the murderer? It had happened before that he had been 110 per cent sure of a murderer's innocence and had to eat virtually every word he had said at the meetings when the final proof came to light – but still, Lindberg? Axel would love to see that arsehole rot in prison, but bloody hell, not for something he hadn't done.

He sat down at his desk, took out his laptop and logged in. Lindberg was the top story on all the online newspapers: Noted left-wing activist arrested for murder.

The news about Piver's murder hadn't reached them yet, but it couldn't be long. It was Ekstra Bladet that had the story of Lindberg's arrest, and that Lindberg had tried to get hold of a film showing that Enver Davidi's murderer was a police officer. Should he call Sonne and question him about where that came from? He would demand something in return, and even if he got it, there was no guarantee he would reveal his source – Axel didn't care about the source's name, he just wanted to know if it was someone on the inside. It would have to wait; it would be far too risky to call him from HQ – he had to find another phone.

He opened his email and began reading the reports that had arrived. Darling had done a roster where Axel was named as a stand-in on the surveillance of Laila Hansen – a considerable demotion, but the thought of seeing her once again warmed him.

Alternatively, he could just go home and smoke a very big pipe of hash and forget all about this crappy day.

He fetched a cup of coffee, closed the door and sat down again. Then he cleared a pile of old reports from the surveillance of a hash club out of the way and placed the coffee cup on the thick glass plate that covered his desk. Between the glass and the desktop were memoranda: phone lists; flyers from takeaway restaurants, sushi, Indian and a genuine Italian pizzeria that advertised pizzas with shawarma and bearnaise sauce; a postcard with a motif by Francis Bacon; a holiday photo of Emma on the sea shore with light curls, brown skin, pink bathing suit with frills, chalky-white protruding teeth and blinking eyes; and on the right side the three photos: the little black-haired girl and two young smiling women, Rajan, Miranda and Stina, who had been killed in the early nineties. They stared at him from a place where the darkness was deeper and thicker than anything he knew.

They were still out there. Their murderers. But they should be brought in. And Axel would do anything to be the one who arrested them. Got them punished. Killed, if necessary.

He searched his emails from the beginning of the investigation on Friday morning and began printing out all the reports. He would read them through again, now he had been sidelined. It wasn't the first time he had been held back because of formalities; he would surely rise again and take this whole crazy investigation to pieces.

A window appeared on Axel's screen, indicating that, though he may well have been sent to the bottom of the investigation hierarchy, he was still receiving all the electronic material on the case. He read the words as they appeared on the screen.

"Resumption of hearing of the suspect Martin Lindberg 220964-0119. Present: The suspect and his lawyer, DCI John Darling from Copenhagen Police and DCI Kristian Kettler from PET. Journal: Erna Jensen."

Kettler, of course. Axel accidentally knocked over his coffee cup and watched its contents flow out and cover the pictures of the murdered women and his daughter before it became so thin that parts of their faces loomed up through the brownish-black liquid. He cursed out loud and snatched at a kitchen roll on the edge of the desk, letting it spin out a few feet of paper, and wiped up while looking at the screen. Of course it was those two who were questioning Lindberg – the new couple. It might explain how the boss had been told about his deal with TV2.

Axel couldn't do anything about it now, but as soon as he got the opportunity, he would confront Darling.

He followed the interview while trying to get an overview of the documents on the case. He printed out all Friday's witness statements, 237 in all, by residents around Assistens – not just near the scene of the crime, but the whole way around the cemetery – the press, demonstrators and all his colleagues who had been in there.

Several of the residents in the property opposite the crime scene had been awake most of the night and some of them had been at their windows watching the police in Assistens during the evening and night. Some of their observations were timed precisely, others estimated within a range of several hours, but there were enough that it was worth making a time schedule and combining the data with TV2's helicopter footage. Axel fastened on to three of the statements. One witness thought he had seen a policeman hiding himself from his colleagues patrolling near the chapel. One had seen two men walking entwined, one of whom was a police officer; and a third person had seen a man carrying a bag climbing into the cemetery via an old lamp post on Kapelvej – 500 yards from the crime scene but close to Enver Davidi's hotel, and just 25 minutes before he was killed.

Then he began to skim through Lindberg's interview.

"We have a witness who tells us that you've been asking about the deceased, Peter Smith."

"It's a lie. I don't know who he is."

"But you asked about him on the street during the disturbances on Friday night, didn't you?"

"I haven't asked anyone about him, but I maybe talked to some colleagues about who the police were looking for."

The suspect hesitates.

"Is this from Sonne? That guy's on another planet. At one point we talked about the police looking for an autonomist. It's true that I asked him about the case."

"Before you said you didn't know Peter Smith at all. Now you remember him?"

"I don't know him, but like all the other journalists, I'd heard that you were looking for an autonomist. I didn't know why, but I'm a journalist, for Christ's sake, it's my job to ask about things and investigate rumours. There's no bloody law against it."

"What's your relationship with Sonne?"

"He's just an idiot I've known for years."

Axel began to review all the files they had received from telecommunications companies. There was tracking and wiretapping on both Piver's phone and the phone from Counterpress, which Lindberg denied knowing about. Piver's phone had only been activated at Christiania, while the Counterpress phone had been used frequently on Friday, several times near Counterpress's editorial office, in Østerbro, at Christiansborg and by the railway line between Nørrebro and Nordvest on Saturday morning.

The lawyer asks to have the recording replayed.

The recording is played.

The suspect protests loudly and denies that it is him. The lawyer asks us if the police really believe that it is his client's voice that can be heard on the recording. He says we must surely be able to hear that it doesn't sound like him at all.

John Darling: "That doesn't prove anything. Nowadays you can distort voices as easily as snapping your fingers."

Lawyer: "In that case I think you should get it analysed very quickly. I can hear with own my ears that it hasn't been distorted. It isn't Martin. And if it isn't him on the tape, then you have a big problem; you have nothing substantial on him. I have to ask for a break. I have an important conference call."

Axel's door opened. John Darling came in with Kettler and the prosecutor.

"Is there anything new?" Darling asked amicably. Kettler was radiant.

"No." Axel's face was expressionless. He continued reading.

"We're on our way in to Corneliussen. We're going to the duty magistrate with him."

Axel ignored them. When they had gone through the door to Corneliussen's office, Axel quickly got up, closed the door behind them, walked out through the other door, which he left ajar, and carried on through the next two offices to Lindberg, now being kept company by a young warder from HQ prison.

"I've been told that no one may talk to him."

"Shut up and wait in the corridor," said Axel, showing him his warrant card.

Lindberg scrutinised him.

"What are you doing here?"

"That doesn't matter. You probably won't believe it, but you have only one chance now. And that chance is me. Is there anything you want to tell me?"

"Have you got a screw loose? You know as well as I do that I don't have anything to do with this. I could see it in your eyes while you were listening to that recording."

Axel stayed silent and waited.

"I know you hate me and I know why, but I thought you were made of different stuff. I didn't think you could be bought for a cheap lie. I thought you were looking for the truth. And you and your friends won't find it by locking me up."

"Who could be trying to frame you?"

"I have no idea, but I didn't have anything to do with it. And if I'm supposed to have killed both of these people, why haven't you found anything on me that could be linked to the murders?"

Axel heard the door to his office open two rooms along.

"I'll get back to you," he said, walking out of the door where the warder was waiting.

"You can go back in," he said, then fetched his stuff from his office and went down to the duty magistrate. There was time booked for Lindberg at 17:00 – in about an hour.

After Lindberg had been to the duty magistrate, the atmosphere was at a low point.

It had been one of the more critical magistrates who had listened to the case. There had been enough reporters to fill the small room with its four chairs five times over, but they had been thrown out in the interests of the investigation after the charge had been read out. The magistrate was fine with the closed doors, but she wasn't fine with the wiretap, which Lindberg's lawyer had demanded to have played back in court.

"I'm no expert, but I've made judgements in several surveillance cases where advanced masking equipment was used, and this doesn't sound like one of them. Even I can hear that it isn't the suspect's voice. You have three days to come up with something better or get that recording analysed so that you can establish on the balance of probabilities that it's Lindberg's voice."

The four weeks that the prosecutor had been after had become the shortest possible period of time someone could be held on remand.

As a 16-year-old second-generation immigrant was led in and sat on a chair bolted firmly to the floor with a steel wire, Axel left the duty magistrate's court and went out to the main entrance, where a number of journalists were still waiting.

"Axel, what happened?"

Dorte Neergaard stubbed out a cigarette and ran after him, her eyes in their almost flat sockets shining with concentration under the wide eyelids.

"Happened? You heard what happened. He's being held for three days on suspicion of murder."

"But you don't seriously believe that, do you? I know him – he would never touch a hair on anyone's head, apart from a cop. Why would he have killed that Davidi guy?"

Axel stopped.

"Listen, Dorte. I fucked up the other day, but I gave you something to show you I'm sorry. Now I can't say any more. I don't know where you've got hold of the story that one of the officers was at home screwing his superior's wife, but everyone thinks it came from me and I'm on my way out of the investigation for that reason. So I can't afford to be seen in your company. I don't blame you – nice story, true too – but I have nothing more to say."

"OK... I was also a little surprised at who it came from."

"Who?"

She smiled. "Sources, Axel, we protect them," she said.

"If I were you, I'd be more careful about it next time. Everyone's saying that I had a deal with you to get that TV recording. I don't know if it'll reach your bosses, but if it does, you're as screwed as I am."

44

Wednesday, March 7

He unbuttoned the dress. It sat tight over her stomach and breasts, a black bra and black silk knickers – or were they synthetic? – with a transparent embroidered edge. Her body was strong, her muscles hard, warm skin, the fabric down over her shoulder, she was wet and wanted to be touched and he was welcome. Her breasts rolled out of the bra, they hung, soft and beautiful, the nipples totally hard, almost too hard for him to be able to stand touching them, they were so unbelievably tense with excitement. He grabbed hold of her short red hair, which he could just about grip between his fingers, pulled her towards him, kissed her and stuck his tongue deep into her mouth, spit and saliva running out of the corners of her mouth, his cheek rubbing against her face, he didn't hold back. Then he got tired of that and bit her lips, clutched at her, now he was going to bloody well take her. Now. Laila. Now.

Axel was woken up by the noise from a dustcart braking in the street below him, ten-fifteen beeps that rang out louder than his alarm clock, depriving him of the last remnant of sex with Laila Hansen and leaving him unfulfilled and completely dry in his mouth. The pressure in his bladder forced him out of bed to go and pee.

He wasn't finding much peace at night, which was a perfect storm of hormones, full of women – real women, fantasy women, memory women and future women to whom he was deeply attracted, but he couldn't work out if he should have them or could get them at all – neither in his dreams nor in reality. First, Cecilie, now Laila Hansen. Next, he would no doubt begin having nightmares or wet dreams about Henriette Nielsen.

He went out to the kitchen and sat down at the small tiled table, rebooted his computer and put water in the coffee machine. Cecilie didn't answer when he tried to call her. He checked his emails and read the latest files in the investigation; nothing new out of Lindberg, who was maintaining his innocence. The technical department reported a burned-out black van found by the fire brigade under the Bispeengbuen motorway flyover.

Then he went for a walk, down Nørrebrogade, through the gate of Assistens Cemetery, past the chapel and out through the exit to Jagtvej. There wasn't much left of the Youth House; girls with smudged mascara were sitting in tears on the asphalt. But the disturbances were over. Air and light were a contour-free study in grey.

Although Axel was still receiving copies of the investigation documents, he couldn't do very much on his own. John Darling would hardly bother to keep him informed from now on, so Henriette Nielsen was still his only way in and he had already exploited that to the fullest during his run-in with Moussa.

She answered at the first ring.

"Hi, Axel. What's up? I heard you've been read the riot act. Are you about to desert us?"

"Not quite yet, but I'm not very highly thought of either. Is there anything new on the drugs or Moussa?"

"Not just yet. I've just got in and have checked through the surveillance briefly. We didn't catch anything on them yesterday."

"They know perfectly well that you're on to them, I suppose?"

"I guess they know something, but not everything."

"Do you have a flat on Pladsen? And can I get into it?"

"We have one that's very central, and we have several cameras inside and outside. You're welcome to come up and see it with me if you want, but I don't have time before this afternoon."

"Oh? What's keeping you so busy?"

"Among other things, I have to review some surveillance footage from Bispevej with our video technician. Several of them show a black Ford van stopping and a man throwing Piver's body out on the building site."

"Fuck, what are you saying?"

"Don't get too excited just yet. The clips I've seen don't shed any light on the man's identity. And the Ford was..."

"...found burned out under Bispeengbuen last night," continued Axel.

"You've heard. Yeah, why the hell is that always the place where criminals set fire to their cars?"

"It's habit," said Axel. In the desolate area under the motorway leading out of Copenhagen between Nørrebro and Frederiksberg, cars were often set on fire to erase any traces of DNA.

"Do you know what's happening with Lindberg?" Axel asked.

"He's going to be questioned again today, but I guess they'll get tired of it. We've had our sound engineers reviewing the recording, and though the possibility that it's him speaking can't be dismissed entirely, the chances aren't very high."

"Why?"

"Lindberg is from Copenhagen. The accent sounds more like Gladsaxe."

"Which means it can't be him?"

"Hardly. Dialects aren't something that can be mimicked through whole conversations. We've had a man from Copenhagen University listen to both voices and he thinks it unlikely that it's the same person."

"I assume Kettler knows all this?"

"You bet."

"Why don't they let him go then?"

"They will do when the deadline expires, but they're probably trying to see if they can get something on him before then."

Axel was thoughtful.

"Has anyone been looking at Lindberg's past?"

"You're the expert on that, or so I've heard," she teased.

"Not that part, but is there any connection between him and Davidi? Has he ever written about him? Has he been to Macedonia? Does he know Piver? Does he know the collective where he lived? Would Piver recognise him and go with him?"

"I don't know. That's not my area. But you could check that out without treading on anyone's toes."

Laila Hansen wanted to see him. She had taken time off work and would prefer to keep Louie at home too, she said, but Louie wanted to go to school because there was a football tournament.

He parked the car right behind the dark blue civilian police car, stepped out, walked up to it, put a hand on the roof and bent down.

"Has anything happened?"

"Not since you were last here," laughed one of them, "but thanks, because it means we get to sit here in the warm instead of running around down at YoHo."

"You're welcome to go home now. I'll take over."

"Could you just make it a little quieter than last time?"

The other one smirked, saluted ironically, straightened up and started the engine. Over the roof of the car, Axel could see Laila Hansen standing in the nearest window with arms folded, staring at him with a distant look that seemed lost in inner turmoil. The experience with the three goons from Pladsen had probably not had the best effect on her. He thought of Emma and how he would have felt if she had witnessed a scene like that. Had Louie seen anything? Had he been woken up by the noise or by Axel's colleagues coming to pick up Moussa's boys?

She greeted him at the door and he immediately sensed her unease, as if she wanted to protect herself against him.

"Come in," she said distractedly, but still looked up at his face as he walked past her in the narrow passage, with a look that was full of… yes, full of what?

Tenderness, desire, anxiety, insecurity? He thought her face contained them all, but he was unable to separate them or understand the reason, because he desired her so much; it came from nowhere else, it wasn't a replacement for holes left elsewhere in his life, it was pure, unadulterated lust for her. The feeling was like a storm inside him; he wanted her, to feel her body, lie with her and hold her. Without him knowing where it came from.

There were six hours to go until he would be relieved. And at least four until Louie came home.

"The guy they've arrested – is he the one who did it?" she asked.

"I don't think so."

"Why not?"

"Because I know him. He's a shit, but he's not the type; he doesn't fit into this case, and I can't see what his motive would be."

"Who is it then? Do you have any ideas?"

"No, but we're getting closer."

"Who is he – the man under arrest?"

"He's an old autonomist, now calling himself a journalist, working for something called Counterpress. His name's Martin Lindberg."

"Is it Martin you've arrested? Martin Lindberg? I know him."

"What do you mean?"

"And he knows… knew David."

"What?"

"He met David in Macedonia. David worked for him and some other journalists. And when they got home, Martin came here and delivered money for Louie."

Why the hell hadn't anyone checked this out?

"What money?"

"A thousand kroner David had earned and which he thought I should have for Louie. I told you that." She went briefly quiet, biting a nail. "I think he did it mostly to impress me and show me that he was a good father, but Lindberg came here with the money."

"Fuck me, that's unexpected. I have to go. I have to go to HQ."

45

In the car on the way to HQ, Henriette Nielsen called.

"Are you busy?"

"You could say. What's up?"

"I think you should come down to Pladsen if you have time. I'm in the flat. Moussa's holding court with a handful of reporters on the street just below me."

"What's he doing?"

"Talking, grandstanding, making big arm movements. Your friend from TV2, Sonne, BT and Jyllands-Posten – they're all here. It's not small stuff he's talking about."

No one else but Axel was aware that Lindberg knew Enver Davidi, so he could postpone questioning him until later. That would have the advantage of there being fewer people at HQ so he could have Lindberg to himself.

"Text me when you get here so that I can come down and let you in the back door."

He parked the car in Korsgade and walked into the courtyard, which covered a whole tenement block and was large and open with lawns, playground, outdoor grill, tables and chairs for the residents. He could see Henriette Nielsen standing in the back door 100 yards away.

On the third floor of the turn-of-the-century brick building, he entered a luxury flat, which only had one room overlooking Blågårds Plads – the rest of the flat was facing the courtyard. Axel could see through three high-ceilinged rooms furnished with expensive Danish designer furniture.

"Who lives here?"

"A guy who was going to New York and needed to rent out the flat for a year."

It was possible to look out from two of the three sections of the window – behind the last one, which was covered with mirror tape, two camcorders had been mounted and there was space for a photographer, who was sitting there snapping freely right now.

Axel put on the headphones. Moussa's voice was grinding away. It had a natural self-assurance which was unmistakable, calm and soft, but completely impossible to dismiss in its imperious tone. He loathed everything Moussa stood for but he had respect for his strength, and he knew what was required to reach the position he had.

"We don't have anything to do with the disturbances," Moussa was saying, "there's no truth in it. Take a look at what has happened. Is it the youth from here at Pladsen, or is it all sorts of troublemakers from all over Europe, from Berlin and elsewhere that are causing the trouble? It speaks for itself. It's not us smashing up shops and burning cars, is it?"

When Axel heard Dorte Neergaard's voice, he went over to the window. Moussa was sitting on a café chair in front of Escobar, leaning back and waving his arms and talking with a big smile. It was his prime-time, with Dorte Neergaard in front of him and a camera team behind his back. He obviously didn't want to be filmed with his face showing. Five reporters and a large group of young second-generation immigrants were standing and sitting around them.

"But it's your boys who have run riot down here and, for example, been responsible for smashing up some of the shops in the street, isn't it?" asked Dorte Neergaard.

"There's no truth in that. It's something the police say to shift… what's it called… focus from their own failures. The police are desperate. Two days ago I met a policeman here in the square. He offered me drugs if I would help him in a case they can't solve."

The journalists around the table woke up and the questions showered down on him. Axel became uncomfortable.

"Who was it?"

"Do you have proof of that?"

"What did he want you to help him with?"

Henriette Nielsen's eyes met his.

"I have no further comments, but if he was standing here, I could point him out for you."

The reporters tried once again but Moussa stayed silent.

"How the hell have you miked them up?" asked Axel.

"There are wireless microphones mounted under every café table," she said with a smile that wasn't completely devoid of professional pride.

Moussa continued to assert his innocence and that of the boys on Pladsen in connection with the vandalism. The interview was about to peter out when Dorte Neergaard's voice cut through.

"But aren't you the leader of the Blågårds Plads gang?"

"There are no gangs."

"But there's a hierarchy here with you at the top?"

"I have no comment on that."

"But you and several of these people standing here have been sentenced to long prison terms for violent and threatening behaviour and dealing hash."

"It's not something I want to comment on."

"Why not? Everyone knows. Why don't you want to talk about it?"

"I just don't."

"If you're not a gang, what are you then?"

"You must understand, that's not the way it is. We're just a bunch of comrades who stick together, that's all. It's the police who are trying to cause a stir, using us as an excuse to drive around the streets and carry out a witch-hunt against all these young people. It's been going on for years and young people are getting tired of it, so some of them are reacting. But we're not a gang and we aren't taking part in the disturbances, if you know what I'm saying."

The photographer in the flat looked at them.

"A bastard like that shouldn't have freedom of speech," he said. "How can he just sit there unchecked and throw outrageous accusations at us?"

Axel looked at Moussa and the assembled reporters and casual onlookers in the street below. It would definitely be one of the press scoops of the day – while it was true that criminals were getting an increasing amount of airtime and column space in the media, it wasn't every day that the leader of the most notorious immigrant gang in Denmark spoke to the press.

Eight to ten of Moussa's boys were hanging around near the group or mixing in with it. Dorte Neergaard was in an intense discussion with one of them, and a reporter from BT stood talking avidly with Moussa, while one of Moussa's henchmen had a hand on his arm. They were arguing.

"I've told you not to take pictures of them. You mustn't interview them. They aren't interested in being in the media," said the gang leader in a tone that didn't exactly encourage the reporters to defy him.

Was it true though? wondered Axel. In gang culture, expressing hatred of journalists and verbally abusing them was a status symbol, but didn't every one of these minions and pushers dream of a notoriety they would never achieve? To become something bigger than a single column court report on page seven after a sentence for GBH, threatening behaviour or dealing hash?

Moussa moved away from the café's outdoor serving area with a small retinue of his comrades, as he called them. Axel recognised two of them as Moussa's bodyguards from Monday night. Jakob Sonne followed them, signalling to his photographer to wait at the café; it looked like he was going to give it one last try. It turned into a one-minute conversation with Moussa, who laughed out loud at something the reporter said, patting him on the back as if they were old friends.

Henriette Nielsen stopped him in the stairwell.

"Aren't we on thin ice now?"

"What do you mean?"

"Your chat with Moussa, Enver Davidi's death. There are a lot of things that won't be able to stand the light of day."

Her brow was knotted with frowns down to her nose.

"You worry too much, Henriette. None of it matters if we get our man."

"Does that also apply to our undercover operation with Davidi?"

Axel couldn't afford to lose her trust now, but he didn't want to lie to her either.

"That was some of the most brainless stuff I've seen for a long time, but it wasn't your idea, was it?"

"No, it wasn't."

"I don't protect anyone, Henriette. And I feel no need to spare Kettler and Jessen."

"And I don't want to lose my job because you're itching for revenge on your ex-wife's new man, understood? Don't forget I was there while you talked to Moussa the other night. I've got something on you."

Axel was impressed; he smiled and nodded.

"It doesn't change the fact that you're all responsible for Davidi's death. PET hiring Davidi to infiltrate BGP, and then getting murdered because of your incompetence, wouldn't look all that fantastic on Ekstra Bladet's front page, would it?"

She gave him an icy look.

"You just keep me out of it, are you with me?" she hissed. "Otherwise I'll drag you down with me!"

Axel laughed and walked down the stairs.

"Relax, Henry. I'll be a good boy – it's just the copper blues!"

46

"Have you come here to blow off steam?"

Martin Lindberg had now spent 36 hours in the six-yard-square cell in the Headquarters lock-up, which was usually reserved for threatening and violent prisoners. It showed. There was a tired look in his eyes, spite and anger, but Axel also thought he could detect capitulation.

"No, I haven't."

"You're well aware of what this is, right? It is a refined form of torture. Locking up innocent people in small rubber cells and not allowing them out all day. I had to wait two fucking hours to get a towel yesterday, because some guy went crazy on the floor underneath."

"Now you're talking about innocence. I'm not here to hear your complaints about the conditions in Danish prisons. I'm sure the Ombudsman will be hearing from you. I'm here because there's something you haven't told us."

Axel took the pictures of the dead Enver Davidi – both from Assistens and from the autopsy – and gave them to Lindberg.

"Don't you recognise this man?"

Lindberg looked at both pictures and shook his head.

"No, I don't."

"Look at them! Don't they say anything to you at all?"

No response. Axel shook his head.

"Macedonia. Enver Davidi, also known as David?"

"David? Is that the interpreter?" Martin Lindberg looked confused, almost worried. "What was he doing…? He was deported."

"You know him then?"

"Yes… I mean… not very well. He was an interpreter for me in Macedonia during the disturbances down there in 2001. I was freelancing for Information and anyone else I could sell articles to. And David could speak both languages so he was an obvious choice. I took him over from a guy from DR. A lot of us used him."

"And then you contacted his ex-wife when you came home?"

"Yes. We paid him a couple of hundred a day down there, and he wanted us to take a large part of the money home to his wife, so he gave me her phone number. I contacted her and went out and handed over an envelope and said a few nice words about him, nothing more."

"Which other Danish journalists used him?"

"There were a lot. I don't know who exactly, but while I was there, there were three from DR, Sonne among others, Dorte Neergaard from TV2, Politiken, a young guy from JP. I don't know if they all used him, but David was in demand because he was good at his job – talented and pleasant. But what does that have to do with my case?"

Axel ignored the question.

"What about Davidi? Have you seen him since then?"

"Never."

"What about the ex-wife?"

"I only saw her the one time I went out to give her the money from David."

"What was your impression of Davidi?"

"I don't have anything bad to say about him. He'd made a mistake, which he bitterly regretted."

"His drug case?"

"Yes, he repeatedly said he longed to see his son. And he…"

There was some hesitation in his account of Davidi.

"He what?"

"He asked me to write a recommendation for him."

"Recommendation for what?"

"He was very preoccupied with getting his deportation case reviewed so that he could come home and see his son or get the conditions relaxed. And then he asked me to write a recommendation that he could attach to his application."

"Did you do that?"

He looked down at his hands.

"No."

"Why not?"

"I was a freelancer. I was trying to create a career for myself in the established press. It wouldn't have looked good if it came out that I'd defended a convicted drug offender."

"How did he react to that?"

"He didn't react."

"What do you mean?"

Lindberg sighed.

"I'm not especially proud of this and I would act differently today, but I said I'd send him one when I got home – and then I didn't."

"Did he react to that?"

"No, I think he already sensed it when I said it down there – that he would never get it. He seemed disappointed, but he accepted it."

"How about Sonne, does he know anything about him?"

"Why? What's this about?"

"I'm just asking if Sonne and Davidi had a relationship."

Hesitation again.

"They did. Sonne was employed by DR at that time and acted like the big shot with the whole state TV apparatus at his back, but when he learnt that David had a drugs conviction, his attitude hardened. He was worried it would come out that DR had been using a deported drug criminal as an interpreter."

"Have you two talked about Davidi since he was murdered?"

"No, I haven't talked to Sonne," he said. Too fast.

Axel took out the photo of Stanca Gutu and showed it to Lindberg.

"What about her?"

Lindberg scrutinised the photo of the smiling woman. Then Axel handed him the photo of her from the mortuary. Lindberg cast a brief glance at her and looked at Axel.

"Is that…?"

"Is that who?"

"I don't know – who is it?"

The conversation had taken an absurd turn. Axel wasn't sure Lindberg had recognised her, but he had reacted to the photo.

"Stanca Gutu, Moldovan prostitute, murdered in a hotel room in Tetovo the night between 17 and 18 March 2001. You look like you know her."

"I don't know her. I don't know who she is."

"When were you down there with Davidi?"

"March 2001. I can't remember the dates."

"Funny memory lapse, don't you think? We'll check what you've said here and then we'll have to see what the prosecutor decides. I hope for your sake that you've told the truth, because if not I'm sure the magistrate will come up with another couple of weeks so that we'll have time to investigate everything you've said in detail."

Axel got up to go. He knocked on the door and a prison warder opened up.

"Can you make sure you treat him properly so that we don't get too many complaints?" Axel said to the warder, before going out into the burgundy corridor, where steel mesh had been stretched out between each floor to prevent the prisoners throwing themselves over the edge.

"Oh, Axel Steen, there's one thing I forgot..."

Axel turned around.

"Yes."

"Sonne also went out to give interpretation pay to David's ex-wife. I think they became lovers."

The blood rose in Axel's cheeks.

"What did you say?"

"Just that. Sonne and I aren't friends but he once told me he'd been out there and didn't understand how David could put his life with her at risk for any amount of heroin because she was the best fuck he'd had in a long time."

Axel closed the cell door behind him.

47

Out of the prison to the back of HQ in Otto Mønsteds Gade and through the door in the heavy prison gates. He took out his mobile immediately but held back. Instead, he went up to the corner of HQ and turned away from the building down Niels Brocks Gade. He went into the minimarket on Anker Heegaards Gade and bought a packet of cigarettes and a lighter.

The first drag tasted of pubs and old men, but he smoked it greedily anyway, enjoying how he became heavy and felt his flesh and musculature collapse throughout his body. The cigarette continued to glow for two to three minutes, then he threw it away, coughing heavily.

She picked up after the third ring.

"Why didn't you tell me about Sonne?"

"What?"

"Why didn't you tell me you'd had a relationship with Sonne?"

"Why should I do that? You didn't ask. What does he have to do with the investigation?"

"You're not that stupid. Everyone who's had a relationship with your ex-husband has something to do with the investigation. Not least a man who's been screwing his ex-wife."

"You're back at work now, aren't you, cop? What are you up to?"

"I'll have to tell the guy leading the investigation about it. Then they'll come over and bring you in. You can be sure of that much."

"What are you talking about? You think I killed David? You must be crazy! I don't want to talk to you any more."

Axel took note of her reaction, which made him feel a little better, because her anger appeared to demonstrate that she was genuinely hurt rather than faking a reaction to hold the lies together.

"I'm not saying you killed him. But Laila, why the hell didn't you just tell me you'd had a relationship with him?"

"I guess I wasn't in the mood. I felt we had something. In a situation like that, you don't just stand there listing everyone you've screwed before."

"No, but I should have fucking asked you to if I'd been doing my job properly, and I wasn't."

"I think you did a pretty good job."

Axel ignored that.

"Do you still have contact, you and Sonne? Did he know that Davidi was coming? What's his relationship with Davidi?"

"Sonne and I were together for about a year. I needed some comfort. I was really lonely, for Christ's sake, and Louie liked him. We now have a friendly relationship. He didn't know that David was in Denmark – not from me at least. He knew David from Macedonia, like Lindberg. I don't think their relationship was anything special."

"You don't know if anything happened between them down there?"

"No, I've never heard anything like that." She hesitated. "What happens now, Axel?"

"I write a report and then you'll be asked to come in for an interview. You'd better look for a babysitter. I doubt that they'll wait until tomorrow."

"Will I hear from you again?"

"Yes, you'll hear something, but not right now. I'll call you."

Axel rang off and lit another cigarette, thinking about the new information. Lindberg. Laila. Sonne. Could it be one of them? It seemed improbable to him.

So who was left? Moussa or someone from his mob? Or PET? An insider from the police?

Was Lindberg telling the truth or was he trying to shift the focus away from himself? Either way, Jakob Sonne owed them a serious explanation. He had been right at the forefront of the coverage of Enver Davidi's murder and at no point had he said he knew him.

Axel went up to Homicide. There were lights on in several offices, both in Darling's and Corneliussen's. He remembered Darling's orders at the PET meeting three days ago to go into depth on Laila Hansen's background: "I want to know who she's been screwing."

Why hadn't he just told it how it was? And asked someone else to take care of that part of the investigation?

On the other hand, he had asked her the first time he interrogated her and she had said that there was no one of importance – including himself.

He went straight into the office where Darling was bent over his computer.

"Ah, there you are. Do you want to hear about the latest developments?" said the big cop.

Axel sat down.

"I didn't think I was part of the inner circle."

"Come on. We have a witness who's sure he saw Enver Davidi climb over the wall into Assistens, and another one who saw him walking with the murderer – entwined, as he put it. It sounds like the murderer has led Davidi to the wall and that fits with your footage from TV2…"

"So what?"

"Hang on a minute. We've watched recordings from Monday when Piver's body was thrown onto the building site. It's a hooded man, the pictures are pretty murky and you can't see his face but he's purposeful and throws the body down without looking around before driving off again. The car was set alight under Bispeengbuen barely half an hour later."

"Where's the car from?"

"We don't know. No black Ford Transit has been reported stolen during the last couple of months, but it could easily have been nicked without the owner having discovered it."

"What year and model?"

"It's from 1985, second generation, I think they call it. Over a thousand of them were sold in Denmark alone that year."

Axel remembered something.

"When did this happen?"

"Monday at 18.41."

"And when was Lindberg arrested?"

"Two hours later."

"I saw an insurance document on an old Ford Transit at Lindberg's place while we were searching it yesterday."

Darling lit up.

"Are you sure?"

"Yes."

"But if it's him, why haven't we found anything else at his place?"

"Maybe because he's got somewhere else?"

"Obviously. We'll have to go through all his stuff again. And check him in all the registers. I'll get people in. I'm afraid I can't take you along in this part of the investigation because I'm not allowed to."

"That's OK. I have something for you, too."

Axel told him about Lindberg's and Sonne's meetings with Enver Davidi in Macedonia in 2001 and about Sonne's relationship with Laila Hansen.

"Why are you telling me that?"

"Because it's important for the case."

"But how have you found out about it? You don't have access to Lindberg."

"No, but Laila Hansen told me. And Lindberg confirmed it."

"You should have come directly to me instead of following it up on your own. Axel, just let go of this case, for Christ's sake. Or you're going to find yourself right at the bottom. If Corneliussen hears that you're still running loose on your own, he'll be furious."

"I know, but it came to me in a natural way."

"If what you're saying is true, then it puts Lindberg under even greater suspicion. He actually knew Davidi."

"Yes, but no more than Sonne. He knew him too. What are you going to do now?"

"I'll get someone to pick up Laila Hansen and question her about her knowledge of the relationships between Davidi, Lindberg and

Sonne, and her relationship with Sonne. And Lindberg will have to make a new statement. And then we have to get Sonne in for a chat. Even though I can't have you along for this part of the investigation, you might want to check the background stuff on Macedonia, unless you'd rather run free."

His freedom of action had shrunk rapidly. Now he was only a researcher – but on the other hand, they were often the ones who found the gold.

48

It was approaching eight o'clock, but Axel had no need to go off duty. He tried to call Cecilie once again, but she didn't answer. This time he left a message and asked her to call back so that they could discuss when he was going to see Emma next.

He received a short text message that she didn't want to talk to him, and that Emma was still in shock after her weekend with him. His rage flared up like napalm.

He dialled her number again.

"Answer the bloody phone! What have you been telling her? Emma was fine when you left me. You can't do this to me."

Then he opened his laptop and checked emails. There was finally a reply from BB. It hadn't been possible to trace the email with the murderer's photo of Davidi, which had been sent from an internet café to Counterpress on Friday afternoon, but there was DNA on the balaclava, two kinds: one of them was naturally enough from Enver Davidi; the second from a source they didn't have registered. There was also DNA in the hotel room from Davidi, plus from some other people, including three police officers, one of whom was Axel himself and the two others were PET staff. There were no answers yet on the DNA samples from the examination of the crime scene at Assistens.

The boot prints just in front of the body were size 44 – one size larger than Lindberg's shoes, Axel noted. During the search of Lindberg's flat, they hadn't found any boots matching the prints, but that meant nothing. They could be somewhere else, or he could have got rid of them. If they weren't his boot prints, it left two possibilities: either Lindberg was involved along with someone else, or someone was trying to pin the murder first on the police and later on Lindberg. However much Axel would like to have Lindberg busted, he was more inclined to believe the second theory.

They were being led by the nose.

Perhaps the key to it would be found back in the spring of 2001.

He called Henriette Nielsen and told her what he was thinking.

"Can you find out if you have anything on Danish journalists in Tetovo in March 2001 covering the conflict between the government and the so-called Albanian rebels?"

"Forget that. There's something happening with Moussa. Your plan seems to be working."

"Has there been word about the gear?"

"Yes, apparently. Not that we've intercepted anything directly, but they're talking about it in the streets – people are restless. Someone wants to sell them fifteen kilos of cocaine and it's happening this week."

"Is Moussa directly involved?"

"No, but some of his top men have blabbed and things seem frantic at Pladsen – maybe you should come and listen to the tapes with me."

"Out in Søborg?"

She sounded completely different, more optimistic than three hours ago on the stairs.

"No, for Christ's sake, I don't want to be seen out there with you now you've been sidelined. I'm in the flat."

"I just have some things to fix, then I'll be over. What about Macedonia and Tetovo in March 2001?"

"Is it important? I can easily get one of our academics to search the archives, check the article databases and consult with the Foreign Ministry if you insist."

His mobile beeped to show Darling was trying to get through to him. He said goodbye to Henriette Nielsen straightaway.

"The chassis number fits. It's Lindberg's Ford Transit. It's the breakthrough we've been waiting for," said Darling.

"What are you going to do now?"

"We're going through all the material on him again. Kettler's coming in and then we'll question Lindberg again. I've asked Corneliussen if you could take part in any of it, but he said it was out of the question."

Axel was going to protest but decided to let go of it and let Darling remain ignorant of the latest development – there was no guarantee that the man who wanted to sell Davidi's drugs to Moussa was the murderer, but it was a possibility. He didn't owe Darling anything.

"What about Sonne and Laila Hansen?"

"I assume they're on their way in."

Axel went out to fetch some water. He walked through the corridor to one of the legendary dark rotundas, which it had taken him a year to orient himself in. There was a story that a person arrested during the war had once taken the wrong door and disappeared while he was supposed to be going to the toilet. He was found mummified in the huge cellar under HQ one year after liberation.

He peed, filled his jug with water and went back. The inner courtyard was dark below him, but he could see two of his colleagues crossing it with Laila Hansen between them.

Am I wrong about her? he asked himself. Is she involved? Their first meeting, the exchange of words, and the long questioning the following day, when she had told him the whole story of her relationship with Enver Davidi, was still razor-sharp in his mind. He remembered every detail – or did he? Was there anything he had overlooked? No, she couldn't have killed him; that was impossible. The technical findings related to the body told another story and the autopsy ruled it out, but could she be colluding with someone? It would be far from the first time in history that a woman had had her ex-husband killed.

He examined the interviews in his mind and came to the conclusion that she was clean. She had clearly been shocked when she learnt that Enver Davidi was dead. The way she spoke about him, their life together, her broken dreams – she deserved an Oscar if she had staged his murder. And she had been surprised when Axel rang her bell on Saturday, but wasn't that surprise just as much due to it being Axel standing on her doorstep – the recollection of a forgotten one-night stand?

He had stayed standing in the corridor with his water jug in his hand. Now they came towards him.

His surprise that she had had a relationship with Sonne had faded into the background, even though it had thrown him off balance when he found out. His negligence hurt – he hadn't figured it out for himself – or was it something else entirely? That he was crazy about her and that it felt like a betrayal. Everything feels like a betrayal to me, he thought.

Then there was Sonne. He certainly hadn't become any more sympathetic towards him, one of the country's best crime reporters, ambitious and very energetic. How well did he know him? Almost not at all.

They stopped three offices away from him. She looked at him. Then he walked over to her and shook her hand.

"I'd like to exchange a few words with her when you're finished. Can you let me know?"

His colleague looked at him in surprise.

"Yes, we can, I suppose, but it depends on what happens."

Her eyes drilled into him. They were saying: I'm on my way to the scaffold. And you aren't helping me. Then she looked away, staring into thin air, but he could still feel her – feel her just under the surface, her determination and her will.

Her look still burned within him. Along with his doubts.

49

Axel drove across Dronning Louises Bro a little past ten. The eight globes were glowing in the dark and the illuminated advertising was still flashing its neon colours from a bygone era into the night. He parked in front of Kaffesalonen by the lake and went up through the backyard where three boys were smashing up an old lady's bicycle with a child seat on the back. One look from Axel and they moved off. Henriette Nielsen let him in through the back door and they went up to the flat together.

"Where's the technical guy?"

"I've let him go."

She nodded towards the other living room, where the armrests of a Børge Mogensen sofa had been lowered.

"I'm going to sleep here tonight."

Axel went over to the window and looked down on Blågårdsgade, whose lifeless tiles lay beneath him – very unlike the hectic flow of people, bikes and street life that characterised it during the day. He could see through the leafless black branches that the square was completely empty. Waste paper danced around in small cyclones in the sunken space where he had met Moussa two days ago. The lights shone warmly and alluringly from Apoteket, and all around the square, lighted windows looked out on the dark space with the pale-blue glow of televisions, like curious eyes.

"What's on the recordings?"

She went over and sat at a computer. Axel went behind her and saw her opening a folder called Henriette N. She handed him a set of headphones.

"What for?"

"We may well have soundproofed the door, but Moussa's boys are everywhere, and if they happen to be walking up the stairs, I don't think it's worth the risk of them overhearing themselves making the next hash deal while we're sitting here slapping our thighs at how we've trapped them."

The folder contained new folders with dates and text – audio, photo or video – 411 in total.

She opened a folder labelled '7.3.2007 audio'. There were several audio files in it, but she double-clicked on one entitled "Fifteen kilo coke" with the time of the interception.

"The one talking is Micki, one of Moussa's old friends from the neighbourhood, ethnic Danish and outside the hierarchy – his status is untouchable. He's served two sentences for dealing hash and three for threatening behaviour. Small, short-haired guy with biceps and pecs which are a little too big – we're talking a small B-cup. He's talking to one of the boys who was with Moussa on Monday evening. Lasso to his friends, Turkish, two sentences for possession of weapons, minor drug offences and disorderly behaviour. They're walking around the square, it's the afternoon, most of it was caught by the microphones under the café tables."

She pressed play.

One voice was heavy with Copenhagen slang, half of the words slurred into each other, and he spoke very fast.

"He's coming with fifteen parcels, know what I mean? He wants the cash for them, otherwise it's all down the drain."

"Sure, man, what..."

The sound disappeared as a car drove past.

"You're in charge of the money. You get hold of it. You keep…"

"When, man?"

"Tomorrow – we have to be ready when they come into Pladsen."

"Why Pladsen? It's a fucking stupid place."

"Shut your mouth. He's decided."

Suddenly two women's voices came in over the drugs chat.

"Look babe, isn't this a nice spot?"

"If something goes wrong... expensive... Moussa... a stupid cop."

"It's a bit cold, but if we're going to smoke, it's best here."

"Where's Moussa when it goes down?"

"For fuck's sake, you idiot, Moussa don't know nothing about this, know what I mean?"

"But why did you say…"

"Mmm, yes, maybe a cappuccino, though I usually have a cortado."

"…you dumb fuck, cut the bullshit."

"I just have to go in to the little house."

Women's laughter.

"…or go home and fuck your mother up the arse, know what I mean? You do what I say, or you'll regret it. They come into the square; we're sitting totally as normal in front of Esco; we get a sign and then you have to make sure you get the money out; you'll have to work out who's going to hold it until then, and then we swap the goods, fifteen kilos. Are you in or are you stupid?"

"I'm in."

"OK. Get lost."

The file was finished.

"Is that it?"

"Yes, that's the best one. There's a lot of other drivel, but only a small handful know anything about it. Afterwards, Micki went into the café where Moussa and three of his most trusted accomplices were sitting. They shook hands, you know, the tribal way, and then he nodded to him, obviously to show he had it under control."

"Why does he go crazy when the little guy mentions Moussa's name? If he knows they're being listened to then he's really damned stupid to say all that other stuff."

"They don't know they're being listened to, but they know there's a big risk of it and so they're not allowed to say anything at all about Moussa and criminal activity. They're just not all very good at controlling themselves."

"No, obviously not."

Henriette Nielsen scratched a nail that was covered with mother-of-pearl-coloured varnish.

"What do you think about them saying 'they'?"

Axel hadn't been thinking about anything else since he heard it. And he was confused and angry at himself that he hadn't thought of several people being involved.

"That's what's most surprising. Either the murderer is colluding with someone else, or the one who's coming with the drugs doesn't have anything to do with the murder," he said.

"Yes, or it means that several people will be coming, but where does that leave us?"

"I can't see that it changes anything. We don't know when it's happening, so we have to be here and we have to be completely invisible and ready to move in. Not too many of us, but enough to be able to pacify them if there's trouble. Will you make a plan with hiding places and positions so that we can cover the whole square, but especially Escobar?"

"Yes."

Axel looked at the video and photo equipment in the window.

"How does it work technically?"

"Everything is recorded and reviewed by four men in Søborg: first sound, then cameras, if someone says something interesting. We can't sit here watching them 24/7 but, at times like this, there's always one person in the flat ready to alert the others if something happens or if we hear something about a delivery."

"And that's you?"

"Tonight, yes."

"I thought you had the plods for that."

"We do, Axel Steen, but I like to keep in touch with every aspect of an investigation. Once you get too good for the leg work, you lose the sense of what's happening on the street. And if you lose that, it all goes wrong."

He could see she had regrets, but he didn't let that hold him back.

"It sounds just like your fuck-up with the Davidi undercover operation and like a very accurate description of your partner."

She looked away.

"He is a bit special."

"He seems like an irresponsible dickhead who has everything in his sights other than solving the case."

"To be honest, I don't always know what he's doing. He sometimes goes off at tangents."

"Who's in charge?"

"He is, but only until he's made enough mistakes. He's very ambitious. And there's no black and white with him, only black."

"How do you mean?"

"Cop paranoia personified. Immigrants, gays, lefties, drug dealers, wind turbine manufacturers and Islamic fundamentalists – it's all just one big jumble in his head."

"Wind turbine manufacturers?"

"Yes, renewable energy – why do we need that when we have nuclear power and oil?"

"And what about you? You're not suffering from the same paranoia, are you?"

She laughed out loud.

"Me? Then I ought to be paranoid about my own life. I grew up in the Youth House."

Axel thought about it and something fell into place.

"Sometimes the converts are the worst."

"But I'm not a convert. I don't have anything against YoHo. I've just found my place in life, my job, what I'm good at. I can't see any contradiction in the fact that I spent four years of my youth in there."

"No, but there are undoubtedly many others who can. Haven't you had any problems with that?"

"No, why should I? I keep a low profile. You're the only person who knows that, in reality, I'm a rabid, lesbian feminist."

Axel laughed because, after all, that was a joke… wasn't it?

"So what are your thoughts when you see the Youth House being torn down?"

She looked at him as if he had asked a stupid question.

"Fortunately, I've had other things to think about."

50

It was almost midnight when he got back to his car. Once he was settled behind the wheel, he called Laila Hansen, but she didn't pick up. Instead of going home, he drove in to HQ. He met Darling on his way in through the columned courtyard.

"We've finished with Lindberg for today. He still denies everything. Claims he had no idea that the victim was Davidi because he knew him only as David, and that he knows nothing about the van. His lawyer says they're in the process of piecing together recordings and photos from the disturbances that can prove he was on the street while the murders were committed, but we haven't seen anything yet. Sonne has given an explanation of his meeting with Davidi in Macedonia. Nothing new in it. He hasn't seen him since."

He looked coldly at Axel.

"Your lady friend is still up there."

Axel went up to the division, into his office, and opened the door to the next office, so that he could hear the interview with Laila Hansen three offices further down.

"You're welcome to ask my son. I haven't been out at night." Her voice was clear.

"Is there anyone else besides an 11-year-old boy who can confirm that you were at home when your ex-husband was murdered?"

He went in and said hello and carried on through, under the pretext of picking up some papers. She was sitting on one side of a small four-man table, the interviewer sitting opposite with his colleague writing beside him. Her look was completely neutral, but as his colleagues made eye contact with him, one of them shook his head slightly, while the other looked disapproving. Axel walked through the room and fetched a report from Darling's office. The interview resumed before he returned to his own office.

"No."

"What about Monday night?"

"You were guarding my house, and your colleague, Axel Steen, was with me too."

"Who, as you've already told us, you've had a relationship with?"

"Who I went to bed with on one occasion a couple of years ago," she said.

"After meeting each other online?"

"Yes. I still can't see what it has to do with the investigation."

But no doubt they'll be able to round the lunch table tomorrow, thought Axel. If his connection to the investigation had been restricted earlier, it was now hanging by an almost invisible thread. You didn't investigate cases in which you had had a sexual relationship with a main witness or suspect. He knew he would be called in to Rosenkvist or Corneliussen as soon as he came in tomorrow, if there wasn't already an email to him from one of them.

"Have you resumed your relationship with Axel Steen?"

She hesitated.

"No, I haven't."

"You haven't been to bed together since the investigation started?"

"No."

"What has he told you about the investigation while he's been with you?"

"All sorts of things. He's interviewed me, told me that Martin Lindberg had been arrested – after all, that's the reason I'm sitting here now."

"Has he given you details of the investigation along the way which you have been surprised about? Has he told you what to say to us?"

Axel was on the edge of going over and kicking the door in and stopping this farce – fuck, what petty, officious nitpickers they were. He hadn't bloody killed Enver Davidi, and maybe Laila Hansen hadn't either, but that's what they were supposed to be figuring out. Why didn't they ask her about Jakob Sonne?

"No, what would that be? He's interviewed me twice about everything in the case and asked exactly the same questions as you. Only not in the same ill-mannered fashion."

Axel sat down at his desk and switched on his computer. He tried to log in to the investigation, but his access had been blocked. Then he opened his email and there were messages from Corneliussen and Rosenkvist, who had both received an email from the interviewer about Axel's relationship with Laila an hour ago. They were requesting a meeting and an explanation respectively.

He replied that he had had a long day but that he would make himself available from twelve noon tomorrow.

He would have to prepare himself for plenty of free time after those meetings.

The interview was over.

One of his colleagues came out to him.

"Jesus, man, you've really fucked up on this one!"

Axel got up and went over to him.

"Have you done your job properly?" Axel asked.

"If you mean have I fucked her, the answer's no," he said.

"Have you got out of her what you're supposed to, or have you been so eager to over-indulge your sanctimonious indignation over me having been to bed with her two years ago that you've missed some clues?"

"You should have reported this straight away and passed her over to other investigators. You know that. Don't try running away from it. You shouldn't have been on the investigation at all."

"Shut your mouth before I shut it for you and chuck you out of my office. You know fuck all about this."

He spun round and went back to Laila Hansen and the other interviewer, who had both overheard the episode.

"I'll take myself home. I don't need you to drive me," she said.

"We weren't going to."

He picked her up on the pavement in front of HQ.

"Was it hard?"

She looked at him as if she was controlling herself so as not to be furious with him.

"You're asking me? Haven't you subjected people hundreds of times to exactly the same as what those two guys just put me through?"

Axel didn't say anything.

"Then you will know that it's not all that nice to sit there being cross-examined about every guy you've ever been to bed with. I got the impression that they almost went after me even more when they found out that I'd slept with you."

"Yes, I'm sorry about that. Maybe it could have been avoided if you'd told me about Lindberg and Sonne from the start."

"What difference would it have made? Would you have kept your hands off me because I was even more of a suspect?"

Maybe. Just maybe. Axel looked at her; her face had become hard – tired and hard.

"Shall I drive you home?"

He pointed to his car. She didn't answer but began walking over to it.

The journey to Nordvest passed in silence. The night was foggy and impenetrable and they slipped through the excessively large, yellowish-lit intersection at HC Andersens Boulevard and Åboulevarden, through the dead landscape of stone and concrete on the motorway at Bispeengbuen and Borups Allé. She blew her nose. Looked stiffly ahead.

The chill was tangible and it wasn't just because of the March night.

Something had been broken; he could feel that in her too. Or was she just exhausted and shocked after the interview? And what was there between them? A fragile bond that had barely been formed. It felt wrong. So much desire replaced by absence and distance. In such a short time. He felt he had lost something he hadn't had and that feeling just made him want to get away – away from the car, away from her, away from himself and away from this damn job with all its shitty complications.

He turned off before the Hareskov motorway, down to Utterslev Torv and into Rentemestervej. There was an unmarked police car waiting in front of her house.

"Are they still looking after me?" she said when she saw it. "Or is it really them I should be afraid of? Am I going to get the same treatment as that time with David?"

"We'll still be looking after you. I'll come by again if you want."

She gave him a look he couldn't interpret and got out.

51

Thursday, March 8

When he looked down at his chest, he could see his heartbeat everywhere, the hairs dancing, the skin vibrating. He raised an arm and looked at the inside of the forearm, the blue-veined wrist, where his pulse was beating its damned rhythm. In the bathroom, he stuck his face right up against the mirror so that he could see the veins in his throat. It was beating there too. The doctor may well have said to him that he had an unusually strong pulse, but this wasn't normal. He would have to have another ECG soon. He went in and sat down with a cup of coffee, took out his watch and counted: 72 beats a minute. Normal resting pulse. Despite the coffee. Why the hell couldn't he just relax and give his poor heart a break from all this fear?

The night had passed without sleep until four o'clock, when he put the mattress on the living-room floor, lit a joint and lay staring into the darkness until sleep came crawling up over his chest and led him away. Prior to that he had spent three hours reading through the interview reports he had printed. He had talked with Henriette Nielsen, who was still OK about letting him take part in the surveillance, unless he was chucked out of the force because of his dick, as she laughingly said as he told her about his history with Laila Hansen.

There was a massive bollocking awaiting him at HQ. And the resolution of the case was further off than ever before.

He tried to collect his thoughts, to think logically. Who would want to kill Davidi?

Someone who knew him. It required contact. There weren't many people to choose from. Laila Hansen could be ruled out because of the technical evidence and because of the video recordings. Lindberg?

Sonne? Neither of them appeared to have had any contact with Davidi up to the murder. That left Moussa's gang and the PET people. He tried to be completely open-minded. What did he know about Henriette Nielsen? That she had run a hopeless operation, where there was bugger all control, but did that give her a motive for killing Davidi? Did it give Kettler a motive?

The other possibility was that Davidi was killed by chance, but who would do it at Assistens in the middle of the night? Apart from police officers? No one. The camouflage with the balaclava and the military boots also contradicted it. It was a planned murder brought to completion in cold blood. And the subsequent murder of Piver supported his sense that this was no amateur. You don't commit two murders by accident.

Jakob Sonne rang.

"There are rumours you've been sidelined."

"There are so many rumours. There's also someone who says you knew Enver Davidi. And his ex-wife."

"That's true. I've explained everything about that to your colleagues. But I was wondering if you had time to meet today."

I'll soon have plenty of time, thought Axel. He didn't much want to, but he was curious to find out what Sonne knew about Davidi.

"Why?"

"I'm writing a big article about the murder. Perhaps you could give me a little background about the crime scene."

"OK then. In half an hour. Let's meet at the café opposite Assistens."

Axel fetched his bike.

The Youth House was being gradually driven away in large trucks by labourers and drivers who still had their faces hidden behind scarves or balaclavas – the exact same uniform as that worn by the autonomists, the very people they feared reprisals from. He showed his warrant card and went round the demolition area; soon it would just be an empty site. What would happen then? Would the excavated ground become a shrine for the young people or would a new building quickly rise from the rubble?

The café was closed, but Axel waited outside.

Assistens Cemetery had once again been opened to the public and it was a great place to go for a walk with Sonne. They could sit on a bench and chat. And he could finish up by showing him the spot where the body of Enver Davidi had been found.

Sonne arrived in a taxi that drove halfway up on to the cycle lane. The reporter paid the driver and stepped out. He looked completely relaxed. He had had his hair cut, but otherwise he seemed just the same as usual – the photographer waistcoat, the thermal clothing. He was almost as tall as Axel, and his face looked bare and more rugged since his hair had been shaved down to a millimetre.

"It's closed," said Axel, nodding at the café. "Let's go for a walk in the cemetery."

"Then I'll have to put a hat on," said Sonne, fishing out a leaf-green knitted army hat from one of his pockets.

They crossed the road and went in through the gate. Instead of going to the murder scene, Axel ignored the glances Sonne cast in that direction and forced him further into the cemetery.

"Tell me about Enver Davidi and your meeting with him in Macedonia."

"There isn't much to tell. I inherited him as an interpreter from a colleague, and he was OK at that."

"How long did you use him?"

"Three, maybe four days – it was years ago. He asked me to take his pay home to his ex-wife, and I did. And that's how I met Laila."

"What happened in Macedonia?"

"We worked, as you do, 24/7, trying to get the best stories home, and David was good because he knew so many people."

"Who did he know?"

"The local imam, people in the mountains; he even knew people in the Macedonian militia. We were detained after a trip up in the mountains, but it was nothing out of the ordinary."

"What happened?"

"The usual. We trudged around for whole and half days trying to get in touch with the UCK, the Albanian Liberation Army, but we never got to interview anyone, apart from some illiterates and some sheep-fucking shepherds."

They turned into the long avenue of lime trees cutting through Assistens; in the summer months a channel of green with a blue roof, now just bare branches sticking to wet, black trunks against a pale grey sky.

"How was your relationship with Enver Davidi?"

"Good. I had nothing against him."

"Did you know from the outset that he was a drug offender, convicted and deported?"

"Very early on in the process, yes. I called my manager at DR and asked if it was a problem."

"And it wasn't?"

"Not in his opinion, but it wasn't exactly something we would boast about either."

"Why didn't you contact us as soon as you found out that the victim was Enver Davidi?"

"Relax. I didn't know. I didn't know him by that name – to me he was David."

There were people with children in carrier bikes, probably on their way to kindergarten, dog-walkers and a grey-haired old man swearing at two immigrant boys on a bike. It seemed like a normal day, but the sound of the crane that was ripping down the Youth House could be heard in the background.

"What about Stanca Gutu?"

Sonne stopped.

"Who?"

There it was again. He reacted exactly like Lindberg. His words denied any acquaintance, but his whole body reacted to her name.

"A young Moldovan prostitute found strangled in a hotel room in

Tetovo on the morning of March 18, 2001. Weren't you down there at the same time?"

"I can't remember."

Nothing about asking Axel why he was interested in Stanca Gutu.

"The murder was never cleared up, but Enver Davidi was questioned about it."

"I haven't heard of it before now."

"Isn't it strange that this occurred at the same time you were down there with him? You and Lindberg. And that you're both lying about not knowing about the case?"

"What the hell do you mean by that?"

"Well, you might not be lying, but you both react to her name."

"I remember David talking about some problems he had to get sorted, but I don't know any more than that."

Every case was sprinkled with witnesses and suspects who embellished the truth, kept details secret or covered their lies with dismissals and brief denials – it was here that consciousness was desperately hunting for an exit while the body told a completely different story. The trick was not to charge in, but to let the other person know that you didn't believe them. And then wait. Wait until doubt and remorse ate at the truth so that it could come out into the open.

Axel changed tack.

"What about you and Laila Hansen? Do you still see each other?"

Sonne half-closed his eyes and looked at Axel, who sensed a clear shift in the atmosphere.

"Rarely, we're just friends. We were together for a year, on and off."

They walked past Niels Bohr's and Kenni Holst's graves, which lay staggered on each side of the avenue with two stones soaring up to a height of almost 14 feet. Axel stopped and asked Sonne if he knew the story about the two gravestones. The reporter shook his head.

Bohr had been awarded the Nobel Prize and lay under a column bearing the owl of wisdom. While the latter, whose grave they were standing in front of, had been the owner of a Harley Davidson, had an insignia on his back and lay under an equally high monolith made of Bornholm granite, surrounded by primitive Roman torches, which his brothers in the Hell's Angels had collected a million kroner for. It was actually supposed to have been twice as high, but the cemetery's management had refused to allow it. The stone resembled something cut out of an Asterix book. The torches were rusty and bore witness to the fact that Kenni's brothers had long since forgotten him.

"What about Laila? What did you make of her relationship with Enver?"

Sonne raised his voice slightly, as if Axel had turned onto a private path.

"I don't have anything bad to say about her. She seemed to be finished with him, but she wasn't bearing any grudges. She's good. A decent person."

"How was your relationship?"

"It's good. Don't you think she's beautiful?"

Is? Axel felt the conversation tilt. Sonne looked at ease and Axel felt like wiping the smile off his long bony face. Why had she been to bed with that idiot? Did he know anything about Axel having been to bed with her?

"Why did it end?"

He was about to say something but then held back.

"I wasn't a good catch, too busy, you know – she had a little child and needed someone who could be there all the time. That wasn't for me."

They turned off the avenue and moved in among the trees. Axel led the way, past Dan Turell's grave, where there was a chillum, coins and several pens, Scherfig's stone tortoise in the thicket and Kjeld Abell's monument. Then they continued out to the ochre wall by Nørrebrogade. "How was she about that?"

"To be honest, she was probably a bit sad. She was very demanding," he said, adding "also sexually" as he studied Axel, who felt like stuffing the confidential, laddish tone down into the reporter's stomach.

"So you dropped her?"

Sonne shrugged.

They had almost reached the gate out to Nørrebrogade, where Enver Davidi had been found. Sonne pulled a half empty bottle of water out of one of the lower pockets in his waistcoat, emptied it and threw it into a rubbish bin.

"I'm not a suspect, am I?"

"No, no."

"You seem very interested in her. Why don't you ask her yourself?"

And why don't you shut your face, you conceited jerk? thought Axel.

"I've done that, but you might have seen it differently. We listen to all sides in an investigation. Sometimes a different view of things helps us to understand what's going on."

"You promised to tell me about the crime scene, to show me what you know. Have you forgotten about that?"

Axel hadn't forgotten, he just had no intention of keeping his promise, but when they got to within three yards of the scene of the crime, he changed his mind. Maybe Sonne could help him anyway.

"OK. He was sitting here with his hands bound behind his back with strips and a balaclava on his head, which the perpetrator had put on him after strangling him. May I see your hands?"

Sonne gave him a quizzical look.

"Come on."

The reporter stuck them out.

Axel touched them and turned them up so that he could see his palms. They were completely undamaged.

"Yes, it could easily have been a pair of big mitts like yours. He was strangled quickly and brutally and he'd been beaten beforehand. Can I see your knuckles?"

"No you bloody can't!"

"Keep your hair on. It's just a joke."

Sonne turned his hands around.

There wasn't a mark on them.

"That's exactly how the murderer's knuckles would look, because he had gloves on."

"How did he get in here? Do you know?" asked the reporter, writing in his notepad.

"Yes, we know all about that. We know that Davidi got in via an old lamp post on Kapelvej. He was apparently carrying a pretty heavy bag, probably containing some drugs, and then he met his murderer here. Come and see."

Axel took hold of Sonne's sleeve and pulled him over to the chapel.

"Look here on the wall. There was blood and some skin that matches Davidi, as do the fibres on the shattered wood," said Axel, pulling him between the columns so that they stood on the tiles in front of the splintered door.

"Nothing from the murderer, but look here – there were lots of traces, the same kind as over at the murder scene, hair, cells, fibres from clothing. A meticulous, careful murderer, but I promise you we'll get him on DNA, when the samples are ready."

"OK. When will that be?"

"Soon, two to three days – yes, we just need to find the perpetrator and have his DNA analysed, but the knot is tightening. And look here…"

Axel again grabbed hold of the big reporter and dragged him over to the wooden hatch that led to the underground passage.

"They've been down here, maybe because they had to hide from a patrol, and it's down here he's beaten him."

"How do you know how long they were there?"

"Bloody hell, have I forgotten to say that? We've got them on tape. We have a perfect timetable on them. We can see the murderer in the cemetery, and a little later we can see him walking with his victim over to the wall, but Davidi doesn't look like he's volunteering."

Sonne looked tense.

"Don't you owe me a favour now?" Axel asked. "One good turn deserves another. I've given you the whole case. But you have information that I'd like. I need to know the source of your information about Lindberg's arrest."

"You know the drill. I can't tell you that."

"I'm not asking you to say who it is, but at least to pin down where the source is."

"I don't have any sources at PET, but I have plenty in your place, so you'll have to guess."

Darling or Corneliussen. Probably the latter.

52

Homicide Division was deserted. Three days after Piver's murder, the press was full of criticism of the police, accusing them of sending the young autonomist into the arms of his killer and neglecting the investigation of the two murders by using too many resources to imprison activists from the riots. Rumours swirled everywhere that the police were behind the murder of Enver Davidi. Sonne had written a scathingly critical article and TV2 News had done a timeline of the case, which was running on a continuous loop and raised a number of uncomfortable questions. The Police Commissioner had found it necessary to make herself available for interview to reassure people that the police were doing their best and that there were no indications that Davidi's murderer was a police officer. Rosenkvist had had to go to a studio and explain the case as well as he could. He had appealed to the public for help, looking directly into the camera with his serious, brown eyes. His comb-over was like a dried-up snail trail across his liver-spotted crown.

"Who has seen Enver Davidi? Who has seen Peter Smith?" he asked, while pictures of both of the victims were displayed on screen.

In the internal mail, Axel read that Rosenkvist had assembled everyone to a meeting before his appearance on TV and asked for maximum effort in clearing up the murders. All their material had to be gone through again.

Axel looked at his watch. It was quarter to twelve. He went over and knocked on Corneliussen's door.

His boss was sitting in his tilting chair, speaking on the phone. He waved Axel in and ended the conversation.

"Yes, there are higher powers looking over you, so I can't suspend you, but it doesn't look good. First, the press leakages to Ekstra Bladet and TV2, and now it appears you've had a relationship with the deceased's ex-wife."

"Spare me all that tosh. I've followed up on everything there was to follow up on in this investigation and that's more than can be said about the people you've put on it. How far have you got with Lindberg?"

Corneliussen's mouth resembled a stitched-up chicken's anus before it exploded, a spiral of saliva arcing across his mahogany desk.

"You shall not insult me or your colleagues. It isn't our fault that this case hasn't been resolved yet, but it's your fault that we look like idiots in the press. And you're going to pay for it. You have a meeting with Rosenkvist now. And I'll be fascinated to hear what you're going to be doing in the future. I've recommended you for a transfer."

Axel strode out. He looked at his watch. There were 10 minutes until he had to go up to Rosenkvist. He sat down at his desk and began reviewing emails. There were significantly fewer of them now that the flow from the investigation had stopped.

But there was one from the editorial office at Counterpress and it contained a number of audio and video files. That was what Darling had mentioned yesterday and it had probably landed in Axel's inbox by mistake. He opened the videos and photos one by one. They were either taken by Martin Lindberg or showed pictures of him. If the times were right, he couldn't have killed Enver Davidi. One of the clips showed him standing with a group of spectators and some television photographers at a junction by Blågårdsgade at the time Davidi was being strangled. Another one proved that he had been in a debate meeting on the disturbances in a community centre in Inner Nørrebro at the precise time that someone drove up in his van and unloaded Piver's body onto the building site in Nordvest.

Axel went on the intranet and saw that Lindberg was still in custody at HQ. Then he went to the public prosecutor's office, which was almost as deserted as Homicide, but in the third office he found the lawyer who had been responsible for Lindberg's remand in custody the other day.

"You still have Lindberg?"

"Yes, it looks a little complicated. Are you back on the case?"

"Yes," lied Axel.

"He's been questioned all night – about his meeting with Davidi in Macedonia. There's nothing there to use. And we've had to drop the phone call with Piver. It's unlikely that it's his voice. That leaves us with circumstantial evidence, but no proof."

"I've received an email you have to look at. It consists of seven recordings that prove that Lindberg couldn't have killed Davidi and that he has a watertight alibi when Piver was dumped in Nordvest. It's from Counterpress, but it looks real enough."

The lawyer looked at him despondently.

"Are you sure?"

"Yes."

"Then I'm afraid we'll have to let him go. I don't have anything that can justify an extension of the deadline."

Axel went back to his office and forwarded the clips to the lawyer.

Then he went up to the executive corridor. It was the fourth time in the course of less than a week. At least three times too many.

Rosenkvist sat looking at him with that smile that wasn't really a smile, but more a mask behind which power reposed.

"It isn't looking good for you. I don't understand why you make life so difficult for yourself. All these fights, all these little stories about press leaks and now a relationship with one of the people involved in the investigation. What's going on?"

"I don't have a relationship with anyone involved in the investigation. Now. That was almost two years ago. It was a single night."

"Thank you, I don't need the details, but I'll probably have to go along with Corneliussen on this and pull you out of the investigation completely, even though there are still people within the system who are interceding in your favour."

He paused for effect and a smile spread across his blue jaws.

"On the other hand, we can't afford to waste our best resources."

He placed his fingers against each other in a gesture that was intended to signal deliberation, but Axel knew that he was once again hearing a verdict that had been reached long before.

"I was wondering if you could team up with Henriette Nielsen. I could lend you out – that is, completely unofficially – to assist PET to the extent that it interests them. Their drugs operation has a certain amount of crossover with the murder investigations."

"Yes, I guess so," was the only thing Axel could find to say.

"Yes, because that's the way we need to look at it, isn't it? Enver Davidi comes into Assistens with 15 kilos of cocaine and is killed."

Axel told him about Lindberg and Rosenkvist agreed.

"There's nothing more on Lindberg and there aren't any more corrupt, squatter-hating officers, but there are drugs worth how much? 15 million kroner? Enough to kill many people in my eyes."

"We're expecting a delivery of the drugs Davidi was carrying. Today. At Blågårds Plads. Is that what you want me to be part of?"

"Yes."

"May I take one man with me?"

"Yes, as long as it isn't someone from Homicide."

"Can I refer to you?"

"Yes."

This wasn't the right time to ask what the hell was really going on, who had been pulling strings and protecting him, but Axel had a feeling that Henriette Nielsen had a hand in it.

"The rumours that we're involved in Davidi's death have to stop now. I want the case closed, Axel."

He had only just left Rosenkvist's office when she called.

The exchange of the drugs was to take place at Blågårds Plads at 16:00. In three hours.

Axel was in a hurry. He dropped in at Narcotics and found Bjarne, whom he wanted with him at Pladsen, and asked him to get in contact with Henriette Nielsen. Then he went over to Homicide to pack his things. There was a meeting in Darling's office, 10 to 12 men, the big cop was doing the talking and delegating duties. Everything had to be reviewed from the bottom. For once, Axel wasn't sad at being left off the team.

He drove towards Nørrebro and parked by the Lakes. Henriette had made an appointment with him at Åboulevarden at 13.30, where she was ready and waiting with two of her colleagues in a camouflaged van.

Axel was walking down Blågårdsgade when his phone rang. It was Cecilie.

He walked into a rear courtyard and answered it.

"I have an offer for you, which I'd like you to consider."

He went cold as he listened to her unfolding it.

"Mediation? I'm not going to bloody mediation with you."

Axel felt like throwing the phone as far away as he could.

"It isn't dangerous. There is a lawyer and a children's expert present. It's your choice. That's it. Otherwise I'll make a request to have your parental custody rights revoked and your contact restricted."

He could feel the voice screaming inside his head, the voice he knew so well from the days, weeks and months after she left him, the voice made of stone and fire, which just carried on rising in volume until he exploded.

"How dare you come to me talking about bloody mediation when you're the one who walked out on me and your child without any sort of warning…"

She tried to get back into the conversation, but Axel just turned up the volume, the words tripping over each other, and the conversation became a noisy, unbroken inferno of hatred.

"…and then you come over one day like a purring kitten wanting to fuck and talk about the old days, and now you want to take my daughter from me, you selfish bitch…"

She went silent. Axel was breathless with rage.

There was silence on the line.

"Cecilie, are you there?"

"Don't you ever call me that again. It's your choice. Either you lose your parental custody rights and have even less contact, or we try to find a solution. It's your last chance. Think about it."

She hung up.

Axel turned around. There was a boy watching him. With big frightened eyes.

"What?!"

The boy ran off.

53

There was nowhere to hide at Blågårds Plads. Not for a cop.

The best hiding place on the whole square was a French pissoir in 19th century cast iron, but it was more than 100 yards from Escobar and it was impossible to close it without attracting the attention of the local meths drinkers. Nor were the roofs obvious surveillance posts because, in tune with the neighbourhood building style, they sloped down from towering red ridges.

The flat on the fourth floor could be used to monitor the square, but it wasn't practical for the operation itself. They wouldn't have time to get down to the street and intervene when the deal took place. It was just as unthinkable that they could be ready and waiting in a side street, follow it all on a screen and move in as soon as it looked like something was happening, because the streets that came up to the square were all kept under surveillance by 10 to 12-year-old boys from the neighbourhood, who would shout "akrash, akrash" as soon as a vehicle that had the faintest smell of police approached. Henriette Nielsen knew all of this, so she and Axel were now in the back of a Toyota Alphard behind opaque windows, parked next to the low granite wall by the sunken square. There were 20 yards over to Escobar and they had a view of the entire square on all sides. In the front sat two of her colleagues from PET wearing red and grey overalls from Dong Energy to match the logo on the car.

Henriette Nielsen presented them as Brian and Liam, also known by the composite name of Briam – no surnames. They said brief hellos. Axel thought he recognised Brian from an arrest in which Copenhagen Police had needed help from the anti-terror squad, and he assumed they both belonged to the police's elite force.

They were going back and forth to an open electricity feeder pillar beside the car. To Axel's eyes they didn't look like electricians. They looked like what they were: a couple of agents from PET in disguise, who with every little movement radiated a highly tuned physique and a suppleness that couldn't be camouflaged by a luminous orange waistcoat and a white safety helmet; but maybe he was the only one who could see it. He hoped so.

"I hate Nørrebro," said Brian, as they sat in the front seat.

"Yeah, fucking hell, what a hole," said Liam.

"It's a swamp – criminals and addicts, the lot of them," said Brian, letting his eyes wander from the meths drinkers on the benches around the square to some immigrant boys kicking a ball around.

"Alkies. Pushers."

"Autonomist arseholes."

"Moonlighting. Everywhere."

"Look at him over there," said Liam, nodding towards the antiquarian bookshop, as a man in his thirties with a rolled cigarette in his mouth came out and put a crate of books on a table in front of the store.

"Or Mustafa over there with the lady's bike – is that his mother's?" said Brian, pointing to an immigrant boy riding around on a bicycle with a child seat on the back.

"Not on your bloody life. He's stolen it."

"If you took 10 random people here on the street and reviewed their criminal records, eight of them would have previous."

"More than that," said Liam.

"And five of them would be pakis."

"And you wouldn't be able to read their criminal records because of all the stains on their character."

Axel watched as the two men high-fived, giggling like two naughty school boys.

"It should be cleared – the whole shithole. Pulled up by the roots," was Brian's conclusion.

Axel thought about saying something to them but cast an inquisitive look at Henriette Nielsen instead.

"Can you just take it easy, boys, and concentrate on the task?" she said, putting a hand on Brian's arm.

But Brian wasn't done.

"This is hopeless, Henriette. It's a hopeless hiding place. We may have an overview, but we're sitting ducks. And why isn't there any backup?"

"There isn't enough space or need for backup. We're staying where we are and your task is to blend into the background and be ready at the first word from us. So stop giving me all that bullshit!"

Brian turned around and looked at Axel.

"Someone's taking the piss out of you – it stinks to high heaven. Why the hell would anyone hand over drugs and money here in broad daylight?"

"That's exactly why. Precisely because you're asking that question."

"I don't believe it."

It was two o'clock and nothing was happening yet. No sign of Moussa. They sat quietly in the car. Every 15 minutes there were messages from their colleague in the surveillance flat. They were all equipped with the latest in radio communication, not the laughable earpiece that the riot squad wore, with wires plastered firmly to their necks, but small wireless earphones the size of a hearing aid, a microphone attached to the collar or jacket and a transmitter in a pocket.

They could see the footage from the hidden cameras at Escobar on two screens mounted on the back of the seats in front of them. In total, seven had been installed, four in the café, one in the kitchen, one in the toilet and one in the passageway to the toilet.

Axel wasn't surprised at the PET people's scepticism – he was doubtful too. Of course it wasn't normal to exchange drugs in the middle of Blågårds Plads in broad daylight, but drug deals no longer took place in lay-bys or breakers yards, where you could be gunned down and cheated of money or drugs, but in public places where there were a lot of people and no risk of being conned. And Pladsen was ideal because it was as good as impossible for the police to be there without being noticed. As good as.

He looked around the inside of the car with all its equipment. Wouldn't they attract attention if they stayed here for two or three hours? And could he stand being locked up for so long in this high-tech can and being forced to listen to the Katzenjammer Kids' words of wisdom?

There was a crackle in the wireless earphone.

"Van on the way into the square from Todesgade. Black delivery van, Toyota Hiace. Older model. Checking the licence plate," Axel heard.

He looked to the left and watched the van as it drove past the playground and continued at a snail's pace round the square. The tables in front of Escobar were empty. It drove slowly towards them, rounded the tree on the corner of Blågårdsgade and stopped.

"Two men in the front seat. Autonomist types," said Brian, bending over the feeder pillar outside, as if he was cutting a wire a long way inside the box and therefore had to turn his face right up towards the van. It was 10 yards away.

"Status on the licence plate, for Christ's sake?" rasped Henriette Nielsen.

It took a moment, then the message came from her colleague up in the flat.

"Anders Nielsen, no previous convictions, arrested three times for disorderly conduct, last time on Friday."

The man in the passenger seat of the black van jumped out with a bag in his hand and trotted over towards Escobar.

"Man on his way to Escobar with a full plastic bag. Liam, follow him, it might be the drugs."

The guy went past Escobar and continued to the paper shop next door. A consignment of cocaine in a plastic bag – it wasn't impossible, but it looked more like empty bottles.

Henriette Nielsen looked at Axel.

She had small pearls of sweat on her upper lip.

The man who had gone in the paper shop came out again without the carrier bag, but with two beers in his hand, a lit cigarette and a big smile on his face. He climbed into the van, gave the driver a cigarette and opened both beers. They chatted, looked around, and their eyes fixed on Brian, who was sitting fiddling with some wires he held up towards the light.

"It was a bag of empty bottles – he bought two beers," said Liam, as he came over from the shop.

Axel rolled the tinted window down an inch. Pladsen was bathed in a grey light showing that spring was far away; the air was cold, no more than four or five degrees. Round about on the benches and the granite wall, young black-clad people were now in the majority. Blågårds Plads was a notorious meeting point for the autonomists, but there were more than usual. He felt just as trapped in the car as the two PET people and would rather be sitting in the café, ready to intervene, but Moussa, and everyone else for that matter, knew his face.

"Mercedes model CL 500 heading down Blågårdsgade from Åboulevarden. Looks like Moussa's."

Everybody looked towards the point where Pladsen meets Blågårdsgade. The shiny grille appeared; Axel could see the clouds mirrored in the windscreen. The streamlined, silver-white car flowed silently over the street tiles and stopped a little way inside the square. At the same time, the van began to drive off. It rolled up beside them and blocked the view completely.

"Get rid of it, for Christ's sake," whispered Henriette.

The van driver – a guy in his early twenties, crewcut with a harelip, wearing a black anorak – stuck his head out of the side window.

"Something wrong with the power supply?" he said to Brian, who was still kneeling at the box. He was the only one who could see Moussa's car.

"No, we just have to change a relay and check everything. Power's still on."

"Fair enough," said the guy, laughing. "Carry on." He saluted with his fingers against an invisible cap and the van rolled on.

Nothing happened with the silver-white Mercedes. No one went over to it; no one got out.

"It's Moussa's," came the message in the earpiece.

The black van had now stopped by the little stage that rose over Pladsen behind them, and the two young men got out and opened the back door. They took out a loudspeaker. And another one. Then one of them fetched a large roll of black cable, threw it over his shoulder and began rolling it out, heading towards the bookshop.

"What are they doing?" asked Henriette Nielsen.

"If it's what I think it is, it's bad timing for us."

"What do you mean?"

"All the young people in black around the square. It looks like a demonstration. Isn't it a week since the Youth House was cleared?"

Axel took out his mobile and called the comms centre. Meanwhile, he saw Moussa get out of his car, light a cigarette and stroll calmly towards Escobar.

He got through to Sten Jensen.

"Have we been notified of a demonstration at Blågårds Plads today?"

"One moment."

While he waited, he watched as, in the space of just two minutes, six or seven of Moussa's friends and henchmen appeared. Two came out of the same stairwell that PET's surveillance flat was in; two emerged from Escobar, one from Flora's, and one appeared to have been playing football with the boys on Pladsen. Several more arrived. Modern telecommunications, thought Axel. We might well have new and improved ways of listening in on these scumbags, but on the other hand, they could assemble a hundred men with a group text in the space of two minutes.

"We've been notified of a demonstration at the square at 15:00 by an Anders Nielsen," said Sten Jensen on the mobile.

"What about?"

"The Youth House, I assume… no, wait a minute, there's something here: Freedom for political prisoners. Release Lindberg!"

"You're bloody joking."

"No, there's no doubt about it. It's here in black and white."

Henriette Nielsen looked at him.

"What's Lindberg's status? Has he been released?"

"I don't know. Shall I check it out?"

"Yes. And make it quick."

"Why haven't we been told?" fumed Henriette.

The two PET men looked at Axel, as if it were his personal mistake that they would now have to compete with a demonstration on top of the expected drug deal.

Axel ignored them and watched Moussa standing there smiling, while his friends took it in turns to come over and raise their fists, smacking them against each other, followed by a half-hug. Like some kind of fucking mafia boss. Henriette pointed out Lasso and Micki among them.

Moussa went into Escobar followed by three of his people. The rest settled down in the chairs outside the café.

Axel's mobile phone rang. It was Sten Jensen from the comms centre.

"Lindberg was released half an hour ago."

"OK."

"But that's not the worst of it."

Axel could see on the screen that Moussa was sitting at an oblong table near the window, his friends were gesticulating, and one of them went up to the bar. The room was empty apart from the waiter, two women breast-feeding and Bjarne from Narcotics. Axel's hedge bet. He was sitting by a tiled chimney in the middle of the room in an armchair, pretending to read, dressed in worn army trousers and a home-knitted sweater in five colours with patches on the sleeves, foot-shaped light-brown leather boots with a zip – an outfit he had carefully put together from a charity shop – and he had half-long hair on the basis that you can always have it cut off if you have to look like a businessman, but you can't stick it on if you want to disguise yourself as a hippie.

"He's been greeted by a hundred scumbags dressed in black hoodies outside HQ, and they're heading in your direction now," said Sten Jensen.

"Fuck, just our fucking luck!"

The two young men from the delivery van switched on the sound system and loud punk music pounded out over Pladsen. Axel couldn't hear if the lyrics were English or Danish, but the refrain was clear enough: No justice! No Peace! Fuck the police!

Lasso, who was to hand over the money, sat on a café chair in front of Escobar, smoking along with four other youths. Moussa was sitting quietly drinking coffee with his friends. It looked like a cosy chat.

"Can anyone see money, a bag, parcel or similar on him?" Henriette Nielsen asked in the earpiece, tense and concentrated.

The press photographers had arrived and were circling Pladsen, while a cluster of reporters stood around a table outside Flora's. Axel recognised several police reporters. Sonne was wearing his waistcoat and carrying a large photo bag, making big arm movements with a cigarette between his lips. A van from TV2 rolled up behind them and Dorte Neergaard jumped out of the sliding door with a cameraman.

Behind the tinted windows in the car, it had gone totally quiet. Everyone was waiting. Henriette Nielsen poked him in the side and pointed behind.

All the press people were standing up and craning their necks, and several of them began jogging down Blågårdsgade towards Nørrebrogade.

"What the hell's going on?"

Axel rolled the pane down a little further. Now he could hear the sound of shouting as they came steadily closer. He drank the damp spring air into his lungs and wished that he could move freely instead of sitting trapped in this little tin can, because the sounds made him desperate, the well-known battle cries.

"Ein, zwei, drei – Nazi Polizei! Take back the streets – from violent police!"

The earpiece crackled again.

"There's a demo on its way towards you. With Lindberg as its figurehead."

The assembled autonomists, a couple of hundred of them, cheered and whooped and flocked together to greet their comrades. The sound of shouting was amplified in the narrow corridor of the street and Axel experienced simultaneous waves of adrenaline and fear. It sounded solid, angry and powerful, stirring and thrilling, more violent than anything he had known. And it was a sound that spelt danger. That's how it had been fourteen years ago and it had never changed.

Killings – mutilation, rotting bodies and violent sex crimes, bring them on, but spare me from street battles and flying cobblestones.

Lasso was still sitting quietly in front of Escobar, chain-smoking.

Brian got back in the car.

"I don't think this'll work, Henriette. You don't even know who's going to deliver the drugs. It's a waste of time. It'll end in trouble if we have to intervene with all these nutters around us. They hate us with a passion."

Henriette Nielsen was calm.

"There's still half an hour before the drugs are to be handed over. Take it easy."

The demonstration flowed into Pladsen. It was a mixture of people there out of curiosity and fellow-travellers in the milieu, topped by the hard core of at least a hundred of the most militant, completely dressed in black, with scarves masking their faces, some wearing crash helmets. Martin Lindberg was among them. He was in the same clothes he had had on in prison but he looked surprisingly invigorated and fresh. The press thronged around him.

"What support do we have if all hell breaks loose?" said Brian.

Henriette Nielsen took out her walkie-talkie.

"Alfa 12, what's the status on response for the demo?"

"There are fifteen cars in the streets around the square, 20 more as backup. We're well prepared if we have to move in," came the reply.

Axel checked the screens. There was no movement in Escobar. Moussa was still sitting with three of his people drinking coffee. It was nearly four o'clock.

Everyone was here now. Lindberg. Moussa and his boys. A crowd of a thousand demonstrators, swelled by casual onlookers, filled the whole square. And the press was in the front stalls. But where were the drugs? And who was going to hand them over and collect the money?

Lindberg was lifted up on the stage and a roar rose from the crowd. He looked out over them, his eyes roamed over the car, Escobar, the crowd, as if he was taking it all in. One of the young men from the delivery van handed him a microphone.

"Friends! Comrades! Activists! Don't give up! They've destroyed Jagtvej 69, but they can't destroy us!"

Cheering.

"There is a straight line, a blood-red straight line, from May 18, 1993 to what happened last Thursday. This is about a state that doesn't care about its citizens, about young people left in the lurch by politicians lusting for votes, and about us only being allowed to be here if we conform. But we won't!"

The crowd howled.

"But it's about the police, too. About assaults, violence and the grotesque way they tried to conceal their own mistakes fourteen years ago. You'd think they'd have learnt from it. But what are they doing today? Two innocent people have been killed and everything indicates that the police are involved, but who are they after? They're after us. A man was brutally and unjustly arrested on Nørrebrogade, beaten and abused, and what do the police do? They charge him with violent conduct."

His voice was drowned in the booing. A chant rose from the crowd.

"Uniformed fascists, we'll burn them down to ashes!"

Lindberg waited patiently, smiling before continuing his tirade against the police, state and society.

The car was surrounded by protesters and the view to Escobar was blocked.

It was four o'clock.

"OK, time's up," said Axel. "I'm getting out of this damned car."

"Wait," said Henriette Nielsen. She took out her gun to check it.

But Axel couldn't wait. His H&K was sitting in its shoulder holster under his jacket and it didn't need checking.

He opened the door so that he could squeeze out without anyone looking into the car. He came out on the side facing the square and the throng of people. The air was charged with anger and violence. He now had the car between him and Escobar. He caught sight of Kettler moving through the crowd along with two other PET agents disguised as demonstrators. The normally suit-clad agent looked completely wrong in jeans, tennis shoes and a black hoodie. What the hell was he doing here? Axel looked towards Escobar, where Moussa had come out on the street with the three men he had been drinking coffee with. They stood watching the demonstration.

Dorte Neergaard was on her way over to him followed by a cameraman and a soundman. Sonne was heading in the same direction.

Axel was shoved, pressed against the side of the car and held firmly.

He heard Kettler's voice in his ear.

"What the hell are you doing here?"

Axel pushed back and stood face to face with Kettler and his two colleagues. They were looking nervously over their shoulders.

"I might ask you the same question, you idiot. You look so much like cops that even I feel like giving you a pasting. Now get lost before you expose the operation."

Kettler looked tense, but he couldn't hide his surprise. Fragments from Lindberg's speech could be heard.

"What are you talking about? What operation?" he said.

"You approved it, you dope, now get lost."

The PET man looked completely blank.

"Not with you involved. Is Henriette here? Where is she? Is she sitting in there?"

He knocked on the door and grabbed the handle but didn't have time to tug at it before someone put a hand on his shoulder and dragged him backwards. Axel turned his head and looked into a balaclava.

"Fucking pigs," it screamed. "Fascists."

He was pushed against the car again. They were surrounded by people dressed in black, furious, screaming, hitting out at the three PET people, pushing them and pressing them away from the car so that they were absorbed by the crowd. Axel was free of them, the activists' attention was focused entirely on Kettler and his colleagues, who were being carried away towards Pladsen in a forest of screams, bodies and arms trying to grab them.

Then three shots were fired close by. Axel went for his gun but stopped himself in mid-movement as he could smell gunpowder and realised that it was from a firework.

He turned around and looked across at Escobar. Moussa was standing in front of Dorte Neergaard shouting, making his points in front of her face with a raised index finger.

"Fucking… you piss off right now!" Axel thought he could hear the gang leader shouting through the noise.

Sonne was standing behind Dorte, smiling with both palms up as a sign that he wouldn't hurt anyone.

"Moussa's angry with the journalists. He wants them to leave. Sonne's trying to calm him down," was the message in the earpiece from the man in the flat, who could pick up fragments of their conversation from the microphones under the tables.

"Can't that idiot just get lost so he doesn't muck up the deal," said Henriette Nielsen in the earpiece.

Sonne put his photo bag on the ground next to a chair, as if to show he didn't want to take any pictures. Then he took three steps towards Moussa.

"I can't hear what they're saying," said the man in the flat.

Sonne was now standing once again with his hands held up reassuringly, then he took a couple of steps backwards, picked up his bag and moved away from Moussa and his men. Several of them also tried to move away.

At that moment, a black Cafax coffee delivery van drew up in front of the café. A crewcut man in uniform stepped out, opened up the rear door and took out a large cardboard box. It looked heavy. He put both arms around it and walked towards the door of Escobar. One of Moussa's boys opened it for him.

"Get ready, everyone," said Henriette Nielsen.

Axel had seen something that didn't make sense to him. He couldn't figure out what it was. He tried to see where Sonne had got to. Did it have anything to do with him? He had to get away from the car, which people were pressing him up against. He pushed two young girls away, reached the end of the vehicle and moved two steps further so that he could find cover behind a tree.

"Officers in distress, officers in distress," sounded in his earpiece.

A distress message is the signal that all available vehicles must come to the rescue because police officers' lives are in danger. Axel reacted instinctively by looking towards the spot Kettler and his two colleagues had been pushed over to. He thought he saw raised batons. Lindberg was thundering against the police from the platform.

They'll have to look after themselves, he thought.

He saw Moussa go into Escobar followed by two of his people.

"They're going into the back room. Liam and Brian, we have to have you round by the back door so they can't escape into the backyard. Bjarne and Axel, get ready to move in," said Henriette.

This is too good to be true, thought Axel. Moussa surely wouldn't just stand there receiving drugs in a backroom in Nørrebro in broad daylight.

At the same moment, a column of police vans with flashing lights rolled up at the end of the street. Henriette Nielsen was on her way out of the car.

Axel looked over his shoulder towards Kettler and now he realised that the raised batons were service pistols. He couldn't believe his eyes. Were they going to shoot?

Then people began shouting that the police were coming. Axel could see the blue flashes mirrored on the walls of the houses at the other end of Pladsen. The demonstrators began running towards him. There was a lot of people and all their attention was focused on the police cars now amassing in the side streets.

The Cafax man came out of Escobar again, went over to his van, opened the rear door and pulled out two large black bags and a small box. He went back into Escobar.

"They're really bloody smart," said Henriette. "He's going into the back room. Moussa and one of the boys are opening a bag of white powder. We move now. We have to take all four of them."

Axel could hear the sirens and knew that it was only a matter of seconds before the police vans would roll into Pladsen. The sirens came closer; the fireworks thundered away. Henriette Nielsen appeared in his line of sight on the left with her pistol drawn. There were three loud bangs. This time Axel wasn't in any doubt. It was gunfire. People were screaming.

They charged in through the door at the same time, but Bjarne was already in the kitchen where he was covering Moussa, the Cafax man, Micki and a young immigrant.

"They've been caught red-handed. There's snow all over the place," was the message in the earpiece.

Liam and Brian opened the back door and stepped in with loaded sub-machine guns.

Henriette Nielsen screamed at them to get the Cafax man on the ground.

"Arms behind your back – now!"

"Fuck, you're going to pay for this, you bastards! The party's fucking over," said Liam, pushing his snub-nosed machine gun into the back of the man lying whimpering on the floor.

Something was wrong.

Axel could see it on the gang leader's face immediately. That smile wouldn't be found on a man who had just been busted with his hands in a bag of snow.

"What do we have here? The bitch and the comedian! How are things?" he laughed, clapping his hands so that clouds of white dust danced in the air between them.

The Cafax man was weeping, but Moussa and his two companions didn't seem in the least affected by the large numbers of police with weapons drawn.

"Welcome, my friends. Shall we bake a cake? Sponge cake with a lovely icing?" shouted Moussa, throwing the white powder up into the air.

Axel could smell icing sugar. It may well be used to cut coke, but possession of it wasn't yet a crime in itself.

"Mugs!" cried Moussa in triumph.

54

They stood motionless in the room, rooted to the spot by the realisation that Moussa had made laughing stocks of them. Henriette announced that all four of them were under arrest. Brian and Liam put strips on them.

Axel went over and opened a door into a cold room. He turned towards the others.

"Take them with you. Now," he said to Henriette. "Just the coffee man and those two." He pointed at Moussa's two helpers.

"What do you mean?"

"Just do it. I'll take Moussa. I won't do anything to him. I just want to talk to him."

Brian, Liam and Bjarne dragged the others off with them. Henriette left the kitchen hesitantly.

Axel went over to Moussa.

"So, comedian, it's you and me now?"

"Yes," he said, grabbing the strips and dragging him up by one arm.

Moussa moaned.

Henriette Nielsen stuck her head back in.

"Get lost now and get everyone else out too," rasped Axel.

Sirens and shouted orders streamed in from Pladsen.

He grabbed hold of Moussa's shoulder with one hand and helped him on his way with his other hand on his back, so that his head was pressed against the galvanised door of the cold room. Then he pulled him back a little, flung open the door and threw Moussa onto the floor inside.

"Which bit of what I said to you the other day didn't you understand?"

"What are you talking about, cop? Why are you so upset?"

"I'm not upset. I'm fucking furious. And I don't have time for all your crap. I made you an offer. And if you fuck with me, I'll come after you."

"What difference would that make? You're already right up my arse. Do you think you're making it worse?"

Axel drew his pistol and went over to him.

"Yes. And you know I am. What is it you usually say? 'I'll bust your skull.' Is that what it takes to make you realise I'm serious?"

Axel released the safety catch.

"You're an amateur, cop. I got your message the other day," said Moussa angrily. "I made sure you were in place and I arranged for the gear to be delivered before your very eyes. So you can fucking sort the rest out yourself."

Axel hesitated and looked deep into brown eyes that weren't yielding an inch. Was it true? It was fifty-fifty. But why would Moussa say that if it was a lie? He wasn't the type who was afraid of being beaten up by a crazy cop.

"If you're lying…"

Moussa shook his head.

"Moussa doesn't make deals with cops, you understand that, right? And definitely not in front of my own people. Now the gear's been delivered. And it's gone, are you with me? It's gone for good, but the man who delivered it – you'll have to find him yourself."

Axel took his thoughts back to the scene he had just witnessed on Pladsen. Moussa in front of Escobar. The henchmen disappearing in several directions. What had he missed?

"Haven't you recorded everything? Don't you have microphones all over Pladsen, in Escobar and cameras in all your shit surveillance flats?"

Axel could hear knocking on the cold room door. Henriette Nielsen shouting to him.

"Wait," said Moussa. "Give them a show. And remember one thing, comedian, you owe me!"

Axel looked at him. He grabbed his thick curls and pulled his head up towards him.

"Open your mouth!"

"You're sick, man," laughed Moussa.

"Open your mouth!"

Moussa opened his mouth.

The door was kicked open and Brian and Henriette tumbled in.

Axel pushed his pistol into Moussa's mouth.

"What the hell was it you didn't understand the other day? Eh? I want the man, I said – don't you get that? Who is he?"

Moussa coughed.

"Stop, Axel – stop now!" yelled Henriette.

Axel let Moussa fall to the floor.

"Take him, for fuck's sake. Get him away from me."

Moussa's eyes were perfectly calm.

"What the hell's got into you?" rasped Henriette, but Axel could see she was fine with it. Brian nodded in acknowledgement.

"Did he fall on the way out?" he laughed. "And hit his head on the fridge?"

"Did he say anything?" asked Henriette.

Axel shook his head.

55

Axel left the back room. Moussa, his two henchmen and the Cafax man were taken to HQ, but it would only be a matter of hours before they'd be out again. The square outside had been more or less cleared of demonstrators. Smoke was drifting through the streets and he could see flames from a barricade down on Nørrebrogade.

As Moussa had passed him on his way out to the police van, he had spat at him, but his look said something else. A debt that was standing and accruing interest.

Axel sat on a bench and began to rewind; the last week, the last day, the last hour, the last minute. He leafed feverishly through his memories. What had he missed?

At that moment, Martin Lindberg came out from Blågårds Apotek.

Axel went over to him.

"I have to talk to you. Just five minutes."

"I can't see that we have anything to talk about."

"I haven't been trying to pin that murder on you, you know that, and now I need your help."

"What makes you think I want to help you?"

"This isn't about you and me. It's about two victims and one murderer who's still walking around out there. And he's been doing everything he could to land you in the shit – and if I'm not very much mistaken, you know who it is."

Now Axel had his attention.

"Why do you think that?"

"Macedonia 2001. What happened there?"

"Why do you say I know who it is?"

"Because it must be someone who knows both you and Davidi."

Lindberg thought.

"So all this is because someone's deliberately out to get me, you mean?"

"Yes."

"And it's not you arseholes trying to pin a murder on me that you're guilty of yourselves?"

Axel just looked at him. He could see that not even Lindberg believed what he had just said.

"What happened in Macedonia?"

"We were arrested."

"Who's we?"

"Sonne, David, me and an Albanian journalist."

"Why?"

"We had gone up in the mountains. It was way out of line, but we didn't have much experience and wanted to have something to take home with us. David was against it, but we insisted, so he went with us. We wandered around up there for a whole day, but we were arrested as we walked back into town again."

"Why?"

"Why? Because there was a war on. They drove towards us in a tank with a dozen or more police soldiers walking bent down behind it with sub-machine guns. That's when I understood that it wasn't just for show. They threw us down on the ground, body-searched us and took us away with them."

Lindberg looked more nervous than Axel had ever seen him before.

"Then what happened?"

"Then we were released. We were very relieved."

"What about Stanca Gutu? What do you know about her?"

"Nothing. I didn't know her."

"Know her? That's a strange way of putting it. What did you all have to do with her death?"

"I don't know what happened, but David knew some prostitutes, and I think he took Sonne along with him. Later they became enemies."

"Sonne and Davidi?"

"Yes, David didn't want anything to do with Sonne. I was on my way home so I don't know what it was all about."

"Have you talked about this with Sonne since?"

"No, never. Maybe the odd allusion to it, but they weren't the sort of experiences we've exactly been desperate to relive over a beer."

Axel left Lindberg and went down to his car. He tried to recall what it was that had captured his attention, but escaped his comprehension, just before they had moved in. He replayed the final minutes before they stormed Escobar.

Moussa had talked first to Dorte Neergaard, then to Sonne. Sonne had put his photo bag down and tried to reassure Moussa, who had seemed agitated. Then Sonne had moved away with his bag. Immediately afterwards, Lasso had also left. Something began to dawn on Axel. Had Lasso been carrying something when he left? Could he have taken the photo bag? But Sonne had had it with him. He had taken it from the chair where he had put it… but he hadn't put it on the chair. He had put it on the ground next to the chair. It wasn't the same bag! He thought back to the other evening when Sonne, along with a group of reporters, had been talking to Moussa and had hung around afterwards and spoken to him alone.

Was it Sonne who had delivered the drugs? If that were the case, they had to get hold of him now. Axel called the comms centre and requested a search for him, asking to get people posted at both his home and his workplace. Then he got in the car to drive the 500 yards over to Sonne's flat. He felt no need to share the visit with his colleagues.

56

Jakob Sonne lived in a large attic flat, where Blegdamsvej runs into Sankt Hans Torv. The wrecks of burned-out cars from the weekend's riots in Nørre Allé were the only blemishes in the idyll shared between some women with prams and a bunch of drunks enveloped in their intoxicated world in the ash-grey twilight.

Axel noted that his call to the comms centre had already resulted in action and nodded to two fellow officers parked in a civilian car 25 yards from the entrance. He pressed the button on the entry phone, and when nobody answered, he started pushing all the buttons from the ground floor up and waited for a phone to be picked up, whereupon he said he had to deliver a letter. He was let in with a grunt. The light-green paint in the stairwell was peeling off the wall and was covered in marks from people moving in and out; the cracks in the linoleum floor looked up at him from the fifties.

On the second floor, an elderly lady was standing waiting for him, wrapped in a housecoat and the reek of browned cabbage. The corners of her mouth hung all the way down to the doormat in disapproval.

"You don't look like a postman," she barked.

He showed his warrant card.

"I'm afraid I must ask you to go back into your flat," he said with his most gracious smile.

"Who are you going up to?" she whispered.

Her eyes shone with questions, but he just nodded and continued up the stairs.

On the fourth floor, he slowed down and took out his bump keys.

Sonne's door was on the next floor and when he saw a big potted palm in front of the other door on the landing, Axel realised that Sonne had the whole floor to himself.

He listened at the door and thought he heard something. Did Sonne have a cat or a dog? Hardly likely. Axel knelt down and silently raised the lid to the letterbox.

He could see into a well-lit hall. To the left was a kitchen, to the right an open door to what looked like an office. There were papers scattered all over the floor and the sounds were coming from in there. He waited. Then he saw a hand at the end of an arm. It rummaged around in the papers, lifted some up, held them, threw them back. But it certainly wasn't Sonne.

The hand belonged to a woman – that much he could see. He had a flash of recognition. She got up without him being able to see anything except her legs, dressed in jeans and black trainers. Then she threw three ring binders on the floor, sat down and began leafing through and tearing out the pages.

Axel closed the letterbox, got to his feet, put on a pair of plastic gloves and examined the lock. She must have a key. He found the tool he thought would fit. He slowly slid it in and began twisting it back and forth, listening for the clicks. It took just under a minute before he was home and ready to open the door.

The sounds from inside the flat had stopped.

Axel waited. Longer than he had time for. He opened the door, stepped into the hall and was shocked to see Laila's face. Her red hair was longer, her eyes looked at him with an openness that accommodated hope and anxiety. She was staring at him from a large photo in the middle of the hallway, surrounded by framed newspaper clippings with small byline pictures of Sonne, photos of Sonne at work during street battles and abroad with flak jacket and helmet, and a diploma for a journalistic prize – he registered it all just as the woman who had been sitting on the floor in the office came charging towards his back. Axel took one swift step forward and spun round, and she slid off him and went flying across the floor with a baseball bat in her hand. It had struck him on his shoulder, but he could only feel the blow, the pain being drowned in the endorphin rush. She was quick on her feet and ran purposefully into the living room, but Axel caught her up as she failed to round the doorframe fast enough. He grabbed hold of her shoulder and threw her up against a cupboard so forcefully that it knocked the wind out of her. She was ready with her nails, but then she realised who he was. Or maybe who he wasn't. She slid down onto the floor and put her arms around herself as if for protection.

"You. What the hell are you doing here?" he said.

Not a word. When he had seen her in the flat on Nørrebrogade six days ago, he had been surprised by her fighting spirit and defiance. It was typical of certain circles of young people who had had a lot of clashes with the police, but Liz had seemed different, as if there was a joy and enthusiasm underneath which she struggled to suppress. When they had met her at Lindberg's flat and she had heard that Piver was dead, she had disintegrated before their eyes. And she clearly hadn't had it any better since. Her skin was grey, her eyes bloodshot and panicky, but there was still a strong will burning inside her.

"What connection do you have with Sonne? Why are you messing with his papers?"

"I'm not saying anything."

Axel sat down in front of her.

"Listen to me. This isn't the usual game with the police; it's a double murder investigation, and you're in all the places you shouldn't be."

She didn't react.

"Do you also have a key to Sonne's flat? Are you having it off with him too? Piver, Lindberg, Sonne. You're generous, aren't you?"

There was fury in her eyes.

"I don't have anything to do with him."

Axel straddled her and looked into a bedroom where the door to the back stairs was ajar – it had been forced open.

"What the hell are you doing here?"

"Why should I help you?"

"Because I'm about to catch your friend's murderer."

"By putting Martin in jail? Even though you know he hasn't killed anyone? It can't be Martin – he would never do such a thing. You hate him, you shot him once and testified against him so he was put in jail."

She looked like she was going to spit in his face, but he put a hand over her mouth.

"Don't spit at me, you'd regret it. Listen. I'm not trying to get Lindberg busted for something he hasn't done. He's been released. And we have a new suspect. And right now, you're in his bedroom."

Axel pulled her up from the floor and pushed her against the door of the cupboard. She suddenly looked totally overwrought.

"And now you have to leave, but first tell me what you're doing here."

Axel could hear the door to the backyard slam.

She whispered.

"He came to us on Friday after you left. Rosa gave him Piver's number."

"I know, but why did you come up here?"

"Because I hoped I'd be able to find something," she said disappointedly.

There were footsteps on the back stairs, moving upwards.

"What were you looking for in his papers?"

She gave him a quizzical look.

"Anything at all. Letters, addresses, something or other."

"What did you want with them?"

"I remembered that Martin once said there was nothing he wouldn't do. And then it was him who first talked to us and he was very interested in Piver. Maybe I could find something that would help Martin. You're not doing anything."

"And you didn't find anything?"

"No."

Now the steps were perhaps two floors beneath them. Axel took her under the arm and pushed her out into the hallway.

"If I don't shout OK within the next minute, run as fast as you can down the main stairs and shout for the police – you'll get help right away."

He went back, keeping to the walls where the floorboards creaked the least. He cast a quick glance out onto the back stairs, where there was another door into the flat. If the person on the way up the stairs was an enemy, they would be on guard as soon as he saw the door had been forced. They would either run off immediately or come into the flat prepared to meet an adversary. If they knew the flat, they would edge in from the left and expect someone to be waiting for him behind the door. Axel gambled on a surprise attack. He took up a position behind the doorframe on the other side, drew his pistol and listened. The footsteps came closer.

57

He sensed a hesitation in the footsteps. The person was now approaching the landing. Just another few feet.

The sound of someone breathing. It was time. The moment he had been waiting for. He could feel his heart pounding, but for once it was a great feeling. He had all the time in the world and there wasn't a sound from him. The longer it went, the more it would tax the person out there.

Did Sonne know they were after him? Or did he think he had been burgled? The police radio, fuck – he hadn't thought of that. Of course, Sonne would have heard that he was under suspicion and was prepared, but what was he doing here?

The floorboards on the backstairs creaked and Axel knew that the person outside was changing position. Now.

He leapt out.

"Stay where you are!" he shouted.

Henriette Nielsen was standing on the stairs two steps below him with a drawn pistol pointing at him. He saw her face, the barrel, her finger on the trigger, and knew that he had been a fraction of a second from death. Her blue eyes were deep in concentration and stone hard, and the thought struck him that he would have been dead before he had managed to shoot.

"Shit, what are you doing here?" said Axel, lowering his weapon.

"I went up to our flat on Pladsen and looked through the surveillance tape. Sonne put his bag down. Lasso took it and Sonne took another one."

"Why didn't you call me?"

"Why didn't you call me?" she replied coldly.

He shouted "OK" into the living room.

"Is he here? Who's here?" she asked, putting her gun in its holster.

She glanced at the door in surprise and then at him.

"Did you break in?"

"No, we have an uninvited guest who's carrying out her own investigation," said Axel, showing her through the living room to Liz, who was leaning against the front door looking completely exhausted.

He brought Henriette Nielsen up to date on their meeting and what Liz had told him.

"She has to give an explanation of the incident, but otherwise she's clean, except for a charge of breaking and entering. She needs to be taken to HQ."

Henriette Nielsen looked angrily at him.

"I'm not your prisoner transport. I'm here to search the apartment. If you want her in HQ, you'll have to damn well drive her yourself," she said, walking into the room where Liz had been on her knees rummaging through Sonne's papers.

Axel was bursting with rage. She came out again and began pulling on plastic gloves.

"What's up with you? Why are you looking at me like that? Send her down to the guys on the street and get them to take her in," she said over her shoulder and walked back into the other part of the flat.

She had delivered the drugs to Davidi and wasn't for anything in the world going to miss out on the chance of busting Sonne for the crime, and she needed it after the blunder with Moussa. Axel hadn't bargained for that; ice-cold ambition now that they were homing in on their goal.

They both knew what they were looking for. Sonne was gone but he had to have somewhere else besides the flat.

Axel used his radio to contact the guys in the car in front of the property, saying that he was sending down a detainee who they should transport to HQ, low risk. Then he asked Liz to go down to the street where some police officers would meet her.

They began examining the flat room by room. In the pile of papers in Sonne's office, they found bills for three different mobile phones. Axel called in and got traces put on all the numbers. On a wall in the kitchen were yellow Post-It slips and a postcard from Corfu from Laila and Louie: *Hello sweetheart. We're enjoying the sun. Looking forward to seeing you again. Kisses Laila and Louie. P.S. There's a water slide and children's club here!* It was from 2002. There was also a cutting about the police's alleged assault on the demonstrator at Nørrebrogade on Thursday afternoon and on top of it a bunch of keys that Axel pocketed, but there were no eye-catching clues, no weapons, no drugs, no camcorder, no remnants of blood or anything else to indicate that Piver had been beaten here in the flat.

Axel began going through a large pile of papers in the office; old letters, documents, cuttings. 'Macedonia' was written on a cover that contained a number of articles and columns from March 2001. War reporting in high-flown, dramatic language.

Ever since he had left Blågårds Plads, he had been going through all the details of the investigation, trying to tie them to Sonne. How had he got his hands on the drugs? And if he had got hold of them, had he also killed Davidi? What had happened in Macedonia?

The papers didn't give any answers. Stanca Gutu wasn't mentioned, but Axel was sure her death was important.

Henriette Nielsen appeared in the doorway triumphantly waving a piece of paper in her hand: a deed for a summer cottage in Asserbo.

"Now we've got him," she said. "Now we've fucking got him."

At that moment, Axel's radio crackled.

"Just wanted to hear what the deal was with that autonomist girl you sent down."

"What do you mean?"

"Well, there are two men standing here who were supposed to be picking her up."

"So?"

"But she's already been picked up. Another cop went into the entrance and came out with her."

"So you've just botched it up?"

"I just thought it was a bit weird. He took her over to a civilian car and drove off with her."

"Who was he?"

"I didn't recognise him."

"But you were the ones who were supposed to have taken her in. Didn't you send for a van?"

"Yes, but I thought maybe it was by agreement with you."

"What did he look like?"

"He was in full combat uniform with a cap on his head, tall, crewcut, with a sort of… I don't know quite how to describe his face."

"Marked, bony?"

"Yes, exactly."

"Fuck, fuck, fuck, have they gone?"

"Yes, 10 minutes ago."

"Get a description of them out right away. That was Sonne."

58

Sonne was gone and Liz with him. A call had been put out and photos of him and the girl had been sent to all the media. There were numerous responses from people who thought they had seen them, but they all turned out to be wild goose chases. Lindberg was once again at Police Headquarters, along with several of Sonne's colleagues, Laila Hansen and another ex-girlfriend. They were to be questioned on what they knew about the journalist. Moussa and his two accomplices had been released, but Lasso, who had slipped away on a scooter in the chaos, had been arrested without the drugs an hour later.

The case was the top story on TV and all the online newspapers. The reporter who had been one of the leading newshounds for many years had himself become front-page news.

The anti-terror force, which was already on full alert, had been sent out to the summer cottage in Asserbo. Henriette Nielsen was the operation leader, accompanied by Darling, Corneliussen and Rosenkvist. Now they were going to close the case. With bows and ribbons and stars on. Axel wasn't part of it. He was still *persona non grata*.

Henriette Nielsen had been completely changed when she left for Asserbo. She had pulled him aside and almost threatened him; he was to contact her if he got so much as a whiff of Sonne or the drugs – not least the latter. She wanted to fucking be there.

Axel drove out to Assistens and parked his car outside the gate where Enver Davidi had been found almost a week ago. He walked in and looked at the spot. All traces of the murder had now been removed.

Then he went walkabout; past Dan Turell's and Kierkegaard's graves, back to the lime-tree alley, finishing up at the chapel where Davidi had met his killer – it was still a mystery to him why he had come to meet him at Assistens. It made no sense. Davidi, who according to Henriette Nielsen was almost paranoid about leaving the hotel room.

He crossed the street, went into a newsagent and bought a packet of cigarettes and a lighter. Back in his car, he sat a while and then lit a cigarette. He put the lighter in his trouser pocket and took two drags. It tasted like a pub at night. He threw the cigarette away and chucked the packet out of the window. He wasn't going to start smoking again.

The clouds lay over Nørrebro like a low grey fog that could turn into torrential rain at any moment, but further out, the sky was orange and yellow over the city, illuminated from below by the sun's twilight rays from the west.

Sonne in Macedonia. Sonne with Enver Davidi. Sonne with Laila Hansen.

Was Sonne the insider he hadn't been able to find? Not a policeman but a reporter who could get through the police barriers and who had access to the media, so that he could stage-manage this whole shitty story about an autonomist killed by the police? And then put the blame on Lindberg? He ran back through the case in his mind, but still thought it sounded too absurd, although more and more was falling into place.

Sonne had got hold of Piver's number when he interviewed the two girls in the collective. And then he had pretended to be Lindberg in the telephone conversation with Piver, who, believing that he would be meeting one of his left-wing heroes, had fallen straight into the trap and met his murderer instead.

But how had he got hold of a phone from Counterpress? And how had he got into Assistens and met Davidi? And had he brought the combat boots, handcuff strips and balaclava with him for the occasion? How had he persuaded Davidi to meet him there?

His mobile rang. It was Darling ringing to tell him that Asserbo had been a dead end. When the anti-terror force had arrived a little before six o'clock, they had found an elderly married couple who had bought the house off Sonne some three years earlier. They knew nothing about him apart from the purchase and there was no trace of Piver or anything suspicious in the house.

Two beeps told him that a new call was waiting.

"I'll get back to you – I'm getting another call," said Axel, and clicked on the second call. It was Sten Jensen from the comms centre.

"What are you all up to?" he asked cheerfully. "Soon I won't have any bloody vans left to send to Nørrebro."

"What have you got for me?"

"I have a trace on one of those mobiles you called in about a couple of hours ago."

"What?"

"It was used out at Rentemestervej 14 minutes ago."

Laila's address. Axel reached instinctively for his pistol. Was Sonne there now? But she was in at Headquarters. How about Louie?

"I'm on my way."

"No need. It's been used again since then, out on the railway tracks by the Nørrebro line. There are warehouses and all kinds of other crap – old shunting yards and industrial decline. The same place as that phone from Counterpress was turned on once last Saturday. If you drive out to Rovsingsgade and turn off, you should hit it straight on. The signal's accurate within about 100 yards, but it's just there at the end of the road right up by the railway tracks."

59

It was nearly nine o'clock as he headed towards Nordvest. He drove out along Tagensvej and Rovsingsgade, then into Vingelodden until he arrived at a large, abandoned railway freight yard. He parked next to an industrial container for cardboard, stepped out and walked in through an open, latticework gate.

It was several years since there had been trains on the track, which was now desolate and overgrown. To his left was an engine shed built of red brick and black half-timbering; to his right were three peeling containers that had once been red, surrounded by three-foot-high bushes and small trees. No car.

The shunting tracks and sidings were interwoven in the dark. Railway wagons stood alone on the tracks, brown with age and rusty as if they had been left there right in the middle of a journey. In the background was the overground suburban line from Hellerup to Vanløse.

Axel checked the keys he had found in Sonne's flat. Apart from a large padlock key, they were for ordinary door locks.

The doors to the engine shed had been broken in and the windows smashed. He walked around the building but couldn't see anything that looked like a locked door. Darkness had fallen, but there was a clear sky and moonlight. He hurried inside; the sound of broken glass under his feet followed him all the way around the building, but after 15 minutes he had to accept that there were no locked rooms.

Then he heard it. A shout. Everything begins with a sound, he thought. He stood completely still and tried to work out where it had come from.

Again.

"Help!"

Across the floor to the nearest window, his crunching steps slicing into his eardrums. He stepped out onto a ramp that led down to the surrounding terrain. The darkness was thick, but his eyes had become accustomed to it during his examination of the building. Now he could see the car, parked behind the last of the containers, a good 100 yards away with its grille pointing towards him.

He waited until an overground train drove past, bent down as low as he could, and ran the first 30 yards along the engine shed under the cover of the wheels rumbling against the rails. Then he crouched waiting for the next train. There was nothing to see, but he could still hear shouting. Was it a woman screaming at the top of her lungs? Was it Liz?

As the next train rolled by, he ran over to the containers. On the way, he fell into a large hole full of water and stumbled to his feet, but he got over there before the buzzing of the electrical wires and the screaming of wheels against rails disappeared along with the train on its way towards Vanløse. He pressed his back against the side of the middle container and looked around. Now there was no mistaking the sound. He could hear a voice speaking angrily, but it sounded muted, as if someone was moaning and begging for mercy from within. There wasn't time to secure the terrain around the containers. With his back to the container, he moved step by step to the gate. It was ajar.

"NO, NO, DON'T!" came a desperate scream from inside.

There was something that didn't add up.

"You're going to die, you little shit. I've wasted far too much time on you," he heard a man rasp. Then came the dull sound of blows against flesh and he assumed that Sonne was beating Liz. Another train went past. Axel took a step back and flung the door open.

"Stop!" he screamed.

It was pitch black in the container. Axel didn't have his torch with him.

Sonne's voice continued regardless.

"There wasn't a copy of the video, you little scumbag. You were bluffing. Time to say goodbye!"

Only now did Axel realise his mistake.

There was no one in the container. No Liz, no Sonne. It hadn't been Liz's voice he had heard, but a recording of something that was probably Piver's last moments.

He sensed a movement out of the corner of his eye, and then he was hit on the arm, which broke like a twig. He heard his own scream and lost his footing as he put a hand to the broken arm and saw his pistol lying on the ground two yards away. He threw himself towards it, even though he knew it was a waste of time. It was kicked further away by a boot and the baseball bat hissed down towards him once again. This time he saw it coming and managed to shift his head to one side, so that it only hit him on his shoulder. There was no mistaking the cracking sound – he had his second broken bone in less than 10 seconds.

"Now be quiet or I'll smash your head in."

Thousands of hours spent being afraid of dying – now he was as close to death as anyone could come and he couldn't feel a damn thing. Except life.

Sonne stood in front of him in full combat uniform.

"You're finished, Sonne. You're being hunted all over the country. You only have one chance and that's to turn yourself in."

Sonne didn't react. He took a step away from Axel, a smile on his face. Axel twisted his shoulder in an attempt to get hold of his mobile, making him groan with pain.

"Lie still!"

Sonne examined Axel's pistol, took off the safety catch and waited.

So this was it, apparently. Not a heart attack, not a blood clot in the brain, not an ambulance ride with desperate paramedics around him, not an emergency doctor shooting defibrillator shocks into his chest, but put down like an animal in an old railway yard by a reporter from the country's biggest daily newspaper. Sonne pointed the pistol at him. Smiled.

The seconds were ticking noisily away inside Axel; what thought would pass through his mind in his last moment? Who? Cecilie, Laila, Emma? Emma, of course, Emma, Emma, Emma, but it was Cecilie's face that reared up, it was her he wanted to reach out for, it was her who should see him, it was his last wish, and acknowledging that filled him with deep shame. Let me die then, for fuck's sake!

But it wasn't his time to die.

Not yet.

Sonne took aim above Axel's head and shot as a train rattled past.

"Like that… yes… I don't need the baseball bat any more. I thought I'd be able to remember how to use one of these guys. Learnt it once on a further education course with the Police and Court Reporters Association, where we went out shooting with the PET people. And by the way, that's where I got hold of this dashing uniform."

Axel had to keep him going.

"How did you get into Assistens?"

"I just walked in. It wasn't difficult. No one stopped me. I even came across a guy sleeping up against a tree. Personally, I thought it was the perfect outfit."

"Why did you kill him?"

Sonne looked as though he were in his own world. He had a worried frown on his brow.

"Arms above your head and turn over. NOW!"

Axel did as he was told, groaning out loud as he tried to stretch his broken arm over his head. The pain was so intense that he was struggling to think clearly. When he was lying on his stomach, Sonne came over to him.

"Arms behind your back," he said hoarsely.

"I can't, for fuck's sake – it's broken," gasped Axel.

He could feel the pistol barrel on his neck.

"Come on!"

Sonne pulled his healthy arm behind his back and then grabbed the other one and dragged it in the same direction, making Axel scream.

If Sonne was going to put strips on him, he would have to use both hands. That was his chance. Axel couldn't use his arms, but he still had his legs. He tensed himself and got ready to turn over so that he could kick out at the body over him. When he felt that the barrel had been removed, he counted the seconds until Sonne would take hold of his hands to bind his wrists together. But though Sonne might well be crazy, he certainly wasn't stupid. He turned and stood with a leg on either side of Axel's head, so that he had his front towards his body. Axel didn't have a chance of reaching him. Then he felt the plastic strap tighten around his wrists.

Sonne looked at him, as if weighing up the situation.

"Where's your radio? And your mobile?"

He turned Axel over, put the pistol to his throat, examined his jacket and found the radio, which was switched off. His mobile was in his back pocket.

"No mobile?"

"It's in the car."

Sonne lit a cigarette. He dropped the radio and stamped on it. The pistol in one hand.

"How did you get hold of Davidi?"

"It doesn't matter now. I found him and then I arranged a meeting with him."

"At Assistens? In the middle of the night?"

"Yes, why not? He looked really surprised when he saw me."

Axel imagined Davidi's shock when Sonne appeared in full combat uniform.

"But why?"

Sonne looked worn out, as if his actions had now corroded his armour and settled down over his whole face, the rust of fate.

"I hated that bastard. He shouldn't have come up here. He should have stayed away, then none of this would have happened," he said.

Axel heard another train approaching and tried to reach his mobile again.

"Where's Liz?" groaned Axel.

"She's fine in the boot," laughed the reporter.

"You can't kill her. It has to stop here," groaned Axel.

"Shut your mouth! The only one who should stop is you. You have nothing to say. She'll go the same way as you."

Axel knew there wasn't much time left. He had to prevent Sonne from dragging her down with him.

"You won't get away."

"Shut the fuck up. Now we have to figure out how we're going to send you two on your way. I thought that a little brisk bonfire was an obvious option. That way we can also clear the container of clues."

"Let her go, Sonne. She has nothing to do with this. Let her go, for Christ's sake."

"For Christ's sake," imitated the reporter in a girlish voice. He opened both doors to the container. "Enough talk. Time for you to go in here. And warm up."

He grabbed hold of the shoulders of Axel's jacket and began dragging him into the container. He threw him into a corner, switched on a light and closed the doors. The walls were covered with soundproofing. A carpenter's bench with tools at one end, a bloody glove, gaffer tape, a camcorder, a computer, a police radio, two police helmets, yet another baseball bat, and in the middle of the space was a metallic café chair with a splash of blood on one armrest. There was enough crime scene here for the entire forensics department, thought Axel. If they ever got to see it. The floor was overflowing with rags and rubbish – empty coke cans, cigarette butts, pizza boxes and liquorice bags.

"Cosy place I have here, isn't it? That young autonomist didn't think so though. You know he had me on tape? That was too fucking bad for him. If he hadn't had it, he wouldn't have disappeared along with it. And you lot would still be suspected of killing David."

"What about Laila? Did you realise Davidi had come back to stay?"

"That doesn't really matter now, does it? He's dead."

"It's her this is all about, isn't it?"

Interest shone out of Sonne's eyes.

"Why do you think that?"

"I've seen the picture of her in your flat. It's hanging there among all your trophies, you sick bastard."

"You're crazy about her too, right? I could see it in your face while you were asking me about the case. I've seen you hanging around her house, but you don't have a chance."

Axel's arms were numb with pain; he tried to get hold of his mobile in his pocket with the fingertips of his good arm, but the lighter was in the way.

"But why kill him?" asked Axel.

"David was raving away about getting a second chance in Denmark, about getting Laila back, about living with her and Louie again."

Axel had almost got the mobile out of his pocket. He had to try to keep the conversation going.

"I gave him a chance. I told him: Go home or I'll turn you in to the police right now. Then he laughed out loud and taunted me. 'Go ahead!' he said. 'Call them, you murderer. I'm working for the police now. I have a deal with them. You're out of your depth again, Jakob.'"

Axel had manoeuvred his mobile phone far enough up out of his pocket that he could feel the keys. He was listening to Sonne, but at the same time concentrating on calling back the last number he had called: his colleagues in the car outside Sonne's house.

"I had no idea it was you dirty pigs who'd brought him up here. I thought he was lying, but then he showed me his passport and told me that you'd just given him fifteen kilos of cocaine to sell under police observation. He had the cocaine with him in a bag that he wanted to hide in the cemetery. He laughed at me. He said I might as well forget everything. Then I hit him and dragged him down into the hole, as you've already worked out. I paralysed him with the taser and put strips and my boots on him. I had the balaclava in my pocket and thought I could hide his face in it. I was going to drag him out with me or something like that. And then I took him over to the gate, but it was locked. I don't know what I intended to do, but even there, with blood all over his face, he kept talking. He was raving about Louie and Laila and that his deportation sentence would be revoked and that he would reveal everything about what happened in Macedonia if I didn't stay away from him and his family. Then I slammed him up against the wall and pressed really hard around his throat."

He stared out into the night.

"It was actually a release. To feel how his larynx crushed and his neck almost broke, how he gurgled and died. If you only knew how much I've hated him all these years."

"What about Stanca Gutu?"

Sonne laughed out loud.

"You'll never find out about that. And it doesn't matter a shit. Have you tried asking Lindberg? He could have told you, but he didn't dare, did he? Self-righteous moron."

Axel's mobile phone rang. Sonne stopped his flood of talk and looked furiously at him.

"I thought you said it was in the car."

He managed to press a button and hoped he had answered the call. Sonne was over him in two steps, kicking him in the stomach three times in a row and turning him over. Axel screamed with the pain in his shoulder. Sonne found the mobile, threw it on the floor and hammered the heel of his boot into it. Plastic splinters flew around the container.

"OK, I'll just fetch the petrol – then I'll be finished with you."

He left the container.

Axel pushed himself up to a standing position and quickly went over to the table. He probably had less than a minute before Sonne brought back what he needed. There was a USB stick lying beside the camera. Axel turned around and manoeuvred it down into his other trouser pocket with the undamaged, bound hand. The closest he came to a weapon was a pair of scissors. He tried to grasp them, but it was difficult; he got hold of one eye and the scissor blade.

Sonne stepped forward into the doorway with the pistol in one hand and a petrol can in the other.

"I heard something. Turn around!"

Axel turned and Sonne took a step towards him. Then he pushed off with all his power against the bench, clenching the scissors in his undamaged hand, the blade cutting into his fingers, and catapulted back towards Sonne. He hit him, but not with the scissors. Sonne fell over towards one side of the container while Axel was sent flying into the other wall, where he lost his footing and rolled over on the floor. Sonne was on his feet first and stood over him.

"I've fucking had enough of you."

He dropped the petrol can and aimed the pistol at Axel. He kicked Axel in the stomach and pulled him all the way to the bottom of the container. Then he took two steps back, put the gun on the workbench and screwed the lid off the petrol can. He began splashing petrol around the container. The fumes were powerful and stung in Axel's nostrils. Sonne walked round the whole container and poured the petrol out. Then he stood up in front of Axel. Barely four inches from his foot.

It was his last chance.

Sonne looked at him and lifted the petrol can over his head.

"How did you get David to meet you at Assistens?" shouted Axel, sliding further down towards Sonne's feet.

"Shut your mouth."

The can was half empty and only a small splash landed on his face. Axel got hold of his lighter and got it out of his trouser pocket. The moment Sonne raised the can higher to empty it completely, Axel pulled his legs from under him, and the reporter landed on his arse with petrol gushing out over him. Axel saw the shock on Sonne's face, kicked out wildly at him, catching him in the stomach, and pushed himself up the wall. He had petrol on his face and body from rolling around in it on the floor. He had no chance of reaching the pistol on the workbench, but Sonne did, and Axel knew that he would shoot him as soon as he got hold of it.

Sonne was on his way up. Axel pushed himself out from the wall and hammered his knee into Sonne's chest, but the fight had been decided in advance, uneven as it was. Sonne could use both his hands. He pushed Axel away from him, and he fell back against the wall. Axel measured the distance. There were three yards to get out of the container; he imagined the flaming hell – it wasn't possible. But it had to be. Axel saw Sonne's eyes searching for the gun, the arm stretching over the worktop to reach it, the hand crawling the last few inches. Axel felt the grooves in the lighter's little wheel, pressed on the gas tap. In a second, they would make it all explode.

"Die, you bastard!" he screamed to stall Sonne for a final second.

Then he lit the lighter. He closed his eyes and mouth, breathed out through his nose and ran as fast as he could.

The space around him exploded. It felt like the fire was embracing him and preventing him from going any further.

But no, he wasn't going to take his leave now, he was high, he had a choice, his own choice, all his fear was gone. Come on, death, let me touch it, let me fight, I'm not giving up.

He felt like he was running through water, heavy water, that was pressing the strength out of him. His hair was crackling. His face was burning on one side; it felt as if it was freezing to ice, but he knew it was the petrol burning his eyebrow, ear and hair. The skin on his face was being singed and was curling up layer by layer. There was fire in his shoes and trousers, and he ran and ran towards the reflection, the shining surface 10 yards away, the pool of water he had fallen into on his way towards the container. He flung himself down into it face first, followed by his body with his burning clothes.

60

Friday, March 9

"Hello, Axel, how are you feeling?"

The Swede was towering over him. The sensation was horizontal, floating, painless, the neon lights in the ceiling sliced into his eyes. Was he lying on an autopsy table?

"Where am I? What are you doing here?"

The Swede laughed.

"No, my friend, I'm not going to dissect you. Not yet. But if you don't look after yourself better than this, I can guarantee you'll be down to me pretty soon."

Axel tried to feel his body, but it wasn't there. There was only a tight feeling in the skin on his face, no pain, just a numb, parchment-like tightness of the skin. He couldn't see clearly. There was a duvet and a drip, an arm in plaster, the sound of a heart monitor. He shook his head. Then he realised he couldn't see out of one eye.

The Swede's face suddenly took on a serious look.

"I was called out to the scene of the crime. A rather burnt body. Then I heard about you and came in here. How's it going?"

"I don't know. Where was he?"

"Who? The body? He was lying outside a container. He was dead when they got there. They found you with your head down in a pool of water."

"What's the time?"

"It's five o'clock in the morning. You've just come out of the recovery room."

Axel tried to lift one arm but had to give up. He wanted to touch his face.

"You'll have to wait a few days with that. You have two fractures."

The Swede looked kindly at him, but the wrinkles on his brow told a different story from the smile.

"How do I look?"

"Burnt. If I'm honest, you look like a barbecued chicken on one half of your face. You won't get out of this without a scar, but apart from hair, skin and eyebrows, there's probably nothing major as far as I can read from your journal. Your ear hasn't melted and your eye is apparently undamaged."

"What did they find out there? Did they find Liz? And the money in his car?"

"I know nothing except that they found a girl in the boot of a car. She was alive. What happened out there?"

Axel told him how Sonne had taken him by surprise, what he had said and how it had ended.

"You got him," said the Swede drily. "As usual. But you might be advised to consider whether this is the way you want things to go in the future."

"Where are my clothes?" said Axel.

The Swede smiled but had misunderstood him.

"Are you nuts? You aren't going anywhere now."

"It's not that. Where are my trousers?"

The Swede looked around the room. Opened the cupboard and took out a bag.

"Is this it?"

He opened the bag and Axel recognised the jacket and the trousers.

"Bloody hell, what a stink," said the Swede. Axel wanted to reach out for them, but he couldn't.

"Is there a USB key in the back pocket?" he said.

The Swede rummaged through the trouser pockets, found the key and held it up.

"This?"

"Take it. Look after it for me."

The Swede put it in his pocket.

"How about Emma? Does she know I'm in here?"

"I called Cecilie and told her what happened. They'll pop by later today."

"Thanks."

"I understood from her that you've had a clash around Emma's visit to the morgue. I told Cecilie that it wasn't all that serious. Do you think there's any chance of a reconciliation?"

"I don't have the slightest idea. She wants to force me into mediation. If I don't agree, we'll be going to the family court where she'll expose me as the hash-smoking father who lets the bodies in the morgue watch over his daughter while he's assisting in the dissection of the latest murder victim."

"Have you considered the possibility that she's doing it for your daughter's sake and not to annoy you?"

"Et tu, Brute."

"I just think Emma needs the two of you to get things working between you – more than she needs a war. Maybe you'll also feel a bit better if it calms down. This sort of thing has a tendency to eat you up from within."

Axel looked out of the window. It was hard to argue with the Swede.

"I'll write you a prescription for some sleeping pills, so that you can tell her you're dropping the hash."

At that moment, the door opened and a doctor came in. Axel was relieved.

"He's not supposed to be having visitors yet. He needs sleep. His body has been in shock and he needs rest for the burns to heal."

The Swede held up his hands in surrender. The doctor went over and turned a screw on a cover to one of the tubes. Axel immediately felt something streaming into him, a balmy sense of peace; he giggled and drifted off.

When he woke up again, it was morning. He was alone in the room. The eye bandage was gone and he could see fairly clearly again. He lay there looking up at the ceiling and then became aware of the smell. There were flowers on the table. And on the window sill.

He tried to assemble the pieces. There were a lot of them and most of them fitted together. Davidi had come up in the belief that PET would give him a second chance. He had played along as far as he could and, indeed, much further than that, and they had been so overexcited to have an insider and get results that they didn't give a shit about what would happen to him afterwards. Everyone in the police had shaken their head when they moved the specialists from the Flying Squad into investigating drugs, trafficking and organised crime over at PET. Now the intelligence service had to achieve something. There was no denying that it had. Henriette, Kettler and Jens Jessen. They hadn't investigated Davidi's past thoroughly enough and before they had got going with the operation, it had overtaken both them and him in the form of a vengeful, hate-filled reporter who had had a relationship with his ex-wife. Or was Sonne's desire for her just revenge for something that had happened in Macedonia? Whatever – he wanted to get rid of Davidi at any price.

Axel thought back to Sonne, whom he had known for years. He had always trusted him; he was able, but small details suddenly stood out in a different light.

Sonne thought he had got Davidi where he wanted him, that he could send him straight back to Macedonia, but Davidi had pulled the rug from under his feet when he told him he was collaborating with the police.

Exhaustion and confusion lay like a blanket over Axel as he rummaged around for answers. He was in need of some clarification and wished he could get up from his bed and get the last pieces to fall into place, but his body lay like a slaughtered animal and he was in pain under the duvet, while the burns on his face seared painfully with every little twitch. Axel fell asleep again. Or did he? He thought he saw Laila Hansen standing at his bedside with his hand in hers, a thumb rubbing the back of his hand. He tried to say something but drifted away again, while trying to retain the image of her eyes, her wide lips and the bristly, short-cut hair, longing to feel it against his palms, between his fingers, and to hold her face. She talked about Louie, they were going to move away to get some peace. Yes, that was a good idea, thought Axel. The boy was sad and she hoped he would recover soon.

"How are you?" she asked.

"Bloody awful," he replied. And how about us – how are we? He didn't know if he had said it out loud, but she had smiled without saying anything.

Suddenly, Emma's voice was there. He opened his eyes and saw his daughter sitting on the edge of the bed. Huge brown eyes, slightly open mouth and two protruding front teeth.

Where was Laila?

He reached out for Emma's hand. It felt warm and small in his, the fingers soft and completely smooth.

"Daddy, why do you have that plaster on your face?"

Cecilie came into his field of vision with a metal vase full of flowers.

"We came as soon as we could. Are you OK?"

She was hectic, pacing back and forth between the bed, the windowsill and the chair where her bag was lying.

"Wasn't there just someone in here?" asked Axel, feeling a bit disoriented.

"No. Who would that have been? You were talking in your sleep."

She gave him a look that was cold and distracted.

What had he said?

"But why do you have a plaster by your eye, Daddy?"

Axel looked at Emma.

"I'm just fine. I've been burnt a little on my face. They say it will get better."

"But Daddy, did you catch him – the thief who did it?" said his daughter.

"That's enough, Emma," interrupted Cecilie. "I talked to the doctor. He says you'll be OK."

It sounded like she was saying the situation was under control. And so are your feelings, thought Axel. Why on earth did you come?

Axel nodded to his daughter.

"Did you catch the thief? Did you, Daddy?" she asked with eyes wide open in anticipation.

"Yes, I did. We're done with him now."

Cecilie sat down on the chair behind Emma, frowning at him with a little finely tuned, totally unnatural smile sitting stiffly under her cheeks.

He watched her face, studied it carefully, hoping something was happening, or was it just an old habit? Where was that crack in the armour that had been there the other evening? He looked for the vulnerability and tenderness he had seen in her eyes, as if he could crawl into it and find the old Cecilie in there.

Perhaps it was just concern about his condition, her child's father, which had brought her there.

She opened her mouth and was about to say something, but he got in first.

"Last Sunday – what was all that about?"

Cecilie got up and went over to the window. Her back to him.

"I thought… I just thought… shouldn't we just let that lie for the time being?"

She had returned to the order of business; the new order that could be found under "responsible and mature divorced parents who are capable of co-operating about the child".

"I've booked a time for the mediation; I hope you want to take part," she said, as if she had been inside his head.

Never a moment's peace, just being chased around. He wished he was alone with his daughter.

"To be perfectly frank, Cecilie, I've had other things on my mind."

"I know, but we're sticking to it, aren't we?"

"Yes. It's probably a good idea. I'd really like it to run smoothly," he said, and went silent as he felt the words squeezing up like lava through his mouth.

"There's something I've been wanting to ask you. Have you told

Jens Jessen that you found that hash out at my place after we'd been making love all night?"

She looked as if he had slapped her round the face.

"Axel, let it be. That isn't why, is it? My coming to you didn't have anything to do with him. Don't punish him for what happened. He's all right. And don't punish me for it either. I was weak. And you were too. We'd forgotten how it was."

We? Of course, it was now called "we", so that the responsibility wasn't hers alone.

She sighed, bit a nail and then suddenly looked angrily at him.

"But now you've certainly reminded me of it. Don't get mixed up in my life. It's 'no trespassing', Axel, even if you're going to be working with him. I've given you this chance with the mediation. Don't waste it!"

Emma looked confusedly from one to the other. Axel squeezed her hand in his. He hated that stupid bitch. And loved her.

"Daddy! Can I touch the plaster on your arm? Can I write on it?"

Axel nodded and lifted his arm. His lungs felt full of mucus. Emma took hold of the bed rail and crawled up to him with a felt-tip in her mouth.

"There should be a heart. And a butterfly. And then it has to say Emma."

He watched as she painstakingly did her drawings, trying to concentrate on her despite being annoyed that his feelings for Cecilie always came between him and his child.

On the steel table next to the bed, there was a bouquet of white roses in a vase with an ordinary envelope. A face was drawn on it, accompanied by "Get well soon. From Laila and Louie".

There was a knock on the door.

Rosenkvist came into view, then Jens Jessen, Kristian Kettler, Henriette Nielsen and John Darling.

"I hope we aren't disturbing you," said Rosenkvist.

"No, no," replied Cecilie, "we were just leaving. Come on, Emma."

She gave Jens Jessen a squeeze on his shoulder as she went past. He did boxing steps in front of Emma, who in turn found her way between his combination and hit him hard on his thigh. He laughed foolishly.

Then they were standing around his bed. Axel shook his head, as though he needed to get his sight working.

"Am I dreaming or am I awake?" he said.

Scattered laughs. Rosenkvist ignored it.

"You're awake," he said.

"Are you sure I'm not in hell?"

"You're the hero of the day, Steen," said Rosenkvist. "If that's your idea of hell, let's just say that's where you are. We're here to see how you're doing. Think of it as collegial solicitude. As we've just held a co-ordination meeting, we agreed to come and visit you as a group."

Co-ordination meeting – it smelt of serious stain-removal. But it would take more than that to wash away the stains that PET and their idiotic operation with Davidi had smeared the force with.

Jessen broke in.

"Yes, exactly, and we understand from the doctors that you'll get back to full fitness. We're happy about that, really happy, all of us, if I may say so, but we're a little curious, in fact super curious, if I may put it that way, about what happened," he said, his facial muscles quivering in all directions like the lights on a pinball machine going crazy. What did she see in that boy scout?

Axel told them about the confrontation with Sonne in the container, minutely and slavishly. He could see on their faces that Sonne's blind hatred for Enver Davidi brought them joy. Both Jessen and Rosenkvist nodded. It was a motive, a driving force that had been completely outside their control. He left out all the details about Stanca Gutu – he wanted to sort out that part of the case himself. It took him half an hour to go through the whole chain of events and then Darling took over.

"All the clues from the container were burnt, but Liz Jensen was found in the boot of Sonne's car. Maybe he'd intended to use her as a hostage if he needed to get away. We also found a bag of mobile phones, two from Counterpress, two which Enver Davidi had used, and three unknowns, which you found the papers for in his flat, all on top-up cards. There was a taser, a jack-knife and two computers containing some material that explains his anger towards Enver Davidi better. They had a clash over a young woman in Macedonia. We're not sure what it's all about yet, but we're working on it. It appears there was serious bad blood over something."

"That fits with his outburst towards Davidi. Sonne said that Davidi taunted him before he killed him. He got a shock when he realised that Davidi had the all-clear because you'd brought him up here," said Axel, looking at the three PET people, who all looked extremely uncomfortable.

Henriette Nielsen broke the silence.

"Yes, we've been checking Sonne's background, and it turns out he had a breakdown after Macedonia. He was hospitalised and was in treatment for three months, but then discharged himself. The doctor who treated him described him as quite ill."

John Darling pulled a folder out of his bag and threw it on the bed.

"Here are print-outs from his computer. There are old love letters to Laila Hansen. It seems that their relationship broke down after just under a year, because he was flipping out and unable to control his temper. He apparently put a stranglehold on her while they were having sex. He's been spying on her. Maybe he never gave up hope of getting her back, and something about Davidi's arrival flipped a switch in him, so that hope was ignited again."

"What you're saying is that he killed Davidi because he was in love with Laila Hansen?"

"Maybe. It's too early to say anything about that. I read it as him hating Davidi enough to kill him. Davidi knew something about him and taunted him about it and threatened to reveal it. Whether or not Sonne fell in love with Laila Hansen to rub salt in the wound, well, you'd have to talk to a therapist about that."

"So now you're just going to clam up about it?"

Rosenkvist folded his hands and cracked his fingers one by one.

"I think we have a clear case. Old divisions and hatred garnished with an unhappy love life."

Axel felt sick.

"And what about our own role in the case?" Axel asked.

Jessen smiled his manic smile – he almost seemed likeable because he was the only one who didn't look like one of the stone faces on Mount Rushmore. Rosenkvist was the highest-ranking officer in the hierarchy and that kind of question was his speciality.

"It has nothing to do with the case. It wasn't us who killed him."

"But it was us… or rather, them," said Axel, pointing at the PET people, "who brought him up here. He would be wandering around in the best of health down in Macedonia if it hadn't been for their agent plans."

Jens Jessen began to speak in a hail of tics.

"Of course, you can see it in many ways, and mistakes were made. It happens in these kinds of delicate operations, but the very nature of the case means that we need to… well now, how should I phrase it… close the lid on that operation, close it and carry it down to the end of the archive where the more sensitive cases are kept."

Axel shook his head.

"I thought you said I hadn't arrived in hell."

Rosenkvist's eyes were filled with contempt.

"Your desire for the truth is impressive. And you've done a fine job solving this case. But it's over as far as you're concerned. And we aren't going to have more holes drilled in it than necessary."

His face looked like it was covered with a shell of thin ice.

"You will now have a few months' sick leave while Darling puts the finishing touches to the case with Nielsen and Kettler."

He paused for effect.

"We're holding a press conference on the case today. It's a bit delicate, of course. One of the noble representatives of the press. It doesn't look too good, but it could have been worse," said Rosenkvist, looking around at them.

The conversation was over. Neither Darling nor Henriette had any urge to stay, and both went over and said goodbye to Axel, while the other three said their goodbyes at a distance and left.

When they had gone, Axel turned on his side. He lay looking out over the lowest of the two main buildings of the Rigshospital at a section of blue sky – the first he thought he had seen for a long time – when he heard the steps. He turned around and looked up into Rosenkvist's face.

"I forgot to tell you that this is your last chance. If anything comes out, you're finished. And what's more, I'll make sure you're so discredited that you'll never get a job again. You've made mistakes. I'm turning a blind eye, but if you cross my path again in a way I don't like, I'll crush you. Do you follow?"

"I don't know what mistakes you're talking about."

"You'll find out the day you see your face on a placard under the headline 'Chief investigator had relationship with murderer's lover'. Or should we say 'Policeman comforted widow with sex'. You choose!"

Axel raised his eyebrows. He couldn't help laughing.

"There's one last thing. We found the camcorder in the boot of Sonne's car. That young autonomist… what's his name… Peter Smith's camera. Have you seen it?"

Quicksand. Axel tried to win time.

"It's not his. It was a shopkeeper on Nørrebrogade who set it up."

Rosenkvist swatted the information away like a fly on his brow.

"Never mind, have you watched it all the way through?"

"No, when could I have done that?"

"The technicians say that the recording's been copied over onto a disk or a USB key. I've checked the list of what you had on you when you were admitted. There was a USB key in your clothes."

"I have no idea what you're talking about."

"Where are your clothes?"

Axel pointed at the cupboard.

Rosenkvist took out the bag, opened it and frowned down his nose. He rummaged through it, then looked at Axel.

"It isn't here."

"As I said, I have no idea what you're talking about."

"I hope for your sake that you're telling the truth."

He felt like saying he did have it and that Rosenkvist was the last person on earth he would give it to. But he had a better idea.

The next day Axel called Lindberg, who said he would come over right away. The old defiance and contempt vanished from his voice when Axel told him Sonne had said that he was the only one who could tell the story about Stanca Gutu.

"There isn't a day goes by without me thinking about it," said the man Axel had hated for 14 years. He was sitting on the chair next to Axel's hospital bed and seemed mellow and burnt-out at the same time.

"We'd had a few totally crazy days, which I told you about. We met the guerrillas in the mountains, we were arrested, and there was tension between David and Sonne. And when we were released from the police station, we were very relieved and euphoric. So, we went to a bar and drank heavily. Later in the evening, Sonne suggested that David should take us with him to his girlfriend. It wasn't for me, but they said we were just going to party, so we went to the hotel."

"Was it a brothel?"

"Brothel, hotel – it was everything. The girls lived on a corridor in small rooms and we were drinking in a lounge at one end. They'd been kept in their rooms by their pimp for days so that they wouldn't meet the foreign press, so they had nothing to do. We got very drunk. The girls… they were…"

He stopped and looked almost like he was in mourning.

"What were they?"

"They were so young and innocent and destroyed at the same time.

I went into a room with a girl who was no more than 17 years old. I didn't want to have sex with her. I chatted with her about her life until I went out like a light. I didn't do anything to her, even though she was begging me to."

"What happened to Stanca Gutu?"

Lindberg looked up at him.

"Sonne was with her. The next morning, David came rushing in and said I should get dressed and get the hell out of there, because the girl in with Sonne was dead."

"Did you see the body?"

"No, but David said she'd been beaten and strangled, and that he'd found her lying halfway down on the floor with a blue tongue sticking out of her mouth."

"But you recognised her when I showed you the picture."

"Yes. That was a mistake. I should have taken responsibility. And told you what I knew. I didn't have the courage."

"What happened between Sonne and David?"

"When I met Sonne later, he'd been given a hiding by David. He said David had threatened to kill him, threatened to reveal what he'd done if he didn't disappear immediately. David told me I should forget everything that had happened."

Axel thought about the poster for 'Stop human trafficking' in Lindberg's flat.

"But you haven't forgotten it."

"No. Never."

"Why didn't you tell me?"

Lindberg hesitated.

"I was embarrassed. I was a failure. It's been difficult to live with – that I didn't intervene, that I indirectly participated in something that damaged other people."

When Lindberg had left, Axel called Frank Jensen in Skopje.

"I've heard from PET," said his old colleague. "They've been asking about Stanca Gutu. I've been holding them at arm's length until I heard from you. And I have something for you."

It was the tale of Stanca Gutu, a young woman from Moldova, sold as an item that would never be returned in the same state. She ended up as the victim of a sexual murder one night at a run-down brothel in a provincial town in Macedonia. Enver Davidi had been alone in the hotel, along with a handful of frightened young prostitutes from Ukraine and Moldova when the police arrived in the morning. He'd been questioned and said he didn't know who'd been with Stanca Gutu; that he'd slept with his girlfriend that night after drinking heavily.

"And was that it?"

"No, it turns out that the case was hushed up and already dropped the following day. The whole world press was down here because of the fighting and the authorities wanted to put a lid on the case. They didn't want any focus on the extensive trafficking of women taking place here. And then there was a local clan leader, Ilir Muriqi, also known as the Young Eagle, whose brothel it was, who intervened."

"How?"

"With money."

"How do you know?"

"I paid him a visit. The Young Eagle's son is in prison for the murder of a NATO soldier in Kosovo. I arranged an opportunity for him to see him. One good turn…"

"…deserves another. What else?"

"The Young Eagle told me that Davidi had approached him and asked for help cleaning up after the murder. He had said that a foreign journalist had been with Stanca Gutu and that it was an accident."

"And why would the clan leader help him?"

"Davidi clearly wasn't just anyone down here. He had status in the community because he hadn't just fallen back into his old habits and become part of the criminal gangs, but had kept his nose clean after he was deported. And the Young Eagle had tried to hire him several times

– without success."

"So Davidi offered his services as payment?"

"I assume so. I couldn't get Muriqi to say how."

"But why did he do that? Why didn't he just let Sonne stew in his own juice?"

"It's not that easy down here. He might have enjoyed respect among the Albanian population, who live almost in a parallel society, but if he'd attracted the attention of the Macedonian authorities, and they'd made a big case out of the murder, he could easily have been thrown in prison. We're collaborating with them, remember that. It would have meant a definitive farewell to all his dreams of coming back to Denmark and seeing his son again. And – according to the Young Eagle – that was the only thought in Enver Davidi's head."

"And money could get rid of a dead girl?"

"Money, favours, a slice of the cake – I'm not going to try and find out anything about that, because then my days here would be numbered, but that's how it works."

"How do we know that's what happened?"

"We don't know. We only have his word for it, but it usually holds around here when you have something to bargain with. He also got the eagle."

"What?"

"Davidi got the eagle tattooed on him when he joined the Young Eagle's organisation. It's a little thing they have running. The Albanian national symbol. You know, like the Russians or the Hell's Angels. You get your criminal competence sign printed into your skin, so you know where you belong."

The eagle on David's chest with the date.

Axel thanked him and ended the conversation.

On the third day, he had a visit from John Darling. He had come to record Axel's explanation of Sonne's death.

Did he admit to committing both murders? Darling wanted to know. Axel recalled Sonne's remark about Piver, who had ended up in the whole mess because he had got the footage of Davidi's murder.

"Yes, he admitted them both. No doubt about it. He did it. He killed both of them."

Axel told him what he knew about Stanca Gutu. That made Darling happy. The pieces were falling into place.

The big man stood up and looked out of the window.

"It's strange to think that we knew him. I must have spoken to him a hundred times. Without feeling anything – other than that irritation you always have with journalists who are bugging you all the time."

"Isn't that the first lesson we're taught, with murder? You discover that you never really know anyone completely."

"The newspapers aren't holding back about him and there is so much speculation about Sonne's motives and connections that even the most hardened conspiracy theorist would be envious. And on top of that, the first stories about his background and career have begun to appear."

"What are they saying?"

"The usual stuff. He pulled the legs off spiders as a child, arson, humiliations in the army, you know. And some old colleagues of his are saying how he was supposed to be the big hot-shot war correspondent, but never got anything apart from Kosovo and Macedonia, before coming home completely changed and having to go on sick leave and eventually being fired. Mood swings, fits of rage and concentration problems, before he was given a second chance, first as a temp at Ritzau, then BT and finally Ekstra Bladet's Crime Editorial, where he's been working for four years. Those bastards won't give us access to his office and computer because of freedom of the press, but the High Court will be giving a ruling this afternoon, which I expect to go our way."

"What about his motives for the murders? Are they writing about them?"

"Yes. He worshipped a woman with a child and became jealous of her ex-husband. That's been prominent. I don't know who's leaked that, but it isn't me. No one has heard anything about Stanca Gutu."

"What do you think about them keeping the entire Davidi operation secret?"

"That's PET all over, isn't it? That's how they work."

"You don't think it should come out?"

"Are you feeling suicidal?"

"But shouldn't they be held responsible for their cock-ups?"

"I know you're not exactly in love with Jens Jessen but do try to keep your personal feelings out of this. If it turns into an investigation, then we'll be the ones taking the rap. Us or Henriette. Have you ever heard of the shit flying upwards?"

Axel sighed.

"No, only if someone turns on a fan."

"Then it doesn't fly upwards. It hits everyone. And that would happen here too. Forget it."

"I noticed you didn't say anything the other day. What was that meeting about?"

Darling began telling him, but Axel could feel that he was losing interest. He was finished with that part of the investigation and couldn't be bothered to hear anything more about strategic considerations from PET and the police leadership about what should be revealed to the public and what should be kept in-house.

"We're going to have a new boss," said Darling suddenly.

"What!"

"Corneliussen has been relocated."

"To PET?"

"No, he's been shifted out to the National Police traffic division."

"What!"

"Rosenkvist has had all calls from HQ to TV2's Dorte Neergaard and to Sonne investigated, and it turns out that Corneliussen has leaked both the story of the officer who screwed his divisional leader's wife and that Lindberg had been arrested for the murders."

"Yes… why would he do that?" Axel found it difficult to understand.

"Well, who got the blame for it? You did. It must have been to get rid of you."

"What an idiot. Who are we getting now then?"

Darling smiled.

That same evening, Axel had another visitor. Henriette Nielsen came with flowers, but her errand wasn't just out of concern.

"What are you going to do?" she asked after a little idle chat.

They both knew what she was talking about.

"Is that why you're here?"

"Yes."

"And now you want to do a deal?"

"I want to know where I stand. It's my case. Not all the fuck-ups are mine but I was the one who handed over the drugs to him and I was the one who lost him."

"I'm not going to do anything to drag *you* through the dirt."

"That isn't good enough. If anything comes out about the case, I'm the one who'll take the blame. You may think you can wound Kettler or Jessen, but it's me who'll be left holding the baby."

"I don't feel any need to wound anyone. Besides, I have a feeling that I have you to thank for not being removed from the investigation completely. Even though I have no idea how you managed to convince your boss I should be allowed to carry out surveillance at Blågårds Plads."

"You have no grounds to thank me," she said coldly.

"Come on now, don't be so modest."

"I'm not being modest. I haven't helped you. On the contrary. I wanted to get rid of you when you started poking your nose into our operation. Besides, you're impossible to stop once you've got an idea in your head."

Axel appreciated her honesty, but who the hell was it then?

The answer came right away.

"If you have anyone to thank, it's Jens. He insisted on you staying on the case and collaborating with us, while your own bosses wanted to kick you to hell and back. He's been holding his hand over you the whole time – God only knows why."

61

Friday, May 11, 2007

It was a beautiful May evening as Axel left Police Headquarters and set off on his bike towards Nørrebro.

The investigation of the murders of Enver Davidi and Piver was completed. The case was solved and closed. But not for Axel. There were still some loose ends.

He had read the final conclusions. The DNA from Assistens, from Sonne's car and on Piver's body linked the dead reporter to the murders with a certainty that would have held all the way home in court.

It emerged that the police were in possession of a recording showing that Sonne had killed Enver Davidi. It didn't show the actual murder, but it showed a man in police uniform dragging Davidi with him, disappearing behind the wall and reappearing after 90 seconds. He took off his cap, as stated in the report, and the face was consistent with that of the suspect. The video had been found on a camcorder in Sonne's car. The footage began on Thursday, March 1 at 21:00 and lasted until the next morning, at which point the second victim had allegedly removed the camera.

Axel had the same reel of film, but his footage started earlier on the morning of Thursday, March 1, and contained clear evidence of an assault of the grossest kind by the police.

A couple of weeks ago, Lindberg had appeared in a major newspaper interview and told the story of Stanca Gutu's murder and his own experiences in Macedonia. It was a raw, honest interview, in which he didn't hide from the fact that he had a bad conscience over even being in a brothel with a handful of young women who had been sold as sex slaves.

Axel swung in through the gate from Nørrebrogade and walked up to the first floor. The red-painted door with the three yellow Christiania stars stood open; the editorial room was empty. That suited him fine. Axel had actually just intended to hand over the USB key, but as he entered Lindberg's office, he discovered the journalist lying reading on a leather sofa behind the door with a stack of papers on his chest. The look over the black spectacles frame was surprised; there was a cigarette behind his ear, Chinese slippers on his feet, an earring, stubble, worn jeans and washed-out T-shirt. It was possible to cultivate one's anti-style so much that it became a style in itself.

Lindberg threw the stack of papers on the floor and got up.

"Axel Steen. I thought we were done with each other – but maybe we never will be?"

Axel looked at him. He had despised him for 14 years, the personification of the intense hatred for the police that he had met that night. It had cost the lives of two of his friends. Lindberg was 18 May in flesh and blood. It hadn't completely gone, but there was something else, something more important and urgent to be done.

"I have something for you," said Axel.

He took the USB key out of his pocket and gave it to Lindberg, who looked confused.

"What's this?"

"You'll find out soon enough."

"Is it the file that disappeared?"

Lindberg looked at him in surprise. Surprised, then sceptical. Then fired-up.

"But why?"

"That doesn't matter. I'm sure you'll know how to use it."

Axel left the office to the sound of a computer being turned on.

He swung in by Dosseringen and cycled down the path by the lake. He parked the bicycle and sat down on a green bench. The worst was yet to come.

He looked over at the boulevard buildings on the other side of the lake. Søtorvet lay like a Parisian dream, with its corner towers, domes, spires, zinc roofs and balconies. A gateway into old Copenhagen, but also a well-appointed indication that Nørrebro, with all its chaotic construction and untameable life, ended here. He liked to think that not much had changed since Meldahl conceived the Søtorv mansions 130 years ago. On the side towards the city, two sculptures of the gods of the Tiber and the Nile stretched out imposingly in verdigris green bronze in accordance with the Roman models, while the Nørrebro side was marked by a hot-dog van and a granite sculpture of two young people facing each other in serious conversation, the man with his head in his hands and the woman open-faced with her hands clenched in front of her.

He took out the conclusions and read.

It all fitted with that extraordinary blend of luck and calculation from Sonne's side and misunderstandings, stupidity and happenstance on their part, which had made it possible for the reporter to slip through the fine-mesh net that a murder investigation is composed of.

Counterpress had been like a traffic hub of activists, NGO workers and journalists during the disturbances, and Sonne had visited the editorial offices as early as the Thursday before the murder of Enver Davidi in the company of a large group of foreign journalists. One of them had noticed that he had been rummaging in a box of mobile phones and chargers. It was concluded that he had used that opportunity to steal several mobile phones, including the one he used to cast suspicion on Lindberg.

Traces of cocaine had been found in Sonne's car, along with a large sum of money, which it was assumed came from Moussa, but it hadn't been possible to prove it – and the drugs were nowhere to be found.

The houses and lime trees along Øster Søgade were reflected in the lake's glossy black mirror, so that it looked as if they were growing down in the water. It didn't look like a reflection, but a palace sticking out from beneath the city, surrounded by islands of light green and brown rotting reeds; every single detail vibrated in the water even more enchantingly than the French stone model rearing up over Søtorvet. What was down there? Axel's gaze glided over the walls, which merged with the lush islands of pond weed and algae: an underwater, overgrown Louvre.

A gust of wind rippling the water wiped out the city in the lake; the small ripples crawled towards him in a movement that just kept coming, wave after wave. A seagull was rocking up and down on the swell, then took off and flew screeching over to the corner of the lake, where an elderly Turkish man in a brown jacket and a cloth cap was throwing pitta bread into the water and the mallards, swans and coots were fighting over the scraps.

He looked towards Dronning Louises Bro with its eight globes and the four corpse-white flagpoles that stuck up in the air; a pedalo had stuck fast under one of the bridge's three arches. The granite side facing the lake was tagged with graffiti: 'Venom', 'Killcrew' and 'Revenge', as a reminder that Nørrebro began here.

He reviewed the phone lists. He could see endless rows of figures, numbers and times for all those involved in the case and their calls – including himself.

So he had attracted that much attention. It made him angry. Had they sincerely believed that he had had something to do with the murders? He continued leafing through until he came to the call lists, where the conversations between the people involved could be seen. Sonne. Lindberg. Laila. Davidi. Himself. He had called Laila and Sonne. He thought back to the conversations as he scanned down the mass of information that in itself meant nothing.

Sonne. Laila. Davidi. A triangle. The main actors in the case.

On Thursday, March 1, Davidi had called Laila. Twice during the day. In the evening she had called Sonne. Soon after, she had called Davidi. And then Sonne. Three conversations within six minutes. Four hours later, Davidi was dead.

In the period between the last conversation and his death, Henriette Nielsen had handed the drugs over to him at the hotel and determined that Enver Davidi was suddenly feeling positive about the whole operation again. Now Axel knew why.

He took his bike and started riding out along Nørrebrogade. It would take him 20 to 25 minutes to get to Rentemestervej – more than enough to think it all through.

He had been sure about her, so sure that he had driven out to her five days after he had got home from hospital. She had greeted him, looked at him, lifted her hand and touched the still-red scars on his face, asking him how he was with a tenderness that went straight to his heart. They had drunk tea in the small kitchen and she had been frail and hesitant. Louie had come home from football and Axel had talked to him about football and pistols, and Louie had showed him his splatter guns. Louie had asked if Axel had caught Jakob, and Axel had said yes. The boy had chewed on it a bit, looking at Axel with question marks in his eyes. When Axel said Jakob had let them down, Louie had turned to Laila as if asking her for confirmation that that was what had happened. When he had been put to bed, she had told him about the relationship with Sonne, how alone she had been before she met him, how helpful he had been. Even though, from the beginning, she had felt that he had been hurt and broken by his experiences, he had been caring and very attentive, good with Louie, and that was what she had missed. She had fallen in love with Sonne – she had looked apologetically at Axel as she said it – even though she had known it wouldn't work between them. The relationship had ebbed out slowly. Sonne had become strange, withdrawn and had crossed the line towards Louie a couple of times, shouting at him, and Laila had broken it off after an episode where he had been violent towards her in bed. Axel had known what she had been talking about.

A long evening had ended with a hug and a promise to see each other again.

Axel cycled past the Blågårdsgade intersection, the asphalt still ruined and scarred after the large number of fires. The traffic was heavy, a flood of cyclists poured along the lanes on either side of the road.

The following day he had been to mediation with Cecilie – it had passed without any angry exchanges. He had told her that he was taking medicine for his insomnia and anxiety and, surprisingly, she had been completely satisfied. Their arrangement still stood. He had gone to Ikea and bought a new bed, with a princess veil to hang over it, for Emma. As he knelt on the floor, fighting his way through a hell of Allen keys and nuts, his front door had been pushed open and Laila Hansen had stuck her head in.

There hadn't been any words.

They had ended up on the dining table. It had been a little too high; his balls had felt they were being sliced against the edge of the table as he penetrated her, but it had been fine. She had scratched him on the chest where he couldn't stand anyone touching him and he hadn't discovered it until afterwards.

He passed Assistens, looked in at the spot where they had found Enver Davidi two months earlier and looked up at the hole in the row of houses where the Youth House had been.

"We are the ones the others don't want to play with" had been on the wall opposite for a decade. Now they didn't have a place to play any more. And the letters hadn't just been painted over but replaced by graffiti with the text "my dick my dick my dick".

They had seen each other twice the week afterwards, then three times, then four. Axel had got to know Louie, and last week he had had Emma with him out there. It had gone well.

It was completely upfront, he felt. As upfront as it could be now. Given that they were both the people they were.

There was still a hole in him where Cecilie had been, but it no longer felt so all-consuming. He had begun to fill it with some confidence and belief that he could succeed.

He cycled under the overhead railway line at Nørrebro Station, continued out through the bazaar-like atmosphere to Nordvest and Bispevej, past the site where Piver's body had been found.

Yesterday evening, he had looked after Louie while Laila attended a staff meeting. Louie had struggled to fall asleep.

"It's always been like this," said the boy, not wanting to be a problem.

They had talked about his father. Louie had shown him all the miniature wooden constructions from matches and ice-lolly sticks that Enver Davidi had assembled in prison and given to his son. Their house, the kindergarten, the playground. There were little matchstick figures of Enver, Laila and Louie on a swing, in a window, waving in the front door, with their arms around each other in front of the house. There was also a miniature of the church where Enver and Laila had been married, of the lakeside pavilion, where they had held their wedding celebration, and of a building Axel recognised: a chapel with four pillars. In front of it, a man was kneeling in front of a woman. "That's where Dad proposed to Mum," said Louie with an apologetic smile.

Jens Bang's gravedigger house at Assistens. Just like that. Simple enough. Not to see the wood for the trees.

"Mum told Dad she'd meet him there," said the boy.

"When?"

"Back then. Before he died."

"What did she say?"

"I couldn't sleep, and I heard Mum call Dad and say she'd meet him there. At the chapel. Where he proposed. That's how she said it. Our place."

Louie had gone silent for a little while.

"But she stayed here. Because she couldn't leave me alone."

Axel stood the bicycle up against the fence in front of the red brick house on Rentemestervej, where the bindweed was shooting through with its light green leaves. The sky was violet and full of the airy hope of spring, but the lightness only made it all worse. There were candles in the living room window. He walked into the yard and knocked on the door.

Laila Hansen came out and opened it, stood in the doorway with a smile and looked up at the sky. Jeans, a white short-sleeved shirt that looked great against her cropped red hair; he could see her bra under the fabric.

"It's amazing, isn't it? Like summer."

He wanted to walk past her but she stretched her arms out towards him and held him, so he felt he had to give her a hug, a half-hug, before tearing himself away and walking past her into the kitchen. He turned around without making any move to sit down or take off his jacket.

"Is Louie asleep?" he asked.

"Yes," she said, going over to him. "What's the matter?"

She came very close, looked enquiringly up at him while fiddling distractedly with two shirt buttons in the middle of his chest. Then she looked at the buttons and he knew she realised what was coming.

That was the moment he knew so well. Just before the words came. What would he get?

The slightest admittance of guilt, just about balancing on the line between the facts and a fog of lies and concealment? Or would she crack under pressure and throw all her cards on the table? Maybe something in between. Anything but the full story from beginning to end didn't count: her full guilt from beginning to end. Yes, I planned it. I asked Sonne to kill him. He would believe that. But all the nicer versions, the half admissions, the diminished responsibility with its considered calculations of risks and refuges – that he would not believe. Even if it was true, he would doubt it, analyse it, bore into it and doubt it again. Over and over again. Doubt would consume him. At the police academy, they called it the witch test. If you take responsibility for it all, you're telling the truth; if you only take on half, you're lying. That's how police officers react. Axel was no exception – that was why he was good at his job.

It was the moment. Just before the words came. He had experienced it a hundred times before and loved it. But not this time.

"You're looking at me strangely. What's happened?"

He looked around. There was a book by Haruki Murakami on the table, next to a saucer with a block light, three of Louie's football shirts, sewing stuff and name tags, everyday life that he now had to destroy.

He thought of Enver Davidi. And Piver. And knew what he had to do.

No matter what she might say.

"Tell me why, Laila. Tell me why you set it all going."

She looked surprised, as you do when you face an open accusation that could mean anything and therefore instinctively feel hit, but then her face fell into place in a defensive position.

"What do you mean?"

"Tell me why you called Davidi and got him to meet you at Assistens. Tell me why you had him killed."

Axel fancied that he could see resignation in her eyes, even though it hadn't expressed itself in words yet.

"What are you talking about? I didn't have David killed."

"You called him up and asked him to meet you, and then you got Sonne to do the job instead. Laila, tell me – why?"

She looked at him with a gaze that was pleading with him to stop.

"I didn't know he'd kill him. I had no idea. I just asked him to talk to him."

"But why Sonne? Why didn't you do it yourself?"

"David threatened me. He wanted to come back to us. Haven't we gone through enough, Louie and me?" she shouted.

Axel stayed silent. The tears tumbled down her cheeks.

"He said he'd come home for good, that everything would be as before. I told you this the first time we talked."

"No, you told me he said big things would happen. And they did too. He was killed. Now I just want you to be honest with me and tell me what happened."

She tore at her hair, raking it around, her tears smearing the mascara across her cheeks.

"He came here one day. Louie was at school. I just couldn't cope. I went completely cold inside. When he started telling me about his plans, I got desperate. He wanted me to take him back, so that we could live somewhere else under police protection and new names, and… I don't know what. We have our own life now, David, I said. It's over. It can't be undone. Then I'll take Louie away from you, he said. You have no choice. And he would get him, he claimed, because he was working with the police."

She sat on a chair with her hands clenched in front of her, her forearms resting on her thighs, her gaze fixed on the floorboards.

"But that would never have happened. That's not how it works."

She stared at him with red eyes.

"Isn't it?" she shouted. "Can you guarantee that? You can't guarantee a damn thing, can you? You took him from us 10 years ago and now you come and deliver him again without asking us. And you want to guarantee it will all be for the best. But what if we don't want him back? What if we're happy he's out of our lives? Did anyone take that into account? No, they didn't."

"So you did it yourself?"

She wept, deep sobs, that shook her whole body. One, two minutes. Looked up at him.

"I was afraid, for Christ's sake, afraid for my son. I couldn't stand the thought that he would have to live with that uncertainty again. He shouldn't have to pay the price for David's fuck-ups. Not again."

Axel looked out into the yard. The darkness was blue.

"So I called Jakob and told him that David had been here and threatened us. He'd fix it, he said. Then I called David and arranged the meeting."

"If they just had to meet and talk, why not let Sonne call him himself? And why Assistens?"

Now the sand came blowing over the truth, covering it under its small grains.

"I don't know. I suppose I wanted to make sure he would come."

"Didn't you know that he was under police surveillance, that he was terrified of going out and that they would follow him all the way? Of course you did. Because he'd told you that. And what did you do? You used your ace card, you knew it would work." He wrung the last words out. "Our place. Where you proposed to me. At the chapel. Wasn't that what you said?"

She went completely still. Didn't move.

"It wasn't like that," she said, but he could see that she knew there was nowhere else to retreat to. She must think that they had a recording of the conversation.

"Why haven't you used that before? Why haven't you taken me in if you have that conversation?"

Axel ignored her question.

"So you knew he'd come back with PET's assistance, you knew all sorts of things, but you pretended not to. You lied and hoped it would work out."

"No, I didn't. I knew almost nothing. Everything I've told you is true. I haven't lied. I didn't know that Jakob would go crazy and kill him. I just wanted him to talk some sense into him – believe me, Axel!"

"I can't."

"But it's the truth."

"If that's the truth, why didn't you just tell me?"

"I don't know… I'm a coward, I suppose… I was in shock."

That was a possibility, of course. Shock. Axel thought back to the first occasions that he had been with her during the investigation, how she had appealed to him, and how he had seen it as a sign of interest and desire, instead of what it was: a woman whose life had exploded in her face, who was only holding it together with the tips of her fingernails. And later. He remembered how she had given herself to him with such voracity, how she had clung to him as she came in a whimper of tears and kisses. He had taken it for passion, thinking he had released something in her, and hadn't seen what it was in reality: relief that the threat was slipping further and further away. She gave him a look that could have chopped down trees.

"Axel, listen to me. I've made a mistake, I know, but I haven't killed anyone. I fell in love with you. It may well be that you don't want to hear about it now…"

"I don't. Forget it."

She bit her lower lip, more pressure on the tear ducts. Axel sat down on the other side of the table.

"I didn't kill David. I didn't know anything. I didn't know that Jakob would kill him, believe me, I was out of my mind trying to work out what to do. David had said he'd get his deportation order rescinded if he would help the police, but the price would be a new identity. Don't you understand what that means?"

"Yes, I understand, but I don't understand why you didn't just tell me."

"I was afraid."

"How did you persuade Sonne to do it?"

"It wasn't difficult. I promised… I said I would give us another chance if he helped me, if he got David to disappear… I didn't mean it, but I was desperate."

Axel's heart was pounding away. He felt like screaming.

"What did Sonne say to you afterwards?"

"He called and said I didn't have to think about it any more. It was sorted. They were the words he used. Then later, when I heard that David was dead, I called him and asked what he'd done. He said he'd had a conversation with David, that David had agreed to leave us alone and that he didn't know what happened afterwards."

"And you believed that?"

"I don't know what I believed – I was falling apart. My son had just lost his father and the thought that it was my old boyfriend who'd killed him was unbearable."

She shook her head.

"Do you believe me?"

"No, and it doesn't matter. You may well be telling me the truth, but I'll never know."

"I tried to tell you, Axel, several times. Every time you came, I thought that now I'd tell you about it. Something always got in the way."

From their very first meeting, she had been on edge, as if everything was about to slide away underneath her, not just at the interview, but every time he saw her. She had constantly been threatening to fall apart, like a naked woman who at the last minute grabs her clothes around her. The feelings she had no control over lay just beneath the surface; he had underestimated that. She should have the benefit of the doubt, but he couldn't give her that. There were other considerations.

"What about Piver? Doesn't he mean anything?"

"But I didn't know it was Jakob who'd killed him. I didn't even know that Jakob had killed David."

"You're making yourself out as dumber than you are. If you'd come to us right away, Piver might have been alive today."

She shook her head and sobbed.

"I couldn't know that, Axel. I did the best I could, but I didn't know what had happened. I can see that I should have said, but I was afraid of being pulled down with it. And I had Louie. I had to think of Louie. I thought it would all go away."

"Things like this never do."

Axel got up.

"What now?"

"You'll have to report yourself."

She gasped.

"And what if I don't?"

"Then I'll do it."

She started crying out loud again.

"If you're telling the truth, then you probably can't be punished. If you didn't know anything, you're not an accomplice."

Axel didn't know if that was right, but he didn't care.

"And what about us two?"

"You knew something crucial and you didn't tell me. You have 24 hours. If you haven't reported yourself, they'll come here and fetch you."

She understood. Smoothed her trousers the same desperate way as the day he had come and told her that Enver Davidi was dead.

He turned round at the door.

"Just before Sonne died, I asked him how he got Davidi to meet him in the cemetery. He wouldn't answer that directly. He protected you to the last, but he said that Davidi was really surprised to see him. I didn't understand that. It's only now that I realise that it was because Davidi had been waiting for you, the love of his life. You didn't come – you sent his murderer instead."

He walked out of the door, out to his bike, cast a glance back at the house, through the living room window, into the kitchen where she was sitting at the table with her face turned towards him. He unlocked the bike.

She needn't have promised Sonne that she would give him another chance. He had his own reasons for getting Enver Davidi to disappear. But she had done it. She had used her love as a bargaining chip to reach a goal. She had covered for a triple murderer.

Axel got on his bike and cycled into Copenhagen. The night sky was pale blue and absolutely endless. An aircraft came floating in over Nørrebro from the west on its way to Kastrup, filled with people who knew nothing about Enver Davidi, Stanca Gutu, Laila Hansen, Piver or Jakob Sonne. Or Axel Steen. That was fair enough.

There was nothing more to be done. He had solved the case. He had survived. He had gone after the truth and brought it out into the light, as far as he could. And he had reached out for love.

Was that where it all went wrong? That truth and love were two incompatible entities? Life had taught him that and yet he had tried to forget it, even though something in him had always known that it wouldn't work.

But he had tried.

He came out onto Frederikssundsvej and cycled under the overhead railway line into Nørrebrogade, along with a procession of shiny cars with white wedding pennants and a newlywed couple in the front of an open sports car. The bride's teeth were shining in the night in competition with her jewellery. Young men were hanging out of the car windows, singing and waving big red and white flags with the green Lebanese cedar in the middle, horns were honking and the drivers swerving from side to side across two lanes. Axel got off his bike at the church opposite his flat and stood watching the wedding procession until the sound of the horns and shouts could no longer be heard, the flashing brake lights disappeared, the cars disappeared, and only the night remained.

Also by Mirror Books

Motherland

G.D. Abson

The first in a gripping series of contemporary crime novels set in St Petersburg, featuring the brilliant and principled policewoman, Captain Natalya Ivanova.

Student Zena Dahl, the daughter of a Swedish millionaire, has gone missin in St Petersburg (or Piter as the city is known locally) after a night out with a friend. Captain Natalya Ivanova is assigned to the case. It makes a chang from her usual fare of domestic violence work, however, because of the family's wealth and profile, there's a lot of pressure on her for a quick result

But as Natalya investigates, she discovers that the case is not as straightforward as it first seemed. Dark, evocative, violent and insightful, MOTHERLAND twists and turns to a satisfyingly dramatic conclusion.